Beautifully Broken

LAURA LEE

__This book is dedicated to my father.__ Thank you for teaching me the meaning of hard work and giving me the strength to pursue my dreams. I miss you every day, Dad.

Rest in peace.

one

The secret to getting away with a fake ID is going to a dive bar. Stay away from grocery stores and classy places—they usually have scanners that can spot a fake a mile away. The last thing I need on my eighteenth birthday is a night in county jail. Or worse, I wouldn't get the drinks that I so desperately desired. Lucky for me, dive bars are practically my only choice here on the Central Oregon Coast. I'm legally an adult now and that's cause for celebration. Normally, I'd call up my friend, Dylan and he'd supply the alcohol...and the orgasms. The perfect combination to make me temporarily forget about all the shit I have to deal with. But that's not what tonight is about. Tonight, I am officially free from the system. I no longer have to go to a group home, or be fostered by someone who's more interested in a paycheck than parenting when my mom gets arrested for solicitation or possession of a controlled substance. She's tried getting sober over the years, hence my entire childhood being one fucked up game of ping pong, but her addiction always wins. Heroin trumps daughter. Every damn time.

I never knew my father. Neither did my mother, I suspect. Besides the night he impregnated her anyway. The only thing I know for certain is that he's Latino. I definitely didn't get my dark features from Mom. Cybil and I couldn't be more opposite physically. While she's tall, fair, and willowy—I'm short, dark, and curvy. Not that I'm complaining, mind you. My curves are in all the right places and they help me appear older than I am. In case you didn't catch it, yes, I call my mother by her first name. She doesn't want any of her regular clients to know that she's old enough to have a teenage daughter. She's only thirty-four, which isn't old if you ask me, but she tells people she's twenty-four. It makes her more *marketable.* If anyone asks, we're roomies. They're usually too inebriated and/or horny to question it.

"What'll you have, pretty lady?"

I raise my head and see the bartender approaching. His bushy eyebrows lift expectantly.

"Tequila rimmed with salt," I reply as I lean over slightly, giving him a better view of my cleavage. In my experience, the portions are pretty generous when the bartender sees something he likes.

He stares at the boobage on display and gives me a

smarmy smile. He grabs a bottle of Don Julio and begins filling the oversized shot glass to the rim. "Sure thing, sweetheart."

He continues to leer as he sets my drink on the bar. Well, look at that; I didn't even need my ID.

"Thanks," I say. "You got any lime?"

He opens the garnish tray and plucks out a few wedges, placing them in a bowl. With his gaze still on my chest he asks, "Anything else I can do for ya?"

He's really asking what *I* can do for *him*...and for what price. There's a surprising amount of illicit sex in small towns, you know. I guess that's what I get for choosing a place next to a seedy motel that rents by the hour. Too bad for him, I don't have a habit to support. Not that I haven't had the chance—there's no way you live the life I've lived without being exposed to every-thing under the sun—but I've seen firsthand how powerful drugs can be and I have no desire to become another sad statistic. The irony of my current scene is not lost on me but I don't have a drinking problem, if that's what you're thinking. If you must know, sex is my chosen vice. The main difference between me and my mother is that I don't use it as a form of payment or to *get* paid. Getting off simply helps me turn down the volume for a while. Silence truly is a beautiful thing in my crazy, chaotic world.

I down the drink in one long gulp, chase it with the lime, and bat my eyelashes. "How about another?"

There's no way I'm interested in this jerk but flirting will keep the drinks flowing. Flirting like a pro is the one useful thing my mother has taught me.

He pours another and waits for me to bring the glass to my lips again. Before I can comply, a big guy on the corner shouts, "Yo, Stan! I'm empty!" Big Guy emphasizes his statement by clanking his mug loudly on the grimy surface.

Slimy Stan, as I've now named him, winks at me. "I'll be back, sweet thing. Don't go anywhere."

I roll my eyes as he walks away to bleed the tap. I lift my glass and say, "Happy fucking birthday to me."

The tequila burns my throat as a deep voice rumbles behind me, "Why is such a beautiful woman drinking all alone on her birthday?"

My shoulders stiffen as I set my glass down. I turn around to fend off this douche but I'm frozen once I see how gorgeous he is. Screw the alcohol. *This* is what I need tonight. My eyes travel across his flawless face, highlighted by turquoise eyes, a strong jaw dusted with stubble, and full lips. He licks said lips and I shiver when I think about what that tongue could do to me. My eyes continue their descent over a pair of broad shoulders that taper to a trim waist and long legs. He's wearing a faded Led Zeppelin tee and a pair of dark jeans. Both show off his toned physique brilliantly. He's built, but not bulky. Ruggedly handsome too—like an old-fashioned movie star. Simply put, he's *breathtaking*. Also, unquestionably out of place in this shitty establishment.

He smirks when he notices my obvious perusal. "May I have a seat?"

I gulp, feeling strange little flutters in my stomach. I nod my head toward the adjacent stool. "Please do."

"May I buy you another drink?" he asks. "Perhaps something a little more... diluted?"

I laugh. "I'd hate to break this to you buddy, but it doesn't work like that."

He crinkles his brows and runs a hand through his sandy blonde hair. "Care to elaborate?"

I smile. "If you're looking to get in my pants, the less diluted the alcohol, the better."

Sexy little crinkles form around his eyes as he returns my smile. "Is that so?"

I nod. "Absolutely."

He signals Slimy Stan. "Bartender, can we get another round? I'll have a bottle of Rogue IPA, and my friend here will have..."

I trace my fingers over the rim of my shot glass. "The same."

Stan scowls when he notices my new friend. He quickly masks his displeasure and says, "Sure thing."

Sexy Eyes flashes his perfect grin again. "So, Birthday Girl, do you have a name?"

"I do," I say, "but I'm not giving it to you."

He frowns. "And why's that?"

I tip my freshly delivered bottle to my lips. "Because I have a strict no-name policy for one-night stands." It's true; I do. It's less complicated that way.

His eyes widen in surprise but I don't miss the underlying interest. "Well, then you have no worries. I'm not interested in sleeping with you. So what's your name?"

I laugh to cover the sting of his rejection. "So, let me get this straight. You're telling me that if I wanted to drag you into a dark corner right now and fuck your brains out, you wouldn't be interested?"

He nods his head slowly and places his hand over mine. "That's *exactly* what I'm saying—I'm not interested in a mindless fuck. *With you or anyone, for that matter.*"

Jesus, my panties are soaked from just listening to his resonant voice, even if the words are toxic to my fragile self-esteem. I bite my lower lip and give him another good once-over. "You're not tripping my gaydar —which if I may say so, is pretty damn accurate—so what gives?"

He rubs his chin thoughtfully and smiles. I can't help but fixate on the subtle scratching sound the motion makes. "So, a man has to be gay to turn you down? I never said I wasn't interested in *getting to know you.* Asking your name seems like a great way to start."

I'd be lying if I said I wasn't intrigued by this guy's approach. "It doesn't matter which name I give you—I could easily lie to placate you. But why bother? Let's just call this what it is and move forward. Sound like a plan, Sparkles?"

He laughs. "Sparkles?"

"I give people nicknames," I explain with a shrug. "Your eyes—they're *really* blue...and sparkly. Hence, Sparkles. No real names. No complications."

"You couldn't come up with something a little more...manly?"

I wink. "Nah, I like Sparkles."

He laughs. "As amusing as this game is, I'd like to at least know the reason behind your no-name policy."

I slowly cross my legs as he watches with blatant interest. "I already told you; it's less complicated that way."

He narrows his eyes at me. "Well, that's a cop-out if I've ever heard one. Could you at least give me something a little more original? Or better yet, how about *the truth*?"

Nope, because if you knew how fucked up I am, you'd go running for the hills. This conversation is teetering dangerously close to the edge of an abyss that I can't afford to fall into again. I put my fake bravado in place and give an exaggerated sigh.

"Look, Sparkles. Can we forget about any games and just get on with this?"

"And what exactly is *this*?"

I lean forward and slowly move my hands up his

powerful thighs. "I want you." Holy hell, I really do. I can't remember ever wanting to lose myself in someone this badly. I go a little bit further to whisper in his ear. "And I *know* you want me, despite your earlier denial. Do you think I can't see your jeans tightening? Hear your breath hitch?" I lick the shell of his earlobe. "See your pulse racing as your eyes trace my every move? Why don't you take me somewhere so we can make that happen?"

He braces his hands on my arms and shifts me back onto my stool. He assesses me briefly before asking, "Is it really your birthday?"

I smile wide, easily predicting his next question. "It is."

He raises a single brow. "Which one? How old are you?"

"Twenty-two," I answer without skipping a beat. "How old are *you*?"

His Adam's apple bobs as he takes a pull from his bottle. "Twenty-six." He pulls out his wallet and throws a couple bills onto the bar. He stands and reaches out to take my hand. "C'mon, Birthday Girl. Let's get out of this shithole."

I beam in victory. "Lead the way."

two

I begin walking toward the right when we get outside.

"Where are you going?" Sparkles asks.

I nod toward the sleazy motel. "Which room is yours?"

He looks insulted. "You think I have a room *there*?"

I shrug. "Sure. I mean...why else would you be in that bar?"

He pulls out a set of keys and hits a button to unlock the shiny SUV five feet away. "I had a flat. I went inside to wash my hands after changing the tire."

I fold my arms across my chest. "A flat?"

He kicks the back tire. The obvious *spare* tire. "Yep." He slowly looks me over. "I'm not sure I want the answer...but what were *you* doing in there?"

Trying to forget. "I was waiting for you."

I'm not the best liar but I'm a great deflector.

He laughs and opens the passenger door. "Okay, Red, I get the hint. You're not big on personal questions."

"Red?"

"I have to call you something," he says. "Your dress and your lips...they're red." He gulps as his eyes lazily roam my body from head to toe. "They're also driving me crazy."

"Good crazy?"

He nods enthusiastically. "Definitely good crazy."

I laugh. "Well, if you don't have a room, where are you taking me?"

"There's an all-night diner a few miles down the road."

"Honey, if you want pie, I've got something better to offer. Why don't we just get a room?"

His eyes widen. "Red, of that I have no doubt. But I'd like to buy you a meal and talk for a while."

I try to hide my shock that he doesn't want to get right down to it like everyone else always does. Nobody's been interested in me for *conversation* before. Doubt really starts to creep in as to whether or not I can handle this.

"That's really not necessary."

He nods toward the car. "Actually, it is. Call me old-fashioned, but I'd like to know a little bit about the women I'm intimate with." He holds up a hand when he sees me smile. "I'm not saying that's going to *happen*, but if you'd like to take this any further, which you've already implied you do, I'd like to break bread and share some conversation first."

Damn it. I want him so much and he knows it. I have to figure out a way to take back the power before I transform into a heaping mess of vulnerability.

"Fine. We'll eat first." I dig my car keys out of my purse and unlock the beat-up Civic that's parked right next to his vehicle. "But I'll follow you."

His lips twitch. "Whatever you want, Red." He walks around to the driver's side and starts his ignition.

I turn my key over as well. "Whatever you want, Red," I mutter.

This guy had better be fucking dynamite in the sack. I can feel Pandora's box opening in my brain and I'd rather not disturb it. All sorts of crazy comes out when that happens.

I follow him up Highway 101 to the north end of town. I knew exactly where we were going once he mentioned an all-night diner. There aren't many options around these parts. I've spent a lot of time sitting in the worn vinyl booths at Rose's. I just hope that no one recognizes me. The place becomes a stoner's paradise after midnight which means I have less than an hour to convince this guy to get naked. Not that I'm a stoner; we've already covered that. But there isn't a whole helluva lot to do in this sleepy town so my friends are. Well, the two that I have anyway.

We each pull into a parking spot and exit our cars. I suddenly get nervous and think about bolting when Sparkles says, "Wow, I wasn't sure if you were really going to follow me."

His incredulity reminds me of why I'm here. It's so contradictory to the confidence that seeps out of his pores. I don't know how to explain it, but this guy is different. It's clear that he's a decent human being. Not that it matters when all is said and done, but it's nice to change things up once in a while. Ya know?

I clear my throat. "Uh...yeah." *Shit.* Awkward much?

He smiles and nods toward the entrance. "Shall we see if they have cake, Birthday Girl?"

I already know the answer but I play along. "Sure. Why not?"

He holds the door open for me. Huh. Clearly this guy didn't get the memo that chivalry is dead. "Ladies first, Red."

I step across the threshold, making sure to lightly brush against him. "Thank you."

He shoves his hands into his pockets and rocks back on his heels, adjusting his growing hard-on. Don't get me wrong; he's being discreet. I just know men. I know how to read every little nuance that says they're aroused. Sparkles is playing hard to get, for reasons I still haven't determined, but he's undeniably affected. He feels this crazy energy that's bouncing between us just as much as I do. Our eyes meet and I swear it feels like the earth just came to a grinding halt. My muscles tense, my chest tightens, and I get this strange tingly sensation right beneath the surface of my skin. I'm frozen in place, staring into azure pools, the color reminding me of the Caribbean. *My God*, his eyes are the most beautiful pair I've ever seen. Have you ever heard the saying, *'The eyes are the windows to your soul'*? I've always thought that was a cheesy line but this guy—*these eyes*—make me seriously reconsider my opinion.

"You okay?" he whispers.

I straighten my shoulders to shake out of my stupor and project a confidence I surely don't feel at the moment. "Of course, honey. I'd be better if we were ripping each other's clothes off, but I'm being a good girl." I press my cheek against his and add, "For now."

His large hand wraps around my right hip. "Something tells me you've *never* been a good girl." He takes two steps back, once again, putting too much distance between us.

I was once, but that was a lifetime ago. I push back the memory and force a smirk. "Touché."

A curvy older woman with bright red hair steps in front of us. "Hey there. Welcome to Rose's. Table for two?"

Sparkles takes my hand, giving me the shivers again. "Yes, please."

I try to calm my racing pulse by discreetly taking deep breaths as we follow the hostess. Why am I so fucking anxious? *Get your shit together, Kat. Sweaty palms and panic attacks are not sexy.*

Ariel's Grandma throws two menus on the table unceremoniously. "Sharon will be right over to take your orders. Can I get you a drink?"

Sparkles waits until I'm seated before sliding into the bench across the table. "Coffee okay?"

"I'll have hot chocolate." I know it's totally childish, but I love the stuff. Plus, the trace amount of caffeine in it won't dull my buzz. I really need one of those right now to counteract my damn nerves.

He nods in approval. "That sounds really good. Make it two hot chocolates, please."

I smirk. "You seem more like a coffee man to me."

"I am," he says. "But I'm in the mood for something...sweet."

I grab the dessert menu and flip through it silently until our cocoa arrives. "No cake...but they have every kind of pie imaginable."

"I like pie." His tone has double entendre written all over it.

"I bet you do." So does mine. Sparkles is getting playful. That's a good sign.

"So, Red. Are you from around here?"

I nod. "Born and raised. But you're not. I definitely would've noticed."

He smiles. "You think so?"

"Pft," I scoff. "Please, Sparkles. Don't pretend you don't own a mirror."

He releases a deep belly laugh that sends tingles to all my girly parts. "I'll take that as a compliment." The hostess sets our two mugs of hot chocolate on the table.

"You should," I say as I take a drink. "So...where are you from then?"

"The Bay Area," he says. "Sausalito to be more specific."

I dip my finger into the whipped cream and suck it off slowly. "What the hell would possess you to move *here*?"

He clears his throat. "Who said I lived here?"

Sparkles watches me with rapt attention as I lick my finger again. "So you're just passing through then?"

"I didn't say that either."

I roll my eyes. "All right, Mr. Evasive, I get the hint. You don't like personal questions either."

He shakes his head. "Not true. But I think it should be a give-and-take type of conversation."

I pull my neckline down slightly and lean forward. "So...like *tit for tat*?" I pull back with a wink.

He glances hungrily at my chest before meeting my eyes. "Yeah...I like the sound of that. I'll even start if it makes things easier. My name's Gavin. What's yours?"

"Hey y'all. Have you decided what you'd like to order?" Geez, this woman sounds like she's been smoking two packs a day for the past fifty years.

I don't need to look at her nametag to confirm that our waitress has arrived. "Hi, Sharon. I think my friend and I need another minute."

Sharon smacks her gum. "Take your time, hon. Just holler when you're ready."

"So," Sparkles, er, Gavin clears his throat. "You know my name now. What's yours again?"

"Nice try. Why don't we stick with Red?"

"It was worth a shot." He rubs his chin again. *Damn, that's sexy.* "Okay, how about starting with something else? Why are you celebrating your birthday all by your lonesome?"

"I'm not all by my lonesome anymore."

"Fair enough," he says and smirks. "Let me rephrase...since you're not wearing a ring, I assume that means you're unmarried. Correct?"

I wiggle my fourth finger. "Correct. Definitely not married."

"Boyfriend?"

"Nope," I answer with a pop at the end.

He smiles. "Girlfriend?"

"Not any that I get naked with."

"Shame," he tsks.

I laugh. "Sorry to ruin the visual for you. *My turn.* Are *you* married?"

"I *was*," he says. "Until she cheated on me with my best friend of twenty years. The divorce was final a few months ago."

"Oh," I stammer. I'm caught off guard by his honesty and the stark pain in his eyes. "I'm sorry."

"Don't be," he assures me. "Clearly neither one of them cared about me as much as they claimed...at least I know the truth. I've moved on."

Total bullshit but I let it slide because no one likes airing their dirty laundry. Lord knows I can understand that. "So...no rebound girlfriend?"

"No *anything* girlfriend. I'm one hundred percent single. Let's get back to you. What do you do for a living?"

Oh, I'm about to be a high school senior. No biggie. "Too personal...I don't want you stalking me at work." I laugh. "Next question."

Gavin smiles. "Okay, so our chosen professions are off limits. We've established that we're single and where we're from. What do you like to do when you're not working?"

"I like to read."

He looks surprised. "Reading, huh? What are some of your favorites?"

"Anything I can get my hands on really. Poetry, the classics, thrillers, mythology, dystopia..." I lick my lips suggestively and add, "romance."

He smiles. "See, I knew there was more to you than just a pretty face. You're smart."

I shrug. "Reading doesn't signify intelligence. It's simply a great form of escapism—especially when you're broke. My library card is well-loved."

"Ah, Red. Don't do that."

"Don't do what?"

"Downplay your intelligence. It's obvious from the way you carry yourself. You're observant, witty, and well-spoken." He folds his hands behind his head. "If you ask me, it makes you even sexier, which I wouldn't have thought was possible."

I smile at the compliment. "Let's get back to you. Where *do* you live?"

"About three blocks away."

I smile at his willingness to divulge that information. "Hey, Gavin?"

"Yeah?"

"Are you ready to order some pie?"

He signals Sharon. "I sure am."

Gum Smacker is back. "You two ready to order?"

Gavin nods for me to go first. "I'll have a slice of pumpkin pie, please," I say. "With lots of whipped cream."

Sharon writes my order on her notepad and looks toward Gavin. "And what about you, sweetie?"

His eyes twinkle as he stares directly at me. "Pumpkin is my *favorite*. Load mine up with whipped cream too, please."

She blows a hair out of her face. "Be right back with that."

"Is pumpkin really your favorite," I ask, "or are you just being cute to get in my pants?"

He smirks. "I thought we already established that your pants are wide open for me to jump right in." He briefly peeks his head under the table. "Although...these pants that we speak of seem to already be missing. Sadly, I can't take credit for that."

"Clever," I say. "Maybe I should've said *panties*, since I'm wearing a dress and all."

He pouts. "Well, that answers that question."

"What question?"

"Whether or not you're wearing any *panties* under that dress," he replies.

And right on cue, Sharon is back delivering our pie. Her brows reach her hairline at Gavin's comment but she chooses to walk away without a word. We both laugh at her quick retreat.

I nudge his foot under the table. "Hey, Gavin?"

"Yeah?"

"You don't know what *kind of panties* I'm wearing." I take a big bite of pie. "*Yet.*"

He chokes a little on the piece he was chewing. "Wow, you really don't have a problem with being direct, do you?"

I shrug. "Not usually, no."

I inhale my pie at an embarrassing pace. "Damn, this is good," I mumble through a full mouth.

Gavin eats his as well but with much better table manners. "It is. Although, my mind is now thinking about *panties* and not pie. That's weird, don't you think?"

"You sure like saying *panties*, don't you?" I wink for added effect.

He swallows his bite before speaking. "Quite honestly, I never gave it a second thought until five minutes ago. At the moment, my thoughts about them seem to be bordering on obsession."

"Panties in general?" I ask. "Or anyone's in particular?"

He smiles. "Oh, I definitely have someone in mind. I can't stop wondering what color they are on this particular...person." *Flirty Gavin is fun.*

"Well, I don't know *who* this lucky girl is," I play along, "but one thing I can tell you is that *my* favorite color is red. Red lips, red dress, *tiny* scraps of red lingerie. I also enjoy lacy things...the way the fabric rubs against certain areas of my body feels *really* nice. Even if they are uncomfortably wet at the moment."

Gavin groans in response and shifts in his seat. "Jesus," he mutters.

"Hey, Sparkles?"

He clears his throat. "Yes, Red?"

"Have we done enough talking yet?"

He stands, drops a twenty-dollar bill on the table, and offers his hand. "My place work for you?"

"That sounds perfect."

three

He opens the passenger door to his Tahoe and this time, I hop in. "You're not worried about my car getting stolen?" I joke. You'd have to be a moron to steal that piece of shit. It's older than I am and covered in rust from prolonged exposure to the salty air.

Gavin smirks. "I'll drive you back to get it later."

I grab a fistful of his t-shirt and pull him inches away from my lips. "After we have hot, sweaty sex, right?"

He stares at my lips. "Right. After that."

I release his shirt. "Alrighty then. Let's go."

He closes my door and walks around to climb in the driver's seat. "You sure about this, Red?"

"Why do I get the feeling you don't normally do this? A guy doesn't usually give a willing girl so many chances to change her mind."

"Because I don't," he says matter-of-factly. "Taking a virtual stranger home is a first for me."

"Right," I scoff.

He raises an eyebrow. "Which part is so hard to believe?"

"All of it," I reply.

He puts the car in gear and reverses out of the parking spot. "Why's that?"

I gesture toward his finely sculpted body. "Because you look like *that*. I'm sure you can have any woman you want."

Sparkles flashes a blinding smile as he drives into the neighborhood behind the diner. "I'm flattered, but it's not true."

"So, you're telling me that you haven't had sex with anyone since your divorce?"

"I didn't say that," he chuckles. "I said never with a stranger. The last woman I was with...it was a brief friends-with-benefits type of thing right before I moved here. Before that, I was with my ex-wife, Hailey, and before her, my high school girlfriend. That's it."

I do the math in my head. "So, you're saying that you've only slept with *three* women in your entire life?"

"Yep." He pulls the car into a driveway. "Is that a problem?"

I think about how many guys I've been with since I lost my virginity at fifteen. I couldn't give you an exact number, but if I had to guess, I'd say it's almost *ten times* that many. "Not as long as you don't have a problem with *my* number." He starts to open his mouth but I cut him off. "Before you ask, I can't give you one. Not that I don't want to; I *can't*. But I'm always safe. *Always*."

Gavin pulls his key out of the ignition and contemplates that for a moment. "No judgment, Red. We all have a past, right?"

I release a breath I didn't realize I was holding. "Right."

"This is it." He nods toward the house as we both step out of the car.

I look up at the quaint cottage-style home which is pretty typical for any beach community. The porch light allows me to see a bench under the overhang with flower beds in front. The yard is perfectly manicured and lined with an honest-to-God white picket fence. Overall, the place seems to be in remarkably good condition. I can hear waves pounding against the rocky shore so I'm sure it has a great ocean view during the day too.

"Nice place. Vacation rental?" Rentals are pretty popular along the coast during the summer months.

"It used to be," he nods. "I've only been here a week so I haven't had much of a chance to put my stamp on it. It was move-in ready, though, so I'm not complaining."

"You *bought* it?" Cybil and I have lived in a run-down apartment my whole life. Well, when I wasn't bouncing around the system anyway. I couldn't imagine being able to afford this place. Although it's not very large, maybe fifteen hundred square feet at best, it's well-cared for with a view. That's not cheap real estate, even in shitty Depoe Bay. Usually places like this are owned by wealthy people who rent it out for a week or two at a time.

Gavin shrugs. "I made a nice profit on my house in Sausalito after the divorce. I wanted to stay by the water but in a much smaller town. This place fit the bill."

"But why *this* town?"

"I got a job," he replies. "I applied for several positions along the coast and this one came up first."

"And what job is that again?"

He smirks. "What was it you do for a living, Red?"

Oh right...we're not discussing that. "Touché."

Opening the front door, he says, "You coming?"

I step toward him with a cheeky grin. "If you do your part right, I will be."

So fast I can barely register the movement, he grabs a fistful of my hair and fuses his mouth to mine. *Holy fuck!* His lips are just as soft as I imagined but there's nothing forgiving about this kiss. He dives into my mouth with no hesitation whatsoever. His velvety tongue caresses mine, mimicking what I hope our lower bodies will be doing shortly. His hard muscles press against me in the doorway, the frame digging into my back while his large erection grinds into my stomach. This man is pure cockiness right now. There's no doubt about who's in charge as he works me into a fever pitch.

What kind of game is he playing? And why am I so effing turned on by the possibilities?

He pulls away, leaving me panting for breath. "Does that give you an idea of what to expect?"

I nod dumbly. "Uh huh."

He opens the door fully and gestures for me to come in. With a boyish grin he adds, "Good."

He leads me through the foyer, past a large dining room, into an eat-in country kitchen. I smile when I see the ceramic roosters perched atop the cabinets.

"So, you have a thing for cocks, huh?"

His eyes follow mine and he barks in laughter. "Not really my scene...but I've recently developed a fondness for you *saying* cock." He punctuates his statement with a wink. "The *roosters* came with the house, I swear. They'll be one of the first things to go. They don't exactly scream bachelor pad. I'm afraid they're already affecting my game."

"Maybe just a little," I agree.

He wags his brows. "Then I'll just have to rectify that."

"Oh yeah?" I ask playfully. "And how are you going to do that? Now that I think about it, they *are* pretty emasculating."

He places his hands on my hips, leans into my neck, and inhales. "You smell incredible. I want to *devour you*."

God bless Victoria's Secret body splash. I rake my hands through his hair and press him into my skin. I moan when I feel his tongue trace the nape of my neck.

"Then *do it.*"

He lifts me onto the counter and my legs instinctively wrap around his waist. Our eyes meet and I'm stupefied by his awed expression. He brushes the back of his knuckles against my cheek with great care. "What is it about you, Red? Please tell me I'm not the only one feeling this...this *connection* between us."

I gulp. "You're not." I tighten my grip with my legs and pull him closer. "I'd really like to make that a *literal* connection right now though."

He presses his forehead against mine. "Please tell me your name."

"No," I whisper.

"Why not?" he groans.

His lips are so close I can't help but lick the seam. "I already told you."

He returns the gesture and pulls back with a little bite. Framing my face with his hands he says, "Break your stupid rule. I *need* to know your real name."

I shake my head in refusal. "Sparkles, don't ruin this."

He scowls. "How would knowing your name ruin anything?"

Tears prick at my eyes. "I have the rules for a reason. Please don't press the issue."

His eyes flicker back and forth as he assesses me.

"What happened to you? Why are those beautiful eyes so haunted?"

No one has been able to get through the iron mask I wear. What is it about this man? Why can *he* see me like no other? Am *I* doing something different that's making me so transparent? I'm frustrated and a tear escapes despite my best efforts to contain it. Gavin catches the salty liquid with his thumb and leaves a chaste kiss in its place.

He pulls back to look at me again. "Red, talk to me."

"*Don't,*" I plead. "Please, just make me forget. Kiss me. Touch me." I take his hand and place it on my breast. "*I need you to touch me.*"

The conflict warring inside of him is apparent. His hand is frozen at first but his hormones eventually win as his fingers absently start kneading. Light at first, then the pressure builds. I moan when he brushes his thumb over my stiff peak. The thin cotton of my sundress does nothing to hide my reaction to him. Slowly, he tests the weight of me in his palm, tracing his fingers around my curves. His other hand joins in the action and does the same with my right breast.

"You're so perfect," he whispers.

I'm terrified of losing control of my emotions. He's looking at me with so much reverence it's unnerving. He makes me feel things I've never felt before. I desperately need to change course before I fall down this rabbit hole any further. I jump off the counter and peel my dress over my head. Now all I'm wearing is a red strapless bra, a matching thong, and a pair of beat-up cowboy boots.

I take one boot off and throw it behind me. "Where's your bedroom, Sparkles?"

He watches me like a starving man looking at an all-you-can-eat buffet. I know I've gained the upper hand when he says, "Third door on the right."

I remove the other boot and drop it on the floor. With what I hope is a bit of flair, I reach behind my back and unclasp my bra. Once it joins my boots, he palms himself through his jeans. I don't think he even realizes he's doing it, but it's hotter than fuck. I leave my panties on for now, because those don't come off until the condom comes on. That's another one of my hard rules. I don't break it. *Ever.*

I walk backwards down the hall, never breaking eye contact. "Well, are you going to join me? Or should I get started without you?"

He scrubs a hand down his face and groans. "Woman, you are driving me crazy."

I press my breasts together and trace my areolas with each index finger. "C'mon Sparkles, I really want to get started *with* you." My lips form into a pout, drawing his gaze back up to my face. "I want to feel your cock in my mouth...my pussy...hell, even my *ass* if you want." If nothing else, that last one should get him.

He briefly looks toward the ceiling as if he's

searching for some divine guidance. "Jesus Christ, a man can only take so much," he mutters.

I smirk. "Jesus ain't got nothing to do with this, honey. Although, I do hope you'll have me calling out to God sooner rather than later."

He sighs. "I'm trying to be a gentleman here, but you're making that really damn difficult."

I'm standing right outside his bedroom door now. "I don't want you to be a gentleman. What I want, is a good, hard fuck until neither one of us can walk. I want to feel you inside of me for *days* after we're done." I give him a coy smile for added effect. The contrast between my words and expression now match the dichotomy between my face and body. The lines are obviously blurring on his end because he's now less than a foot away. I go in for the kill shot. "Fuck being a gentleman, Gavin. Fuck *me* instead."

four

Gavin's teeth clash against mine as he moves in for a kiss. We're both instantly ravenous—I'm clutching his shirt, pulling him closer. The fingers of his one hand twist around my locks while the other hand pushes on my lower back, seeking friction for his straining erection. We're both breathless, tongues dueling, moaning into each other's mouth, being consumed by this electric charge that blasts between us.

He wraps his hands around my biceps and turns me away from him. His lips dance over my nape, down my shoulder. Hot breath leaves a path of goose pimples across my over-sensitized flesh. He palms my breasts, one in each hand, molding them as he pulls my back into his chest. I inhale sharply as he rolls my hardened nipples between his fingers. One hand moves down... lower and lower still until he reaches the top of my panties. He pauses for just a moment before sliding between the lace and my heated skin. My knees go weak when he parts my plump, lower lips with his middle finger and begins massaging me in circles.

"Oh, Gavin!"

He tightens his hold when he feels my body turn to putty. "You like that, Red?"

I think I mumble something but I'm not positive. My heart is thundering in my chest. I swear I can hear my pulse drumming in my ears. I can't recall ever being this turned on before and we've barely started. Why does this man and his magic hands have so much power over me?

"Tell me your name and I'll make it so much better."

His command jolts me out of my trance and I know that I need to gain control of this situation. I break free from his hold and spin around.

"You're wearing too many clothes," I say as I tug on his shirt.

My distraction seems to have worked because he's pulling his shirt over his head while I'm unfastening his belt and the top button to his jeans. We both watch as I slide the zipper down, the sound deafening in the silent room. Our eyes meet as I push the denim down to his ankles. He steps out of his pants and kicks them to the side. I take a moment to appreciate the beauty in front of me as we both stand here in our underwear.

His chest is chiseled to perfection; better than I

imagined. I run my fingers across his pecs, lightly brushing over his nipples. He takes a deep breath when I trace the ridges of his abs down to that little patch of hair that leads to happy places. His dark blue boxers are tented, hinting at the impressive package concealed beneath the cotton. A sliver of heat knifes through me as I run my hand over the bulge, feeling large veins running along the shaft. He jerks beneath me, an automatic response to my touch.

"Fuck, Red," he gasps.

Needing to see all of him, I peel away the waistband and roll it down. His cock springs free, thick and long, glistening at the tip.

"So pretty," I murmur.

He chuckles. "I'm not sure if I should take that as a compliment or not."

I hum in appreciation. "Oh, you *definitely* should."

Gavin hooks his thumbs under the waist of my panties. "Now *you're* wearing too many clothes."

I grip his hands, preventing him from moving. "These don't come off until the condom is on. I'm always safe; remember?"

I try squashing down the memory of the only time my partner didn't use a condom and the subsequent nightmare that ensued. I can see the question in Gavin's eyes but he doesn't vocalize it. He can probably sense what a flight risk I am if he digs too deep. He nudges me backwards until the backs of my knees hit the bed and I fall onto the pillow-top mattress. My thighs automatically spread for him, opening myself to his unwavering gaze.

"Well, I guess I'll have to be creative then."

Before I can ask him to explain, his head dives between my legs until his wet mouth is directly over my core. His nose burrows into the lace making me tingle in all the right places.

"Jesus, you smell good," he groans. "So fucking good."

My eyes close involuntarily as his tongue darts out to lick me from the bottom up, over my underwear. I feel his fingertip skirting up my inner thigh before brushing against the lace. He shifts me so my legs are now hanging over his shoulders, baring me even more. My eyes pop open as I feel him move my panties to the side. I watch as he traces my opening with his finger. Once. Twice. Three times around. And then he takes the pleasure to new heights by plunging his finger in deep while sucking my clit into his mouth.

"Oh, fuck!" I scream as my back arches off the bed.

Gavin pumps his finger in and out, crooking it just the right way to hit that spot. He licks and sucks my swollen flesh and then slips a second finger inside of me. I'm so full it almost aches, but pleasantly so. The pressure is mounting to an impossible degree as he works my body over. His tongue flicks out, over and over, faster and faster, never relenting.

I'm screaming incoherently at this point, not caring about anything other than this moment.

This man.

My need for him.

I've had a lot of sex over the years and nothing has felt this good before. *Nothing.* He slides an arm under my ass, pressing me into his mouth. I'm riding his face unabashedly, so close to release I can taste it. His fingers and tongue work in perfect harmony, driving me to the brink of insanity.

Before I know it, I'm shaking. Imploding. My thighs are clenched around his head. My hips move up and down. I whimper and moan, not wanting this feeling to ever end. I want to cry as I come down, feeling like I just ran an emotional marathon. I'm already spent but Gavin makes it clear we're just getting started. He moves our bodies to the middle of the mattress, reaches for a drawer on the side table, and removes a foil packet. He sits back on his knees and smiles as he rips it open. His lips are glistening with my arousal; his ears are red from being squeezed. I'm mesmerized as he rolls the latex down his impressive length.

"Condom's on so these are coming off," he demands as he rolls my panties down my legs.

I feel him hard and hot against my opening as his torso stretches over mine. He leans down to steal a soft kiss before pulling back and watching me intently as he lines himself up. We never break eye contact as he slides in at an excruciatingly slow pace. Neither of us makes a sound when he's fully sheathed inside of me. As I'm adjusting to being stretched so wide, we just stare at each other, having a moment of silence.

Of stillness.

Of oneness.

This is so beyond anything physical that I start to panic. I'm desperate for him and that scares the living shit out of me. I can't bear the thought of severing our connection so I do the only thing I can think of.

"Gavin, I need you to move. Please fuck me. Hard."

I can see the strain on his face. "Are you okay?"

"Yes," I nod emphatically. "I just need you to move. Please just *move*."

He pulls back and surges forward in one long, hard shove. I wrap my hands around his neck, pulling his mouth to mine, kissing him with everything I've got. He's moving now, faster and harder with each thrust. He fills me so completely that I whimper each time he withdraws. My inner walls tighten, trying to keep him locked inside of me.

"Fuck, Red. *Fuck!* You feel so good. So tight."

He buries his face in my neck and pulls my legs higher to adjust the angle. I gasp as he goes deeper than I ever thought possible. My fists clench the sheets as he pounds into me again and again. He's panting. I'm screaming. The bed is creaking ominously. I roll my hips to meet his rhythm and I feel dizzy from the overwhelming ecstasy. I'm close—so close—but I try holding off so I can feel him coming with me. I can tell he's almost there so I move a bit faster, clutch him a little tighter, until his hands grip my hips almost painfully. He squeezes his eyes shut and I *know* that the pressure is building, that he's ready to detonate at any moment.

I curl my ankles together behind his back and pull him into me just a little bit deeper. He groans as he rocks into me, grabbing my face with both hands.

"Look at me, Red."

My eyes lock onto his hooded lids as I feel him let go. My climax pulses through me at the same time and we fall together. He crashes his mouth into mine and I can't help but return the desperation. He rolls in and out, slowing his pace more and more as we kiss. Our tempo goes from frantic to leisurely to pure serenity. Gavin stills inside of me as we both catch our breath. After a minute or so, he slides out and falls to his side.

"Holy Mother of God," he whispers.

"No shit," I agree.

He turns his head toward me and smiles. "I'll be right back." He nods toward his softening erection. "I need to take care of the condom."

"Okay."

I watch his muscular ass as he disappears through the ensuite bathroom door. *Holy shit!* What was that? I've never experienced anything like that before. It was so much more than sex. *It was fucking extraordinary.* I hear running water in the other room and figure that he must be taking a shower. *Great time to make an exit, Kat.* I hop off the bed to search for my panties. *Damn it, where did they go?*

"Not that I'm complaining about the view, but what are you doing?"

Shit! I jump as I hear his voice, awareness of my position setting in. I'm on all fours with my bare ass wiggling in the air as I reach under the bed. I sit back on my knees and feel my cheeks heating. "I was looking for my underwear."

"Why?"

"Why?" I repeat. "Um, because it might be a little drafty outside without them."

He steps closer and offers his hand to help me stand. He has a wet washcloth clenched in the other fist which I suppose explains the sound I heard. Once I'm fully upright, he pulls my chest against his and wraps me in a bear hug. "Stay the night, Red."

Another hard rule of mine is no sleepovers, but that doesn't stop me from sinking into his embrace. He feels too good not to. "I can't."

His fingers slowly climb up my spine as he kisses my neck. "I'm not nearly done with you yet. We both still seem perfectly capable of walking."

I smirk as my earlier words taunt me. "I *did* say that I wanted to keep going until we couldn't do that."

He pulls back with a smile. "You did." He cups my cheek with his big hand and I can't help but lean into it. "So you see, we have no choice. You have to stay the night. It'll easily be dawn before we get to that point."

I place a kiss on his palm. "Well, I can't go back on my word." I sigh dramatically and flop back onto the bed. "Go ahead; ravage me if you must."

"If you insist." He launches himself on top of me and begins playfully bouncing the mattress. We both laugh hysterically as the headboard crashes against the wall repeatedly. All humor quickly fades when a certain part of him stirs to life again.

I gasp when I feel his hardness press against my thigh. "Wow, talk about a fast recovery."

He tugs on my bottom lip. "You seem to have that effect on me."

I stroke his length from root to tip. "Condom," I say breathily.

Gavin reaches into the nightstand drawer and withdraws a packet. "I'm on it."

"Hurry," I beg. "I need you inside me."

He sheathes himself and runs his eyes over my body. I swear I can feel his caress through his gaze. "Not as much as I need inside of you, Red." He pulls my hips toward him and positions himself against my entrance. "Tell me your name or we're not doing this again."

"No fair!" I whine.

He rubs the head of his dick against my slit. "I'm

serious, Red. As much as I want this, I want your name more. Your *real* name."

I whimper in frustration. "Gavin, please!"

He slides in slowly, making both of us groan in pleasure. Cradling my cheeks with both hands he pleads, "I'm not moving until you tell me. *Please.*"

I mewl as he rubs his thumb over that little bundle of nerves. With his fingers, he brings me to the edge of a slippery slope as he remains completely still inside of me. The pressure is building so high it borders on pain without the release my body so desperately seeks. I arch my back, trying to encourage him to thrust but he holds true to his word.

Our eyes are locked, brown to bright blue, and I have a terrifying realization. This man is everything I don't want, yet everything I need. No one looks at me the way he does. He sees the damaged parts of me that I work so hard to conceal. The confusing part is that despite this, he looks at me like that doesn't matter. He looks at me like he can fix me...like he wants to be the one to make me whole again. *Is that even possible anymore?* I shake my head in denial.

"C'mon, Red," he coos. "I promise it'll be okay. Just give me your name and I'll make you come so hard you won't have the energy to regret breaking one of your precious rules."

He pulls out almost completely when I hesitate. I look down to the spot where our bodies are joined. His thick cock is painted in my wetness; my inner folds are parted to receive him. I feel drugged by the erotic picture we make. There's no other explanation for what happens next.

"Kat...my name is Kat."

"Kat," he repeats. He flashes a blinding smile, seemingly satisfied with my answer. "Are you ready to come now?"

I don't even have a chance to reply before he sinks into me, instantly causing me to shatter.

five

I startle awake and it takes me a moment to remember where I am. The rising sun slices through the blinds, affording me a view of the man beside me. Gavin sleeps soundly with his heavy arm thrown over my chest. He looks slightly younger and definitely a lot less jaded. I wouldn't have thought it was possible, but he's even more striking. Flashes of last night run through my brain on repeat. *My God, this man knows how to fuck.* If I truly am only the fourth woman he's been with, he must've had lots of practice with the other three. I frown when a stab of jealously causes my chest to tighten at the thought.

Graphic images of bodies writhing and moaning assault me; memories of the most profound sexual experience of my life. I sigh dreamily thinking about it. *What is going on with me?* My life isn't a damn romance novel! I chalk up my ridiculous behavior to the fact that he's just so damn gifted sexually. I have a sex hangover, plain and simple. I need to get the hell out of here before he wakes up! I've never had to deal with an awkward morning after conversation and I don't intend to start now. I have no idea what time it is, but the daylight tells me that I'd better move my ass.

I slide out from underneath him and slink quietly down to the floor. I hear Gavin shifting and risk a glance to find him rolling onto his side, still snoozing. I never did find my panties but I couldn't care less as I duck walk out of the bedroom and down the hall. I quickly pull my dress over my head, shove my feet into my boots, and throw my bra into my purse that's still sitting on the kitchen table. I take one more glance down the hall as I head to the front door. As I step outside without getting caught, I smile to myself victoriously.

I hoof it the three blocks it takes me to get to my car and think about how this is my first official walk of shame. I've never apologized for my actions or have been anything but upfront about what I want from men. Before Gavin, no one has ever questioned my desire to leave immediately after the deed is done. Shit, most guys *appreciate* it. Before Gavin though, no one has even remotely tempted me to stay. I silently admonish myself for being so stupid. It's bad enough that we traded names. I know not to trust a stranger well enough to sleep beside them. I couldn't have been out for more than a couple of hours, but that's two hours too many. Nothing good ever comes from being that vulnerable. If anyone knows that all too well, I do. And I wouldn't wish the nightmares I've lived through on my worst enemy.

Rose's parking lot is fairly full when I get there. I ignore the curious gazes of patrons through the windows as I unlock my car and get inside. I back out of my spot without another thought and head home. Today's home is different than yesterday's. My latest round of foster parents left a lot to be desired so I packed up my meager belongings and told them I was leaving. The fact that they didn't even try to talk me out of it should tell you how invested they were. I mostly keep to myself...do my best to fly under the radar, but I've learned to speak up for myself when necessary. When my sleazy foster brother, Lucas, their biological son, suggested I provide the *entertainment* for his drunken house party, in the form of blow jobs, I had enough. I told him to go fuck himself and he in turn, told his parents that the party was my idea. That I was the asshole that took advantage of their weekend away to celebrate their wedding anniversary. That *my* friends were the ones who puked on the carpet and dumped Grandma Betty's ashes off the mantel. Of course I tried telling them the truth about their precious son, but they weren't having it. It's a lot easier to blame the person you don't share DNA with, I suppose. It'd be nice if my own mother got that memo one of these days.

I pull into the assigned space of the crappy two-story walk up that Cybil and I have lived in for as long as I can remember. She had her license revoked from too many DUI's so I'm the lucky one who gets to drive our shared vehicle. Which also means that I'm the one responsible for gas and insurance. Cybil thinks that if you don't get behind the wheel, you aren't financially liable. Never mind the fact that I have to run errands or chauffeur her to and from Newport, the next town over, for court appearances.

I take a deep breath as I look at my home sweet home. The white paint on the U-shaped building should have been refreshed at least ten years ago. Now, it's mostly a dingy gray with some yellow spots here and there. There's a concrete staircase on each end leading to the second level apartments. The exterior seems to be modeled after a cheap motel but the inside isn't too bad. Sure, it's outdated, and the place reeks like cigarettes from years of smoke, but I have my own bedroom which is a luxury when you're bounced from one foster home to another. More importantly, there's a heavy-duty lock on the door so I don't need to worry about any of my mother's clients mistaking my bedroom door for hers.

I unlock the front door and prepare myself for what I might see. In the past, it's been something as innocuous as Mom being passed out on the couch fully clothed.

More often than not though, there's someone in some stage of undress or inebriation. Then there was that one time when there were *six* fully undressed people having a grand ol' time; so much so, that they didn't even notice when I walked through the door screaming at my mother for having an orgy in our living room. Just a day in the life of Kat Kennedy.

I sigh in relief as I walk into an empty space. "Cybil?"

I open the fridge and scan the contents for anything edible. Sadly, my choices consist of mustard, cheap beer, or leftover pizza. I lift the lid to the pizza box and quickly regret doing so. Clearly it's the same one from my last night here over four months ago. Well, now it's more like a science experiment but you get the point. I mentally add grocery shopping to my list of things to do.

I walk down the short hall and give the handle to my bedroom an experimental tug. I'm surprised to find that it's still locked after all this time. Usually, if Cybil gets too hard up she'll break in to see what she can sell. Business must've been good in my absence.

I knock on the door to her bedroom. "Cybil? Are you home?"

I hear shuffling behind the door so I know she's in there. I also hear muted voices so I know she's not alone. After a moment, she opens the door wearing a short peach robe that doesn't cover much on her five-foot-ten-inch frame. "Katherine! You're back!"

She pulls me into an uncharacteristic hug and I'm momentarily stunned. "Yep, in the flesh."

She pulls back and looks at me. "How long has it been? A few weeks now?"

I roll my eyes. "*Four months, Mom.* I've been gone for four months. Nice of you to notice."

She ignores my jibe. "Well, you look lovely, darling. Have you gotten taller?"

"Really, Cybil? Don't you think I'm done growing by now?"

She gasps. "Oh my fuck! I know what's different! You're older! You had a birthday, didn't you?"

"I sure did. The big one-eight. I can legally buy your cigarettes now. Yay me!"

She smiles. "Oh, that's wonderful dear. You'll be able to fully support yourself now."

I raise my eyebrows. "And how would you suggest I do that? Part-time baristas don't get paid very well, Mom. I can't even afford gas without my tips. School starts soon. I can't work more than twenty hours per week once that happens. This is my senior year. I have too many things on my plate as it is. I need to maintain my GPA if I have any chance of getting a scholarship. As the parent in this relationship, you should understand that."

My eyes shift to the man coming up behind her. He places his meaty paws on her shoulders and scoots her behind him. He's not a bad looking guy...he's slightly taller than her so I'd guess he's around six feet or so. He's in his mid-forties maybe, with a full head of hair and an impressive build. I know this because he's standing in front of me wearing a pair of boxers and nothing else. "Who's this lovely creature, Cybil?"

My hackles rise. "I'm her *daughter*. Who the fuck are you?"

He laughs. "Oh, Katherine, right? Yeah, your mom has told me all about you. She warned me you had a bit of a bite."

"She has?" I have a hard time hiding my shock. Not at his veiled reference to my attitude, but the fact that she mentioned me at all.

He swings an arm around her shoulder and pulls her into a side hug. "Yes, of course she has. She also told me how gorgeous you are and clearly she wasn't exaggerating."

"Thanks," I reply snidely. "You still didn't tell me who you are."

My mother beams as she shoves her left hand in front of my face. The left hand that bears an awfully large rock. "Katherine, this is Marcus. He's going to be your new step-father. We're getting married!"

"Oh, you've got to be kidding me," I mutter.

She rubs his back affectionately. "Not at all, Baby Girl. Marcus has one of those big houses on the cliff overlooking the ocean. I'm finally moving out of this dump at the end of next month. I spoke to the landlord and he said you can keep the place if you can prove enough income."

"Of course, you're also welcome to come live with us," Marcus adds. "I know that you're legally an adult now, but as I understand it, you have one year left of high school, correct?"

I eye him suspiciously. "Yeah, I do. Which leaves me few options in the way of full-time employment."

Marcus smiles. "There's plenty of room for two beautiful women in the house. I may be able to help you with the income part should you decide to stay here. You're quite fetching and in my business, that means money."

I cross my arms over my chest. I don't miss the way he stares at my braless breasts when I do. "Oh, really? And what business would that be?" Is my mother seriously considering marrying a *pimp*? And is he really propositioning me to follow her lead? Could my life be more fucked up at the moment?

"He owns that gentleman's club off the main highway," Cybil offers. "You know the place...*The Pitiful Princess*?"

"Ah," I muse as everything clicks into place. My shields automatically go into defense mode...also known as bitch mode. "I do know the place. Although I like to refer to it as, *Girls with Daddy Issues*. I mean, seriously? What's with the name?"

Marcus's laughter booms through the apartment. "I

like you, Katherine. I didn't mean to offend you; I'm simply trying to point out your options. You let me know if you'd like a tour of the place. Most of my dancers are students at the community college. Almost every one plans to transfer to a university once they make a little more money. They're smart girls. They know that we're the only game in town which makes their tips go through the roof. There's no other place around here where you can work three short nights a week and take home full-time income. I have a reputation for only hiring delectable young co-eds such as yourself. Men come from two counties over to see them."

"Yeah, and to get a blow job on the side," I huff.

"Katherine!" Cybil scolds.

I roll my eyes. "Save it, *mother*."

Marcus grins. "I assure you, Katherine, I do not run that kind of establishment." He looks at me thoughtfully. "What you choose to do in your own time, is your prerogative, of course."

"Of course." *Yeah, buddy, I can read between those lines just fine. That's twice now in twelve hours that someone has assumed I can be bought.* "Look, I've had a long night and I'd really like to reacquaint myself with my own bed. I'll let you two get back to what you were doing."

Cybil lights a cigarette and takes a drag. "Okay, Baby Girl; you get some rest. It's good to have you home."

Yeah, it's great. Just great.

six

My alarm sounds so I hit the snooze button. When it goes off again, I crack one eye open and reluctantly check the time.

I bolt upright in bed. "Shit!"

I'd hit the snooze button five times! *How did that happen?* I have exactly twenty-one minutes to get to work. Not a great way to start your week. I really like my job but these occasional early morning shifts kill me. I slept half the day away yesterday after my happy homecoming which totally fucked with my internal clock. I couldn't fall asleep until after two so now I'm running on less than three hours and I don't even have time to take a proper shower. I'm actually looking forward to starting school next week so I can have some routine in my life. How fucked up is that?

As I get dressed, I mentally calculate how long it will

take me to drive. As I'm brushing my teeth, I decide to forgo any makeup. My tips are much better when I put on the pretty, but I simply don't have time today. They'll just have to settle for the fresh-faced teenager look. I pull my long locks into a ponytail and run out the door.

I pull into the lot where the coffee cart sits with one minute to spare before we're officially open. *Damn it!* I need at least fifteen minutes of prep time. There are already two cars waiting in the drive-thru. I unlock the trailer and move around as fast as possible brewing the drip coffees, unwrapping the pastries, powering up the register, and organizing the flavored syrups the way I like them. It's 6:13 when I officially open for business. With fake enthusiasm, I lift the shade and slide open the window to take my first order of the day.

Unfortunately for me, today is the day when our owner is the first car waiting. My smile immediately falls when I see how pissed she is. Marilyn runs a tight ship and this isn't the first time I've been caught opening late.

"Uh, hi, Marilyn. What can I get for you?"

She looks into her rear view, most likely at the lineup of cars behind her. "Time is money, Kat. How many times do I have to tell you that? Six cars have driven away already because you can't seem to abide by the posted business hours."

"I know, Marilyn. I'm really sorry; I accidentally turned off my alarm."

She rolls her eyes. "We'll talk about this after your shift. I'll be back then." With that, she squeals her tires out of the gravel lot.

I square my shoulders and paint on a smile as the next car arrives. I somehow manage to get through the first rush with my sanity intact. Once I have a lull, I take the time to think about the possible consequences facing me at the end of my shift. I've seen Marilyn pissed before, but never *that* pissed. I'm so screwed if she fires me. I need this damn job. I'm already dealing with a cereal and Ramen noodles food budget. I qualify for assistance from the district so I'll get free breakfast and lunch once school starts but that doesn't pay for gas and insurance. *Or rent,* I remind myself. *Fuck!* I slam my fist on the counter when I consider the real possibility that I'm walking away from this place without a steady paycheck.

"Ow!" I scream as the pain slices through my knuckles. Great, now I have to make it through the rest of my shift with anxiety *and* a swollen hand.

"Hey, Kitty Kat," Dylan calls as he walks into the trailer.

"Ugh, you know I hate it when you call me that," I complain, shaking my aching hand.

Dylan and I have been friends with occasional benefits since I started working here a year ago. He's the only guy that I've banged more than once since the inception of my rules. Until the other night, that is. I shake my head to chase away the memory of my night with Sparkles. It's never going to happen again so why dwell on it? Dylan and I have an understanding which is why I keep him around. His fresh out of the surf style makes him easy on the eyes and his boyish charm is rather... well, *charming*. I usually don't mess around with guys from school since I've been burned so badly in the past, but he's cool and he doesn't kiss and tell. Not with me anyway, since doing so would ruin his chances of hooking up with someone else.

I grab some ice, place it in a towel, and wrap it around my knuckles. This does not go unnoticed.

"What'd you do to your hand, babe?"

I wince from the sting of the ice. "I punched the counter."

He laughs. "What'd the counter do to you?"

Looking at the digital clock on the register I ask, "What are you doing here so early? Your shift doesn't start for another hour."

"Why are you avoiding my question with a question?"

"Dylan," I sigh with annoyance. He knows my deflection technique by now. Normally he goes with the flow and moves forward.

"Kitty," he mimics my tone.

I'm given temporary reprieve when a customer pulls up. One skinny half-caff mocha later, I turn toward him. "Quit calling me that. You know it pisses me off."

He walks up to me, runs his hand down my arm and says, "Ah, but you're *so hot* when you're pissed. I get hard just thinking about it."

I roll my eyes. "I screwed up. I woke up late so I opened for business late. *Again.* Your mom was here and she was *pissed.*" Yep, Dylan is Marilyn's son. "I got the impression that she's going to can me after my shift."

"Seriously? You want me to talk to her?"

"Seriously," I repeat. "And no, I can deal with it. Thanks for offering though."

"Man, that blows."

"Tell me about it," I agree. "Now you can answer my question. Why are you here so early?"

He shrugs. "It's always dead this time of day. I thought we could have a little fun."

Okay, I know what you're thinking and it's not as bad as it sounds. All right, *maybe* we've taken advantage of the fact that customers can't see us from the waist down a time or two. But in my defense, Dylan is *very* talented orally.

"What happened to Britney?" Britney is the girl he's been seeing for the past month or so.

"Britney is being...difficult."

I laugh. "What you really mean, is that Britney hasn't given it up yet."

He throws his hands up in exasperation. "Exactly! I mean, what's the deal? You've seen my cock. How could any chick resist that? Justin Bieber ain't got nothing on me! One night, we got drunk and she gave me a hand job but that's it! No below the waist action since. She won't even blow me, Kat. How cruel is that?"

"Oh, *so* cruel," I mock.

"Right?" he says, clearly not picking up on my sarcasm. "So what do you say? You up for a little oral exchange to pass the time?"

I watch as he begins unbuckling his belt. "As tempting as that offer is, I'm going to pass."

His hand pauses as he looks up in disbelief. "What? Why not? C'mon, baby, I'll even offer to make you come twice before you suck me off. You know it will help get your mind off of everything."

I shrug. "I'm just not feeling up to it." No way am I going to tell him that I don't want to lose myself in sex for the first time since...*before*. Normally, stress triggers my cravings, no matter how recently I've been with someone. I still don't know what *I* think of that. I certainly don't need anyone else to psychoanalyze me.

He smiles. "How about I just take care of you, then? You know your pussy is my favorite."

"*Any* pussy is your favorite," I retort.

"Not true. You can be a prickly one sometimes, but your pussy is sweeter than all the other girls combined. Yours is definitely my fave."

I smirk at his attempt to sweet talk me. "As flattering as that is, I'm still going to pass. You have a girlfriend,

Dylan. You know that's a hard limit for me—I won't be anyone's piece on the side."

Dylan sinks down into the small chair we have propped in the corner. "Well, shit."

I laugh. "Sorry, bud. Raincheck?"

"Yeah, I guess," he pouts. "What's the deal, Kat? You okay?"

The nice thing about Dylan is that his concern is genuine. I've learned that I don't need insincere people in my life anymore so I'm selective with my friends. His honesty is what makes him one of the chosen few even if he does think with his dick more often than not.

"Yeah, I'll be okay. I'm just preoccupied with other stuff."

"Like what?"

"Well, whether or not I'll have a job at the end of the day for one," I reply. "My reunion with Cybil didn't go so well either. She actually got engaged while I was staying with the Martin family. He's some rich guy that owns the big strip club in town. She said she's moving into his giant house on the bluff next month. Can you believe that?"

He thinks about that for a minute. "Wait a minute… where does that leave you? Where are you going to live? You can't afford rent without her assistance from the state, right?"

"Right," I confirm. "They said I can move in too but I'm not sure I'm okay with that option. Her fiancé,

Marcus, doesn't give off the best vibes, ya know? The dick actually offered me a job as a stripper in his club. If wanting to see your soon-to-be stepdaughter naked isn't sleazy, I don't know what is."

"Babe, that sucks. Are you sure you don't want me to talk to my mom? Maybe if she knew the situation, she wouldn't be so hard on you. Maybe she could even give you more hours."

I take his hand. "Dylan, that's sweet. I appreciate the offer; I really do. But I'm a big girl and I need to figure this out. I've been through worse. In the grand scheme of things, this is nothing."

He narrows his eyes. "What does that mean? What worse things have you been through? Are you talking about all that shit that went down a few years ago?"

He's referring to the time when I was rumored to have willingly filmed a gang bang with half the soccer team in the locker room during my freshman year of high school. We weren't friends back then, but there wasn't anyone in town who didn't hear about *that*. While the story was false, there's usually an element of truth in any lie. That was one of the most traumatic experiences of my life and rumors had nothing to do with it. The *truth* is what scarred me so intensely that I feel sick just thinking about it. I try my best to lock that shit up in the deep recesses of my brain so I don't wind up in a mental institution.

"Yeah, well, that time in my life wasn't exactly fun. It

still follows me. You know that, Dyl." I don't bother correcting him; it's better to let him think that was my problem. It's actually the reason I don't give out my real name when I hook up with a guy. The people in this town certainly don't need any more fodder for their gossip circles. My Scarlet Letter is big enough already.

"Shit, my mom is here," Dylan mutters.

I look at the clock and notice that Marilyn is early. We watch as she parks her car and walks to the trailer.

She peeks her head inside the door. "Dylan, what are you doing here so early?"

"Hey, Ma. I was bored so I thought I'd come in."

She scrunches her brows. "Well, honey, I need to speak with Kat for a bit. *Privately.*" She looks around the coffee cart. "As you can plainly see, there isn't any room for that to happen with you here."

Dylan gives me a worried look and then stares at the floor. "Uh...okay. I guess I'll go grab a quick lunch and come back." He glances my way again. "You sure you don't need my help, Kat?"

I gulp. "I'm fine, Dyl. Go on."

Marilyn is carefully watching our exchange. "Yes, Dylan. Go enjoy your lunch. We shouldn't need more than thirty minutes or so. I'd like to take advantage of our low-traffic."

Dylan exits the trailer and slips into his truck. Marilyn waits to speak until he's pulled away. "Why don't you gather your things, Kat?"

I tighten my ponytail. "Um, my shift isn't over for almost an hour. What about the customers?"

She waves her hand dismissively and ties an apron around her waist. "I'll take care of any customers that may come by. Just gather your things and have a seat so we can talk."

I quickly do as she asks and take a seat in the corner. "Look, Marilyn, I really am sorry about this morning. I'm not sure how, but I turned off my alarm at some point."

She wipes down the counter and begins rearranging the syrups. "Well, be that as it may, you and I both know this isn't the first time this has happened. In fact, it's the *third* time. You know what they say about three strikes, don't you, Kat?"

A car pulls up, putting my defense on hold. After the customers drive away I say, "Please, Marilyn, I really am sorry. I promise I won't let it happen again. I need this job."

She rolls her eyes. "And I need a reliable employee, Kat. You made the exact same promise last time. It's nothing personal, but I'm going to have to let you go."

"Nothing personal, my ass," I mutter.

"Excuse me?" Marilyn shrieks.

"Nothing." I grab my purse off the nearby hook and stand. "So that's it?"

"Your alarm passcode has already been disabled and I have a locksmith coming later today. I'll have your final check ready for you by tomorrow. You can swing by to pick it up or I can mail it to you. Which do you prefer?"

Wow, she's efficient. I guess I really didn't have any hope of keeping my job. "I'll stop by on my way to the bank tomorrow."

She nods. "That will do." I place my hand on the doorknob when she says, "Oh, and Kat?"

I turn toward her. "Yes?"

"I know you and my son are...*friends.*" She says the last word like she ate a piece of bad fish. "He'll be eighteen next month and capable of making his own decisions, but I'm going to ask this anyway."

Oh, this is gonna be good. "And what's that?"

"Well, with you leaving *Perk Up*, there's really no need to continue your association with him. He needs to focus on his schooling this year and you seem to be a rather large...distraction in his life."

"A distraction," I repeat.

She stiffens her shoulders. "Yes, an unnecessary one in my opinion. I'm not stupid; I know what teenage boys think about all day long. I was your age once too, you know. But I don't think Dylan needs to buy what you're selling, if you catch my drift."

I mirror her stance. "I'm not *selling* anything, Marilyn. To Dylan or anyone else."

She gives me a condescending glare. "You know what they say...about the apple falling close to the tree?"

I return her glare. "Wow, so that's what this is about.

Let me guess, your husband had an affair? With my mother perhaps? Or someone like her? Is that why you just got divorced? Is this some sort of revenge?"

"How dare you!" she shouts. "You little—"

I hold my hand up. "You know what, Marilyn? Save it. I have enough people looking down on me in this town. I'm outta here."

I barely make it to my car before the angry tears break loose.

seven

"Stan give me anutha'," I slur.

Slimy Stan releases a hearty laugh, revealing a mouth full of metal fillings. "Sweet thing, you're cute as hell like this, but you are three sheets to the wind. You've been here for almost five hours. I feel like it's my professional and ethical responsibility to cut you off."

"Oh, don't bullshit me," I say. "We both know your moral code is lacking."

He places a glass of water on the bar. "Here, honey, drink this and I'll call you a cab."

"I don't have money for a cab," I complain. "Hell, I don't have any money to pay for the drinks that are making me all spinchy. Why is it so spinchy in here anyway?"

He laughs again. "Are you trying to say *spinny*, darlin'? Is your head spinning?"

"That's what I said! SPINCHY!" I clunk my head on the bar. *Ouch.*

I can feel Stan's foul breath on my neck. "Darlin', I ain't running a free watering hole here. Why don't you go sleep it off on the couch in my office and we can discuss payment after closing?"

"Run my card," a deep voice demands. *Hey, I know that voice.* I crack one eye open as I see him come into my peripheral. Gavin removes his wallet from his pants and practically throws his credit card at Stan. "Charge her entire tab to my card. I'll take her home."

"Now look, buddy—" Stan begins.

"No, *you look*," Gavin leans over the bar and lowers his voice, somehow making it sound even *more* menacing. "Don't think I'm afraid to report what I just witnessed here. I'm sure that wouldn't be good for business. *Am I right, buddy?* Now run my damn card and I will take her home."

"You okay going home with this guy, Princess?" Stan asks.

I lift my head off the bar and smile at Gavin. "You're sooooooo sexy. I'd go home with you any day. Oh wait, I've already done that." I giggle as I turn toward Stan. "It's all good Spinchy Stan. Sparkles can take me. He's really pretty. And he has a *really big* d—"

"That's enough, Kat," Gavin scolds.

"I've always wanted a cat," I sigh wistfully. "I could never have one though because my mom would probably forget to feed it when I got sent away. Gavin, you should totally get a cat! Then I could pet your pussy! Get it? Pet your pussy? It's funny because I'm the one th—"

"Just keep your damn mouth shut until we get out of here," he growls.

"I should change your name to Grumpy Gus," I mumble.

Gavin signs the receipt and grabs my arm to pull me off the stool. "Let's go."

I stumble as he drags me behind him. "Slow down there, Sparkles. You're like, a foot taller than me. I can't walk as fast as you."

I yelp as he lifts me up and throws me over his shoulder. "Problem solved," he grumbles.

"Ooh, are we going to role play?" I ask. "Are you pretending you're a big, strapping fireman? Because I could totally get into that." The blood starts rushing to my head making me feel sick. "Oh God, I think I'm going to puke."

I feel a blast of cool air as I'm deposited onto the concrete just in time to ralph up everything I've eaten today. "Unh," I groan.

Gavin holds my ponytail back as I continue to barf in the middle of the parking lot. And a little bit on my shoes. "Jesus, Kat. What the hell were you thinking getting drunk alone in a place like that? Do you always behave so dangerously?"

"What were you doing there anyway?" I manage in between retching.

"I spotted your car in the lot as I was driving home," he replies. "I thought I'd drop in to see if you had an explanation for sneaking out on me the other night. Considering the fact that you reek like a distillery and vomit, I'm guessing now's not a good time."

"Can we save the verbal spankings for later?" I ask weakly. "Like when I'm not heaving up a major organ?"

"Somebody's ass definitely needs a spanking around here," he grumbles.

"Oh, and let me guess...you know just the person for the job, right?"

"Are you done?" he asks impatiently. "Do you think you can handle the drive home?"

I stand up and walk fifty feet or so before reaching his car. "Yeah, I think I'll be okay. You might want to keep the windows down just in case."

He helps me into the passenger side and buckles my seat belt. "Where do you live?"

I fling my arm out in the general direction of my apartment. "That way."

Gavin sighs. "That's not very helpful. Give me your license; I'll get the address from that."

"No can do," I say, "It's a fake. My real address isn't on *that* license."

He furrows his brows. "What? What's a fake? The

address on your license? Why would you have a fake address on your license?"

Oh shit. Clearly I've become a little too loose-lipped in my drunken state. "Go toward downtown, take a right on Collins. Shitty white apartment building five blocks back from the main road. Can't miss it. It's right behind the old Baptist church." I lean my head against the open window, gulping in the salty air.

"Kat, wake up."

"Wha—" I jump awake, looking around to gather my bearings. Apparently I passed out on our short drive to my house.

"Is this the right place?" Gavin asks as we idle in the driveway to my complex.

"Unfortunately," I mumble.

He pulls into the lot. "Which apartment is yours?"

I point to the left. "Number three. Ground floor."

He heads toward the empty spot marked for my unit and parks his car. "Do you live with anyone? Is there someone home that can take care of you tonight?"

I laugh. "Cybil *might* be there but she wouldn't know how to take care of me if her life depended on it."

"Cybil?"

"My mo—, um, I mean, my roommate. She's pretty useless."

He frowns as he pulls his keys from the ignition and gets out of the car. I stare blankly as he walks around to my side and opens the door. "C'mon, Kat."

"What are you doing?"

He sighs. "I'm making sure you get inside okay."

I gesture to my building. "You can't go in there."

"Why not? Got something to hide?"

"You have no idea," I mutter.

"What?"

I give up and get out of the car. He's already seen me shitfaced; how much worse can seeing the inside of my apartment make things? "Fine, but don't say I didn't warn you."

Sparkles holds his hand out expectantly. "Keys?"

I dig them out of my purse and hand them over. I take deep breaths to prepare for what he's about to see. As the door creaks open, I'm hit with a cloud of smoke and raucous laughter. *Awesome, Cybil has company.*

Gavin cautiously steps inside with me close behind. I look around his big body to see what we're dealing with. Mom and two of her friends are sitting around the coffee table smoking cigarettes and drinking beer. Oh well, it could be worse...at least they're fully clothed. Gavin's eyes narrow on the center of the table. The exact spot where Cybil's friend—Mandy, I think—is leaning over, snorting white powder up her nose through a hollowed-out pen. Even in my current state, I can see how bad this looks. *Fuck.*

Gavin glances back at me and glares. "Friends of yours?"

I nod toward Cybil. "Friends of *hers*." I step in front of him and begin pulling him toward my bedroom. "This way."

"Baby Girl!" Cybil calls. "Who's the hot piece of ass?"

"None of your business, Cybil!" I shout behind me. All three women cackle maniacally in response.

I peel Gavin's clenched fist open and grab my keys to unlock the door to my room. I see the question in his eyes but he doesn't say anything. All bets are off once we're closed inside and I turn the locks.

"What the hell is going on here, Kat? What was that out there? Is that what you're into? And why the hell do you have a *goddamn deadbolt* on your bedroom door?"

I flop onto the full-sized mattress perched on the floor and groan as a fresh wave of nausea hits me. "Sparkles, please not now. I feel like ass."

I feel the bed sink as he sits down and sighs. "Kat, I can't do this. I can't...be with someone that has an addiction."

I roll onto my stomach and shove a pillow over my face. "First of all, we're not dating, so you have nothing to worry about. Secondly, that's *her* thing—not mine. I've never touched a single drug in my life." *Not willingly anyway.* "As you can imagine, her lifestyle comes with certain...challenges. The lock is there because I believe in taking precautions."

He lifts the pillow off my head. "Care to elaborate?"

"Not really." The fog surrounding me is getting thicker by the second, making it increasingly more difficult to keep my eyes open. "Look, Sparkles. I appreciate your concern, but I'm fine. I think it's time for you to go. Thanks for the ride...and the drinks. Although I'm seriously regretting the drinks right now." I feel like I'm recovering from dental surgery. I know I'm slurring—my mouth feels thick with cotton—and I may or may not be drooling.

"Good," he says. "Maybe you'll think about that next time you decide to do something so colossally stupid. Jesus, Kat. What if I didn't show up? What would you have done with that bastard who was propositioning you?"

I curl into a ball, desperately wanting this conversation to be over. "I would've figured something out... I always do. Besides, I don't normally drink like this. It's been a really bad day."

"What does that mean?"

"I don't want to be a stripper," I whine. I roll over and instantly regret it when the ceiling starts spinning again. "Ugh, I'm going to throw up."

Gavin jumps off the bed and before I can figure out what he's doing, he's shoving something in front of me. "Here."

He grabbed the small wastebasket from the corner of my room. As I'm puking up what's left in my stomach, he leaves the room and returns with a cool towel that he places on the back of my neck. At first, I try to resist the help, but truth be told, it's kinda nice.

"Shh, it's okay, Kat. I'm not going anywhere. I'll take care of you."

The last thing I remember is thinking how much I wished that could be true.

eight

Yellow sunlight streams through the window as a chill breaks out over my skin. I stretch and realize that I've stripped down to my bra and underwear. *When did I do that?* I glance around my room and thankfully, find it empty. I get out of bed, wrap an old afghan around my body, and stumble down the hall into the bathroom. I feel slightly more human after brushing my teeth and showering, although my head is still pounding.

I practically leap out of my skin when I step into my bedroom and see Gavin sitting on the edge of my bed.

"Jesusmotherofshit!" I shout. "Where did you come from?"

His face is expressionless. "How are you feeling?"

I close my door and pull the towel more tightly around my body. "Humiliated."

He cocks his head to the side. "What do you have to be embarrassed about?"

Everything? I decide to narrow it down a little bit. "You know...for being all belligerent and needing a rescue last night...subjecting you to projectile vomiting..." I gesture toward the hallway. "And for having to see all that shit with Cybil and her friends. I get the feeling you're not used to hanging around people as trashy as we are."

"Stop," he growls.

I'm startled by the venom in his tone. "Stop *what?*"

He stands up and braces his hands around my biceps. "Stop putting yourself down. Lumping yourself into the same category as that woman you live with. I barely know you but I do know you're *nothing* like her."

His nostrils flare as he stares down at me. I'm suddenly very aware how little fabric stands between us. He seems to come to the same realization as his eyes travel down to my chest and back up again.

I gasp when he slides his thumb over my bottom lip. "Gavin—"

"Shut the hell up, Kat."

His mouth crashes into mine before I have a chance to protest. Waves of pleasure rush over me, making me realize how much I missed his touch. His kiss is bruising, so hard it's almost painful, but at the same time, I can feel his restraint. He's communicating with me through his actions. He's angry with me; that much is obvious. But despite this, he's telling me that I'm safe with him. That he would never hurt me. That I can trust him. I never knew a kiss could be so expressive until now.

He pulls back, leaving us both panting for breath. "What is it about you, Kat? I haven't been able to get you out of my head. You admitted that you feel it too, so why did you leave?"

I avert my eyes, unable to hold his penetrating gaze. "I told you, Gavin. I don't do this."

He lifts my chin with his finger. "Don't do what?"

"Date," I shrug. "Relationships. It's too complicated. *We fucked.* Don't romanticize this and look for something that isn't there."

He narrows his eyes at me. "That's bullshit and we both know it. This thing between us...it's more than just chemistry."

"It's not," I deny. "That's not how things work with me."

"Why not? What happened to you? Is this because of a guy?"

If only it were that simple. I sigh as I open the door. "Trust me, Sparkles. You don't want to know what made me who I am today. I'm damaged goods and that's the only information you need. If you knew what was good for you, you'd forget we ever met. I know this is a small town so let's just agree to walk the other way if we happen to bump into each other again. Do you think you can do that?" I open the door wider, silently inviting him to leave.

He looks at his watch. "I started my new job yesterday; I have an hour before I have to be there so I'll leave for now. I have a really busy week so I'll give you a few days, but this conversation isn't over."

I groan. "Gavin, it really is. There's nothing else to say."

He nods toward the plastic bag that's perched on my wobbly old desk. "I ran out and got some things to help with your hangover. We'll talk later, Kat."

I peek inside the bag as he walks away and see a bottle of ibuprofen, Gatorade, and a greasy breakfast sandwich. *The hangover trifecta.* I throw on some clothes, take a couple of the pills, and eat. As annoyed as I am by Gavin's persistence, I can't help but smile at his thoughtfulness. I've barely finished my sandwich and already feel much better.

I reach under the mattress and grab my journal. I started seeing a court-mandated therapist after everything went down freshman year. I was pretty tight-lipped about the whole thing with everyone—including her—so Dr. Gibbons suggested that I keep a journal whenever I feel the need to talk. If you haven't already figured it out, I have trust issues; therefore, I don't openly share my feelings which she says is unhealthy. I thought it was a bunch of psychobabble at first, but writing my thoughts onto a piece of paper has actually been quite cathartic. I even wound up trusting her over time, enough to share some pages during our sessions.

I find an empty spot and grab a pen. I sit cross-legged on my worn mattress, pouring my thoughts and feelings onto the paper. Before I know it, I've written seven pages about leaving the foster system, meeting Gavin, getting fired and subsequently being rescued by Gavin, along with a list of local places that I need to check, to see if they're hiring. I look back through what I've written and count five pages dedicated to Sparkles and how he makes me feel both terrified and electrified. I've never met someone like him—someone who makes me feel so raw and vulnerable, yet safe. It's confusing as hell; hence, the lengthy journal entry.

I check the time and decide to head over to *Perk Up* to grab my final paycheck. Dylan should be on shift right now which is much better than the thought of facing Marilyn. I grab my purse and head out into the kitchen to refill my water bottle before taking off.

"Mornin', Baby Girl," Cybil mumbles as she sips her coffee.

I take a moment to look her over as she leans against the counter of our small galley kitchen. Her bleached hair sits in a messy top knot and she's wearing a pastel-colored sports bra with tight matching capris. She looks a little tired but surprisingly good. *Sporty. What the hell?* Cybil doesn't do sporty. "Hey, what are you doing up so early?"

She smirks. "Most people would consider ten o'clock late."

"True," I agree. "But most people don't keep schedules like you do." I can't remember the last time she was awake before noon.

She lifts a delicate shoulder. "I'm turning over a new leaf."

I fold my arms over my chest. "That's not what it looked like when I came home last night."

She pulls a zippered hoodie over her shoulders. "The coke was Mandy's, not mine. I haven't touched the hard stuff since Marcus and I started seeing each other. Like I said, new leaf. I'm trying to be better."

I give her a doubtful look. "We've all heard that before, Cybil." I glance down and notice that she's also wearing brand new running shoes. "What's with the new clothes, Cyb? Since when do you go for the *fresh from yoga class* look?"

Cybil runs her hands down her sides. "It's cute, right? Marcus took me shopping. He said all the girls from his club wear clothes like this when they're not working." She turns around, giving me a view of her rock-solid butt. "Plus these pants make my ass look fantastic, don't they? Marcus is surrounded by twenty-year-old tits and ass every night. I need to be able to keep up. My body isn't what it used to be."

Ah, that explains it. "Please, Cybil, you look amazing

and you know it. If Marcus can't see that, then leave him."

She releases a lyrical laugh. "Oh, darling daughter, you have so much to learn about men. Especially men like Marcus."

"Thanks, *Mom*, but I have no desire to learn anything about men like Marcus."

"I have to work damn hard to look like this at my age, Katherine. Marcus is used to being surrounded by beauty. He wouldn't want to provide for me unless I can look just as good, if not *better* than those girls that work for him. You'll see when you get pregnant one day and you have to watch in horror as your body changes."

I stiffen as the words leave her mouth, waiting for her to realize what she has just said to me. Three...two...one...and *there it is*! Her eyes widen for only a second, but it's enough to know she realizes what she has done.

"Oh, Baby Girl—"

I hold my hand up. "*Don't,* Cybil. We agreed to never talk about that shit again and you know it!"

Wow, she actually manages to look remorseful. "I know, honey, and I'm sorry. I'm really, truly sorry. I guess I forgot for a minute."

My fists clench. "How nice for you...that you can just *forget*. You see, I don't have that luxury. It's rather hard to *forget* being forced to deliver a baby that isn't nearly ready to enter the world. It's hard to *forget* how she felt growing inside of me...feeling every little kick and turn, only to watch as she takes her final breath and stops moving entirely. It's rather hard to *forget* how she *came to be in the first place!*" I swipe angrily at the tears that are pouring down my face.

Cybil grabs my arm. "Katherine, I know! I'm sorry! I didn't mean to bring it up. I wasn't thinking!"

I pull away from her. "That's your problem, *Mother.* You don't think! At least not about anything that matters." I throw my purse over my shoulder and head for the door. "Thanks for the lovely *chat*, Cybil. I'll see you later."

I slam the door and walk toward my parking spot. My *empty* parking spot. *Fuck.* With everything going on this morning, I completely forgot about my Civic being stuck at the bar. To make matters worse, it's starting to rain. *Of course* it's starting to rain. I take a fortifying breath, pull my hood over my head and begin the three-mile-trek to collect my car.

nine

"Do you have a name picked out?" the ultrasound tech, Susan, asks as she applies warm gel to my protruding stomach.

I shake my head. "No...um, I'm giving the baby up for adoption."

She gives me a sad smile. "Oh, I'm sorry for bringing it up, sweetie; I must have missed that on your file."

"It's okay," I assure her. "I mean, I'm okay with my decision...who's capable of being a good parent at fifteen anyway? I found a really great couple that have been trying to conceive for six years. The adoption will be open so I'll get to see pictures as he or she grows up. I just want what's best for the baby. In my situation, that's not me."

Susan squeezes my hand. "This is a very brave thing you're doing, Katherine. Don't let anyone tell you otherwise."

"Thank you," I whisper.

She perks up as the machine whirls to life. "Are you ready to do this? You're twenty weeks now so I'm going to take a peek and make sure everything is on track with the little peanut. You'll see me taking some measurements and such. If you'd like, I can explain what I'm doing along the way."

"Sure."

"Provided baby cooperates, I should be able to determine the sex as well. Would you like to know?"

"Do most people want to know?"

"It depends," she replies. "Some do; some like to be surprised. Do you know if the adoptive parents have a preference?"

"Um, I don't know. Maybe you should tell me and then they can decide if they want to know or not."

Susan smiles again. "Okay, honey. We can do that. Just relax while I check baby out and we'll go from there."

I wipe a rogue tear from my cheek as I slip out of my daydream. After getting my car, I drove straight to the one place where I can think clearly. With no access road, the only way of getting here is by leaving your car on the side of the highway and hiking down an embankment. I've been here hundreds of times and not once have I encountered another person. It's a small, nondescript piece of land that becomes rather ominous during a storm, but still, it's my own little piece of paradise in this Podunk town.

As I sit on the rocky beach, thumbing my heart-shaped locket, I finally feel like I can breathe. The waves pound angrily against the shore, as seagulls swoop and dive for their next meal. I close my eyes and inhale deeply—the smell of brine mixed with evergreens fills my nose. I open my eyes and stare at the whitecaps out in the distance. As much as I hate living in a small town, where everyone knows your business, I don't think I could ever stray too far from the water. The ocean, in all its vastness, has a way of making me feel like any problem I'm having is insignificant.

I found this spot one week after giving birth to Amelia...to my daughter. Even though she was conceived in the most brutal way, I loved her with all my heart from the moment I knew she existed. I was giving her to a family that could provide a better life because I loved her so much. I couldn't stop thinking about how different my own life could have been, had my mother done the same.

When Amelia passed away in my arms, I held her tiny red, alien-like body to my chest, and promised her that I would do right by her. She never had a chance to live so I would lay her to rest in the one place that to me, held so much beauty and serenity and...vitality. I held her ashes in the small, biodegradable urn as I walked into the water up to my waist. As a wave came into shore and made its way back out again, I tipped the box over and released her remains into the sea. I remained motionless as she was carried out with the surf, officially becoming one with nature.

I sat on this beach for hours afterward and cried until there was nothing left inside of me. I haven't cried a single tear over her since...until today. I'd be lying if I said I didn't seriously consider joining her that day. I almost walked back in so many times that I lost count, but in the end, I couldn't take my own life. I couldn't dishonor her memory like that. Still, with the pain being too much to bear, I became a shell of my former self, merely existing in a haze from that point on. I numb myself with liquor and men because coping with reality is too hard. Let's face it; growing up with my mother and in the system caused me to be in survival mode from early on, but since that day, it's been on a much greater scale. I gave up caring about what anyone else does or thinks.

My only goal in life is to do what I have to, in order to get out of this place for good. Through a lot of hard work, I've managed to maintain a 4.0 GPA, making me eligible for scholarships. College is my one-way ticket out of here so it's the one thing I do give a shit about. Nothing and no one is going to stand in my way. Not even a sexy, sweet, enigmatic man that I can't stop thinking about.

ten

I've spent the past four days pounding the pavement looking for a job. I've tried coffee stands, souvenir shops, grocery stores, hell, even a place that sells fudge. With every business I went to, the response was the same: *Sorry, we're not hiring during the off-season.* That's one downfall of living in a beach community; the job possibilities are slim when tourism is low. At least for someone with limited availability.

My senior year begins the day after tomorrow. I've enrolled in several AP classes so this year will require more of my time than ever before. My guidance counselor helped me select the best course load for scholarship applicants, but getting into a university is pointless if I don't have funding to pay for it. None of this would be a problem if I didn't have to worry about housing expenses when Cybil moves out. I need to find a job that offers a swing shift if I'm going to fully support myself, which unfortunately limits the amount of time I'd have to sleep. My alternatives, going back into the system until graduation, or taking Marcus up on his offer, are not something I want to consider. Lack of sleep is definitely the better choice.

I'm beat as I walk through the front door and more than a little irritated to find that I'm not alone. Marcus, along with another man around his age, and a *much* younger woman are sitting on the couch.

"Hello, Katherine," Marcus purrs.

I ignore him and walk to the kitchen to refill my water bottle. It's a trick that I've learned over the years; hydrate well and you don't feel the hunger pangs nearly as much. As I turn to head into my room I'm surprised to find Marcus right next to me.

"Excuse me," I say with annoyance.

"What's the hurry, Katherine?" he asks. "Come join us; I want you to meet some people."

I roll my eyes. "No, thanks. I'm really tired so I'm just going to hole up in bed for the night."

His eyes roam over my body. "Feel like having company?"

I gawk at him. "Excuse me?!"

Marcus laughs loudly. "I meant for *conversation*, Katherine. I feel like we should get to know each other."

"No, thanks," I grumble. "Where's Cybil anyway?"

"She got a call from a client about a half hour ago. She won't be back for a while."

I cross my arms over my chest. "A *client?* She still has those?"

He smirks. "It's business, Katherine. Trust me when I say your mother is *very* good at what she does. And she's paid handsomely for it. What's more, she *enjoys* it. Who am I to stop her? It's how we met after all."

I hold my hand up, prompting him to stop with the overshare. I jerk my chin to the couple in the living room currently trying to paw each other's clothes off. "Who are they?"

"That's a business colleague of mine, Brandon. The lovely lady on his lap is one of my dancers, Amber."

I quirk a brow. "I thought you said you weren't in *that* kind of business, Marcus."

"Amber is here of her own free will. She and Brandon...*date* on occasion."

"Do you think they could move their *date* away from my couch?"

He ignores my question and leans into me. "Why don't you come over and socialize for a bit?"

With distaste, I look toward the living room. "No, I'm good. Really." I look at the clock on the microwave. "In fact, I forgot that I actually have to be somewhere."

"Really?" he challenges. "I thought you said you were tired."

"I am," I reply. "But I made plans to watch crappy

reality TV all night with a friend of mine. I'll probably be too tired to drive home, so I can just crash there."

"Would this be a *male* friend?"

I twist the cap off my bottle and take a sip. "I really don't think that's any of your business." I start to walk around him. "Now if you'll excuse me, I need to get going. I'm already late."

"Have fun, Katherine," I hear him call as I close the door.

I get in my car as fast as possible and peel out of the complex. *Shit!* Where the hell am I going to go? I can't afford to drive around too much. My tank is only half-full and I don't have any money in my budget to fill it more than once a month.

I drive aimlessly for about ten minutes or so before pulling into a driveway and shifting into park. I look up at the charming little home and wonder how I got here. This was never my intended destination but I'm sitting here like an idiot nonetheless.

I thunk my head on the steering wheel. "What the hell am I doing?"

I cannot go to him. It would give him the impression that I'm interested in something more than our one-night-stand. *Which I'm not,* I remind myself. This was a mistake. *Why can't I seem to make myself leave?*

"Kat, what are you doing?" Gavin says while tapping on my window.

"Damn it!" I scream while jolting up in surprise. "You need to stop scaring the shit out of me!"

He motions for me to lower my window. I crank the old handle until it's halfway down. No automatic features for this girl.

"Hi," I say, trying to hide my embarrassment. "What are you doing here?"

He smirks. "Hi. It's *my* house. What are *you* doing here?"

Oh, geez, how lame can I be? Why does this man make me so discombobulated?

"Uh..."

He laughs and opens my car door. "Come inside, Kat."

I try pulling my door closed but he holds onto it. "No, thanks. I don't know why I'm here...this was a mistake."

He leans into the car and reaches across my body. *God, his woodsy cologne is so damn sexy it's intoxicating.* I'm distracted by his proximity so I don't realize what he's doing until it's too late.

"Hey," I complain as he pulls my keys out of the ignition and pockets them.

Gavin steps aside and gestures for me to exit the vehicle. "You're here for a reason, whether you want to admit it or not. Come inside. I was just making a sandwich; there's plenty to share."

My stomach growls loudly at the mention of food. To

my utter embarrassment, he notices and raises an eyebrow. I remove my seatbelt and step out of the car without a word. Gavin closes the door and extends his hand in my direction. I stare at it in confusion.

"It's just a hand, Kat. I won't bite." He winks and adds, "Unless you're into that sort of thing."

I feel the blood rushing to my face as a shiver courses through my body, remembering the feel of Gavin's mouth on my bare skin. This garners another laugh on his end. I groan at my inability to save face as I take his hand and follow him through the front door.

He leads me into the little dining nook off the kitchen and nods toward a chair. "Make yourself at home while I put something together."

I take a seat and watch as he moves about the kitchen, gathering items to assemble sandwiches. My nerves are starting to get the best of me so I decide to ask for some liquid courage. "Do you have anything to drink around here?"

He pokes his head into the stainless steel refrigerator. "Anything specific on your mind?"

"Beer?" He's definitely a craft brew kind of guy so I figure my odds are pretty good.

He reaches down low and retrieves a bottle. "I have this new fall ale from the local brewery. That work for you?"

I smile. "That's perfect."

He pops the top and hands it over. After I take a sip he asks, "What do you think?"

I savor the hint of apple as I swallow. When I do drink beer, it's rarely anything this fancy. You definitely get what you pay for. "Mmm, it's really good."

He stares at my lips as I speak. There's an electric current in the air as I do the same to him. He clears his throat and resumes his task. Placing a giant hoagie in front of me he says, "Hope you're hungry."

I discreetly check to make sure I'm not drooling. "Wow, I don't know if I can fit my mouth around that sucker."

"I'm sure going to enjoy watching you try," he teases. He finishes preparing his sandwich and joins me at the table. "Well? I'm waiting to see what you think of my culinary skills."

I laugh. "Are you sure you're not just waiting to watch me wrap my lips around this suspiciously phallic roll?"

His eyes twinkle in amusement. "Am I that obvious?"

"Totally."

Our banter is so effortless that I forget about my shitty day while we eat. He's careful to keep the conversation light; he seems to instinctively know that my flight response will kick in if things get too serious. We laugh and flirt shamelessly while I devour my food. Being with Sparkles is nice...comforting even. I can't remember the last time I felt so at ease. After our meal, we both crack open another beer and move over to the couch in the living room.

"You feel like watching a movie?" Gavin asks. "I can see what's playing On Demand."

Oh hell, why not? It's not like I have anywhere else to be. "Sure."

He smiles and begins flipping through the menu on TV. We agree on an action flick and settle in to watch. I'm careful to remain on the opposite end of the sectional so we're not touching. He's exercising restraint for sure; I can definitely feel his attraction but not once have I sensed that he's about to make a move. I'm more concerned about my own inability to control my hormones. About halfway through the movie, I get chilled so I grab the throw off the back of the couch and snuggle into it.

I stifle a yawn as my eyes become unfocused. "It's pretty late; I should probably get going."

Gavin pauses the movie. "What? Why?"

I wrap the blanket around my shoulders. "Gavin, you know why."

He sighs and scoots closer. "No, I don't know why, Kat. Why don't you explain it to me?"

"Don't do this," I groan.

He comes even closer and takes my hand. "Don't do *what*? I thought we were having a nice evening."

"We were," I agree. "We *are*." He starts rubbing his thumb over the webbing between my thumb and forefinger. Suddenly I'm wide awake and my senses are on high-alert. I continue to watch as his thumb glides back and forth. I release a little moan as my eyes roll back. *Since when is that spot an erogenous zone?*

"Kat," he whispers a hairsbreadth away from my lips.

He smells like clean masculinity and crisp ale. I feel my resolve weaken as I stare into his beautiful eyes. He seems to sense it the moment I part my lips. "What are you doing to me?"

He closes the gap between us and tugs on my lower lip. "I could ask you the same thing."

"Gavin," I plead.

"Shh…stop overthinking it."

I wrap my arms around his neck and pull him into me. "Give me a reason not to."

"With pleasure," he growls.

He lifts me until I'm straddling his lap. I gasp as he presses me into his straining erection and I brazenly grind into him as our mouths connect.

Something is poking me and it's not the good kind of something. "Ouch! What is that?"

Gavin reaches into his pocket and removes my car keys, throwing them to the floor. His hands roam down my thighs to the back of my calves, before circling my ankles. He lightly taps my foot, prompting me to rise. He's still sitting on the couch while I stand directly in front of him. He never breaks eye contact as he lowers my leggings and helps me step out of them. He pops the button to his jeans, slides the zipper down, and lifts up slightly to remove them. As I watch him with rapt interest, I lift my tunic over my head to which he counters by taking off his own shirt.

His hands wrap around my hips as he pulls me into him, softly kissing my stomach. My fingers comb through his hair as his lips leave a wet trail down my abdomen, teasing the hem of my panties. Fingers feather over the sensitive skin of my inner thighs.

"God, Kat," he pants. "No matter how close you are; I can't get enough. I need to be inside of you."

I lean down and press soft kisses along his jaw. "I want that too. *So much.*"

My hands ghost over his chest, down to his abs until I reach the waistband on his boxers. I can't get over the thrill of how he makes my entire body tingle with anticipation. He inhales sharply when I free his erection and groans when my fingers curl around his bare skin.

I sink down to the floor. "I want you in my mouth first though."

Gavin groans again as I pull his underwear down to his ankles. He kicks them aside and throws his head back on the couch.

"Kat, you don't need to do that."

I lick my lips as I stare at his cock. "Oh, yes, I really do."

I lower my head and place soft kisses over the blunt

tip, then flatten my tongue and lick him from root to tip before taking the head into my mouth.

"Oh, hell!" he shouts. "If you insist."

I smile as my lips stretch around his delicious girth and hum in approval. I swirl my tongue around the tip before sucking him deeply into my mouth. I wrap my fist around the root and pump in perfect rhythm with my mouth. His hands tangle in my hair and his hips jut out, pushing his cock down to my throat. My free hand cups his balls while I extend my finger to press against the magic spot right behind them. He's fucking my mouth in earnest now—panting, cussing, telling me how good it is.

"Jesus, Kat. You need to stop or this will be over in seconds."

I hollow my cheeks one last time, sucking hard before releasing him with a pop. I smirk when I see the strained smile on his face.

"Get your ass back up here," he growls.

Gavin pulls me back into his lap and smashes his mouth into mine. He reaches behind my back and unclasps my bra. I gasp as the cool air hits my skin, my nipples hardening as soon as the cups fall away. His eager fingers knead my flesh, tracing over the pink tips. I tremble as he sucks a bud into his hot mouth, hooks a finger into the band of my panties, and rips them away in one powerful movement. I press down when I feel the head of his cock notch against my opening. He kisses up my jaw as I sink onto him inch by magnificent inch.

I sigh. "You feel incredible."

He thrusts into me in reply but then suddenly freezes. His eyes pop open and he stares at me, unblinking.

"Condom," he says. "We need a condom."

Oh, shit! How in the hell did I not notice that? My God, this man makes me lose all rational thought.

"I'm not sleeping with anyone else. I'm clean and on the pill," I pant. See? Not a drop of sense in my head right now. "Have been for years."

He grabs my hips, moaning as he pulls me down to the hilt. "Thank God. You feel too good to stop now. I am too. Clean, I mean—not the pill. Obviously, I have no reason to be on the pill. And there's no one else for me either."

I lift up, swivel my hips, and slowly inch myself down again. "Less talking, Sparkles. More moving."

He moves me up and down, short probing strokes alternated with deep thrusts. Just as we've developed a delectable rhythm, he pauses. My inner walls grip him, starving for more.

"Gavin, *please*," I whimper.

"Look at me, Kat."

As I heed to his command, he surges upward, causing a bolt of electricity to run through the entire length of my body. He tightens his grip, clutching me to him, impaling me over his cock again and again until I'm screaming. As lust clouds my vision, I struggle to maintain eye contact. He's filling me so wholly—his presence overwhelms my mind and body. His eyes pierce straight through my soul. I'm consumed by him—by everything he is and everything we are together. White hot pleasure ricochets throughout my body and I'm coming harder than I ever have before. Gavin follows right behind me, repeating my name over and over.

My forehead is resting on his shoulder as I try catching my breath. Warm tears trickle down my cheeks, opening the floodgate for my uncontrollable sobs. Gavin gently grabs my face and kisses away each salty drop.

"Shh, Kat. I know…it's okay. I'm right here."

I wipe my cheeks, embarrassed that I'm being so emotional. "I don't know why I'm crying. I feel like an idiot."

He pets my hair soothingly. "Don't. That was *intense*. I get it. Are you going to be okay?"

I don't know how to answer his question. With our eyes locked, I feel so exposed…so vulnerable. This man makes me want things that I can't have. He makes me want to tell him everything, to release all the ugly memories I have inside of me, just to have someone who knows what I've been through. Someone who can comfort me when I have nightmares. Someone who can help me glue all the broken pieces back together. I know my thoughts are reckless—I barely know this guy—but every instinct in my body is screaming at me to let him in. To let him *see*. That's when I know it's time to get the hell out of here.

I awkwardly dislodge myself from Gavin's lap and stand up. "I have to go." I start gathering my clothes, getting dressed as fast as possible.

He stands and pulls on his discarded boxers. "Now, wait just a damn minute. I am not letting you walk away from me again."

I pull up my pants and place a hand on my hip. "You don't get to make that call."

"Are you kidding me right now?" He rakes his hand over his head and tugs on the ends of his hair. "What the hell is wrong with you, Kat? Is this par for the course? Should I be grateful that I'm at least awake when you ditch out this time? How can you leave after what just happened?"

"We fucked, Gavin," I say harshly. "That's all." Clearly my defense mechanisms are kicking in.

He scowls. "That was not fucking and you know it, Kat. I've never...I've never experienced a *connection* like that before. It was even stronger than the first time we were together. It was fucking surreal."

Yes, it was, but I don't tell him that. "No need to

pretty it up on my account. We both got off and now that we're done, it's time for me to go."

"You're so goddamn confusing!" he shouts. "I've never met someone that throws around as many mixed signals as you do."

I blanch at the harshness in his tone. "Well, pardon me for being so damn complicated. Don't worry; I won't make this mistake again so you can just forget it ever happened." I grab my keys off the floor and head for the front door.

He grabs my arm. "Kat, wait. I'm sorry; I didn't mean to be a dick. Stay so we can talk about this. *Just stay, damn it.*"

Tears prick at my eyes. "I can't. Trust me when I say it's for your own good. You don't want me, Gavin."

"I'm a grown-ass man. Don't you think I can decide that for myself?"

"I'm well aware of how *grown* you are." *And how fast you'd run away once you found out I'm still in high school.* "Unless you plan on forcing me to stay against my will, I'm out of here."

He looks affronted as he releases me. "I would *never* force you to do *anything* against your will. What would possess you to even say something like that?"

I see the wheels turning in his brain and decide that I need to make a quick exit. I open the door and look back one last time. "Forget I said anything. Goodbye, Gavin."

I think he's still contemplating my words as I step outside because he doesn't attempt to follow. I squash down the disappointment as I get in my car and drive away. I head straight back to my apartment and see that the lights are still on. Having no desire to walk into God-knows-what, I opt for sleeping in the cramped backseat instead. My brain and my body are completely spent and I need at least a few hours of rest before I can deal with anything else. As I fold my arm under my head, I think about how comforting the blanket from Gavin's couch would be right now. Or even better, how comfortable my head would be lying on his chest. Oh, well, when has my life ever been easy? I close my eyes and will myself to fall asleep and forget he ever existed.

eleven

Today is the first day of school. I walk through the bustling halls of McKinley High after first period calculus. Whoever had the idea that math should be taught before noon was a sadist—my brain already hurts. I stash my book in my locker and close it, ready to head to AP Literature.

"Oh-Em-Gee, Kat! I've been dying to talk to you! You really need to get a cell phone so we can text."

I roll my eyes at Bree, my only real friend besides Dylan. We've had this conversation many times and I give her the same reply that I always do. "Yes, Bree; we've been through this. I'd be happy to get a cell phone if you'd like to pay for it."

She returns the gesture and gathers her long locks into a ponytail. "Har har, *Kitty*."

On the surface, Bree is your stereotypical American

high school girl. She's blonde, beautiful, and a cheer-leader with a perennially sunny disposition. Nothing seems to faze her. In reality, she comes from a broken home with some seriously fucked up parents. She moved here when they went to jail for meth distribution and her aunt offered to take her in. I've learned that damaged people seem to gravitate toward one another. It's like we can recognize each other's pain and need someone with whom we can just be our authentic selves.

I start walking toward class. "Very funny, Bree-otch." Hey, if she can use an annoying nickname, so can I. "What's up? We only have a few minutes before the tardy bell rings."

Her hair swings back and forth as we walk. "Your second period class is Lit, right? With the new guy?"

I glance at my schedule. "Yeah...Mr. Cooper. Why?"

She flashes her pearly whites. "Because he's gorgeous!" she says in a singsong voice. "I mean, like totally drool-all-over-your-desk gorgeous. I had him for first period and my panties practically melted off my body! I swear I'm going to dream about blowing him under his desk tonight."

"Nice. Thanks for putting that visual in my head."

"Oh, trust me, you won't have any trouble coming up with your own pornographic images to replace it." She steps into her next class and gives me a finger wave. "Good luck concentrating, Kitty!"

Dylan comes up and swings his arm around my shoulder. "What was that about?"

"That was Bree being Bree. That girl always has sex on the brain."

He laughs and squeezes me into a side hug. "Just *that* girl, huh?"

"Oh, shut it, Dyl. C'mon, we're about to be late."

We run down the hall and slide through the doors right before the bell rings. Dylan also has several AP classes so our schedules are pretty similar this semester. We spot two adjoining desks toward the back and take a seat as the teacher begins taking roll. I grab my notebook out of my bag and face forward waiting for my name to be called. I freeze as my eyes travel toward the front of the room where our new teacher, Mr. Cooper, is commanding attention. Bree was right; the man is gorgeous. I slowly sink into my seat and watch as each student raises their hand after their names are called. I'm pretty sure shock is the only reason my feet are still firmly rooted in place. Every cell in my body is urging me to run far, far away.

"Tyler Janus," Mr. Cooper calls.

Tyler raises his hand. "Here."

Our teacher looks down at the paper in his hands. "Braeden Jones."

Braeden lifts a finger. "Right here."

Mr. Cooper looks at Braeden and nods. "Katherine Kennedy."

I hold my breath as he looks around the room waiting to match a face with the name. I sink a little lower into my chair as he repeats himself.

Dylan pokes me in the shoulder. "Wake up, Kat. He's calling your name."

"Is there a Katherine Kennedy here?" Mr. Cooper asks, projecting his deep voice a bit more.

I hesitantly raise my hand. "Kat," I say with a trembling voice. "My name is Kat."

Mr. Cooper's head whips in my direction and he immediately hones in on my desk. His bright blue orbs widen in recognition. I'm sure it's only a matter of seconds but it feels like an eternity as his jaw clenches and his face reddens in anger. I swear to God it feels like every set of eyes are on me and there's a neon sign flashing above my head that says, *"Hot for teacher"*.

He clears his throat and tears his gaze away from me. "Hannah Lewis."

"Here," she says.

I pull my hair forward to act as a curtain and stare at my cuticles. *I am so screwed.* And not in a good way. I laugh to myself when I think about how this could've all been avoided had I told him that I was a barista and in turn, he would have shared his new job with me. I would've instantly cut the night short and likely never thought about it again. Instead, I now have firsthand knowledge of what this sinfully sexy man looks like naked. How he tastes. How well our bodies fit together with no barriers between us. The sound he makes when he comes. *I could never forget that sound.* I risk a glance toward the front of class and see that I'm not the only one affected by this disturbing bit of information. Mr. Cooper—*Gavin*—is burning holes through me as he reviews the syllabus with the other students. *I am so, so screwed.*

After what was quite possibly the longest forty-five minutes of my life, class is dismissed. I grab my bag, prepared to get the hell out of here.

"Miss Kennedy," Gavin calls. "Please stay behind for a moment."

"Fuck," I mutter.

Dylan laughs as he hears the expletive fly out under my breath. "What'd you do, Kitty? It's only the first day."

I glare at him. "Can it, Dylan."

He smiles and leans in to whisper in my ear. "Meet me under the bleachers at lunch?"

I look up and notice that Gavin is watching our interaction with interest. And something a bit more...*hostile.* "Dylan, get out of here. You'll be late for your next class. I'll talk to you later."

He laughs as he pulls back. "See ya later, babe."

Gavin waits until the last student leaves the room. "Close the door, Kat."

"Look, Gavin, I know—"

"I said, *close the fucking door,*" he says through gritted teeth.

I shut the door as fast as possible and take a deep breath before turning around to face him.

"Lock it," he growls.

I look over my shoulder in confusion. "What? Don't you have another class coming in?"

He charges toward me so fast I flatten my body against the wood. He reaches down and turns the lock as he hovers over me. "You lied to me."

I know it's wrong on so many levels, but my nipples instantly harden from being this close to him. It's like I've turned into a freaking Pavlovian mutt. "Gavin, I know you're mad. But I can explain."

His fists clench as he notices the new pair of headlights that I'm sporting through my belted shirt dress. "Mad?" he sneers. "Oh, I am *so* much more than mad. What the hell were you thinking? I could lose my job when I report this to my boss, Kat!"

I shake my head. "Is that what you're so upset about? I haven't told anyone. I would *never* tell anyone. And you can't either! How was I supposed to know that you would be my freaking teacher? Trust me, I have just as much to lose as you do if anyone finds out about this. You can't tell Principal Edwards. *Please, Gavin*. This town is so small. They already know too much."

He studies me as he takes in my words. "How old are you?"

I lower my head and whisper, "Eighteen."

"Jesus," he mutters. A few seconds later, he takes my

chin between his thumb and forefinger. "How old were you on the night we met?"

I look him straight in the eye. "Eighteen. It was my eighteenth birthday."

He rakes a hand through his hair and takes a deep breath. "We met in a bar. Last time I checked, the legal drinking age was twenty-one."

"I'm aware," I say with a clipped tone.

He glares at me. "Now is really not the time to push my buttons."

"Really?" I challenge. "Are you going to give me detention?"

His nostrils flare. "Kat, *don't*."

"Don't *what*, Gavin?"

"Don't play games with me! I can't believe this is happening."

The bell rings, indicating the start of class. "Why isn't anyone pounding on the door?" I ask.

He begins pacing the small space in front of me. "This is my planning period."

Ah, that explains why he wasn't worried about locking us in. No one would question his need for privacy during this time. I know it's twisted, but I can't help thinking about what Bree said earlier as I glance at his desk. I could easily imagine being on my knees in front of him, freeing his perfect dick from his slacks and taking him into my mouth.

He looks at the desk and back at me again. "What are

you thinking about?"

"You probably don't want the answer to that, *Mr. Cooper.*"

He closes his eyes for a moment and takes a deep breath. Upon opening them he says, "What class are you supposed to be in right now?"

"No class," I reply. "This is my senior project study period." At McKinley, all seniors have a project due at the end of the year which is like a master's dissertation, but on a smaller scale. We work on it throughout the year and have a free period each day dedicated toward making progress. We have a closed-campus so most students spend that time in the library.

He walks over to his desk and takes a seat in the chair. "That's...*convenient.*" His eyes roam over my body. "So is that dress."

"Did you really just say that?"

He props his elbows on his knees and holds his head. "Habit," he explains. "When I'm with you, I lose all rational thought. There's something about you that makes me feel...reckless." He tugs on his hair and groans, which I'm learning is his way of coping with stress. "I'm sorry; I shouldn't have said that."

I walk over to his desk and rub my hand through his hair. He falls into my touch and rests his head against my stomach. "Gavin...I'm sorry. I'm sorry about lying... about putting you in this position. And I'm sorry that I freaked out the other night and left like that. I know what you mean about feeling reckless. Since I've met you, I've seemed to throw all my carefully crafted rules out the window. I have those rules for a reason, yet with you, they don't seem to matter."

He puts his hands on my hips and looks up at me. "We can't do this."

I place my hand on his cheek. "I know. Please promise me you won't say anything to Mr. Edwards. He can't know about this."

"You have nothing to worry about, Kat. I'm the one in the difficult position here. Anything that I tell him would be confidential."

I shake my head furiously. "That's not true. That office is the central hub for gossip in this town. Believe me, I know from personal experience. I know they're not *supposed* to talk about students, but they *do*. Please don't report this. We did nothing wrong—we didn't know. *They can't know*, Gavin. I can't go through it again."

His eyebrows shoot up. "You've had an affair with a teacher before?"

I grimace. "No. *God, no.* It was something else— something I don't want to get into. Please just trust that a new scandal would do nothing but distract me. I can't afford a distraction this year. I need to maintain my grades. I've worked too hard to blow it now."

He releases a sigh. "You don't look eighteen. You certainly don't *act* eighteen. Hell, you're more mature than half the thirty-year-olds that I know."

I give him a sad smile. "I was forced to grow up pretty quickly."

"I'm gathering that."

I take a step back and clear my throat. "Well, I should probably get going now. I'm going to stop by the office to see if they can transfer me into another class."

He shakes his head. "This is the only AP option."

"Seriously?"

"Yeah." He stands up and places his hand on the back of his neck. "You need this course for college admissions, don't you?"

I nod. "The guidance counselor said it would help on my scholarship applications."

"It would."

"Oh. Well...I don't think we really have a choice. Do we?"

He sighs. "Look, Kat. I know this has the potential to be awkward, but it doesn't have to be. You need this class and I'm a damn good teacher."

"Wow, a modest one too," I tease.

"I mean it. I chose teaching because I wanted to make a difference. A positive difference. If you missed out on an opportunity because you had to drop this class, I'd never forgive myself. I'm not saying it's going to be easy, but I can be professional. We're both adults. We just need to chalk this up to being a really messed-up coincidence and move forward. Do you think you can do that?"

I look into his eyes and see the sincerity in them. "I can try."

He gives me a boyish grin. "Should we hug it out?"

"Do you normally cuddle your students?"

"No, but I'd make an exception. Just this once, of course." He opens his arms to invite me in.

"Of course," I laugh as I get sucked into his embrace. He pats me lightly on the back which quickly escalates into something not nearly as innocent. "Gavin, this doesn't feel very professional."

My skin tingles when he pulls back and traces his fingertips across my collarbone, grabs a hold of my shoulders, and prompts me to turn away from him. He runs his fingers down both of my arms and circles my wrists, placing my hands on the edge of his desk. My knees buckle when I feel his chest pressing into my back followed by his hot, wet mouth trailing kisses down my neck.

"Gavin, wha—"

He leans into my ear. "Do you want me?"

"Yes," I pant.

His fingertips dig into my hips so hard I'm sure they'll leave marks. "This has to be the last time. To get it out of our systems."

My panties are soaked just thinking about what's going to happen. "I'm good with that."

Gavin bunches my dress over my hips and groans as he rolls my panties down to my knees. He plunges a finger in deep, seeing how ready I am for him. "You're so damn wet."

"I know," I moan as he moves his finger in and out. "Please don't make me wait."

"Don't worry; as much as I love the idea of teasing you, I have no patience for that right now," he says.

I hear him unbuckling his belt with his free hand as he continues working me into a frenzy. Before I can form another cognizant thought, he's inside of me and I can no longer focus on anything else. Nothing else exists but this moment. His hand on my lower back, pressing me into the desk. The thick head of his cock pressing tightly inside my core, hitting just the right spot, sending delicious shivers of arousal throughout my body.

I'm gripping the edge of the desk while he pounds into me over and over again. As a loud moan escapes my lips, Gavin's hand claps over my mouth, silencing my cries of pleasure.

He stills. "Shh, Kat. You need to be quiet."

I nibble his palm until he releases his hold. I think I literally might die if he doesn't start moving again. Spontaneous combustion is a real thing, right?

"Gavin," I whisper. "Please move. I'll be quiet; I promise. Just *move!*"

He stretches over me, intertwining his fingers with mine, and continues slamming into me at a furious pace. I know this is dangerous. I know that someone could walk down the hall or knock on the door at any moment.

I know that I should care, but I don't. Consequences don't matter right now.

Being caught could ruin both of us but I simply can't process that while he's grinding into me, filling me in the way that only he can. Every part of my body is attuned to his. Every inch of me is consumed with how it feels to have him inside of me. He activates all my neurons; I'm buzzing from the sensation overload. I'm lost in the raw, overpowering pleasure he gives me.

"You feel that?" Gavin asks in a guttural tone.

"Could you be more specific?" I pant.

Thrust.

"How perfectly we fit together."

Thrust.

"How much this pussy loves being filled by me."

Thrust.

"I can feel you quivering, Kat. You're about to come, aren't you?"

Thrust.

I can barely think right now, let alone speak. His dirty talk has my sanity hanging on by a loose thread. Gavin's cock is so long, so hard, so merciless. My pussy is throbbing in the most delightful way; I can feel my wetness seeping out of me.

"Admit it, Kat," he presses. "You can't get enough of this either. You're so tight; so wet for me. Always so fucking wet for me. Just let it go, Kat."

Thrust.

"Show me how much you love being bent over my desk right now."

Thrust.

Thrust.

"Come all over my dick, baby."

Oh God! His words send me flying over the edge, my climax so unexpected it takes my breath away. I start to scream but he swiftly clamps his hand over my mouth again as his pace quickens, chasing his own release. When he comes, I feel every bit of it. Every stream shooting into me. Every pulse of his cock as he rides it out. He collapses onto my back and we're both frozen in place. The only sound in the room is our labored breathing.

"Who knew you had such a filthy mouth?" I whisper.

He chuckles and places a soft kiss on the back of my neck. "You bring it out in me, I guess."

The bell suddenly rings, causing us both to tense. Gavin carefully pulls out of me and stands upright to tuck himself back into his pants. I straighten as well and try smoothing out the wrinkles in my dress. As hot as it was only a minute ago, the air is now pregnant with unease. We agreed that we needed to do this for closure, but that felt like anything but. Unspoken words hang in the space between us, begging to be voiced. Right when I get the nerve to speak up, Gavin beats me to it.

"So…" he says as he squeezes the back of his neck.

"So…" I repeat.

"I guess that will do the job, huh?" he says. "For closure, I mean. We'll be nothing but professional from this point forward?"

"Professional...right."

He looks like he wants to take it back but instead he says, "Well, I guess you should probably get out there and head to your next class."

"Um, yeah. I probably should."

Gavin clears his throat and walks me to the door. He opens it and gives me a sad smile. "Have a good day, *Miss Kennedy*."

"You too, *Mr. Cooper*."

As I'm rushing to Spanish class, I can't help but think how hard it's going to be keeping things *professional* after that. I'll never look at that desk the same way again.

twelve

"**K**at, look! There he is! Bree says excitedly.

I turn my head in the direction she's pointing. "Who?"

"Eyes on me!" she scolds. "Don't be so obvious! He'll know we're talking about him."

"And how am I supposed to know *who* we're talking about when you won't let me look?"

She bites into a French fry. "Mr. Cooper! He's on lunch duty today. Damn, he is sooo hawt! I'd do him in a second."

Oh, shit. I squirm in my seat as memories of being bent over Gavin's desk flood my head.

"Who are you trying to sink your claws into now, Bree?" Dylan slides onto the bench next to me, puts his arm around my shoulder and pulls me into a side hug. "Hey, Kitty Kat. Why are you so flushed?"

Damn it! "Uh, I'm hot. It's really hot in here. Don't ya think?"

He leans in to whisper in my ear. "Admit it; you're just thinking about how much you want my giant cock, aren't you? I'd be more than happy to help you out with that, you know."

"Holy shit!" Bree whisper shouts. *"He's looking right over here!* Why does he look like he's about to murder someone? God, that makes him even hotter! It totally gives him a bad boy vibe."

I don't need to turn around to know the look Bree is seeing. I can *feel it* and it's directed right at me. Or more probably, Dylan. I shrug him off so Gavin doesn't get the wrong impression. *Not that it matters*, I remind myself. You know, since nothing can happen between us again.

Dylan looks behind him and scrunches his face in concentration. "Who the hell are we talking about?"

Bree fans her face dramatically. "Mr. Cooper."

"Gross, Bree," he says. "He's a teacher. And an old man."

"He's not that old," Bree scoffs. "Thirty tops. I'd still fuck him in a heartbeat."

Twenty-six, actually. And so would I. I bite my lip before I accidentally vocalize my thoughts.

"You're such a little slut," he says.

Bree rolls her eyes. "Oh, puh-leez. We all know that the last thing any of us should be doing is slut-shaming.

Especially you, Dylan. There's nothing wrong with having a healthy sexual appetite."

Dylan pulls me back into him. "I agree with you there. Right, Kat?" He leans into my ear again. "I know that look in your eyes. You want to take me up on my offer from earlier, don't you?" He places his hand on my thigh, making me flinch. "C'mon, baby. I officially broke up with Brittany last night. I know how you feel about cheating but that's no longer an issue. I bet if I slid my fingers up that short little dress of yours, I'd find you soaked. Wouldn't I?"

I scoot away from him. "Don't be a pig, Dylan."

"Miss Kennedy," Gavin growls. "Is there a problem?"

"Shit!" I yelp.

Gavin crosses his arms over his chest. "Is there a problem here, Miss Kennedy? Is Mr. Taylor bothering you?"

Dylan laughs. "No problem, Teach. Kitty and I were just playing around."

Gavin raises an eyebrow. "Kitty?"

Dylan gives me a shoulder squeeze. "Yeah, my little Kitty Kat. We were just goofing around. No problem here."

Gavin's eyes narrow on Dylan's hand. "Is that right, Miss Kennedy?"

I hang my head, trying to hide my blush. "Yep, no problem."

Gavin straightens his spine. "I see." He points to Dylan. "Keep your hands where I can see them, Mr. Taylor."

As Gavin walks away, Bree says, "Oh, he looks just as good from the back as he does from the front."

"He's an asshole," Dylan grumbles.

Bree makes a lewd gesture with a fry. "I'd still fuck him. Any. Day. Of. The. Week."

He glares at her. "You're a whore, Breanna."

"So are you, Dylan," she retorts. "You're just jealous because there's new competition in town."

"Fuck that," he says. "I don't go after old pussy. Any chick that I'd want wouldn't touch his shit with a ten-foot pole."

"Yeah, right," Bree scoffs. "If I met him outside of school, I'd ride him like there was no tomorrow. So would Kat."

I hold my hands up. "Hey, leave me out of this, you two!"

Dylan shoots me a scowl. "Why did he want to see you after class anyway?"

"Uh..." I stammer. "He...uh...wasn't happy that I wasn't paying attention during roll call. He wanted to let me know that he expects me to be less distracted going forward." *That sounds plausible, right?*

Dylan makes an '*I told you*' gesture. "See? Total asshole. Right, Kat?"

I shrug noncommittally. "I don't know; I think he was just doing his job." I'm sure it would help my cause if Dylan thinks I hated our teacher but I can't force myself to speak poorly about him.

"Whatever," Dylan mutters.

"See?" Bree smiles triumphantly. "Kat totally agrees with me. She'd bang the teacher too."

I throw my hands up. "I said to leave me out of your petty little argument!"

"Why are you getting so defensive?" Bree asks. "Geez, Kat. Is it Shark Week or something?"

Dylan laughs. "Must be."

I stand up. "Oh, screw both of you guys. I'm out of here."

"Oh, Kitty, we were just kidding!"

I hold my hand up. "Don't *'Kitty'* me, Dylan." I take a deep breath to center myself. "I'm sorry for being a bitch, okay? It's been a rough couple of weeks. I'm heading to the library. I'll talk to you guys later."

"Oh, you know we love you, bitch," Bree says. "Meet me out front after the final bell, okay?"

I nod. "Yeah, see you then."

I spot Gavin watching me as I leave the cafeteria. He looks like he wants to follow but stops himself at the last second. I can see the questions running through his brain and the last thing I need right now is another confrontation. I head to the library as fast as possible and hide out behind the stacks until the bell rings. It never seems to fail; when it comes to fight or flight, I always gravitate toward the latter. I'm disgusted with my behavior. Clearly, this situation is going to be more difficult than I thought.

thirteen

I'm the last one to arrive for second period. The only open seat is right in front of Gavin's desk. You know, the same one that we screwed on less than twenty-four hours ago? I look up as I walk into the room and see him sitting down, looking at the empty chair in front of him with a smirk. *Did he plan this somehow?* Ignoring my attraction to him is going to be difficult, especially in such close proximity. I thought we both agreed that we needed to stay far away from each other. What the hell?

"Good morning, Miss Kennedy," he purrs as I sit down.

I blush. "Morning, *Mr. Cooper.*"

His deep voice addresses the room as soon as the bell rings. "Good morning, class. Let's get straight to today's lesson. I trust that you all completed your required summer reading?"

There were some yesses mixed with uncomfortable grumbles throughout the room. Clearly not everyone completed the course pre-work. Thankfully, I'm not one of them.

Gavin claps his hands together. "In literary works, cruelty often functions as a crucial motivation or a major social or political factor. For your first essay, we're looking at a play from your required reading list in which acts of cruelty are important to the theme. You are expected to analyze how cruelty functions in the work as a whole and what the cruelty reveals about the perpetrator and/or victim."

He looks throughout the room before flipping the projector on. On the white board is the name of the piece we will be analyzing: *Othello.*

A collective groan moves across the classroom. I clap a hand over my mouth to stifle the laughter that escapes when I realize that the man I'm fucking is making me write an essay.

Gavin lifts an eyebrow. "Care to share what you find so amusing, Miss Kennedy?"

Besides the absurdity of our situation? I clear my throat. "Nope. I have *absolutely* no comment."

His eyes lift to the other students. "I'm going to use this assignment to gauge where everyone is at; therefore, it won't be graded. Normally, I'd be happy to help you with your work but this is the exception to that. If you're writing it by hand, it should be at least three pages on single-sided lined paper. If you choose to type your paper, then it should be at least one-and-a-half pages in length using twelve-point Times New Roman font. Your essay is due on Monday. Any questions?"

A blonde named Sarah raises her hand.

Gavin nods in her direction. "Yes, Miss White?"

She chomps her gum and twirls a piece of hair around her finger. "Which do you prefer, Mr. Cooper? Hand-written or typed?"

"It's your choice, Miss White. I know not all students have access to a computer or printer at home so I don't require work to be typed."

"But which do you *prefer*?" she insists.

He scowls. "Miss White, I don't care to repeat myself. Is that understood?"

Sarah pouts as several others giggle. "Yes, Mr. Cooper."

His jaw ticks. "Good. Any others?" After his question is met with silence he adds, "Remember, do not merely summarize the plot. You need to analyze the theme we've discussed. You're welcome to use your resources around the classroom but not your fellow students. Bring your copy of *The Complete Works of Shakespeare* tomorrow. If you need something to use today, there are printed copies of *Othello* sitting on the table in the back. I expect them to be returned before you leave this room. Now get to work."

Wow, he's kind of a hardass. And it's really sexy. I grab

my notebook out of my bag and pick up a pen. Most of the other students are milling around the back of the room waiting to snag a copy of the play. I don't have my book with me, but I'm quite familiar with the piece because I read it five times over the summer.

I get to work outlining my thoughts. I've found that outlining first always helps me produce better essays. Gavin—er, *Mr. Cooper*—leans against his desk and crosses his arms over his chest. He's wearing charcoal slacks and a bright blue button-up shirt today that makes his eyes glitter even more than normal. I bite my pen as I watch him run his hand over his scruffy jaw. I blush when I remember how that scruff feels against my inner thigh.

As if sensing my salacious thoughts, he grins as he walks over to my desk. I have to consciously focus on my work to avoid staring at his crotch as he comes closer.

He places a hand next to my paper. "You don't need a copy of the play, Miss Kennedy?"

I try not to be obvious as I breathe in his cologne. "No, *Mr. Cooper*. I'm familiar with it."

He glances at my notes about Iago's manipulative ways and how he fuels each character's cruelty throughout the story. He taps my paper. "I see that. Nice work. I'm looking forward to seeing the finished product. Maybe I'll get a little more insight into what makes you tick."

No one has ever been curious about my mind before.

I know he's a teacher so he's *supposed* to be invested in my schoolwork, but this feels different. This isn't the first time he's expressed interest in getting to know me. I know things have changed now that I'm his student, but his tone suggests otherwise. *What a mind fuck.*

I continue making notes as I try to ignore my hot teacher through the end of class. As I'm packing my bag, Dylan comes up to me and pulls me out of my chair.

"C'mon, Kat. I'll walk you to the library." He leans in to whisper, "And maybe we can make a pit stop along the way."

I pull away from him to see Gavin glaring at Dylan.

"Miss Kennedy, I need you to stay behind a moment, please."

"Again?" Dylan challenges.

Gavin crosses his arms over his chest. "Do you have an issue, Mr. Taylor?"

Dylan rolls his eyes. "Of course not, Teach. You can talk to my girl all you want."

His girl? What the hell? "Dylan, I'll see you at lunch. Okay?"

Dylan looks from me to Gavin, then back to me again. "Okay, Trouble Maker. Second day of school and you're being held after class again. What'd you do to get under the new guy's skin so bad?"

"Mr. Taylor—" Gavin interrupts. "You'd better get a move on before you're late for the next class. I won't excuse your tardiness."

"Whatever," Dylan huffs. "Bye, Kitty."

Dylan rounds the corner and my insides warm as Gavin closes the door. He looks about to turn the lock but seems to rethink it at the last second. Damn. I'm a bit more disappointed than I care to admit about that.

"What'd you need, *Teach*?" I intentionally use the same flippant name Dylan has for him. By his expression, I can see that I've pushed some buttons.

He flings his arm out. "What's the deal with that tool?"

I feign confusion. "Whatever do you mean, Mr. Cooper?"

"Kat," he growls.

I bat my eyelashes. "What relevance does my relationship with Dylan have to you?" I know I'm egging him on but I can't seem to help myself. He has no right to pull the jealous boyfriend act and I'm sure he knows it.

"Are you fucking him?"

I gasp in feigned shock. "Mr. Cooper! Is that an appropriate question to ask one of your students?"

He tugs on his hair. "Damn it, Kat. Answer the question!"

"No."

He looks surprised. "No? Oh...I thought by the way he was constantly touching you—"

"I wasn't answering your question," I clarify. "I was

refusing to answer your question, considering it's none of your business."

He glares at me. "I think it damn well *is* my business considering we've had unprotected sex twice in the past few days! I need to know how many little boys you're fucking around with so I know whether or not I have something to worry about."

"Something to *worry about*?" I repeat. "As in, whether or not I was being truthful the other night? You're worried about how much of a little whore I am? Is that it, Mr. Cooper? Have you been asking around about me?"

"What? No. I mean, yes."

"Which is it?"

He clenches his jaw. "No, I haven't asked anyone about you. Yes, I need to know if I should get tested."

I ball my hands into fists. "You know what, *Mr. Cooper*? It's none of your business who I fuck. And if you want to call me a liar *and* a whore, then all you need to know is that I won't be fucking you. *Ever* again! But we already decided that, didn't we, Teach?" I slam my hand down on his desk. "When you bent me over your student roster and pounded into me like you couldn't get enough. Remember that? You should probably hold onto it for the spank bank because that's all you're getting. Think whatever you want about me. Just fuck off, Gavin."

I storm toward the door and hurl it open.

"Kat, wait!" he calls.

"Gavin, may I have a word with you?" Miss Salas, our drama teacher stands outside the door. "Oh, pardon me; I wasn't aware you were conferring with a student."

I widen the door and gesture for her to come in. "He's all yours. We're done here."

As I'm stepping into the hall, I catch a quick glimpse of Gavin. His expression is saying that we're anything *but* done.

fourteen

I throw my backpack onto the couch as I walk into my apartment after school. I've been fuming ever since the end of second period. Who the hell does Gavin think he is? He's made it very clear that we cannot continue seeing each other, yet he has the gall to behave like that? This is exactly why I tried pushing him away to begin with! He's so intense—*we're* so intense together. I don't need this kind of disturbance in my life.

A loud knock on the door startles me out of my musings. I hold my breath as I see the man through the peephole.

"Kat, I just saw you walk in there. Open the damn door."

"I have nothing to say to you, *Mr. Cooper*."

He knocks louder this time. "I'm sure I'm making quite the scene out here. You probably want to let me in before it gets worse. Oh, look, your neighbor three doors down is watching me."

Damn him! Of course he'd use my fear of gossip against me. And he has to mention the one neighbor I know would use this as a conversation starter. I swing open the door and step aside with a huff.

"Get in here, asshole."

He smiles triumphantly as he walks into my living room and perches himself against the back of the couch. "Now, Miss Kennedy, is that any way to speak to your teacher?"

I slam the door and roll my eyes. "Please. You and I both know you're not here as my teacher."

He shrugs. "Hey, you're the one who pulled out the '*Mr. Cooper*'."

Crossing my arms, I say, "What do you want, *Gavin*?"

Cybil stumbles out of her bedroom looking a little worse for wear. "Baby Girl, what's all the noise about? I have a wicked hangover so I'm trying to rest before work." She spots Gavin and instantly morphs into business mode, smoothing down her hair and smiling seductively. "Oh, I'm sorry, honey. I didn't realize you had company."

Gavin takes her in and offers his hand. "We didn't officially meet the last time I was here. I'm Gavin."

"It's lovely to meet you, Gavin," she purrs. "I'm Katherine's roommate, Cybil."

"Cut the shit, *Mother*," I scold.

His eyes widen in surprise as he looks between me and Cybil. She's dressed in a pair of sleep shorts that ride halfway up her ass cheeks and a tank top that leaves very little to the imagination. I can see him trying to fit all the puzzle pieces together. He's taken note of the label I've given her but it's not quite jiving with her appearance. As I mentioned before, Cybil and I look *nothing* alike and she's at least a decade younger than a typical high school student's parent. With the way she dresses and acts, she seems even younger still.

"Mother?" he questions.

"Yep," I confirm. "She's my mommy dearest. I bet that answers quite a few questions, huh?"

"Katherine!" Cybil says. "Don't be so rude!"

"She's your mom? *Seriously?*"

"Tell me, Gavin," Cybil interrupts. "How do you and my darling *daughter* know each other?"

Gavin pulls on his hair. "Uh..."

"He's my Lit teacher, Mom," I offer. "I'm fucking him for an easy A."

Gavin's jaw drops. "What the hell, Kat?"

Cybil laughs. "Oh, don't mind her; Katherine likes to joke around." She looks at me pointedly. "Though she could certainly work on her style of humor."

"You know me...I'm just a big ol' jokester," I mumble.

He sighs. "Kat, can we please go somewhere to talk?"

I raise my eyebrows. "Do you really think that's wise? Anyone from school could see us, Teach."

Cybil chuckles. "Oh, Katherine, give the poor man a few minutes. I'm going back to bed so you can talk here."

"Great," I mutter.

He waits until she closes her bedroom door. "So… that's your mom, huh? I didn't think I'd be meeting the folks so early in our relationship."

"Ha ha. We don't have a relationship, remember?"

"Right," he agrees halfheartedly. "Look, Kat, I wanted to apologize for being a jerk earlier. I was out of line."

"I'll say."

"This whole situation has thrown me off kilter, you know? Everything feels like it's spiraling out of control. I do trust you and I definitely don't think you're a whore. I didn't mean to act like such a caveman—I couldn't stand seeing that little punk put his hands all over you and I reacted."

I soften a bit. "Dylan and I are just friends."

"Friends who have sex," he speculates.

"Friends who have *had* sex," I correct. "Past tense. It's been a couple months since we were last together and I have no intention of going back for more." *Although I didn't realize that until just now.*

"So when he looks at you like he's undressing you with his eyes—which he does *all the time* by the way—

it's because he *knows* what's underneath your clothes? I really wish you'd said I was imagining the whole thing."

I take a moment to think about how I want to say this. "Gavin, what are you doing? Why does it matter who sees me naked? We both agreed that nothing could happen between us after yesterday. Have you changed your mind or something?"

"I *can't* change my mind, Kat...even if I wanted to. It's bad enough I did what I did yesterday."

"It took two of us to do that, you know."

He sighs deeply. "True, but I'm the one who's in a position of trust at that school. It doesn't matter that we're not breaking any laws. Eighteen may be old enough to consent, but being with you still compro-mises my professional code. This is only my third year of teaching and I've already broken the cardinal rule. They warn us about being attracted to our students when you choose to teach secondary ed. They go into great detail about how to avoid this exact situation. Yet here I am."

"And you blame me for that?"

"No, I don't *blame* you. We met over the summer and I've never taught at McKinley before. I would've defi-nitely been more cautious had I known your real age, but it is what it is. Hell, who am I kidding? I probably wouldn't have cared even if I *did* know. I can't seem to help myself where you're concerned. Age is relative anyway—my parents have a fifteen-year gap between them and they're the happiest couple I know. In my opinion, the only time it matters is when it's illegal."

"Well, good for you that I was legal to the day then, huh?" I smirk. "You're much too pretty for prison."

He narrows his eyes at me. "Not funny."

I shrug. "Just trying to lighten the mood."

"No, you're using humor as a defense mechanism."

"I already have a shrink, Gavin. I don't need another one."

He flinches. "Why do you have a shrink?"

I gesture toward our surroundings. "Do you really have to ask? You've met my mother and she only scratches the surface of my fucked-up life."

"Why do you live with her anyway?"

I probably look as confused as I feel. "What do you mean?"

"Why do you live with someone who is clearly... unfit? What about your father?"

"I don't have a father; never have."

He gives me a sympathetic look. "Kat, I'm going to put on my teacher hat here. You have resources. I know you're eighteen, but you're still in school. You don't have to be in this situation."

"Trust me, I know all about my *resources*," I sneer. "I've been in and out of foster care since I was a toddler. I know it works out for tons of people, but all I've seen are the flaws. I voluntarily left when I became a legal adult and I have no intention of signing myself back in. Under *any* circumstances."

"But what about maintaining your grades? Getting into college? I'm sure living under the same roof as that woman makes it challenging."

"Take off the teacher hat, Gavin. I don't need another guidance counselor either."

He blows out a breath. "I'm just trying to help."

I cross my arms over my chest. "If I need your help, I'll ask...but don't hold your breath. I may be young, but trust me when I say that I've lived through *a lot*. And I've survived this long with stellar grades to boot. Surviving is what I do."

Gavin steps closer and uncrosses my arms. Wrapping me in a hug, he says, "Surviving isn't *living*, Kat."

I melt into him despite all the warning signals going off in my brain. I count ten deep breaths before I step away.

"I think it's time for you to leave."

"Okay...you're right. We can't be alone like this; I don't trust myself. But know that I'm here for you—in a strictly platonic capacity, of course."

"Of course," I mock.

"Right," he nods. "I think it's best from this point on if we keep our distance as much as possible. I meant what I said about being professional—in class, if you need my help, that's what I'm there for. And if you need help outside of it, I'm still there for you; with my classroom door open. We simply have to make sure we never see each other outside of school."

"Wow, you've given this some thought, huh?"

"I think it's necessary. Don't you? I can't fathom any other way to make this work. When I'm near you, something primal takes over. I know you have the same reaction, even though you constantly fight it. If we always have the guarantee of witnesses, there's no way we can compromise ourselves. Kat and Gavin don't exist at McKinley. Starting tomorrow, we are Miss Kennedy and Mr. Cooper."

"So from this point on...it's as if we just met on the first day of school?"

He smiles. "Maybe the third day would be better."

"Right," I laugh.

"Right." He opens the door and steps over the threshold. "So, I'll *meet* you tomorrow then."

"Ten-four, Mr. Cooper."

fifteen

"**W**elcome to our home, Katherine."

I hang my head. It's a submissive gesture that I've learned over the years when coming to a new place. "Thank you, Mr. and Mrs. Anderson."

"Oh, please, Katherine," Mr. Anderson says, "there's no need to be so formal. You can call us Judy and Pete."

"Okay."

I clutch my garbage bag of belongings to my chest. It isn't much but it's all I have moving from one home to the next so quickly. That's what happens when your mom gets arrested for a DUI and you have no other family to crash with. Today's my fifteenth birthday and she insisted on celebrating with a trip to Dairy Queen. Too bad she already got a jump start on the celebration before we left the house.

"Okay, Katherine," my social worker, Martha says, "You

know the drill. I'll check back in with you later in the week. Try to get some rest tonight; it's been a long day."

Judy touches my shoulder gently. "Honey, let me show you to your room so you can get settled. After that, we have a little treat for you. Ms. Perry said you're celebrating a birthday today."

"Oh, no, that's okay. I don't need to put you out any more than I already have."

"Nonsense, young lady," Pete argues. "First of all, you're not putting us out. Judy and I have opened our home to kids like you because we want to help. You are part of our family for as long as you'd like. And part of being included in this family is celebrating our special days together. Judy makes the best chocolate cake you'll ever have."

"Um..."

"Oh, Pete, give the girl a few moments to collect herself," Judy chides. She starts leading me down the hall. "C'mon, sweetheart. We'll get you settled and if you're feeling up to it, we'll have some cake. You don't have to do anything that makes you uncomfortable, Katherine."

I'm stunned. Up until this point, I've never had someone welcome me into their home so warmly. Especially not when they get a call from social services at nine o'clock on a Sunday night.

"Thank you," I whisper.

Could this possibly be the one home that makes a differ-ence? Is my life about to turn around? I smile to myself thinking about the possibilities.

I wake up sweating from my dream and take a few moments to catch my breath. God, where did that come from? I haven't thought about the Andersons in years. After the trial, I pushed them into the tight little box of ugliness that I store in the back of my mind. I made a conscious decision to *not* think about them after that; I didn't want to give them any more of me than they'd already taken. So why now? Why can't I stop thinking about all the horrible things that happened to me in their home?

I run my hands through my hair and flop back onto the pillow. I stare at the ceiling and run through the last couple of weeks in my head. Gavin has to be the reason why my subconscious is strolling down memory lane. He's the only new variable in my life— it's the one thing that makes sense. Since I've met him, all sorts of emotions that I thought were long dead have floated to the surface. What is it about that man? How can one person I barely know affect me so profoundly?

I take a long shower to ward off the chill. It's a little early but I decide to head into school since I have nothing better to do. I make my way through the break- fast line in the cafeteria and glance up at my seating options. Since it's so early, most of the tables are empty. As I scan the room, I happen to spot the one person that I shouldn't be seen with. Despite this, I find myself heading toward him. He's standing against the wall observing the students so I choose the table directly in front of him.

As I take a seat, I say, "Good morning, Mr. Cooper."

My back is to him so I can't see his expression but I imagine he's smirking. "Good morning, Miss Kennedy. What are you doing here so early?"

I shrug. "I'm taking advantage of my free breakfast. It's the most important meal of the day, you know."

"I've heard that a time or two."

"What are you doing here?" I ask. "Don't you have anything better to do?"

He chuckles. "Apparently at McKinley, the new guy gets stuck with cafeteria duty a lot. I'm on the schedule three days this week."

"Is that the administration's subtle way of hazing?"

"It's not so bad at the moment," he replies quietly. "Potentially dangerous, but not unpleasant."

I preen a little. "Really?"

"I take that back," he says stiffly.

Huh? It only takes a second for me to comprehend as Dylan sits at my table.

"Hey, Kitty. You're looking mighty fine this morning, as always."

"Thanks," I mutter, hyperaware of the man standing within earshot.

He smiles. "What? You're not going to return the compliment?" He motions to himself. "You know you're dying to tell me how hot I am."

I laugh. Dylan's cockiness is definitely a constant. "Yet somehow I refrain."

He leans over the table and presses the back of his hand to my forehead. "Are you feeling okay?"

"Mr. Taylor," a deep voice grumbles behind me. "Didn't I already warn you about keeping your hands to yourself?"

Dylan looks over my shoulder and narrows his eyes. "Mr. Cooper, I believe what you said was, 'Keep your hands where I can see them.'"

I stifle a giggle because I'm pretty sure that's *exactly* what he said. Gavin doesn't seem to appreciate the reminder.

"Don't make me say it again, Mr. Taylor." I see him walking to the other side of the room out of the corner of my eye.

"Seriously what the hell is that guy's problem?" Dylan gripes. "He's been riding my ass all week."

"Maybe the PDA policies were much stricter at his last school," I offer lamely.

He scoffs. "Or more likely, he's just an asshole. This is going to be a long year."

You could say that again, I think. Gavin and I set clear boundaries that I'm already pushing. Sure, some of his comments weren't entirely professional earlier, but I was the one who sat so close in the first place. I need to remind myself that being within whispering range is too intimate. Neither one of us seems able to control ourselves around each other. And that's *not* a good thing, I remind myself. Maybe if I say it enough, I'll start believing it.

sixteen

I somehow manage to make it through the rest of September without any further student/teacher transgressions. I can't say I haven't thought about Gavin but keeping our distance seems to be working. In class, he treats me like any other student. He doesn't ignore me, but he respects our invisible boundary lines. It really is as if we met on the third day of school. Hopefully one of these days, my hormones will get the memo. Those still react as strongly as ever whenever we're in the same room. And many nights when I'm alone in bed remembering his touch.

Sadly, I've also ended the month without a viable means to support myself. Every place that's hiring only needs someone to fill shifts during school hours. All except one, that is. I stare at the purple neon sign proudly boasting, "The Finest Gentleman's Club on the

Oregon Coast". As if that's something to be proud of? I take a fortifying breath and open the doors to *The Pitiful Princess*. I'm surprised by the brightness inside. It's only four o'clock so they're not open for business yet, but for some reason, I expected the place to be much darker.

A bald giant right inside the door asks, "May I help you?"

"Um..." *Am I really going to do this?* "I'm here to see Marcus."

Mr. Clean smiles. "I see. Are you here for a job interview, honey?"

"Not exactly...but he told me to drop by if I ever wanted to check the place out."

He presses a finger to his earpiece. "Boss Man, there's a hot little Latina here to see you." He pauses a moment; I assume to listen to *Boss Man's* reply. "What's your name, sweetheart?"

"Kat."

Mr. Clean relays my name and dutifully waits for instructions. "He wants me to bring you to his office. It's this way."

I take in my surroundings as I follow him toward the back of the building. The place is much bigger on the inside than you'd expect. *And classier*, I have to admit. Sure, the occasional platform with stripper poles gives away what you're really here for, but otherwise, it just looks like an upscale bar.

The bouncer knocks on a door marked, *Private*. A

moment later, it opens and a young blonde saunters out with smudged lipstick.

"Excuse me," she says as she walks past us.

What the hell? I look around the room and find a lazily smiling Marcus sitting behind a large black desk.

"Katherine, it's so good to see you! What brings you by?"

Badass Bouncer steps into the hall and closes the door behind him. I lean against the wall, suddenly feeling very strange being alone with Marcus.

"Um..."

Marcus stands and walks over to me. There's no mistaking the chub he's sporting, clearly indicating my arrival interrupted something. *Pig.* No wonder he's not concerned about Cybil taking clients.

"Tell me, Katherine. Did you decide to take me up on my offer?"

"I'm not sure," I admit weakly. "If Cybil still plans on moving out, I don't think I have a choice."

He smiles. "Of course she does. But you're also welcome to come along."

I shake my head. "No...taking my clothes off for money is definitely the better option there."

He barks in laughter. "I really like your fire. So will my clientele."

I shift uncomfortably. "So, how does this work? Do I need to fill out a job application or something?"

"No, it's not quite that involved." He looks me over

hungrily. "You definitely have the assets; now I need to see if you have the stage presence. What are you? A 36D-cup?"

I flinch. "That's disturbingly accurate."

"I'm a man of many talents."

I move to the side as Marcus reaches for the doorknob.

"C'mon, Katherine. I'll show you to the costume room and you can pick out something to wear for your audition."

"Audition? Like now?"

"Is there a better time that works for you?" he asks. "I assumed you'd want to start as soon as possible if you took the initiative to show up. Was I wrong?"

"Nope. My bank account certainly isn't getting any bigger just standing here."

"Let's go then."

He leads me to another private room at the end of the hall with four doors in between.

"What are those other rooms for?" I ask.

We walk inside a large dressing room with racks of clothing on one side and a large vanity on the other.

"Those are the VIP rooms. They're set up for private parties."

"And what goes on in a typical party?" I thumb through one of the clothing racks and see that every bra, corset, and teddy are all in my size. I try not to think too much about what I'm getting ready to do as I grab the first red ensemble that I see.

"Oh, you know, usually bachelor parties and what not. The occasional businessman showing off for a potential client. Couples will sometimes book the room for date nights. Fire code allows a maximum of fifteen people in each room so they're never too big. They can also be used for private lap dances although we have smaller rooms for those. The VIP spaces are reserved for clients who book an extended dance. If you're lucky enough to be one of the girls chosen, that's where you'll make the most money."

"So how much money are we talking about?" I hold the lace against my body and look in the mirror.

"The house takes a twenty-percent cut on all private dances which includes booked parties. A two-hour party costs three hundred per dancer. They can request up to three dancers per party and they pay extra for bar services. Your cut would be two-forty."

"I'd make *a hundred and twenty dollars an hour?*" Holy shit! I had no idea strippers could make this much.

"For a private party, yes. Don't get too excited, Katherine. Parties are usually only held on weekends and the client gets to choose his dancers. That spot usually goes to the more seasoned gals but you never know. We haven't had a fresh face around here in a while. I'm sure you'll stir some...excitement."

I bite my lip to hold back my standard smartass

reply. "So, on a typical night, how much money are we talking?"

"You'll take the stage for two songs per shift and you'll get tips from those," he explains. "After that, you work the floor for private dances. Most girls aim for at least ten per night. Private dances are twenty dollars each for three minutes, so you'd take sixteen a piece. Extended dances are twenty minutes in length and cost one hundred, so you'd take home eighty."

I do the math in my head. "So on a typical night, you're saying I could make a couple hundred dollars?"

"Roughly, yes. On the weekends, slightly more."

"And how many nights would I work per week?"

"Three to four nights, four-hour shifts."

"So...you're saying I could make roughly twenty-five hundred to three thousand dollars a month, working only twelve to sixteen hours per week? Are you for real?"

Marcus grins widely. "That's exactly what I'm saying, Katherine."

I'm trying to school my features but I'm pretty sure he can see my excitement. Stripping is pretty much the last thing I'd want to do for a living, but my God. Can you imagine the possibilities? Not only could I easily afford to pay the bills, I'd also have money to set aside for a newer car and emergency expenses. I'd hate to admit it, but this job sounds more appealing the further I think about it.

"I'll leave you to get dressed...you provide your own

shoes and panties but we provide the rest. You'll find everything you need in this room." I must've made a face because he adds, "Don't worry, each costume is professionally laundered after use. Most clubs don't provide wardrobe; it's one of the many perks of working here. Our house mother can show you some standard moves later; this performance is simply to get a feel for your stage presence. Remember, we're an all-nude club, Katherine, so take it all off. I'll have you work the pole first, and then we'll move to lap dances. To make it a little less awkward considering our association, I'll have you dance for Brandon."

"The same Brandon that was using my couch for nefarious purposes?"

Marcus laughs. "Yes, the one and only. He's our assistant manager. You'll get to know Brandon well. I'll be out front waiting. I'll turn on the stage lighting with some music. Any requests?"

"Surprise me."

I'm sure I'll look back ten years from now and this will be a defining moment in my life. Whether it's a good moment or a bad moment, has yet to be determined.

seventeen

The main room has been completely transformed. It's much darker now, illuminated by purple and red disco lights dancing around like fireflies. A sexy R&B song flows through the speakers, amping up the vibe. This place screams sensuality in its purest form. I'm definitely getting a lesson in humility, as I can certainly see the appeal.

I'm still standing against the dressing room door, mentally preparing myself. I'm wearing a red lace midriff tank, a matching skirted garter belt, fishnet thigh highs, and my ass is just hanging in the breeze since I'm wearing a thong. I take a deep breath and remind myself that I don't have any other options. Especially if what Marcus said about the money is true.

I make my way over to the platform and step up to a

pole. I look up and see Marcus and his associate staring at me with wide grins plastered across their faces.

"You look incredible, Katherine," Marcus says. "Better than I imagined."

I choose to ignore the nausea that sets in with his slimy comment. If I'm going to do this for a living, I'd better get used to it.

I hold my finger up. "We're not using my real name."

"So what shall we call you, my dear?"

I think about it for a second. "Red." Yes, I know it's twisted that I'm using the nickname Gavin gave me, but I feel it's appropriate. Red is confident. Sexy. She knows how to make a man bend to her will. I'm trying to convince myself that using an alter ego will help me get through this.

Brandon chuckles. "Fitting. I like it."

Okay, so you're probably thinking at this point I have no clue what to do, but that's not the case. You see, that's the beauty of the internet. I'm a quick study and there are a surprising number of striptease tutorials on YouTube. I'm not stupid; I won't be trying anything fancy without practice, but I think I have the basics down. I try pretending the men in front of me aren't there as I raise my arm and grab onto the pole. Putting one foot in front of the other, I slowly surround it until I've made a complete circle. I'm sure this would look much sexier in heels, but I'm working with what I have at the moment.

With an unnatural grace I didn't know I possessed, I grab the pole with both hands and arch my back until my hair is touching the floor. I lower myself to the ground and flip onto my stomach. My chest pressed to the floor, I raise my round ass in the air. I do this a few times as I crawl forward with my forearms.

"Very well, Katherine," Marcus coos. "You seem to be a natural."

"It's Red, remember?"

"Right. You seem to be quite the natural, Red. Shall we move on to clothing removal?"

"Sure," I say as I saunter back over to the pole.

With my back turned to my audience, I open my legs wide and squat down against the pole. On the upward move, I turn around and begin working the laces that run down the center of my top. After the final tie has been undone, I let it fall away. I slide the strap off one shoulder, then the other, now fully exposed from the top up. I don't mean to, but I catch Marcus's heated gaze and start feeling sick again. He's looking at me with unguarded lust. This man, who is going to be my stepfather in a matter of months, wants me. There's no doubt he's having highly inappropriate thoughts at the moment.

I freeze for a moment before turning away and working the pole like a boss. *Just pretend he's not there*, I repeat to myself over and over. For the most part it works as I take off one article of clothing after another until I'm standing completely naked. Mind you, I've stripped willingly in front of other men plenty of times, but I've never been on display like this before. Trust me when I tell you that it's a very different animal. Every self-conscious thought I've ever had is needling away at me. Every insult that has been thrown my way is piling up. I don't know how any girl does this without feeling insecure. I certainly have much more respect for the profession now.

"Red, are you okay?" Brandon asks.

I didn't realize I had stopped moving until he spoke.

"Uh...yeah, sure. Sorry, I got distracted for a moment. Should we move onto the lap dance portion of the evening?"

Marcus stands and offers me a short silken robe with the club's logo on the breast. "That won't be necessary, Katherine. We've seen everything we need to see."

What? Did he not like my performance? He certainly seemed into it.

I wrap the robe around my body. "So I guess that's it then? When will I hear back from you?"

"The job is yours, Katherine. Come in tomorrow at five and I'll have you meet with Shawn, our house mother, for the specifics. I'm quite impressed; I've never seen someone more natural at this."

Great. Just what every girl wants to hear.

eighteen

Dylan leans against my locker. "Hey, babe. How was first period?"

"Ugh," I complain. "Brutal. We had a quiz and I'm pretty sure I got a B at best."

He gasps in mock horror. "Oh, no, your perfect record is at risk!"

"Oh, shut up, you know how important my grades are. I'll be applying for scholarships soon; I can't fuck up."

He puts his arm around my shoulders as we walk to class. "I'm sure it will be okay, baby. You're the smartest person I know."

"Thanks, Dyl."

"What are you doing after school? I was hoping we could hang."

Translation: I was hoping we could fuck. This isn't the

first time he's asked over the past few weeks. Even though I decided that I wasn't going to sleep with him again, I haven't had the nerve to officially cut him off yet. He's one of my best friends; I don't want to risk losing that by hurting his feelings. I'm sure we'll have to talk about it one day soon but I'm pushing it off as long as I can.

"Can't," I say, "I start my new job tonight."

He pulls me to the side so we're not hit by the other people rushing to class. "You got a job? That's awesome, babe!" He pulls me into a rib-crushing hug.

I pull back and mutter, "Yeah, thanks."

He looks confused. "What's wrong? I thought this was a good thing."

"It is," I nod. "I mean, the money's good. *Really* good."

"Then why do you have that shitty look on your face?"

Okay, I might as well get this over with. It's not like I'm going to announce my place of employment to the world but there's no sense in hiding it from him.

"Because I took Marcus up on his offer."

He mimes unplugging his ears. "I'm sorry, but I don't think I heard you correctly. Would you mind repeating that?"

The warning bell rings. The buzz in the hall gets louder as the students really start to hustle.

"You heard me. I'm going to be a dancer. The hours are short and the money is more than enough."

"Over my dead fucking body!" he shouts. Despite the volume surrounding us, he's loud enough that we garner more than a few curious glances.

What the hell? Why is he reacting like this? If anyone would approve of a naked lady profession, it'd be him.

"What's your problem, Dylan?"

He grips my bicep. Hard. "Are you fucking kidding me, Kat? Why would you think I'd be okay with you taking your clothes of in front of a bunch of drunk men?"

"Let. Go. Of. My. Arm," I say, seething.

"I'm sorry." He releases me and rubs a hand over his face. "You can't do this, Kat. I won't allow it."

"You won't *allow* it?" I repeat. "Who the hell do you think you are? You and Bree understand my situation more than anyone. I don't have a choice; the benefits far outweigh my pride. You know how much I need the money. Even if I didn't, it's not your decision. It's *my* body, Dylan."

"The fuck it is!" he yells. "I'm not going to share you with a bunch of nasty, lonely men looking to get their rocks off."

"I'm not yours to share!" I scream back.

"Hey!" a loud voice booms. "What's going on out here?"

I look up and realize that the bell must have rung. Dylan and I are the only ones left in the hall. *And the very angry teacher yelling at us.* I didn't notice until now that we'd stopped right outside of our next class.

Gavin crosses his arms over his chest. "Well? I'm waiting for an explanation."

Dylan mimics his stance. "Don't hold your breath, Teach."

"Watch it, Mr. Taylor," Gavin warns.

"Fuck off," Dylan mutters under his breath.

"That just earned detention after school," Gavin says curtly.

I roll my eyes. "Un-fucking-believable."

Gavin points his finger at me. "You too, Miss Kennedy."

What? Is he serious?

"You can't give me detention!" I protest. "I start my new job today."

"Fine. Then you can serve yours during lunch."

"Are you kidding me?"

"Afraid not," he replies. "Now both of you get inside and take your seats. This conversation is over."

Dylan stomps into class as I glare at Gavin in a silent standoff.

He raises an eyebrow and smirks. "Something you'd like to add, Miss Kennedy?"

"So many things," I mumble.

He leans into my ear, causing my blood to boil for an entirely different reason. God, what is it about this man's scent that drives me insane? I feel like I'm melting into a puddle of horny girl goo.

"Have I ever told you that I find you especially sexy when you're pissed off?"

I blink a few times as he turns to walk away. *Did I imagine that?* He's acting as if he didn't just say something incredibly improper. And *oh, so hot.*

He stops at the threshold and looks over his shoulder. "Get inside, Kat. *Now.*"

I have to bite my lip to prevent myself from echoing his statement. *Only I wouldn't be talking about a classroom.*

nineteen

I arrive to detention like the good little student I am. You know, besides the whole detention aspect of it. Gavin looks up from his desk as I enter the room and smiles. I stop mid-stride, caught off-guard by the gesture. Over the past month, he's barely spoken to me and certainly hasn't looked happy to see me. Right now, he's looking at me like I'm the biggest box under the Christmas tree with his name written all over it. His mask slips, revealing blatant desire on top of it. I flush all over and bite my lip to stifle a moan at the memory his expression invokes.

"Come sit down, Kat."

"What happened to Miss Kennedy?"

He stands up and pulls out the chair in front of his desk. "There's no one else here, so there's no need to be so formal."

I shake my head as he gestures for me to sit. "Um, I think I'll sit at my normal spot in the back, *Mr. Cooper*." He assigned seats after our discussion about boundaries and placed me as far away from him as possible.

He grins. "No, I think I'll have you sit right here where I can keep a better eye on you."

What is he doing? He's the one who suggested we keep our distance and now he wants me to sit with him? *At the sex desk?*

"I *really* don't think that's a good idea."

"Why not?"

I place my hand on my hip and give him an *'are you kidding me'* gesture.

"Why not, Kat?" he presses.

"I thought that was a rhetorical question. The reason should be pretty clear, *Mr. Cooper*."

"A teacher can sit next to his student. It's perfectly innocent."

"Right," I scoff. "Not *this* teacher and student. Not at *that* desk."

He rubs the surface of the desk with a lover's caress. "Ah, yes, I have become quite fond of this thing."

I'm catapulted back to the first day of school. The whole thing flashes through my mind in a matter of seconds. Gavin ripping my panties down, splaying me over the flat surface, taking me from behind with more hunger than ever before. His hands and lips are everywhere, like he can't get enough of me, despite the fact that he's filling me so completely. It's unequivocally raw and desperate and *passionate*. I've never experienced anything like it before. I'm guessing he's having similar thoughts because his expression has taken a turn toward carnal.

"Gavin, what are you doing?" My voice is so low it's barely a whisper.

He looks at the door pointedly. "I just want to be near you. I miss talking to you. The door is open; nothing's going to happen." He pats the chair. "Now sit."

I take the offered chair and open my backpack to retrieve the latest novel I'm reading. I flip to the bookmarked page and try focusing on the words while Gavin rounds his desk and sits down.

"*The Shining*?" he laughs. "In the mood for some light reading, are you?"

"I wanted something creepy," I say with a shrug.

"You know, I once stayed in the hotel that inspired the story. It was a really cool experience."

"Really?" I ask. "That would be amazing. I haven't even been to the lodge where the movie was filmed and that's right here in Oregon."

"Not much of a skier? I hear Timberline is a great place to go."

"Not by choice," I answer. "I'd love to take up snowboarding one day if I could ever afford it. Honestly, I've rarely been away from the coast. Not many opportunities for someone like me."

"What does that mean? *Someone like you?*"

He's seen where I live; what I drive. He's met my mother. You'd think it'd be pretty self-explanatory. I give him an incredulous look.

"What does that mean, Kat?" he repeats.

I sigh. "Do I really need to spell it out for you?"

"I think you do."

Okay, now I'm getting angry. Why is he making me verbalize this?

"Hmm, let's see." I use my fingers to tick off the reasons. "For one, I've been bounced around the system most of my life. The majority of that time has been spent in a group home. Two, it should be pretty obvious by my current living conditions that money is tight. Cybil doesn't have a very...conventional job. The only reason we can afford our shitty apartment is because she receives assistance from the state. Any money she does have left is spent feeding her addictions." He winces at that last admission. "Three, now that she's moving out, I won't even have that to rely on. Four,—"

"What do you mean she's moving out?" he interrupts.

"She's moving in with her fiancé at the end of the month."

"And she's going without you?"

"Yep."

"I don't understand."

"Which part isn't clear? She's moving out. I'm not; therefore, I have to figure out how to pay the bills."

"She can't do that," he argues. "You're still in school."

"I'm also a legal adult in case you forgot."

"Oh trust me, I haven't forgotten *that*," he mutters. "I just meant that she can't just leave you to fend for yourself while you're still in school. How are you supposed to pay for anything?"

Oh, shit, I didn't see the conversation leading here.

"I found a gig that pays really well. I'll be working less than twenty hours a week but I'll easily be able to make rent."

He narrows his eyes at me. "What kind of job?"

"It's nothing illegal if that's what you're insinuating."

"You mentioned you're starting today."

"I did," I confirm.

"So, I'll ask again. What kind of job? And where?"

I cross my arms in defiance. "I don't think that's information a *teacher* needs to know. Do you?"

"It is if I'm concerned about your well-being. As a teacher, I'm responsible for students when they're away from their parents."

"Not if the student is eighteen."

"I disagree. I still have the right to be concerned if I think they're putting themselves at risk."

"Thanks for your concern but I'll be fine, Mr. Cooper."

"What are you hiding?"

"I'm not hiding anything," I lie. "I just don't think it's any of your business."

He chews on that for a moment. "Why aren't you eating?"

"I usually get lunch from the cafeteria. Since I'm in here, I can't do that."

"I didn't say you couldn't eat."

"How was I supposed to know? I've never had detention before."

His eyebrows lift. "Never?"

"Never," I repeat. "Why is that so hard to believe?"

"Oh, I don't know...maybe because you're one of the most obstinate people I've ever met? You also curse like a sailor. I'm sure that's ticked off a teacher every now and again."

I smile. "Maybe you bring out my bad side. Ask around; you'll find that I'm an exemplary student."

Gavin chuckles as he rustles through his lunch sack. He places a sandwich on the desk in front of me. "Here, eat this."

"I'm not going to take your lunch."

"It's my fault you don't have a lunch. I can get something later."

My initial instinct is to argue but then I consider that

this will likely be the only chance I get to eat for the rest of the day. I unwrap the sandwich and take a bite.

"Mmm, you make the best sandwiches. I should change your name to the Sandwich Man."

He takes a bite of an apple. "Nah, I think we should stick with Sparkles."

twenty

My new job has been much different than expected. On my first day, I met with the house mother, Shawn, who was a dancer in her youth. Now she's in charge of training, wardrobe, and making sure everything runs smoothly. She's actually very sweet and seems to have a genuine concern for the girls.

The Pitiful Princess apparently has a reputation to uphold, so I'm not allowed to start working the floor until Shawn has decided I'm ready. I've met with her every day after school learning classic pole and lap dance moves. Other girls come in on occasion to lend their expertise as well. Over the past three weeks, I haven't had to remove any clothing in front of an audience. Hell, I haven't even been out in the public spaces yet. I mostly train before opening or in an empty VIP room. Let's face it—the real money is in the tips and commissions so it'd be in my best interest to get out there as soon as possible. Like I said before, I'm a quick study, but this shit isn't as easy as it looks.

I could barely walk after my first week. I had sore muscles in places that I didn't even know *had* muscles. My entire body has been conditioned to the point of exhaustion. I do have to admit that I'm pleased with the results though. I've been blessed with curves on a naturally thin frame but I never really had any muscle definition before. Now, my thighs are tighter, my arms more sculpted, and my previously weak core feels stronger. My posture is even better. I guess the term *dancer's body* isn't exclusive to a discipline that requires clothing. I can only imagine what I'll look like with continued practice.

"Verra' good, lass." Did I mention Shawn is from Scotland?

I just successfully executed an inverted twist called the Russian Lay Back. I've been working on the damn move for two days. I hop on the balls of my feet in excitement. "I finally did it!"

Trina, one of my fellow dancers, holds up her hand for a high five. "Nice job, girl! I think you're ready to get out there!"

"Do you think so?" I ask Shawn.

"Aye," she says. "I think you're ready to start making some money. How do you feel about that?"

How do I feel about that? I can't say I'm excited to bare all to the general public, but I'm definitely excited about having a roof over my head and food in the fridge. Now that I've had some practice, I certainly feel more confident.

"I'd like to try."

"Great," she replies. "I'll tell Brandon you're ready to show him what you've got. If he signs off on it, maybe we can get you on stage tomorrow night. The lads are going to love you; I'm sure of it."

I get home later that evening and find Cybil waiting for me. She's wearing a low-cut black cocktail dress with her hair swept into a twist. Very fancy, especially for a Thursday night.

"Hi, honey. I was hoping you'd get home before I turned in."

"Are you working tonight?" I ask.

"No, I accompanied Marcus to a business dinner. Some Japanese investors are in town and he's showing them around."

I maneuver around the U-Haul boxes stacked by the front door. "What'd you want to talk about, Cybil?"

"Marcus tells me you're ready to hit the stage. I wanted to congratulate you. He's very excited about showing you off."

"Gee, thanks, Mom. I'm so glad you're proud that I'll be shaking my titties for a living."

She rolls her eyes. "You don't have to be a smartass about it, Katherine. You have nothing to be ashamed of. Plenty of women do this for a living. Marcus tells me some of his past dancers have become doctors, lawyers, veterinarians, you name it. There's no shame in exploiting what God gave you."

"You're the expert when it comes to exploiting your body."

"My point was that it's a respectable way to support yourself," she huffs.

"I didn't say it wasn't. Most of the girls who work there are actually pretty cool. But here's the thing— they're stripping to make their way through *college*. I'm the only one still in high school. You're not supposed to worry about being a grown-up until graduation. But let's be real. Shall we? You and I both know I've been the only responsible one around here for a long time, so what's new? You can't take care of a plant, let alone your own kid. I'd be better off without you in my life. You're pathetic."

I didn't see it coming until it was too late. Her slap reverberates throughout the room as the pain sets in. I rub my aching cheek, part shocked that she actually laid a hand on me, and part resigned, not surprised at all that she would take things to the next level. I've had to endure so much from her throughout my life, what's one more thing?

"*You ungrateful little whore!*" she screams.

"That's rich, Mother. I guess you have to be one to know one, huh?"

I wipe the stupid tear from my eye and turn around to walk out the door. Without another thought, I start my car and drive to the one place that I shouldn't go.

twenty-one

I pound angrily on the front door. I hate Cybil for making me feel so weak. I hate her for loving drugs more than she loves me. I hate her for the pain I still feel on my face. I hate her for fucking *existing*. Life would be much easier if she'd just go away.

I knock even louder. "C'mon, Gavin. Open the door. I know you're there; your car's in the driveway."

I blink as the porch light comes on and the door cracks open. Inside the frame stands a statuesque woman, wearing nothing but a long t-shirt.

"May I help you?" she asks in a stupidly melodic voice.

Shit! Why did I assume he'd be alone? Just because I can't seem to move past him, doesn't mean he should have the same problem. Shit! Shit! Shit!

"Oh, um...I'm sorry; I must have the wrong house."

The door opens wider, revealing Gavin wearing nothing but a pair of flannel pajama pants. I can't seem to stop myself from checking out his finely sculpted abs.

"Elle, what's—" We make eye contact. "Oh. Kat, what are you doing here?"

I wipe a traitorous tear from my eye. "Nothing. I shouldn't have come here. I'm sorry."

I try making a quick retreat but he grabs my wrist. "Wait a minute."

I turn around and look toward the beautiful brunette eyeing us with curiosity. "No, you have company. I should go."

He sighs. "Kat, this is my *sister*, Elle. She's visiting from California. Elle, this is my...*friend*, Kat Kennedy."

Sister? I'm more relieved than I should be about that.

"Um, hi," I offer awkwardly.

She smiles. "Hi. It's nice to meet you." She looks to Gavin. "Gav, I'm going back to bed. I have a feeling I'll see you later, Kat."

Damn it, I clearly woke them; I didn't consider the time when I drove here. Oh, who am I kidding? I didn't consider *anything*.

He tugs on my hand, leading me into the house. "C'mon, it's freezing out here."

I dig my heels in. "No, I should go. I didn't realize how late it was."

"Kat, don't make me haul your ass inside. You're obviously upset. Now get in the house and talk to me about it. Coat?" He holds his hand out expectantly as I walk into the foyer.

Fuck, I'm still wearing my clothes from the club. I clutch the coat tighter around my body.

"No, that's okay; I'll keep it on."

He notices my bare legs. "Are you wearing anything underneath?"

Geez, did he think I came here to seduce him? I know, I know; my past behavior says that wouldn't be too far-fetched.

"Of course I am! I'm wearing my...workout clothes."

He extends his arm further, challenging me to hand over my coat. "Prove it."

"Fine," I agree as I shrug my coat off and throw it to him. "But I expect you to apologize for being a jackass."

He catches my jacket and stands immobile, staring at me with wide eyes. I'm wearing a white spaghetti strap tank top from the club with the word *Princess* stamped across my breasts and a pair of black booty shorts. Okay, so it may not be much, but everything is covered at least. I follow his gaze to see what the big deal is. *Oh.* Okay, so I'm not wearing a bra (why bother when you have to take it off anyway?) and apparently, I'm still cold from being outside. My nipples are sticking out like giant beacons in the night.

"You went to the gym dressed in *that*?!"

"I didn't say I was at the gym."

"Well then where were y—" His eyes open further

and he advances upon me. Gently touching the side of my face he says, "Kat, *why the fuck* is your cheek red and puffy?"

What? My face still stings but I never thought to check for marks. Great, how do I explain this?

I cover his hand with my own. "Um..." I'm so embarrassed that he's seeing me like this I'm speechless. I'm *never* speechless.

His expression softens as he cradles my face. "Please talk to me."

"I can't."

He crouches down to look me in the eyes. "Kat, you're going to need to find the words. Because right now, I'm imagining all sorts of possibilities and making a list of people that I need to hurt."

I smile. I know it's wrong, and I know we can't explore anything, but the fact that he seems so invested tells me that I'm not the only one feeling this way. God, why does the one person I'd actually want to be with be the one person I *can't* be with?

"It was my mom," I admit. "I said something that I probably shouldn't have, and she slapped me across the face. *Really hard.*"

Gavin clenches his jaw. "Has she hit you before?"

"No. Never."

He straightens and grabs my hand, leading me down the hall. I remain silent as we cross into his bedroom and he closes the door. He shuffles through a dresser drawer and pulls out a t-shirt and a pair of boxer shorts.

"What are you doing?"

"I'm getting some clothes for you."

"Why?"

He waves his hand up and down. "Because I can't stand here another minute with you dressed like *that* and not act on it. But I'm not letting you leave either. I don't want you to be alone tonight. I thought you might want to take a hot shower before coming to bed."

My heart rate picks up. "Are you crazy? I can't stay here. The fact that I came here in the first place has to be against some rule."

"I don't give a fuck about the rules right now," he says with complete conviction. "You need a friend and that's what I'm going to be. I'll sleep on the couch—I don't care where I am as long as I know you're safe."

I pick up the shirt he laid out for me and pull it over my head. I crawl toward the bed and slide under the covers, sighing when my head hits the pillow.

"You don't want to take a shower first?"

"No. I just want to forget tonight ever happened."

"Oh. Okay. Well...I'll be out in the living room if you need anything."

I sit up. "Gavin, don't go."

He looks at the empty spot on the bed. "I don't think that's such a good idea."

"Please just stay with me for a bit."

He joins me on the bed and lays down on top of the covers. "Do you want me to turn something on from Netflix?"

"Sure. What'd you have in mind?"

He gets a boyish smile on his face. "Okay...if anyone asks about this, I will deny it until I'm six feet under."

"And what's that?"

"I'm going through a *Dawson's Creek* binge right now. Wanna watch it with me?"

I can't help it; I laugh until I'm snorting. "Are you serious?"

Gavin grabs the remote and begins flipping through the menu. "Completely serious. I never joke about *The Creek*."

"Wow...I have no words."

He bumps his shoulder into mine. "C'mon, you'll love it. Have you ever seen it before?"

"Of course I have!" I reply. "Do you know how many *Dawson ugly cry memes* there are in existence? I had to know the source."

"Yeah, I'm definitely Team Pacey all the way. Dawson is way overrated."

I smirk. "Oh my God, when did you grow a vagina? I could've sworn you were a dude."

His expression changes from jovial to angry in an instant. "We both know damn well I'm one-hundred-percent male. Don't make me prove it to you, Kat."

And with that, my expression morphs into equal parts stunned and horny. "Uh…"

He clears his throat and pushes a button on the remote. "And on that note…let's forget I said that and get lost in North Carolina teen angst."

"Okay, but make sure it's an episode that has Mitch in it. Dawson's dad is where it's at."

"You like older men, huh? I'll have to remember that."

I burrow under the covers and yawn. "I walked right into that one, didn't I?"

He smirks. "Pretty much."

"Just hit play, smartass."

"Now that, I can do." He presses play and the opening sequence begins.

As we lay there watching the show, I begin to slowly drift off. I smile softly when I feel Gavin petting my hair. My eyes close as I give myself over to this wonderful feeling. For the first time in my life, I fall asleep feeling completely safe.

twenty-two

The doorbell rings again so I get up to answer it. When I open the door, I see two men around my foster-dad Pete's age standing there smiling.

"Hi, come on in. The guys are just getting set up in the kitchen."

My foster-mom, Judy, is a night nurse at the hospital one town over. She works twelve hour shifts so I don't see her much on work days. Pete works from home with some tech-based job so he's the one here with me more often than not. He's pretty laid back so it's cool. I've been with the Andersons for four months now and I have to admit that it's the most stable home I've known. We have meals together, movie nights, and other normal family stuff. Judy once shared with me that she and Pete opened their house because they were unable to conceive. She wanted children desperately but she had issues with egg supply or something like that. They figured that fostering was the next best thing so they could still make a difference in a child's life.

She even took me clothes shopping before school started. I've never had the luxury of buying multiple outfits at one time just because a new year was beginning. Especially not brand new clothing from the mall. Now than I'm in high school, I'm learning that appearances are more important than ever. If you want to fit in, you have to look a certain way and act a certain way. Being bounced around throughout my life, I've learned some tricks about being accepted pretty easily and they seem to be working. High school has actually been fun. I have lots of new friends and dare I say, my first sorta boyfriend. Judy and Pete say I'm too young to date, but they have let Stephen come over to hang out as long as adults are present. Most kids my age would gripe about having rules and things like supervision, but to me, it's a refreshing change of pace. I like the fact that they care enough to make rules.

Pete is having some friends over for poker so he said I could invite Stephen. While the grown-ups are socializing, Stephen and I will be in the basement watching a movie. Speaking of...the bell rings again and I open it to see my favorite face in the whole world smiling back at me.

"Hi," I whisper.

I can feel my cheeks flushing which is so embarrassing. I don't know why I'm so painfully shy around boys. I'm sure a head doctor would attribute that to seeing some of the men my mom usually hangs out with, but I don't know.

Those guys give me creepy looks every now and again, especially since I grew boobs, but they ignore me for the most part.

"Hi, beautiful."

Stephen pulls me into a hug and I melt. He's so sweet and cute; I don't know how I got so lucky. He's a junior and already the captain of the varsity soccer team. He's super patient with me too. I know he's been with other girls who let him have sex with them but at fifteen, I'm just not ready yet. Don't get me wrong, I definitely have sex-type feelings sometimes, especially when Stephen and I are making out, but we haven't gone past second base.

I invite him over to the kitchen and throw a bag of popcorn in the microwave. Once it's ready, we make our way downstairs with an assortment of snacks and sodas.

"Thanks, babe. You're awesome."

I smile as I settle in next to him and grab the remote to start the movie. He gets a mischievous grin on his face as he reaches into his coat pocket. He produces a little flask and holds it up.

"I thought we could have some extra fun tonight."

"Is there alcohol in there?"

"Yep," he grins. "I swiped some rum from my old man's liquor cabinet. It will go great with the soda."

"I don't know, Stephen. If Pete finds out, he'll be really mad."

"C'mon, baby; he'll never know. The door to the basement is closed and they'll be busy drinking beer and playing

cards for hours. We don't have to have much—just enough to get a good buzz."

I hesitate. "Okay...but just a little."

"That's my girl!"

About an hour into the movie, I'm really starting to feel drunk. Or what I assume is drunk anyway. I wouldn't know considering I've never had alcohol before tonight. I didn't want to sound lame so I didn't tell Stephen that, but I suspect he knows based on my uncontrollable giggling.

"You're such a cute drunk," he says.

"Shh, don't say the D word! Someone will hear you!"

He laughs. "Oh, Katherine, what am I going to do with you?"

Maybe it's the rum that's making me so bold, but I find myself thinking about all the naughty things I'd like to try with him. I remove my sweatshirt in one swift movement, which leaves me in my bra and jeans. My boobs are bigger than most girls my age, so I usually hide them so people don't make stupid comments. Stephen has felt them before over my shirt, but I've never let him see them before tonight.

"Holy shit!" He stares at me in amazement, like I'm the prettiest thing he's ever seen. "Your tits are incredible. They're huge!"

"Do you want to touch them?"

"Hell, yeah, I do!"

He eagerly reaches out and grabs one in each hand. He brushes his thumbs over my nipples, sending a shockwave of pleasure straight to my panties. I moan as he continues to knead them while he presses me back into the couch. He reaches behind my back and unclasps my bra.

"Stephen, no. What if someone comes down here?"

"Shh, don't worry, babe. We'll hear them walking down the stairs first. I just have to see them. You're gorgeous."

I blush as he removes my bra and just stares at my chest for a few beats.

"Do you like them?" I ask. "More than...other girls' that you've seen?"

He bends over and takes my nipple into his mouth.

"Mmm," he moans. "They're perfect. You're perfect, Katherine."

Perfect. I like that. No one has ever made me feel deserving of that title before but with Stephen, I feel it. We make out for a while and things naturally progress. Before I know it, the only thing either of us is wearing is underwear. He starts pulling my panties down and I have a moment of panic.

"Stephen, wait!"

He slows down and places a soft kiss on my hip. "C'mon, babe. I just want to kiss you." He runs a finger over the center of my panties. "Right here. I'll make you feel so good; I promise."

I writhe as he continues stroking me through the wet cotton. "Okay."

He removes my underwear and lowers his mouth to my center. At the first warm touch of his tongue, my back bows off the couch and I scream in pleasure. I'm lost in ecstasy as he works me over with his fingers and tongue. I never knew your body could feel like this. Sure, I've touched myself before —mostly out of curiosity—but it's never felt like this. Out of nowhere, I feel a delicious pressure building in my abdomen right before stars explode behind my eyes.

"Oh, Stephen! Don't stop! Please don't stop!"

"Katherine! What the hell do you think you're doing?" Pete's voice explodes throughout the room.

"Oh, shit!" Stephen shouts as he frantically jumps off the couch.

I quickly grab a blanket to cover myself. "Oh, God. I can't believe this is happening."

Pete looks at Stephen like he's going to murder him. "Boy, you have exactly thirty seconds to get out of my house before I castrate you."

"Uh..." Stephen stammers as he pulls his jeans on. "Uh, Katherine, I'll see you later." Stephen runs up the stairs without another word.

"Not if you know what's good for you!" Pete calls after him.

I pull the blanket over my chest, afraid to meet his eyes.

"Katherine, what the hell were you thinking?"

"I don't know...I've never done anything like that before. I'm a virgin—I swear! It just felt too good to stop."

I hear him sigh. "You need to get dressed. I'm going to send the guys home and then we're going to have a talk. Don't leave this room. Do you understand?"

I nod while I wipe away my tears of mortification. "Okay."

Pete's back after a short while, taking a seat next to me on the couch. I'm too afraid to say anything so I just sit there.

"Look, I know you're curious; it's natural. Hell, I'm only forty-two—I remember what is was like to have your hormones in the driver's seat."

Ugh, this is so embarrassing. "Pete, I'm sorry. I promise it won't happen again. Just please don't tell Judy or send me away. I love it here; I can't stand the thought of being forced to leave."

He picks up a glass from the side table and sniffs. "Have you been drinking?"

Oh, crap. "Yeah...I've never done that before either. I swear I'll be good. Please just don't make me go."

I feel the couch dip as he comes closer. He places a finger under my chin so I'm forced to look him in the eye.

"I'm not going to send you away. And despite my better judgment, I won't say anything to Judy. But if this happens again, I'll need to get her involved."

"Thank you," I whisper.

"You're beautiful, Katherine. And smart. You don't need to let a boy use your body just to make him like you."

"Stephen's not like that," I argue. "He didn't pressure me at all. I'm the one who...who took my clothes off first."

"I appreciate your honesty," he says. "Look, I'll make you a deal. If you want to drink, I'll let you drink. But only in

moderation and while I'm at home so I can keep an eye on you. If you want to fool around with boys, hell, I can't stop you from doing that either. But you need to promise me that you'll be responsible. When you feel ready to have sex, you need to come talk to me or Judy. We'll make sure you're prepared."

"Really?"

"Really. And if you're curious about sex, there's other ways to get answers."

"Like what?"

"Movies, magazines, things like that."

"Like porn?" I ask, shocked that he's even bringing this up.

He laughs. "Yeah, like porn. I'm pretty sure that's how all of my high school friends got their education." He holds a hand up. "Now you need to understand that most of those videos aren't realistic—but if you're anything like I was back then, it will help...get you by without getting yourself into trouble. It's okay to have these feelings, Katherine. And there's no shame in exploring your own body when you're turned on."

"Um...okay." Could this conversation be any more awkward?

He walks over to the desk in the corner that doubles as his in-home office. He writes something down on a piece of paper and hands it to me. "Here's a website that I like. You should check it out."

twenty-three

"Wake up, sleeping beauty."

I stretch languidly as I drift from dreamland back into reality. I look over and see Gavin smiling at me, looking freshly showered and dressed.

"What time is it?"

"Almost six-thirty. I have to get to work but I figured you needed time to go home and get ready."

I sit up. "Um, yeah, thanks."

"Are you going to be okay?"

"Yeah," I assure him. "If Cybil's home, she's definitely not awake this early. Besides, I'm sure it was a one-time thing."

He gives me a sad smile. "Let's hope. I have to head out. Elle is still asleep so just lock the door on your way out. Okay?"

"Okay. Thanks for dealing with my drama last night. And for letting me stay."

Gavin leans over and places a soft kiss on my forehead. "You're welcome here anytime, Kat. I mean it. My door is always open as your friend."

"A non-naked friend?" I clarify.

"Right," he laughs. "We're definitely friends who wear clothes around each other."

"Pity," I tease.

"I'll see you in class, Miss Kennedy," he winks.

"Bye, Mr. Cooper."

I'm sitting in the school cafeteria eating breakfast when Bree sits across from me.

"Will you please start talking to Dylan again? He's such a pain in the ass without you as my buffer."

"Has he loosened up about my job yet?"

"Not really. But can you blame him, Kat? That boy is crazy about you."

"He is not," I argue. "Dylan and I are just friends."

"Are you sure about that? I don't screw any of my friends on a regular basis."

"You know?"

She rolls her eyes. "Of course I do; I'm not stupid."

"Is he telling people about us?"

"Relax, Kat. He hasn't said a word. I can just tell. It's

cool; Dylan's hot. A bit annoying, but I can see why you're attracted to him."

"I'm not attracted to him," I begin. "Well, I mean, I *am* attracted to him, but it's not like that anymore. We haven't been together in a long time. And before that, it was only once in a while to scratch an itch. He knows it's nothing serious."

"Are you sure about that?" she challenges. "Because from where I'm standing, he's pretty smitten, and he has been for a while." She nods to the doorway where he's standing, watching us. "Please go talk to him. He looks like a sad puppy."

"It's too early for this crap," I grumble. I walk over to Dylan and give him a small smile. "Hey."

"Hey, Kitty. How've ya been?"

"Okay. Busy."

"With work?"

"Yep. They've been training me for the past few weeks. I'm finally going on stage tonight."

He frowns but says nothing.

"Nothing to say about that?" I challenge.

"I have plenty to say about that; just nothing that you want to hear."

Well, at least he's learning.

"Look, Dyl, I don't want to fight with you."

"Me neither. I miss you."

"So we're good?"

"We're good," he repeats.

twenty-four

"Okay people, mock midterms are on Monday. Remember, the test is broken down into six parts: multiple choice, character matching, character analysis, style prose analysis, and two sections with short answers. Go through your notes this weekend on the novels we've read so far. Make sure you can clearly and succinctly articulate your own interpretation of the themes and arguments."

I'm captivated as I watch Gavin address the class. I left his bed only a few hours ago and I can't stop obsessing about how badly I want to crawl back into it. After he left for work, I took a shower before going home. It may be a bit stalker-ish but I had to use his soap so I could still smell him throughout the day. I'm sitting here at my desk like a weirdo repeatedly sniffing my skin, hoping that no one notices. As the bell rings and students begin rushing out the door, I'm firmly rooted in my seat.

"Kat, are you coming?" Dylan asks.

"I'll meet up with you later. I have to ask Mr. Cooper a question about the test."

"Why does it matter? It's not the real thing."

"It matters because the actual exam is almost half our final grade and I want to prepare for it as much as possible. I think Mr. Cooper's idea to have a trial run was brilliant."

"Of course you do, my beautiful overachiever. So I'll see you at lunch?"

"Maybe. I might need some extra study time since I'm working tonight and tomorrow."

"Okay...I guess I'll talk to you later then?"

"Sounds like a plan."

Dylan leaves while one other student is left behind asking questions. As soon as she's gone, I stand up and approach Gavin's desk.

"Hi, friend."

"Hi," he smirks.

"So..." I fidget awkwardly.

"So...?"

"So...I was wondering how you felt about having company for lunch?"

"Depends on who you're talking about."

"What if I said it was me?"

"Then I'd say I'd *love* to have company for lunch."

"Okay. So, I'll meet you back here then?"

"I'll be here with bells on," he winks. As I'm walking out the door he adds, "Miss Kennedy?"

I stop. "Yes?"

"Don't forget to grab food this time."

"Thanks for the reminder, Mr. Cooper."

"I'll see you soon. I'll be the one sitting in the teacher's chair."

"See you soon," I repeat. "I'll be the one with the boobs."

I hear him laughing as I make my way down the hall.

twenty-five

"So, your sister's in town, huh?"

We're sitting at Gavin's desk eating lunch, chatting away like two old friends.

"Yeah, but only until Sunday. She dropped by unannounced to check up on me."

"Why's that?"

"Because she's worried, I suppose," he says and shrugs. "It's her job as my big sister. I haven't talked to her much since the move. I've been...trying to sort through some stuff."

"How much older is she?"

"Almost four years. She just celebrated the big three-o, much to her chagrin."

"Wow, you guys are like, ancient."

"You think you're a funny girl, don't you?"

"I have my moments. So...is Elle the only sibling?"

"No, I have a brother too. Jack is also twenty-six."

"*You're a twin?*"

"No," he laughs. "I'm adopted."

"*What?*"

He takes a sip from his water bottle. "My biological mom developed a drinking problem when my dad walked out. She tried the best she could for an addict, I suppose, but eventually the school caught on that something wasn't right at home. I was seven when they put me in the system. She got behind the wheel after too many drinks and died in a car crash about six months later. Social Services tracked down my dad but he wanted nothing to do with me. The Coopers adopted me about two years after that."

"*Shut the fuck up!*" I slam my hand over my mouth to stifle my outburst.

"I don't really know how to respond to that."

"No...I just meant, how did I not know this?"

"Well, now you do."

"But you seem so well-adjusted."

He laughs. "Why wouldn't I be? I have a great family. Sure, I think about those early years every once in a while, but the happy memories I've had since overshadow any negative ones. I'm sorry that the people who gave me life are no longer in the picture, but I'm also glad that I have my parents. I can't wait for you to meet them. I know they're going to love you."

"Why would you introduce me to your parents?"

He gulps. "Uh...I don't know. It was just something to say, I guess. I wasn't thinking. Of course I wouldn't introduce one of my *students* to my parents. That's ridiculous." He crumples his lunch bag and throws it in the trash. "So, what about your family?"

"You've already met dear ol' mom."

"True...and you said you've never known your dad. What about the rest? Grandparents? Aunts or uncles?"

I shake my head. "My mom was an only child. Her parents were super strict and religious which didn't mesh well with her wild-child ways. She ran away at fifteen and I came a year later. When she was drunk one night, she told me that she tried going home when she was pregnant but they wouldn't take her back. They told her that they wanted nothing to do with a Jezebel and her bastard child. I've never met them. I don't even know if they're still alive."

"Wow."

"Yeah, I come from a pretty stellar bloodline, don't I?"

"*Don't*," he growls.

"Don't *what*?"

"Stop putting yourself down. You're so much better than that. Why are you so willfully blind? You're capable of anything; you've proven that by overcoming your circumstances. You're *incomparable*, Kat. Everyone around you is riveted when you walk into a room. How have you gone your entire life without knowing how truly exquisite you are? You're easily the smartest, bravest, most beautiful person I've ever met."

I'm simultaneously breathless, speechless, and terrified of all the thoughts his words induce. I stand so fast that my chair topples over behind me.

"You can't say things like that!" I shout.

Gavin looks toward the open door and lowers his voice before speaking again. "Kat, calm down. What did I say that was so wrong?"

I can feel my eyes filling with tears. I put my hands out to halt him when he starts advancing toward me. "Don't come any closer!"

He holds up his hands and slowly takes his seat again. "I'm staying put. Now please tell me what's going on in that head of yours. And unless you'd like to draw attention to us, I'd suggest you lower the volume."

I look toward the door to make sure we don't have an audience. Thankfully, everyone is still in the cafeteria or their own classrooms. I take a few deep breaths to calm down before speaking.

"You can't say things like that to me, Mr. Cooper."

"And why the hell not?"

"Because it confuses me!" I whisper shout. "Those aren't things that a *teacher* says to his *student*!"

"You know what?" he says. "You're right. But I don't give a damn right now because apparently, it needs to be said."

"No, it doesn't! It makes me feel important. Like I matter."

"*You do matter!*"

"You don't even know me well enough to say that."

"I know enough," he insists. "I see you, Kat. *The real you*—not the person you let everyone else know. Don't you get that by now?"

"Don't give me false hope like that unless you intend to follow through on it!"

"Kat, calm down. Sit down. Talk to me."

I taste saltwater on my lips as fat drops roll down my cheek. "No. No more talking. No more one-on-one time. I can't do this; it's giving me whiplash. I can't be your... friend. I'm your student—nothing more. *This is me drawing the line.*"

I start to back away when the bell rings, signaling the end of the period. Students begin flooding the halls.

"Kat, wait."

I turn away and step out the door. "I'll see you in class on Monday, Mr. Cooper. Have a good weekend."

twenty-six

"I can't do this."

I'm shaking and nauseated, standing in the dressing room at work. Tonight's supposed to be my first performance in front of a live audience. I thought I was ready. I thought I had accepted weeks ago that I would be undressing for dollars, but when the time comes, I don't feel anywhere close to ready.

"Sure ya can, lass," Shawn assures me. "You've got this. You've been practicing for weeks and you look incredibly sexy."

It's Friday night—one of our busiest of the week—so the club is packed. It was full when I walked in earlier, but twice as many seats were filled when I peeked my head out the door a few minutes ago. I dab my lipstick in the mirror and look at my chosen outfit for this momentous occasion. I'm wearing a red vinyl mini dress that loosely laces up both sides. In the front, my breasts are pressed together, practically popping out of the top, and in the back, the deep V opening exposes the barest hint of my ass. A discreet zipper runs along the side for easy removal. A thick rhinestone choker wraps around my neck and clear 5" stilettos adorn my feet. My eyes are smoky, my lips are red, and my dark hair falls to the middle of my back in thick waves.

Shawn thought my signature color should match my stage name so she's outfitted me with a complete line of red costumes. Halloween is next week, which she says is a crazy night, and she's insisted that I'll be dressed as Slutty Little Red Riding Hood. I've just let her run with it to this point because I know nothing about dressing for a striptease.

I meet my reflection and sigh. Normally, I wear little makeup; usually a swipe of mascara and lipstick is all I need. Tonight, my face is painted in heavy stage makeup. It's supposed to highlight my face better in the darkened room. I look like myself, but older and a lot more sexed-up, which I guess is the point.

"I feel like I'm going to be sick."

"Ah, lass, that's normal. First-time stage jitters. No one's actually puked on stage."

"Well, that's reassuring," I mutter.

She releases a hearty laugh and squeezes my shoulder. "You'll be fine, love; I promise."

I hear Trina's song ending and know that my time is

almost up. When the first few beats of Ciara's "Body Party" starts thumping through the sound system, Shawn pushes me out the door.

"Break a leg, Kat."

"DJ Annie has a special treat for all you lovely ladies and gents tonight. Take out those wallets and let's give a warm welcome to our newest Princess, *Reeeeeddddd!*"

The song kicks in as I take the stage and the room erupts in applause and drunken catcalls. *Don't make eye contact*, I remind myself. I detach from the situation as much as possible and grab the pole. *Smile*, I chant inwardly. *Look sexy. Be charming. Focus on the music and the routine.*

As Ciara sings about the boy she can't get off her mind, I swing around the pole, thinking about the man who occupies mine. When she croons about how tired she is of fighting their attraction, I mourn the possibilities of what could never be. Sliding to the floor in a perfectly executed *Fireman*, I tell myself it's for the best. I'm unconvinced as I lower the zipper suggestively and step out of my dress. The regret is suffocating me—of what I've done, of what I'm *doing*. No one seems the wiser though. Now clad in a bright red bikini, my body glides fluidly across the floor, captivating the audience. I have them in a trance as the spotlight follows my every move, proudly putting my curves on display to feed the hunger that thickens the air.

I forcibly numb myself as the song ends, crawling on

my hands and knees to collect my reward. Fingertips linger on my hips as bills are stuffed under the straps of my G-string. Since this is my first dance, I'm not fully nude—that will come on the next set. *The slower the seduction, the better the pay,* Shawn's voice rings in my head. *Entice them, make them desperate for more as the song nears an end. The men will be lining up for private dances. They'll want to set their eyes on your naked body before anyone else. If you stage it properly, they'll pay for an extended session. They know they can't touch you in those rooms; but they can fantasize about it. We're in the fantasy business, Red. And you're their walking wet dream.*

twenty-seven

I'm exhausted as I leave the club, but I made it through the end of my shift so I'm calling it a success. I can't help but smile as I pull my purse over my shoulder, thinking of all the money I currently have stuffed in my wallet. I made over three hundred dollars tonight. Marcus was right when he projected a new face would cause quite a stir. All of the girls leave together so we're lining up at the door waiting to be escorted to our vehicles. As I step outside, I hear my name being called. I look for the source of the familiar voice until I spot him standing with his foot propped against the side of the building. Nick, the big bald guy I met during my audition, tries holding him back but I let him know it's okay as I head toward my friend.

"Dylan, what are you doing here?"

He shrugs. "I couldn't get inside...the bouncer took

one look at my fake ID and laughed at me. I've been standing here for hours because I had to make sure you were okay. Bree told me you were really nervous about going on stage."

I instantly soften when I see his expression. Equal parts remorse, concern, and affection color his face. I can't even find the will to be mad at Bree right now.

"Don't I look okay?"

He takes a moment to assess me. "You look...good. *Really* good."

I'm dressed in sweats but I haven't washed my makeup off or tamed my hair yet.

"Yeah...well, I feel good. I mean, not *great*...but I'm okay. Really. I already have half of next month's rent. That's what matters."

He walks me to my car and leans against the door. "Would it be all right if I followed you home? I was hoping we could hang out. It's been a long time since we've been alone together."

"Dylan, I'm tired. I don't think that's such a good idea."

"C'mon, Kitty. I'm not trying to get laid. I really just want to talk to you for a while."

He's giving me sad puppy eyes again. He knows I can't resist them. "Okay, but just for a little bit."

Dylan follows me home and into my bedroom. It's two in the morning but there are no signs of Cybil anywhere in the house. Hopefully it will stay that way.

She's on the lease until the end of the month, but she's been staying with Marcus more often than not. Dyl takes a seat on the mattress and holds up the plastic bag he was carrying.

"I brought your favorite."

I smile as I take the bag from him and peek inside. Oreos, gummy bears, trail mix, and a bottle of orange juice.

"Oh my God, you're the best!"

I rip open all three bags and begin inhaling the contents as I take a seat.

"That is seriously the grossest combination of food I've ever seen."

I take a swig of juice. "It is not! It's perfect!"

He laughs. "I'll take your word for it."

"You don't know what you're missing." He makes a face as I spit crumbs out of my mouth while talking.

I finish one more cookie before deciding that I need to get cleaned up. I smell like sweat and a mixture of scented lotion with various colognes.

"Hey, are you cool waiting for me to take a quick shower?"

"I'd be better if you'd ask me to wash your back."

"Funny, Dylan."

"Maybe I wasn't trying to be funny."

"Well, that's a nice offer but I think I can manage. I'll be out in less than ten minutes. Make yourself comfortable."

As I scrub the offensive odors off my body, I think about what Bree said—that Dylan's interested in being more than just a friend. I haven't had a boyfriend since my freshman year; I don't even know what that would involve or if I'm capable of it. But I can't deny that things would be much easier if I could summon those feelings for him. We're the same age, in the same grade, and we get along great. Could I go there? Would it stop me from lusting after my teacher? Would Dylan even want to be with me like that? What about his mom? It would no doubt put a strain on their relationship.

There's definitely chemistry between us. It's not nearly as explosive as it is with Gavin, but really, nothing is. Every time Gavin and I have been together, it's like two forces of nature combining. It's incomparable. *Like you*, his voice echoes through my mind. I've already talked myself out of it as I dry off and throw on a clean pair of sweats. I'm not willing to risk our friendship or his reputation by being with him in that capacity. I walk back into my bedroom and freeze in the doorway. Dylan is lounging on my bed, *completely naked* and hard as a rock.

"Um...whatcha' doing, Dyl?"

He gives me a sexy smile. "You said to make myself comfortable. I thought you meant, make myself *comfortable*."

I close my door and turn the lock out of habit. Dylan takes this as a good sign and perks up even more. He folds his hands behind his head and reclines back onto my pillows. A familiar stirring hits me as I take him in. His athletic build is the type that other girls want and other guys envy. He's hung too; the perfect blend of length and girth. More importantly, he actually knows what to do with it. *Not as much as Gavin does*. I shake off the unwanted thought and wonder if I can resume a physical relationship with Dylan and not screw everything else up. I still haven't moved so he stands from the bed and comes over to me. He grabs my hand and brings it down to wrap around his hardness. Together, our hands pump up and down until a drop of pre-cum leaks from the tip.

"Kat, it's been so long." He brushes my wet hair behind my ear and places a soft kiss on my neck. "This tension between us sucks. I think we need to sweat it out."

I consider my options. Dylan is kind and knows how to make me feel good. He's brushing his hand over my hip and kissing my neck, as I continue to work him over with my hand. I lean my head back as he pulls me into him and moves his lips across my collarbone. We've done this before—*many times*—and it's never been awkward. So why does it feel that way now? Wrong even?

I release him and pull away. "Dylan, stop."

He groans. "I don't want to stop."

"*Well, I do*. You said you wanted to talk."

It takes him a moment for the lust-induced fog to clear. "I know, but I got so hard thinking about you all wet and soapy in the shower. We can talk after."

I shake my head. "There's not going to be an after. Please get dressed."

"What? Why? I'm not seeing anyone, you're *never* seeing anyone, so we're free to take care of each other."

"That's not exactly accurate. I...met a guy. Someone that I really like."

He scowls and grabs his jeans. Pulling them up he says, "What do you mean you *met* a guy?"

"I think it's pretty self-explanatory. I want to try being...exclusive." The word sounds foreign on my tongue.

"Kat, you don't *do* exclusive. You fuck them once and move on. All. The. Time."

"Not *all* the time," I argue.

"You're right; only when I'm seeing other girls. And I'm not judging—I know you're really sexual and you have needs. But those other guys don't even know your real name. *I do*. I know the real you *and* I can make you come better than the rest of them."

Not anymore. I don't think he'd appreciate that remark so instead I say, "Dylan, you're my best friend. I don't want to fuck that up. I don't think we should have sex anymore."

"*Ever?!*"

"Ever," I confirm.

He throws his shirt over his head and slips his shoes on. "So you'll take your clothes off in front of strangers but not me—the guy who actually gives a damn about more than just your body?"

"I'm going to pretend you didn't say that. That's different and you know it."

"Don't you get sick of it, Kitty? Don't you want someone to take care of your body *and* your heart?"

I really do. For the first time in years, I do want more than sex. I want it all—just not from Dylan.

"I think you should leave."

"I'm not giving up, Kat. When this guy breaks your heart—which we both know is only a matter of time— I'll be waiting. We'd be good together and you know it."

The sad part is that he's probably right...yet I can't bring myself to stop him from walking away.

twenty-eight

I've been living on my own for almost a month now and it's going surprisingly well. I'm still pulling straight A's at school and I'm doing so well at the club that I only have to work three nights a week. That gives me plenty of time to study and look into the college application process. I'm applying to several different schools in California as well as two in-state universities. I'm not picky; I'll go to whichever place accepts me and gives me the most scholarship money. I'm thinking about majoring in business which I can do pretty much anywhere.

"Kat, my aunt said you're welcome to come over for Thanksgiving dinner if you don't have any other plans."

"Thanks, Bree. I might take you up on that. I can't remember the last time I had a big holiday dinner." *Yes, you can; it was with the Andersons.*

"Hello? Earth to Kat!" Bree is waving her hands in front of my face dramatically.

"Sorry, I guess I was spacing out."

"I'll say," she laughs. "So I'll see you at my place tomorrow then? Aunt Carol said everything will be ready around three."

"Sounds good. I'll be there."

Today is the last day at McKinley before Thanksgiving break. As we reach the parking lot, I realize that I forgot a book in my locker so I break away from Bree to retrieve it. Students are anxious to begin their long weekend so the halls empty out quicker than normal. School is almost tolerable when I don't have to worry about all the assholes whispering behind my back.

"Miss Kennedy, I'm surprised to see you're still here."

God, I love his voice. Every time he speaks, I feel it in my bones. I imagine him saying all sorts of naughty things in that deep timbre, and it makes me uncomfortably wet. Even with our limited interactions, my body still craves his incessantly. Second period has become an exercise in self-control. I've lost count of how many times I've had to be excused so I can rub one out in the bathroom stall. He probably thinks I'm incontinent.

I close my locker and hitch my bag over my shoulder. "Mr. Cooper, long time no see."

He chuckles. "It's only been about five hours."

"Right...it seems longer though."

"I know what you mean." He gives me a sad smile.

We stare at each other in silence, yet at the same time, we're conversing. I feel dizzy as I study gray flecks in his eyes that are slowly undressing me. He licks his lips and my knees go weak because I *know* that he's thinking about tasting my bare skin. The whole conversation occurs within a matter of seconds but it feels like hours. The physical effect we hold over each other is disturbing. The way we're able to communicate without words is disarming. No matter how much we resist, or how much distance we keep between us, we're helpless to change it. We attract each other on a visceral level.

I force myself to snap out of it. "Well, I should probably get going."

He clears his throat. "Right. Do you have any plans for Thanksgiving?"

"A friend invited me over for dinner."

"Mr. Taylor?"

"No." I feel a moment of sadness at the mention of Dylan's name. He's trying to pretend that nothing's wrong but things haven't quite been the same since that night at my apartment. "His mom wouldn't let me anywhere near her house. I'm working tonight then I'm going to spend tomorrow afternoon with my friend, Bree. Do you have any plans?"

"I do," he nods. "I'm leaving in the morning to go back home for the weekend. It's a quick trip but it will be nice to see everyone. I promised them I would try harder to keep in touch."

"Tell Elle I say hello."

He smiles. "I will. Have a good break, Miss Kennedy."

"You too, Mr. Cooper."

twenty-nine

I'm at the end of my first set when I see him. His eyes are cold, assessing, without an ounce of their usual brilliance. He's standing in front of the bar, radiating malevolence. I'm so caught off guard that I stumble as I walk off stage. My hands are shaking so violently that I have trouble working the combo on my tip locker.

"Lass, you were lovely out there, as usual."

"Thanks, Shawn."

"So much so, that a lad has already requested a private dance. *An extended dance.* They're setting him up in the champagne room."

Thank God. It will give me a chance to get away from that arctic stare. Maybe he'll leave by the time I'm done. What's he doing here anyway? I wouldn't have pegged him as a strip club kind of guy.

"I'll be out in just a few. I need to pick something to wear."

I try calming my nerves while I slip a sheer red negligee over my bikini. I haven't had the jitters since my first night on stage so why are they coming back now? *You know why*, I say to myself. You're not nervous about performing; you're nervous about *him*. You're afraid he's going to judge you like all the others. I throw my shoulders back and raise my chin. *Screw it*, I've got nothing to be ashamed of. I'm doing what I always do— I'm surviving. Besides, the champagne room is right next door so it's not likely that I'll run into him anyway.

I walk through the door with a sexy swagger and recite my standard line. "Hey, handsome. Are you ready to have some fun?"

"I'm certainly ready to see what you have to offer."

Gavin sits in the cream leather chaise located in the center of the champagne room, named for its color scheme of rose, white gold, and shades of cream. A bottle of champagne is included with every dance. I walk over to the bucket of ice and pick up a flute.

"May I pour you a glass?"

I'm trying not to freak out. Trying not to wonder what he's thinking right now. I'm not doing so well with either.

"Please do. I'm rather thirsty all of a sudden."

Our fingers touch as I hand the glass over and sparks shoot under my skin. "Enjoy."

He takes a sip and leans back into the chair. "I believe I'm about to. Shall we get started?"

"Sure." I walk over to the sound system and hit play. Each dancer gets to select their own playlist. I simply have to press a button and *viola*; sexy beats begin thumping through the speakers.

The VIP rooms feature a small platform with a pole that lies between a wall of mirrors and the chaise. I allow the beat of The Weeknd's "Earned It" to flow through my body as I step up. I hook one leg around the pole, kick off with the other, and send my body spinning. Midair, I clench the pole with my thighs and flip upside down. I slide down slowly, arching my back sinuously. I open my legs into a wide V until my thighs touch the floor. My heart is pounding but I'm determined not to falter in front of him. I keep telling myself this is just like any other dance.

Our eyes meet as I lift up and make my way toward the chaise. I lean forward, placing my hands on his knees. His large intake of air tells me he's not as cool as he's pretending to be. I crawl up his body until my cleavage is at eye level, peel the champagne glass from his hand, and take a sip before placing it on the side table.

With my breasts practically smothering him I say, "Do you like what you see, Mr. Cooper?"

"Much more than I should."

His pupils are dilated and filled with heat. A thick

vein bulges from his forehead and his jaw is set into a hard line. He raises a hand and places it on my hip.

"No, no," I scold as I remove his hand. "No touching allowed."

"Is that a special rule for me, or for all your customers?"

"It's a house rule. Hands off the entertainment. You can look all you want but you can't touch."

"And that's what you are? The *entertainment*?"

"You tell me." I roll my hips and press my chest into his face. "Are you entertained?"

"You'll find out if you go any lower."

I smile as I lift off his lap and turn around. He groans when I bend forward and touch the floor. I lower my body into a full split, before crawling forward on all fours. I turn toward him and scissor my legs suggestively before opening them wide, allowing him to look his fill.

"Jesus, Kat."

I join him in the chair again, straddle his legs, grab onto his shoulders, and move my body in a wave-like formation. "So, Mr. Cooper, do you come here often?"

"First time."

He grunts as I lower my body and grind into his lap. I give him a cheeky smile when I feel how *entertained* he is. His lack of control emboldens me. My nerves have taken a back seat and *Red* is now at the helm. I slowly lift the nightie over my head and throw it behind me. My breasts are heavy; swollen with need. Typically, I'd wait longer before removing more clothing but the material from my bikini top abrades my hardened nipples. I reach behind me and loosen the ties. His eyes are fixed on my movements as I remove the tiny scraps of material and dramatically drape it around his neck.

"What do you think so far?" I press my breasts together and roll my nipples through my fingertips. "You didn't look very happy when you first came in."

"I wasn't."

I place my hands on his chest and throw my head back as I ride him over his clothes. Goosebumps scatter across my flesh as I envision doing this to him while neither one of us are wearing anything. I normally do whatever I can to refrain from any lap-to-ass contact during a private dance, but my body seems to have a mind of its own at the moment. I grind into his erection shamelessly, watching with pleasure as his eyes sparkle with unfettered lust.

I bite my lip to stifle a moan. "And now?"

He grabs onto my hips again and this time, I don't stop him. "I don't know...blood isn't flowing so well... to my brain right now." He pulls me into him to punctuate his statement.

"Mmm, I happen to like where it's flowing at the moment."

"Of course you do; you know I'm at your mercy right now."

I laugh unabashedly. "Ah, the power of the pussy."

He smiles. "Only yours."

"Speaking of…"

I stand up and prop my leg on the end of the chair to unsnap my garter. Gavin watches as I remove my shoe and unroll my fishnet stocking. He's fixated as I do the same with the other leg. I untie the strings of my bikini bottom but keep them around my fingers, holding them up, delaying the seduction.

"Is that why you came here? For this?" I release the strings and allow the material to float to the floor.

He bites his knuckles. "Fuck. What are you doing, Kat? What happened to that line you were so fond of drawing?"

"It was erased the minute you requested a private dance."

I climb onto his lap, fully nude while he's fully clothed. I'm sure if I looked down, I would see the evidence of my arousal all over his jeans. I grab the glass and take a healthy sip, needing a moment before I put myself out there. His hands are lightly brushing over my back, down my arms, and across my thighs.

I nibble his full bottom lip. "Why are you here, Gavin?"

He gulps. "I saw the sign out front. I had to see if my suspicions were true."

Ah, the wonderful sign Marcus had insisted on posting, much to my dismay. *Come meet our newest Princess,*

Red. This buxom brunette will make all your fantasies come true.

"And now that you know? Now that we're here like this? What's next?"

He hangs his head on my shoulder. "Nothing," he whispers. "Nothing can come next. I shouldn't be here; I just had to know."

I'm instantly irate. I can't believe I fell into this trap *again*. How many times do I have to make a fool out of myself before I learn? I jump off his lap and grab my robe off the back of the door.

"Kat, wait!"

I pull the collar together and open the door as my eyes fill with tears. I hold my hand up to stop him. "I believe your twenty minutes are up."

"No, they're not."

"I don't want your fucking money; I'll have the club refund you. *Goodbye, Mr. Cooper.*"

I slam the door and run into the dressing room right before the waterworks break loose.

thirty

"Where were you during second period?" Dylan asks.

I shrug. "I skipped."

I couldn't bear the thought of facing him this morning. After Gavin left the club on Wednesday, I faked sickness so I could go home early. I couldn't handle the thought of him staying there watching me dance all night. He may have left right after I did—who knows—but I couldn't take the chance. I think the only reason I made it through my shifts over the weekend was because I knew he was out of town.

I'm still angry, but mostly at myself for letting him get to me like this. I feel so lonely without him. I know how ridiculous that is but I can't seem to stop myself. I've had very little growing up, but I've never felt like I was missing much before he came into my life. Now, I feel like there's this gaping hole inside of me that only he can fill. The only time my chest doesn't hurt is when he's nearby. I felt it the first time we had sex. I was bereft the moment he left my body and every minute that he hasn't been inside me since.

"What do you mean you skipped? You don't skip."

"I just didn't feel like discussing *The Scarlet Letter* this morning."

"Where'd you go?" Bree questions.

"Library."

"You skipped Lit class to go to the *library*?" Dylan says. "You realize how ironic that is, right?"

I say nothing and take a bite of my apple.

"Miss Kennedy, may I see you in my classroom for a moment?"

I practically choke when I hear his voice. *Shit!* Did he overhear our conversation?

"Why, Teach? Have I been naughty?"

Dylan smirks at my smartass comment while Bree's jaw hangs open.

Gavin narrows his eyes at me. "*Because you skipped my class this morning.* Unless you'd like to talk in detention after school, you'll come with me now."

"Fine," I huff. I gather my things since lunch is almost over. "I'll see you later, guys."

"Good luck, Kitty," Dylan calls.

Grudgingly, I follow Gavin down the hall into his classroom. When we step inside, he closes the door and turns the lock. I'm fuming by this point so I take the privacy as my license to get everything off my chest.

"What's wrong, Teach?"

"Why'd you skip class, Kat?"

"Why'd you lock the door, *Gavin*? Are you looking for another lap dance?"

He glances at the door nervously as I begin lifting my shirt. He charges forward and pulls it back down.

"*Stop it!*" he growls.

"Why?" I ask coyly. "You don't want to see me naked?"

"*I always want to see you naked!*" He pulls the ends of his hair. "Damn it! I didn't mean to say that. Forget I said that."

I place my hand on my hip. "Something like that is kind of hard to forget, *Teach*."

"Stop calling me that."

"Why? You're my *teacher*, are you not?"

"I won't *always* be your teacher. In just over six months, you won't even be a student here anymore."

"What does that mean?"

He shrugs. "It's a factual statement. There's no hidden meaning."

My head spins as I try reading between the lines. Is he saying that he wants to pursue something after graduation? Is he asking me to wait for him?

"Stop playing games with me. What are you trying to say?"

"I'm not playing games," he insists. "*I can't say anything.* I'm trying to do the right thing here, Kat. Can't you respect that?"

"I'd respect you a lot more if you'd cut the shit and just tell me the truth. I'm a big girl, Gavin. Whatever it is, I can handle it."

Unless he tells me that he doesn't want me. I don't think I could handle *that.*

His eyes fill with fire. "Fine! You want the truth? The other night...when I saw you taking your clothes off in front of all those men? I wanted to *fucking kill them* for seeing you like that! I wanted to throw you over my shoulder and haul your ass out of there. When we were alone in that room...I wanted to claim your body so badly that it would erase every memory of those assholes leering at you on that stage. I spent the entire holiday weekend drinking myself into oblivion trying to forget the look on those fuckers' faces. Trying to forget how much I want you. How much I miss talking to you. Seeing you laugh. Being the one responsible on the rare occasion when your face does light up. The *truth* is that I want to be in your orbit every second of every day. I want to find some way to make this work. And right now, *in this very moment,* I want nothing more than to throw you over my desk and fuck you until you're screaming for mercy."

He's breathing hard by the time he finishes his rant.

So am I. My body is screaming for his. I'm soaking wet, pliant.

"So do it," I whisper.

He doesn't give me a chance to change my mind. *Not that I would.* He grabs me behind the neck and pulls me into a punishing kiss. He picks me up and lays me down on the desk, our mouths never leaving one another's. Miscellaneous items are digging into my back but I ignore the pain because the pleasure I'm feeling is much more intense. We're so lost in each other that we don't hear the bell ring. Or the knocking.

"Mr. Cooper, are you in there?" a voice calls.

Gavin pulls away from me. "Shit!"

I jump off the desk and we do our best to quickly right ourselves. I take a seat and try looking like I wasn't about to have sex on the desk. *Again.*

Gavin unlocks the door and swings it open. Students are piled up, waiting to get in. I notice a few curious glances as they walk into the room but no one seems to notice anything is amiss. Until I make my way into the hallway and see Dylan leaning against a locker directly in front of the door. He's glaring at someone over my shoulder so I turn around to find the target of his ire. Gavin is standing right behind me, returning Dylan's cold stare. Dylan's eyes meet mine and quickly flicker down my body. I nervously look away, fidgeting under his scrutiny. When I realize how guilty I appear, I meet his gaze and act aloof. That's when I see it. His eyes widen—marginally at best—but I know him well enough to read him. *He knows.*

I quickly cross the hall. "Dylan—"

He holds his hand up. *"You're fucking the new guy? You've got to be kidding me, Kat!"*

He slams his open hand into a locker before storming away, leaving me standing there wondering what the hell I should do. I turn around and see Gavin standing in the doorway to his classroom, clearly having witnessed the entire thing.

"What should I—"

He shakes his head, silently telling me to shut my mouth. "You'd better get to class, Miss Kennedy. We can review your questions about *the assignment* after school."

"Right," I nod.

Hopefully shit won't hit the fan before then.

<h1 style="text-align:center">thirty-one</h1>

I linger by my locker after school as the halls filter out. I tried speaking with Dylan several times but he was doing everything possible to avoid me. We had two classes together after lunch and he acted like he didn't even notice I was in the room. If I didn't catch the occasional glare directed my way, I would've thought I imagined the whole incident earlier.

I wait until I've felt enough people have left before making my way to Gavin's room. He's leaving just as I reach his class.

"Miss Kennedy, can I help you with something?"

I remind myself to be discreet. "Um, I was hoping to ask you about the assignment that's due on Friday."

"I'm sorry but I'm not staying after today. I have to meet the cable guy *at home*. I'm having issues with my service."

"Oh."

He widens his eyes. "So I'll see you later?"

"Yeah, I guess." How is he not worried about the massive pile of shit we could be buried under if Dylan says something? I stare at him blankly trying to figure out what to say.

"Okay, so *I'm going home* then. I'll be there *all night.* You know those cable guys; they're never on time."

Ah, I get it now. "Right. Well, I'll see you later then."

Seemingly satisfied that I've read between the lines, he nods. "Have a good evening, Miss Kennedy."

"You too, Mr. Cooper."

I take the long way to the parking lot so we're not seen leaving together. I spot Gavin pulling out of the lot as I reach my car and count to sixty before starting the ignition and following. I pull into his driveway as he's opening the door to the detached garage. He motions for me to park inside and waits as I exit my vehicle. I notice his eyes darting around nervously.

"You're sure he didn't follow you, right?"

"I'm sure. I saw his truck parked at *Perk Up* on my way over. His shift usually starts right after school on weekdays."

He nods, seemingly satisfied that I've taken neces-sary precautions. "We need to be careful, Kat. *Really fucking careful.*"

"That's why I'm here, isn't it? To figure out what we're going to do about Dylan?"

"Right." He gestures for me to step inside and closes the door behind me. "Can I get you something to drink?"

"A beer works."

He raises an eyebrow. "Really? You'd like to add contributing to the delinquency of a minor to my list of bad choices?"

I mimic his gesture. "Are you calling me a bad choice?"

"Point taken." He smirks as he heads into the kitchen to retrieve two bottles of beer.

I take a long swig before heading over to the couch to take a seat. Gavin joins me and stretches his long legs on the coffee table in front of him. He releases a heavy sigh and turns toward me.

"Have you talked to him since lunch?"

I shake my head. "No. He's pointedly ignoring me. He's pissed."

"Because of me? Or because you're with anyone other than him?"

"Probably both," I admit. "What are we going to do?"

"He has no proof, Kat. We just need to be careful not to give him any."

"Easier said than done," I argue. "Dylan knows me... he knows how to read me. He could tell what we were up to by just *looking at me,* for fuck's sake!"

"He *assumes* he knew what we were up to."

I shake my head. "Gavin, you're not taking this seriously enough. Trust me, Dylan *knows*."

"Why are you so sure of that?"

"Because...he knows what I look like when I'm...in the mood." I don't miss the scowl forming on his face as the words leave my lips.

"I still think we should go with full denial. He has no proof. And we're not going to give him any. We'll stay away from each other at school outside of second period."

"I don't know if that's going to work, Gavin. What if he says something to Principal Edwards? Or anyone for that matter?"

"Then we deal with it as it happens. You know him better than I do—obviously— but I think you should talk to him tomorrow. Say whatever you need to say to alleviate his suspicions. Convince him to keep his mouth shut."

"In other words...you want me to flat out lie to him. Dylan is smart, Sparkles. I really don't think it's going to work."

"Kat, we don't have a choice. Unless you don't want to move forward with me?"

"I'm not going to change my mind. If you're willing to take the risk, I am too."

"I am," he says. "I *definitely* am."

"Okay...but it's only a matter of time before he does the math. I told him I met someone—somebody that I wanted to be exclusive with. He knows that it would take someone pretty special to make me consider that."

He flashes a blinding smile. "Anyone I know?"

I roll my eyes. "Just some guy. Although, now that I think about it...he is somewhat of a cocky ass. I might change my mind."

Gavin catches me off guard by launching himself on top of me. The bottle that I was holding bounces off his chest and rolls onto the floor, spilling beer all over the hardwood.

"You're going to pay for that, smartass," Gavin promises.

"Gavin!" I yelp. "Be serious! We need to talk."

He grinds his growing erection into my thigh and begins kissing my neck. "Does this feel serious enough for you?"

I arch my back as goose pimples scatter across my skin. His tongue flicks out, licking my earlobe before biting down. I grab onto his firm biceps, unable to decide if I should pull him closer or push him away. I suck in a deep breath, trying to identify this unfamiliar feeling roaring beneath the surface. My libido is raging like wildfire—it's always like this with him. But the confusing part is that while ensconced in his arms, I feel protected from *everything*. He makes me feel invincible. The pessimist in me can't help but question that. What happens when he decides that I'm not worth the gamble? Because let's face it—the risk is astronomical.

He could ruin his reputation—*his entire career*. I could fall right back into the black hole that once threatened to swallow me whole. I've suffered my fair share of heartbreak over the years but for some reason, the thought of Gavin breaking me makes me feel like there's nothing that could possibly mend me back together afterwards. There's no backpedaling if we decide to venture down this road together. The funny thing is, I don't think either one of us really has a choice. No matter our differences, or the challenges we face being together, we can't seem to stay away from each other. This connection we share is fierce and undeniable.

He runs his hands through my hair, pulling harshly at the ends so I'm forced to focus on the here and now.

"Stay with me, Kat," he whispers softly. "Feel how good we are together. Don't overanalyze it."

I release varying puffs of air, relinquishing control. I feel a smile forming on Gavin's lips as he makes his way over my collarbone down to my cleavage. My breasts spill over his hands as he kneads them with reverence, brushing his thumbs over my puckered nipples. His fingertips make their way down to the hem of my t-shirt before tugging the cotton over my head. He stares down at my newly exposed skin and traces a finger over the lace cup of my bra.

"I've never seen anything more stunning," he says.

I lick my bottom lip as his gaze darts to my mouth. "Well, are you going to stare at me all day or fuck me?"

"Neither."

"What?" I ask. "You were supposed to go for option two."

He leans forward and tugs on my bottom lip. "Oh, trust me, I'm going to be inside of you. Very soon, in fact. But I'm not going to fuck you this time, Kat."

My brows knit together. "I'm confused."

He grabs my chin, directing my gaze to his. "I'm going to *make love* to you. And when we're done, there's no turning back. I want a life with you. I know that we have obstacles in front of us, but I need to know that you'll be standing by my side while we knock them on their asses."

I give him a teary smile. "Bring 'em on."

"I was hoping you'd say that."

He certainly doesn't need me to repeat myself. I'm hanging onto him like a baby sloth hugging a tree as he strides down the hallway to his bedroom. He slides me down his body until I feel the plush carpet beneath my feet. His eyes never stray as he unbuttons his shirt and toes off the brown loafers he seems to favor for work. He grabs the neck of his white undershirt and pulls it over his head in one fluid movement, a feat that only a man with his level of confidence could pull off so smoothly.

I swallow loudly as I step backwards until the backs of my knees threaten to buckle against the mattress. I quickly remove my shoes and jeans before I lose the ability to stand altogether. I'm perched on the end of the bed, clad only in my bra and panties, as I watch Gavin remove the rest of his clothing. His jeans and boxer briefs come off as if they're stitched together, like they can't stand being on his body a second longer. My mouth waters as his proud, swollen shaft is positioned right in front of my face. I try reaching for him but he seems to have other ideas in mind as he hovers over me, pressing my back into the mattress. Our lips are molded together, kissing each other until we're breathless. His hand slides down my body and my thighs widen in response, aching to be touched by him. He rests his forehead against mine and I gasp when his fingers reach their target. With deft movements, he feels how ready I am, priming my body even more as he continues to work his magic beneath my panties. I'm on the edge, quickly climbing into supernova territory.

"Gavin," I pant. "Please. I need you inside of me when I come."

He pulls back to slide my thong down my legs while I unclasp my bra and toss it to the side. He places a soft kiss against the corner of my lips then rests his forehead against mine.

"Are you really with me, Kat? I want to give you so much but I can't lie and say it's going to be easy. We can't have a normal relationship...I can't offer you the things you deserve until you graduate. No one in this town can know—not your mom, not even your closest friends. Are you prepared for that?"

He leans into my hand as I place it against his cheek. "I'm with you, Gavin."

"Are you sure? Because if it's too hard, I'll wait. It'll be the longest six months of my life, but I swear to God I'll wait."

Tears prick at my eyes. "I believe you. *I do*. But I don't want to wait. I can handle whatever comes at us."

"Thank God," he groans.

We both release a sigh as he slides into me. He peppers my jaw with kisses before pressing his mouth into mine. He moves within me slower than anything I've ever experienced. You'd think the pace would be infuriating but with Gavin, it's perfect. Everything about this feels right. It's much deeper than anything physical. It's *soulful*. When we reach our climax together, I realize that I'll never get enough of this man. No matter what happens in our future, he's permanently etched himself onto my heart. I inherently know that I will never be the same after this.

thirty-two

"**C**'mon, beautiful. The Andersons won't be home until morning. Your basement has the perfect setup for a party."

My foster parents are both gone for the entire evening which never happens. I've been here for over five months now and someone is always home with me. Pete is out of town for some business function and Judy is working her usual night shift at the hospital. My boyfriend, Stephen, is trying to convince me to invite his soccer buddies over to drink and play games.

"I don't know, Stephen. Life is good here; I don't want to mess it up by throwing a party while they're away."

"Babe, I promise things will be chill. Just a few guys to shoot pool and play darts downstairs. I'll even keep the drinks to beer only. I really want you to get to know my teammates. Your foster parents will never know."

When I told Stephen we would have the house to ourselves, I thought he'd jump at the chance to fool around. Inviting his friends along never crossed my mind. I can't say I'm not disappointed. I thought tonight was the night we'd finally go all the way. I know a guy like him won't wait for much longer. He could have any girl he wants but he chose me. Who better to lose my virginity to?

"Stephen, I thought we'd be alone tonight. So we could, you know, do stuff."

"Katherine, I have all night. My parents think I'm staying over at Cam's. We'll have plenty of alone time later. I've been telling the guys about you for months now but they've only seen you at games. I want them to know the girl I've fallen for."

"You've fallen for me?" I ask. "Like, you're in love with me?"

"Of course I love you," he assures me. "What's not to love? You're smart, sweet, and ridiculously hot."

"Yeah, but you could have any girl. Why would you want a freshman with a totally messed up background?"

He smiles warmly. "Babe, those girls have nothing on you. You're more on point than they could ever hope to be."

I return a smile. "I love you too, Stephen."

"You do?"

"I do," I nod.

Seriously, how did I get so lucky? After all the totally jacked-up things in my life, I finally feel like I'm part of a real family. On top of that, one of the most popular boys in school just told me he loves me. I feel like this night couldn't get any better as we kiss to celebrate our declaration of feelings.

"I'd love to hang out with your friends. Invite them over."

Stephen wraps me in a giant hug. "Really? Thanks, babe! This night is going to be so awesome!"

Stephen sends a group text to his friends inviting them over in an hour, giving us a little more time to make out beforehand. He tells me how much he adores me in between kisses, lighting my body on fire with his touch. I know without a doubt that tonight is the night and I can't wait to give myself to him. He makes me feel so special. Most boys in school make lewd comments about my boobs or crack sexual jokes about my pouty lips or round butt. Stephen has never made me feel like he wants me just for my body. He compliments me in a way that makes me feel beautiful, not like I need to take a shower to wash the slime away. He truly is the perfect boyfriend and in this moment, I'd do anything for him.

The doorbell rings a while later and Stephen jumps up from the couch.

"That must be them. I'll answer it." He gives me a quick peck on the lips. "I love you, babe."

I beam. "I love you too."

I watch his cute butt as he runs up the stairs to meet his friends. I nervously smooth down my hair and adjust my clothing so his friends won't know that we were fooling around. As they descend into the basement, I see Cam, Jaden, and Will trailing behind Stephen. They're all varsity soccer players like he is and most girls would say equally gorgeous. My eyes are really only on one guy though—the one who somehow manages to make me feel like a normal teenager instead of someone who's had to bear far too much weight on her shoulders.

"Babe, you know the guys, right?" Stephen asks.

"I do. Hi, guys."

Three muttered versions of hello come my way in reply.

Will raises up a case of beer. "You ready to have some fun, Katherine?"

I glance nervously toward Stephen. When he mentioned beer earlier, I thought he meant maybe one bottle each—not the four or five that could be allotted to each person present.

Stephen reads my mind. "Don't worry, babe. This will barely get us buzzed." He gestures to each boy at his side. "Do you see how big and manly we are?"

I join them in laughter. I suppose I didn't consider that. I'm what you'd call "fun-sized" so it doesn't take much to get me drunk. Not like I'd know really—I've only drank the few times that Stephen has offered since we've been together. But still, each one of these guys are well over six feet and easily have fifty pounds or more over me. Logically, a few beers wouldn't have the same effect on them.

Stephen grabs a pool cue. "Babe, why don't you rack the balls for us?"

"Sure," I shrug.

I can feel several sets of eyes on me as I perform the simple task. I look up to find my boyfriend with all three of his friends looking at me like I'm a big juicy steak. I grimace when I notice that my shirt is gaping at the neckline, exposing my pale blue bra. Cam smirks when I straighten my back and adjust the collar.

"Can't blame a guy for looking when they're staring you in the face like that," Cam says and winks.

Appalled, I glance toward Stephen, waiting for him to defend my honor. I frown when he fist bumps Cam instead. What the heck?

I point toward my face. "Let's keep the eyes up here, boys."

All four of them laugh, especially Stephen.

"Relax, babe," he says. "Your rack is amazing; you should be flattered. As far as I'm concerned, you should just walk around topless. None of us would complain."

Okay, who is this guy and what did he do with my sweet, thoughtful boyfriend from earlier? Did he really just say that? The rowdy laughter and high fives going around confirms it.

"Stephen!" I shriek. "What is wrong with you?"

Stephen walks over to me and pulls me into a hug, despite my protest. "Katherine, loosen up. I'm just kidding. I'm the only one in this room that gets to see your rack up close and personal."

I blush and whisper shout, "Stephen, can we please not talk about the things we do in private?"

He kisses me on the forehead. "Of course, babe." He

squats down so our eyes are level. "Do you forgive me?" He pouts, revealing the boyish side of him that I love.

I tuck my head into his chest. "Okay."

Stephen releases a whoop then proceeds to shoot pool with his buddies while I sit back and watch. They're each on their third beers, while I'm still nursing my first. They're acting kind of funny but I can't quite put my finger on why. They don't seem drunk, but they're definitely really happy and...affectionate. They keep joining together for group hugs, almost always smashing me in the middle of their bro-mance circle. After yet another lovefest, Stephen grabs my face and kisses me passionately. I feel something foreign on my tongue, and immediately try to reject the powdery substance. Stephen won't relent on the tonsil hockey so I wind up swallowing the large lump instead.

I pull back and cough. "What the hell was in your mouth, Stephen?"

Stephen tries rubbing my shoulders but I shake him off. "We thought you needed a boost. You're taking forever to drink your beer."

I narrow my eyes at him. "A boost of what?"

"We're rolling tonight, babe. I slipped some in your beer earlier but it's probably settled on the bottom by now. You're supposed to down that shit—not take all night to finish one drink."

"Rolling?" I repeat. "You mean, drugs?"

Stephen laughs. "Yeah, babe. It's just a little Molly—totally harmless. It'll make you feel good."

"No drug is harmless," I argue. "Stephen, how could you? You know about my mom. You know how I feel about that stuff!"

"Relax, girly," Will says. "What's the problem? You'll be feeling great in about twenty minutes. Then we'll all be ready to party."

"The problem is that you idiots thought you could force feed me drugs without my knowledge! What the hell is wrong with you?" I'm screaming like a psycho at this point.

Stephen holds his hands up like he's dealing with a frightened animal. "Katherine, calm down. You're at your house. What's the worst that can happen? Look, why don't you go sit down and watch some TV? We'll leave you alone and play some darts. You just let me know if you feel like hanging with us. Okay?"

"Fine," I grumble as I slump down on the couch. Boys are so stupid. How could they possibly think it would be okay to slip me something? Ugh!

One sitcom re-run later, I'm singing a different tune. I smile at Stephen from across the room and give him a come hither gesture with my finger. He leans over the back of the couch and starts rubbing my shoulders while kissing my neck. To me, this feels like an orgasm rolled in a warm blanket wrapped in a cuddle. I've never felt anything better in my life. I reach back to wrap my hands around his neck and pull him into a hard, demanding kiss.

"You're so sexy," I mumble against his delicious lips. "Have I ever told you how sexy you are?"

He walks around the couch and takes my hand, prompting me to stand. "Come over here where I can see you spread out for me, gorgeous."

Stephen leads me to the pool table and presses kisses across my collarbone until I'm leaning back against the felt. I stretch languidly, savoring his velvety touch and the smoothness of the surface beneath me. Clothing is removed as we make out to allow better access to the good parts. I completely forget we're not alone until I hear someone else speak.

"Holy shit, they're going to fuck right in front of us!" I think that was Jaden.

I pull back from Stephen's mouth and eye him questioningly. He reaches behind me and unclasps my bra.

"It's okay, babe. Let them see how beautiful you are." He looks over his shoulder as he slowly runs his hands down the length of my torso and removes my bra. "Doesn't this feel good, Katherine?"

"So good," I pant.

"Well, if it feels good with me, imagine how it could be with more hands."

He has a point. Wait...what am I saying? This isn't like me at all. I try to make sense of everything but my head feels too fuzzy.

"Come closer, guys. Show Katherine how much you want her."

Jaden, Cam, and Will line up next to Stephen with grins plastered on their faces. I glance below their belts and sure enough, I can see the outline of their erections.

Stephen pulls my panties down, unbuckles his belt, and removes his penis from his pants. He's long and hard as he rubs the head against my opening.

"Do you want me, babe? Do you want my cock inside of you?"

"Not like this," I say. "Not with them watching." Why am I still lying here exposed like this?

"Katherine, these guys are my best friends. We share everything. You can trust them."

"Everything?" I ask. "Even girls?"

"Sure, if the girl is into it." Stephen looks them over. "Show her, guys."

All three guys push their pants down to their knees, allowing their erections to spring free.

Jaden steps closer and strokes himself. "Touch it, honey."

"Uh...no, I really don't think I—" Seriously, why am I not running for the nearest exit? It feels almost like I'm having an out of body experience.

"Oh, fuck yeah," he says as he pumps up and down. "Your titties are amazing, Katherine. I'm going to fuck those babies after I give your pussy a good pounding."

"Wait...are you saying you want to have sex with me too?"

Jaden runs his palm over the tip of his length and moans. "Hell, yeah, babe. We all do."

Stephen pushes him to the side. "Back up, Jay. Her cherry is mine. Then you can have a shot."

"Fucker," Jay mumbles. "Why do you always get to pop their cherries?"

"What does that mean?" I ask.

Stephen pulls me to the edge of the table and drops to his knees. "Shh, baby. Just close your eyes and we'll take good care of you."

thirty-three

"**K**at, wake up!"

I'm tangled in sheets as I come to, trying desperately to free myself so I can breathe. I wind up falling onto the floor as I finally manage to break loose.

"Whoa!" Gavin shouts. "Are you okay?"

I struggle to calm my racing pulse. *It was just a dream*, I tell myself. Nightmare, rather. *Definitely a nightmare.* Gavin must notice my distress because he joins me on the carpet and wraps his arms around me.

"What's going on, Kat?"

Shit, I must look like a freak right now. I can only imagine what he's thinking. I'm sitting on the floor naked with my knees pulled against my chest. My skin feels clammy and I'm sure I have an awful case of bedhead.

"Nothing," I say and shake my head. "Just a bad dream."

He cradles me to his chest and strokes my hair. "Who's Steve?"

I pull away from him. "What?"

"Steve," he repeats. "You were talking in your sleep."

"What did I say?"

"You were mumbling for the most part. I think you may have said, 'Steve, don't do this.' or 'I don't want to do this.' Something like that."

Damn it. How am I going to explain this? I try schooling my features. "Hmm, that's weird. I don't know any Steves."

Gavin frowns. "Kat, if we're going to give this a shot, you need to be honest with me." He helps me back onto the bed and tucks me under the covers. "Now tell me about your dream."

"You don't want to know. Trust me. It wasn't really a dream. More like a memory."

"About some guy named Steve?"

"Stephen," I correct. "He was my boyfriend during freshman year. It was a *really* bad break up. He's the reason why I don't date."

"Well, now I *really* want to know."

I sigh. "Gavin, please...don't. I don't like thinking about it, let alone talking about it. I like the way you look at me now. That would change if you knew."

He brushes his fingers through my hair. "Kat, I

promise that nothing you can say will change how I feel about you."

"Don't be so sure," I argue. "I already told you…I'm damaged goods."

"And I already told you…*I don't care*. I want to know what makes you tick. Whatever happened back then, obviously still affects you now. You're already thinking about it—or at least your subconscious is. I want to know you. If possible, I want to *help* you. I can't do that if I don't know what I'm dealing with."

His sincerity is obvious but I still hesitate. Not many people know the truth about what happened—not even Bree or Dylan. Sure, they've all heard rumors at one point or another—the whole town has. But the only people who know the true extent of my living nightmare are the people who were directly involved. Since I was a minor at the time, my name was hidden from the media. It didn't stop the speculation, though, once a quarter of the soccer team wound up in jail and I became pregnant.

Since Stephen and his friends were old enough to be tried as adults, they weren't spared in the least. Neither was my foster father, Pete. It wasn't that hard to connect the dots, especially since his wife, Judy was incredibly vocal about blaming me for his arrest. She couldn't accept the fact that her husband could be such a pervert. She went from doting mother one minute to woman scorned the next, publicly shaming me, trying to convince everyone that I put him up to it, despite piles of evidence to the contrary. The only reason Gavin is so clueless is because he's new to town. I'm sure it'll only be a matter of time before he hears something.

I sigh deeply, accepting the fact that I'd rather have him hear it from me than anyone else. I roll over, thinking that it would be easier to get it all out if I don't have to face him. Gavin allows me to look away but he doesn't tolerate any distance. He scoots right behind me and wraps his arms around my midsection.

"When I was fifteen, I lived with a really great foster family...people that I thought were great anyway. They were the only solid examples of parents that I had ever had. I had been with them for about six months before my world was turned upside down."

"What does that have to do with Stephen?"

"I'm getting to that," I reply. "Please, Gavin. Just let me say this before I change my mind."

He kisses the back of my shoulder. "I'm sorry for interrupting. Please go on."

"Anyway...one night the Andersons were gone—Judy and Pete. They were going to be away all night so my boyfriend, Stephen, convinced me to invite a few of his friends over. They were drinking and doing something similar to Ecstasy. I had been slowly sipping on a beer but that's it. Until Stephen drugged me."

I feel Gavin stiffen but he doesn't say a word.

"I was mad when I figured out what had happened... but a little while later, my anger melted away. Stephen and I started fooling around and it felt really good. I know now that it was the drugs enhancing the sensations, but I didn't consider that at the time. All I know is that I wanted him. I was a virgin but I thought he loved me. I was prepared to give him my virginity right then and there. When he began undressing me, one of his friends said something, reminding me that we had an audience. I told Stephen I wanted to stop but...he didn't."

Gavin tightens his arms around me. "What do you mean he didn't? He didn't want to stop?"

"No, he didn't. Neither did his friends."

I hear his teeth grinding. "Kat, I really need you to finish this story because I'm imagining all sorts of horrible things that I hope to God aren't true."

"Your imagination probably isn't too far from the truth. It took me a while to see it this way...but the night I lost my virginity...I was raped. By four high school boys."

His head falls between my shoulder blades. "Jesus." He kisses my back and adds, "Kat, I don't know what to say. All I have are useless platitudes."

I laugh mirthlessly. "Oh, just wait. It gets worse."

"How could it possibly get worse than that?"

"My foster dad, Pete, had an internet-based business that wasn't very...legal. He was busted for distributing child pornography during a state-wide sting. There were a bunch of videos online—naked, private videos. I wasn't his first victim. It turns out, he'd been recording their foster daughters for years. He had hidden cameras in the shower, my bedroom, and the basement. I'm sure you can imagine some of the content considering we were all at the perfect age to discover our hormones. What we thought was private...*wasn't*. The entire incident with Stephen was caught on camera and released with the lovely title, *Virgin Gangbang*. Pete turned me into an amateur porn star and I had no clue. According to the feds, my *series* was very popular."

"Fuck," Gavin says.

"Oh, there's more."

"Are you kidding?" He is incredulous.

"I wish," I say. "Like I said before, I didn't see it as rape at the time. Afterwards, Stephen had convinced me that I wanted it. *I had to have wanted it* because I was wet...and I came. *A lot.* I never fought them off—never even tried beyond muttered protests. I just laid there in a dream-like state taking them into my body. *Every* part of my body, Gavin. In retrospect, I know it was the drugs, but I continued having sex with Stephen for weeks until the video surfaced and the police got involved. I was blinded by my desperation to be loved."

"Please tell me those fuckers got what they deserved."

"Gavin, there's one more thing."

"I'm afraid to ask."

"After the police raid, the arrests...I found out I was

pregnant. With the timing, it was most likely the night of the rape. I don't know which one of them fathered my daughter."

"You have a child." He tightens his arms around me and sighs. "Where is she now?"

The tears are falling down my face. I open the locket around my neck and remove the tiny scrap of pink muslin, holding it up for him to see. "This was hers. It was from the hospital blanket—the one she was wrapped in when she died."

Gavin shifts his body and turns me toward him. Looking into my eyes, he asks, "How? When?"

My breath stutters as he kisses the tears away. "My water broke just over the halfway mark...they said my cervix was incompetent. It was a freak thing that just happens sometimes, I guess. She was born too early and there was nothing they could do. I was forced to deliver her, knowing that when they put her in my arms, it was for the sole purpose of what they called, *comfort care*. At twenty-two weeks, there was no way she would survive without significant brain damage. She was *so small*...so red and wrinkly. She only took a few labored breaths before passing away in my arms."

Gavin pulls me into his chest as I cry for Amelia—for the chances she never had. His breathing becomes choppy and I recognize that he is crying too. This man I've only known for a few months is grieving over what I lost—my innocence, my optimism, and most importantly, my beautiful, helpless child. He whispers sweet words into my ear as he holds me, never once loosening his grip. For the first time since everything happened, I don't feel like I'm floating in a dark abyss. Being here in Gavin's arms, I feel anchored to the present. I think about what anchors represent: strength and stability. I realize that Gavin *is* my anchor. He makes me feel like maybe there is hope for the future—like maybe I'm not so broken after all.

thirty-four

I get to school early and hang out by Dylan's locker. I see him down the hall, waiting to gauge his expression as he notices me. I'm hoping he's had some time to cool down—maybe he's talked himself out of believing what he saw. *What he thinks he saw*, I remind myself. If I'm going to convince Dylan that nothing is going on between me and Gavin, then I need to keep my story straight. I know the moment he sees me because he slows his pace and frowns. Well, so much for my hope that this would all brush over.

"Hi," I say as I step aside, allowing him access to his locker.

"What do you want, Kat?"

"Since when do I need an excuse to talk to you?"

Dylan leans forward and lowers his voice. "Since you decided to start fucking our Lit teacher."

Okay, this is it. This is the moment where I need to convince him that he's totally off base.

"Dylan, that's what I wanted to talk to you about. I don't know where you got such a ridiculous idea, but—"

"Don't bullshit me, Kitty," he snarls. "You can lie to everyone else, but don't lie to me."

"What makes you think I'm lying?"

He slams his locker shut, grabs my arm, and pulls me down the hall into an empty janitor's closet.

"Dylan, what are you—"

"Shut up!" he shouts. "Just shut the fuck up for one minute and let me think!"

I stand there silently, surprised by his outburst. I watch as he seems to be working through something in his head. He runs his fingers through his hair as he paces the small space. He finally stills and takes a deep breath.

"Look, I followed you. Okay?"

"What do you mean you followed me? Followed me *where*?" I ask.

"To that asshole's classroom! You were acting weird so I knew something was up. I decided to follow you out of the cafeteria and find out what was going on."

Okay, this isn't too bad. I can work through this. The door was closed which means he still doesn't have any proof.

"So?" I challenge. "I never denied being in his classroom. That doesn't mean there was any debauchery involved, which is what you're implying. Am I wrong?"

"I'm not *implying* anything, Kat. I'm clearly stating that I *know* you're fucking around with Mr. Cooper. What I don't know, is if he's the same guy you were talking about that night in your apartment. That's a question you can answer for me."

"Of course not," I deny.

Dylan scoffs. "Oh, well, that just makes it even better. So you can fuck a teacher while you're hung up on some mystery guy, but not me, huh?"

"I'm not fucking a teacher!" I whisper shout.

He crosses his arms over his chest. "Really? What are you willing to do to prove it?"

I narrow my eyes at him. "What is that supposed to mean?"

"Fuck *me*. Right here, right now. Maybe that will convince me."

I think about what Gavin said...to do *anything* it takes to convince him. The old me may have considered it. This new and improved Kat can't stomach the idea.

"Oh, go fuck yourself, Dylan!"

"Oh, trust me, that's all I seem to be doing lately. Because my stupid ass thought that if I showed you I could stop sleeping around, then maybe you'd take me seriously. You've been different lately...I thought you were ready to try some kind of commitment. Come to find out, you were just as busy as ever adding notches to your bedpost. With that asshat, nonetheless. Pretty fucked up, don't ya think?"

"Nothing is going on between me and Mr. Cooper! How many times do I have to repeat myself?"

Dylan gets right in my face and hisses, "I heard you, Kat. *I fucking heard you.*"

I step back until I hit the wall. "What?"

"I pressed my ear against the goddamn door and listened. What do you think I mean? I heard everything, Kat. The argument, him telling you how much he wanted to throw you over his desk, you *moaning* his name. Do you think I don't know a moan when I hear one, Kitty? Especially *your* moan? Give me a little fucking credit."

"Oh, God." I slam my hand over my mouth, having no clue what to say. What am I going to do? Gavin and I are both screwed if Dylan says anything.

"Wow, I've rendered you speechless," he sneers. "I didn't think that was possible."

"Dylan...please, you can't say anything to anyone."

"Oh, that's rich. Why would I want to protect that asshole?"

"Because it's not just him you'd be protecting!" I try holding it in, but I feel my eyes starting to water. "Dylan, if someone finds out about this...not only will Gavin lose his job, but I'll be at the center of a giant scandal all over again. You can't let that happen."

"*I* didn't let anything happen, Kitty. You and *Gavin* are the ones who decided to fuck up. Don't pin this shit on me."

I grab his arm, pleading with him to look at me. "Dylan, you don't understand. When we met...we didn't know. We didn't know he was my teacher."

"How the hell is that possible?"

Now I'm the one who's pacing. "Because...we met on my last birthday. *At a bar*. I was out celebrating my release from the system. I told him I was older. He didn't know the truth until I showed up in second period on the first day of school."

He looks at me skeptically. "Your birthday was over three months ago."

"I'm aware of that, Dyl."

His face turns red again. "So you're telling me this has been going on for *months*? What the fuck, Kat? My God, all those weird little interactions between you two make sense now."

"No, it hasn't been going on for months. Not really anyway. After he learned the truth, he put a stop to it."

"That's not what it sounded like yesterday," he argues.

"I know...I know. We just decided to stop fighting it. He's different, Dylan. *I'm different* when I'm with him. Better. This isn't anything like my previous hookups. You've got to believe me."

"So he *is* the guy? How old is he anyway?"

"Twenty-six," I answer as a tear rolls down my face. "And yes, he's the guy I told you about. If you expose us, I'll never know if he can fix me. I *really* think he's the one who can fix me, Dylan. Don't you think I deserve the chance to find out?"

Dylan releases a breath. "Damn it, Kitty. Don't cry."

"I can't help it," I sob.

He pulls me into a hug. "Why does it have to be him? Why can't it be me? All you have to do is let me in."

"I don't know," I say. "I've asked myself that same question many times. I don't know how to explain it, Dylan. I knew he was different from the first moment we met. There's this thing about him...it's ineffable. *He gets me.*"

"And I don't?"

I pull back and wipe my face with my hand. "Please don't take it personally. You're my best friend, Dylan. I love you. I can't lose you because of this."

He hunches down to my level so we're eye to eye. "You love me, but you're not *in love* with me, right?"

I nod.

"But you think *he's* someone you could fall in love with?"

"It's too early for that," I say. "But maybe, yeah."

"I can't believe I'm considering this," he mutters. "I hate that guy!"

"You don't know him well enough to say that, Dylan. I actually think you guys would get along if you gave it a shot."

"Ha! Doubtful."

I smirk, thinking about comments Gavin has made

about him. "Yeah, maybe not. But it should only matter how I feel about him, right?"

"I guess," he grumbles.

"So you really won't say anything? To anyone?"

He points his finger at me. "I'm not doing this for him. I want to make that very clear. I won't say anything, Kitty, but only because of you. I may not know exactly what went down freshman year, but I know it fucked you up. I won't be the one responsible for throwing you to the wolves again."

I jump into his arms and hug him tight. "Thank you, Dylan. You have no idea how much this means to me."

"Yeah, yeah," he replies. "But you can tell Mr. Cooper that if he hurts you, I will *fuck him up*."

"I'll be sure to pass the message along."

Dylan looks at the clock on his phone. "C'mon, Kitty, let's get out of here. We're ridiculously late for first period."

I take his hand as we exit the closet with a smile on my face and courage in my heart.

thirty-five

O ver the past few weeks, Gavin and I have fallen into a rhythm of sorts. He was anxious when he first learned that Dylan knew about us, but he eventually calmed down, saying that he trusted my judgment. As hard as it is to stay away, we've managed to control ourselves during school hours. We certainly make up for it afterwards, though. I've stayed at his place every night I'm not working.

Speaking of work, that's one area of contention between us. Gavin *hates* what I do for a living—he becomes distant whenever I mention anything about the club. He says he doesn't want to share me with anyone. I try explaining how I detach myself from the situation but all he sees is that hundreds of men see me naked every week, which makes him grunt and groan like a caveman. He can't deny that it's my only viable means of supporting myself in this shitty situation so he's careful not to cross any lines with his opinion. We agree to disagree about it, I guess.

I smile when my phone chimes with an incoming text.

Gavin: You're mine on Christmas Eve. Don't make any plans.

Winter break starts tomorrow which means that Gavin and I will have lots of uninterrupted time together. He's leaving to go back home on Christmas morning but we'll have the first week with each other. I even asked for time off from the club. Gavin will be gone from Christmas through New Year's so I'm working extra shifts during his absence to make up for it.

I type my reply, still trying to get used to moving my thumbs over such a small keyboard. Yes, I know I'm a disgrace to my generation for waiting until age eighteen to get my first cell phone, but when you're broke, you don't have much choice in the matter.

Me: Do these plans involve being naked? If so, I'm in!

Gavin: There may be a strategically placed bow somewhere, but other than that, nakedness is a guarantee. ;)

I laugh when I imagine him standing there with a big red bow tied around his finer assets.

Me: You sure do know how to woo a gal.

Gavin: You're the only gal worth wooing, Kat. xoxo

Wow, could he have thought of a better response? Things with Gavin seem almost *too perfect*. I'm not just talking about the sex—which to be clear is *phenomenal*—but everything seems better with him in the picture. We've laid awake for countless hours talking, getting to know each other beyond a physical level. He knows more about me than anyone ever has and surprisingly, he hasn't run away in horror.

I think back to a conversation we had just the other night.

"So, why'd you move to Oregon?" I ask.

He runs his fingers through my hair. "I told you before... this was the first job offer I had so I jumped on it."

"I get that," I say, "but I meant, why did you leave the Bay Area? From what you've told me, you really seem to love it there."

"I do," he confirms. "Well, I did, anyway. After I found out about Hailey's affair...with my best friend Joe of all people, I was crushed. I couldn't go anywhere without being reminded of them. I was haunted by their betrayal."

"Do you regret leaving your family?"

"I had a hard time at first. I miss them every day. I really miss our weekly Sunday dinners. My mom's pot roast is to die for. I don't regret leaving though."

"Why not?"

He kisses the top of my head. "Because it led me to you."

I smile. "Did you always want to be a high school teacher?"

"Not really, but it's a good place to start."

I scrunch my face in confusion. "What do you mean?"

"My ultimate goal is to become a college professor…in creative writing, ideally," he explains. "But that would require going back to school for my PhD."

"Do you think you'll do it one day? Go back to school?"

"I hope so," he replies. "What about you? What are your plans after graduation?"

"College, hopefully. It all depends on where I'm accepted and whether or not I get any financial assistance."

"Have you applied anywhere yet?"

"No, but I've been collecting all of the information I need to start."

"Do you mind me asking what your S.A.T. score was?"

"1580."

He shifts his body, causing me to roll off of him. "Are you serious? You can get into almost any Ivy League school with those scores. Holy shit, Kat. I knew you were smart, but damn!"

I smile. "Thanks, but the Ivies aren't a possibility for me. Academically, sure. But they all want extra-curricular activities, people who volunteer to mentor little kids and shit like that. I never had a chance for that, being bounced around the system. Plus, I'm fairly certain I'd never get a worthy recommendation letter in this town."

"I'd give you one in a heartbeat," he says.

"Waxing poetic about my ability to give a blow job won't impress the admissions office, Gavin."

He laughs. "I was being serious, Kat. But now that you mention it, you do inspire me when your lips are wrapped *around my cock. I could write a poem and call it, Ode to a Fellatio Master."*

I roll my eyes. "You are such a nerd!"

He leans over me and kisses my neck. "Yes, but I'm your nerd."

I bring his lips to mine. "You are."

I smile when I think about what followed that particular conversation. I can't help but feeling like it's only a matter of time before the other shoe drops, though. I can't help question what he sees in someone like me. He mentioned that his ex is a Stanford grad as well as an attorney. Seriously! Why would he want a small town girl with epic amounts of baggage when he's been with someone so sophisticated?

I'm pretty confident that I'll be admitted to several colleges with my grades but what if no one offers me a scholarship? Will I be stuck in this town forever? Will I wind up stripping until I can no longer rely on my looks? What will happen then? What will happen if I *do* get a scholarship? Could we handle a long-distance relationship? I realize that these questions typically arise after much more time together but everything with Gavin has moved at light speed. On the surface, you'd see a tawdry affair between a teacher and his student. In reality, Gavin and I are like two halves of a whole. I never thought in a million years that I would be spouting off about soulmates and shit but that's what I feel with him. It's like we were meant to be together. Cheesy, I know, but it doesn't make it any less true.

My phone chimes with another text.

Gavin: You still there?

Me: Yeah, sorry...got lost in thought. What time should I come over?

Gavin: Now?

Me: Xmas Eve is still a week away

Gavin: And? I have no problem keeping you occupied until then.

Me: I promise I'm all yours after tonight. I'm going out with Bree and Dylan. Remember?

Gavin: Come over afterwards.

Me: It will be late.

Gavin: I don't care. I want to wake up with you in my bed.

I'm grinning like a fool as I type my reply.

Me: Okay. I'll text you when I'm on my way.

Gavin: Be safe.

Me: Yes, Mr. Cooper.

Gavin: Don't make me take you over my knee, smartass!

Me: Please do...sounds kinky! ;)

Gavin: Kat, go have fun with your friends before I change my mind and tie you to my bed.

Me: Promise?

The next message that comes in is a picture. I laugh as I open it up and see Gavin frowning at me. I know he's going for stern but it's coming off as sexy, making me want to drive over to his house and mount him instead. I decide to return the favor, giving him something to think about while I'm out. I tuck my shirt under my chin and snap a picture of my boobs currently encased in a lilac push up bra.

Gavin: Woman, you're killing me!

Me: That should get you by until I come over later. Think of me. xoxo

Gavin: Always.

A knock at the door shakes me out of my Gavin-induced stupor. I get up from the couch to answer it and find Bree and Dylan standing on the other side.

"Hey girl!" Bree pulls me into a tight hug. "I feel like I haven't seen you in forever!"

"Breanna, I just saw you at lunch."

She rolls her eyes. "I meant outside of school, bitch. You've been so busy. I miss you."

I look up and see Dylan standing awkwardly at the threshold. He hasn't been in my apartment since the night I rejected his advances.

"Come on in, guys."

They both step inside and make themselves comfortable on the couch.

"So what's the plan?" I ask. "I can see what movies are playing if you want."

Bree releases her lyrical laugh. "Oh, Kitty. Why would we want to sit in a movie for two hours and not be able to talk? The whole point of meeting up tonight was so we could all catch up and have fun. It's been like a month!"

"So what do you want to do?"

Dylan holds up a large paper sack. "We're going old-school tonight, babe. Beach, fire, and liquor."

Okay, that actually sounds pretty incredible. I know what you're thinking...who the hell goes to the beach at night in the middle of winter? Well, when you're a teenager in this town with not much else to do, *that's* what you do. Besides, in the Northwest, the weather at the beach stays pretty much the same all year long with the exception of late summer. And by the same, I mean you'll be wearing jeans and a sweatshirt. As long as it's not raining, it's a good day for it.

"That sounds great," I say. "Our usual spot?"

"Well, yeah!" Bree pumps her fist in the air.

My apartment may be a piece of shit, but it's centrally located. It's only a five block walk from public beach access which is definitely convenient when you're drinking. Bree and I grab the tequila and blankets while Dylan hauls the firewood he brought. We make our way to the sand and sit back while the flames get going. The alcohol and conversation are flowing as my friends pass a joint between them. At least they give me the courtesy of sitting across the fire while they smoke. I don't realize how drunk I am until I get up to pee behind a big log. Now if you've ever tried digging a hole and squatting over it, you know how difficult it is to coordinate that.

Adding drinks to the mix is just asking for trouble, but when you gotta go, *you gotta go*. I sway as I try positioning myself just right so I don't soak my clothes. I realize it's a lost cause as my bare ass hits the sand.

"Bree!" I shout. "I need your help!"

Bree stumbles over to me and starts laughing hysterically once she sees the pickle I'm in. "Oh, man, I've got to get a picture of this."

I point my finger at her. "Don't you dare! I swear to God I will break your phone if you try."

"Fine," she says grumpily.

"Just get over here and help me hold still."

Bree giggles as she does her best to help hold me up while I pee in the sand and drip dry since I don't have any toilet paper handy.

"What are you guys doing over there?" Dylan shouts in the distance.

"Kat needed help peeing!" Bree screams in my ear.

"Ow!" I hold my hand up to my ear as I pull my pants up with the other hand. "Do you have to be so loud?"

I have sand in unmentionable places. I try shaking it loose to no avail. Bree sees this and starts giggling again until she's gasping for air.

Dylan joins us and hands me the bottle of Cuervo. I wrap my lips around it and take a big swig. I shiver as it goes down and then I wipe my mouth.

"You cold, Kitty?" he asks.

Now that I think about it, I am. Being away from the fire pit makes a huge difference.

"A little bit, yeah."

Dylan pulls me into a side hug and says, "C'mon, babe. I'll keep you warm."

thirty-six

Why in the hell is someone using a chainsaw in the middle of the night? Not a chainsaw, I think as I open my eyes. It's still dark out but there's enough moonlight filtering in to see that I'm not in bed alone. When did Gavin get here? And since when does he snore? I sit up and rub my head, trying to recall the events of last night before I passed out. The last thing I remember is sitting by the fire drinking. Damn tequila gets me every time.

As my eyes adjust to the darkness, I look over to Gavin. He rolls toward me and his face catches in the moonlight. *Oh, shit!* Not Gavin. What the fuck is Dylan doing here? In my bed? I start to panic as I take inventory of our clothing. I'm wearing my t-shirt from last night and a pair of panties. I'm not going to risk waking him, but I can see that Dylan's chest is bare. My God, what did I do? Please, please, *please* let him be wearing pants!

Ding dong.

What the hell was that? Is that my doorbell? I look over to my alarm clock and see that it's 4:30 in the morning. The bell rings again and wakes Dylan who stretches and groans.

"Kitty, who the fuck is at your door in the middle of the night?"

"*Who's at my door?*" I whisper shout. "What the hell are you doing here? *In my bed?*"

He sits up. "You don't remember?"

"Remember *what?*"

The bell rings again followed by loud knocking.

"Kat, it's Gavin. Open the door before I knock it down. You're not answering your phone and I'm getting really worried."

"Oh, shit! Shit! Shit! Shit!" I jump out of bed and quickly pull up my discarded jeans that are lying on the floor. "Dylan, hurry the fuck up and get dressed!"

Gavin's knuckles pound on my door even harder. "Kat, I'm serious. I'm about to break down your door."

"Coming!" I shout. "I just woke up. Be right there!"

That seems to placate him for the moment because he's no longer making a ruckus outside.

"Dylan!"

He flops back onto the mattress. "Go take care of *Mr. Cooper*, Kitty. I'm going back to bed."

I shove him. "The fuck you are! Goddammit, get dressed!"

I run into the hall and shut my bedroom door. Dylan's ass had better be putting some clothes on. I unlock the deadbolt to my front door and swing it open.

"Oh, thank God!" Gavin exclaims. "You had me worried half to death, Kat. Why weren't you answering your phone? I was expecting to hear from you hours ago."

"Um…" I step aside to let him in. "I passed out. I guess we drank a little too much."

Gavin's eyes flit across my living room and pauses a beat over the blankets on my couch. Is that where Dylan was originally sleeping? And where is Bree? Ugh, I'm never drinking tequila again!

"So you fell asleep in here? What took you so long to answer the door?"

"I…um…" I stammer.

Just then, I hear the door to my bedroom creak open. So does Gavin.

"Is Bree here?" he whispers in a panicked voice. "Shit, Kat. How are we going to explain this?"

"Your secret is safe, *Teach*," Dylan says gruffly. "Breanna's current fuckboy picked her up hours ago. It's just me and Kitty here. Well, and now you."

Gavin instantly stiffens and looks over my shoulder. By the firm set of his jaw, I'm guessing Dylan decided not to get dressed. I'm too afraid to turn around to confirm it either way.

"Kat, what's going on?" Gavin asks.

His tone is eerily calm. Like when you're in the eye of a hurricane. I risk a glance over my shoulder and see Dylan standing there wearing nothing but his boxers.

"Damn it, Dylan! Where are your clothes?"

"I'm wearing clothes," he argues.

"Hardly," Gavin scoffs.

"What's the problem, Kitty? It's nothing you haven't seen before."

"You piece of sh—" Gavin says as he charges forward.

I somehow manage to wedge myself between them.

I shove Dylan toward my room. "Dylan, go get your fucking clothes on and don't come out until I tell you to!" I place my hand on Gavin's chest. "And you! Go sit down on the couch and we'll talk!"

"Geez, Kitty. Who knew you could be so bossy?" Dylan asks. "It's kind of hot."

"Kat," Gavin says through a clenched jaw. "I swear to God I'm going to kick the shit out of him if you can't convince him to shut his mouth."

"Dylan, one more word and I will kick the shit out of you myself. Starting with your balls. *Now go!*" I stomp my foot and point toward my room to emphasize my statement.

Dylan goes into my bedroom and slams the door

while Gavin stomps over to the couch and sits down. Crossing his arms over his chest, he says, "Would you care to explain to me what happened tonight? Namely, why that asshole is coming out of your *bedroom* practically naked?"

I sit next to him and sigh. "I don't know."

"You don't know?" he repeats. "I'm going to need you to expand on that, Kat."

"I can't," I say shamefully. "The last thing I remember is drinking on the beach with Bree and Dylan. I have *no* idea what happened after that."

"Jesus." He pulls on his hair and throws his head back, closing his eyes. "You're telling me that you have no idea what happened? You completely blacked out?"

"Clearly, I drank too much."

He glares at me. "You think?"

"I don't need your sarcasm, Gavin. I feel shitty enough as is."

"Kat, what the hell am I supposed to say here? We made plans to see each other tonight. Instead, you don't answer my calls or texts and I come here to find Dylan coming out of your room in his underwear? I'm trying not to jump to conclusions but it's really fucking hard when you tell me you can't remember *anything*."

"I know," I groan. "I don't know what to say either, Gavin. I've never had to answer to someone before. This is all new to me. You know that."

"So that makes it okay?" he asks, incredulity in his tone.

"No, it doesn't make it okay," I offer. "I'm just trying to explain where I'm coming from."

He sighs. "How would you feel if the situation were reversed? If you showed up at my house in the middle of the night to find a half-naked woman coming out of my room? And then I can't tell you anything that happened prior to that?"

"I'd be pissed," I admit. "And hurt." I turn toward him. "Gavin, I wish I could give you a better explanation but I can't. I don't remember."

"I don't know what to say, Kat."

"Me neither."

We sit there in silence for a moment before Dylan comes into the room, fully dressed, with his car keys dangling from his hand.

Gavin glares at him. "You're really pushing it, kid."

"*Kid?* Ha! That's rich, Mr. Cooper. Considering I'm only three weeks younger than your girlfriend here."

Gavin stands up with his fists clenched. "Get the hell out of here."

Dylan rolls his eyes. "I'm going, *Teach*. I overheard your little lover's spat and just wanted to clear things up before I leave. For Kat's sake, not yours."

Gavin sits down. "Then by all means, enlighten us."

"Nothing fucking happened," Dylan says. "She drank too much, stumbled home, and I put her to bed. I stayed behind because I couldn't drive at that point. This piece of shit couch is too small for me. I tried sleeping on it, but eventually gave up. I tried Cybil's old room but all her furniture is gone, so I went into Kat's. She slept. I slept. We were both clothed."

"And you thought being in your underwear was appropriate?" Gavin challenges.

Dylan rolls his eyes again. "Again, sorry to point this out—oh, who am I kidding...no, I'm not— but it's nothing she hasn't seen before. *Many times.*"

Okay, I'm really grateful to Dylan for confirming that nothing bad happened but did he have to go there? I grab Gavin's hand when I feel him tensing, getting ready to stand. Probably to break Dylan's jaw, I'm guessing.

"Dylan, thank you for filling in the gaps. I really think Gavin and I need to be alone now."

"Whatever, Kitty," Dylan huffs. "I'll talk to you later."

Gavin and I wait until the door is closed before saying anything else.

"Kat, I'm going to ask you something and you need to be honest with me."

"Go on."

"Do you have a drinking problem?"

"What? Of course not!"

"What else am I supposed to think?" he asks. "This isn't the first time I've found you in a bad situation due to alcohol. People don't normally drink this heavily this often unless they're feeding an addiction. After what I told you about my birth mother, I'm sure you can appreciate how sensitive I am to alcoholism."

"Of course I can *appreciate* it," I snap. "My own mother is a fucking heroin addict. Among other things. I get it. Probably more than most people."

"Well, then please explain it to me."

I sigh. "Look, we were just hanging out. Besides you, they're the only people in this world that I feel safe with. I overdid it because I can actually relax around them. But I don't have to drink much to make that happen. I'm 5'2" and a hundred and ten pounds soaking wet, Gavin. It doesn't take much, especially when I'm drinking liquor. You can't tell me that you didn't drink in high school."

"No, I can't."

"So where do we go from here?"

He pulls me into his side and tucks my head into the crook of his neck. "Look, all I'm asking is that you're more careful from now on. And that you consider me when you're out with your friends. I'm not saying that you need to *report* to me, Kat. I don't want that at all. Just put yourself in my shoes. Okay?"

"You're really not giving up on me?"

Gavin shifts so our faces are practically touching. "Oh, baby, you're not getting rid of me that easily. When I'm in a relationship, Kat, I'm *all in*. I know you don't have any experience with this but that's what I'm here for. We'll work through it together. Okay?"

A tear drops from my eye. "I feel like you're too good to be true."

He smiles. "I think the same thing every time I look at you."

thirty-seven

Gavin's waiting for me with a big smile on his face as I park my car in the garage. I grin when I see him bouncing on the balls of his feet as I walk toward him.

"Merry Christmas," he says excitedly.

I place a light kiss on his lips. "Christmas isn't until tomorrow."

"Christmas Eve counts too," he argues. "Hence the word *Christmas*."

I roll my eyes. "Okay, I'll give you that one. Even though you're technically wrong."

Gavin closes the garage door. "How very kind of you to humor me, Grinch."

"Oh, just what every girl wants—to be called a grumpy green guy."

He gives me a playful smack on the ass as we're

walking toward the house. "Just get in the house, smartass."

"Yes, Mr. Cooper."

I get a pinch on the ass for that one.

"Holy shit," I exclaim as I walk into the house. "It looks like the North Pole threw up in here."

Gavin releases a hearty laugh as I take in the colorful decorations. The exterior lights are subdued but this —*this* is spectacular. In the center of the living room is fully trimmed tree that shoots up to the ceiling, filling the air with a woodsy pine scent. Knickknacks cover every available surface ranging from cartoonish snowmen to realistic men with long white beards. Lights twinkle from each window and giant throw pillows with reindeer on them adorn the couch. The embellishments continue throughout every room I can see. I'd bet money that the entire house is filled with Santa, snowmen, elves, and reindeer. My brain is trying to play catch-up with my eyes. I'm stunned—I've never seen anything like this in real life before. Cybil always said that Christmas was a load of crap meant to help retailers so we've never celebrated. Same goes with birthdays or any other holiday, really. Sure, my foster parents made an effort sometimes, but it always felt like an obligation rather than something born from joy. Gavin's ear-to-ear grin tells me that he derives complete, unadulterated pleasure from this.

"Do you like it?" he asks.

I smile. "It's really pretty. When did you have time for this?"

"Today. I was storing the boxes at my parents' house. I called my mom last week asking for a huge favor and they arrived this morning."

"But why? You're leaving tomorrow; you won't even have a chance to enjoy them."

Gavin leads me to the couch and hands me a mug from the coffee table. "Hot chocolate for the lady."

I laugh as I look down and see the cup overflowing with marshmallows. I take a sip and moan at the deliciousness of it. "Gavin, seriously. Why?"

He shrugs. "I wanted to do something special for you."

I'm sure the shock is plain on my face. "*For me*? Why?"

"Because you're you," he says. "Besides, it wasn't *entirely* for you. I'll let you in on a little secret."

"Besides the fact that you love teenage dramas?"

"Besides that," he laughs. "It just so happens that I *love* Christmas. Like, to an embarrassing degree. Have you ever seen the movie *Elf*? Buddy's excitement is nothing compared to mine."

I laugh so hard I'm crying. Visions of Gavin screaming, *"Santa? I know him!"* run through my head. I set my hot cocoa on the table before it spills.

"My God, you're beautiful when you laugh. I could never get enough of seeing you like this."

I sober instantly when I see the look on his face. "Gavin—"

I'm silenced when his lips meet mine. We kiss unhurriedly, savoring each other's breath. He pulls away when I try escalating things by climbing on top of him. I whimper in protest.

"Kat, we're never going to get to your present if we keep this up."

"You're all the present I need," I whine.

He stands from the couch, depositing me onto the cushions. "As touching as that is, your *actual* present might not agree if I don't bring it out soon."

"Huh?"

He starts walking down the hall leading to the bedrooms. "Go sit in front of the tree. I'll be right back."

I do as he says despite my confusion. My fingers tap the wood floors in a staccato rhythm as I wait. I hear Gavin toward the back of the house fumbling with something. I could swear he's *talking* to someone. What the hell is going on? My question is answered when he appears at the end of the hall holding an adorable, squirming, striped brown kitten.

"Oh my God!" I run up to him and grab the kitty out of his arms. She startles for a moment but then releases the sweetest little purr when I tickle behind her ears. "Hello, baby! What's your name?"

"That's up to you," Gavin smiles. He looks at the

content furball in my hands and adds, "I think he likes you. Which is good because he's yours."

"*Mine?* You got me a cat?"

"Yeah," he nods. "You mentioned that you've always wanted one. I thought he would make you happy."

"He?" I peek under its tail. Sure enough, there are two tiny little kitty balls.

He chuckles. "The lady at the Humane Society said that male cats are better snugglers." He nods his head to the feline pressing his body into my breasts. "He certainly seems to like snuggling your chest. Lucky bastard."

I make cooing noises and kiss the kitty's wet, pink nose. "Oh, don't listen to that guy, baby. He didn't mean to call you a bad name."

Gavin looks at me thoughtfully.

"What?" I ask.

He shakes his head. "Nothing. It's cute seeing you be so nurturing. I wouldn't think that would come naturally considering..."

"Considering I've had shit role models?" I finish.

"Yeah, that," he laughs.

"It is what it is. I've always told myself that if I ever became a mom again, I'll do the opposite of what Cybil would do and I'll be set."

He gives me a sad smile. "Do you want more kids someday?"

"Maybe," I shrug. "Down the road...like *way* down the

road. I'd have to get away from this town and experience life first, though. Ya know? I need to know that I can take care of myself in the real world before settling down and bringing a helpless child into the mix. Plus, my head needs to be in a better place. Only time will tell if that happens."

Gavin pets the kitty on the head. "Maybe I can help with that. The better place part."

I smile at him. "You already are."

"We'll talk more about the baby part after."

I roll my eyes. "It's a little early to ask if you can put babies in me. Don't ya think?"

He laughs. "Yeah, maybe. So what are you thinking for names?"

I look into the kitty's golden green eyes. "He looks like a Frodo to me."

Gavin's lips quirk up in the corners. "Really?"

"What's wrong with Frodo?"

"Nothing. You just never fail to surprise me. You don't seem like the typical *Lord of the Rings* fan."

"*Lord of the Rings, Harry Potter, Game of Thrones*...I love them all. When you live in my world, fantasy realms provide a nice break."

He scratches the cat behind the ears. "Frodo it is, then." Gavin fumbles with the collar around the kitten's neck before revealing a shiny silver key. "I do have another question for you."

"What's that? Why is there a key around his neck?"

"It's for you. I know it seems fast but I want you to move in with me."

"*What?*" I'm too surprised to string together more words.

I stare as he removes the key from the ring around Frodo's collar. "Will you move in with me, Kat? You wouldn't have to work at the club anymore."

"Is that what this is about?" I ask. "You want me to move in with you so I don't have to take my clothes off to pay rent?"

"No," he denies. "I want you to move in because I can't stand waking up without you. I can't stand having to go all day without being able to touch you. Our situation isn't the best but I want to make it better. This allows us to be together as much as possible. I thought getting you out of that apartment and into my bed was a good start."

Tears prick at my eyes. "Gavin, I can't."

His brows furrow. "Why not? It's the perfect solution."

"I don't need a *solution*," I insist. "I need to know that I can make it on my own. I need to prove to myself that it's possible." When I see the hurt on his face I backpedal. "That doesn't mean I don't want to be with you. They're completely independent from each other. Am I making any sense?"

"Not really," he replies. "You're here more often than

not anyway. Why would you pay to keep a place that you barely live in?"

"Because I need to know that I *can*. I need to know that I have somewhere to go if—" I close my mouth before I step in it any further.

"If *what*, Kat? If we don't work out? Is that the problem? You think we won't make it?"

I release a deep sigh. "Gavin, can you blame me? The people in my past don't exactly have the best track record. I'm just trying to protect myself. It's what I do."

He frames my face with his hands and kisses my forehead. "Baby, I'm not going anywhere. I promise."

Frodo wriggles out of my arms as Gavin pulls me into a hug.

"I still can't move in with you. I'm not going to risk your job any more than we already are."

"Screw the job; I can get another one."

I shake my head. "Gavin, I know we haven't exactly gone the traditional route with our relationship, but I just don't want to push it. Okay? I want to be with you. I have no intention of going anywhere either but I'm not going to bend on this. It's too soon to live together."

It's his turn to sigh. "I guess I should gather up Frodo's stuff then, huh?"

I pull back. "I can't have pets in my apartment."

Gavin takes my hand and presses his house key into my palm. "Well, then you'll need this to help take care of him. He can stay here."

I clutch the key to my chest. "You're not mad at me?"

He wraps his arms around me again. "No, Kat. I'm not mad. Disappointed, but not mad. Just feel free to use the key whenever you want. I mean it."

I kiss him lightly on the lips. "Thank you."

"My pleasure."

I trace the hard planes of his chest with my index finger. "You still haven't opened your present."

He smiles. "Where is it?"

I pull the sweater over my head to reveal my naked torso. Gavin's eyes darken when I pull at the red ribbon tied into a bow around my breasts. I start walking backwards down the hall toward his bedroom.

"I believe you mentioned something about bows. Care to unwrap me?"

I barely have a chance to squeal before he scoops me up and closes the distance to the bed.

thirty-eight

The Pitiful Princess is packed tonight. There are more couples than normal, apparently thinking a strip club was the best place to ring in the new year together. This is my fourth VIP dance of the night and there are still two hours before last call. People are definitely in a mood to celebrate by splurging for extras. I'm currently grinding on a thirty-something woman's lap while her husband watches, clearly turned on by the whole scene. I can tell she's a first timer—her face is beet red and she's sitting on her hands, not quite sure what to do with them.

I slowly untie my bikini top and place it around her neck. "Are you and your husband having a good time tonight, honey?"

I talk to the women a lot more than the men because it seems to lower the awkwardness over receiving a lap dance. As far as I'm concerned, she has nothing to be ashamed of. Most couples come here because they're trying to spice things up in the bedroom. If anything, she should be proud that she's open-minded enough to keep their relationship healthy on a sexual level. Not that I'm saying strip clubs are the answer, mind you. Different strokes for different folks and all that.

She blushes further and averts her eyes away from my breasts. "Um, sure. The girls here are all very beautiful."

"Thank you," I say. "So are you. Your husband is a lucky man."

"You got that right," he says with a big smile.

The woman smiles back at him with obvious affection. "Our ten-year anniversary is today. I wanted to surprise him with something...different."

I face the husband and loop my arm around his wife's neck. I roll my body against hers while giving him the sultry expressions that a client expects. "Happy Anniversary."

"Thank you," they both reply in unison.

"Is this your first time here?" I ask.

"Yes," she answers. "I didn't quite know what to expect. I have to admit...it's not as bad as I thought it'd be."

I chuckle as I turn to address her. "Well, that's always good. I'd hate to sour your night."

"Oh, you're not," she assures me. "I'm...enjoying

myself." She looks away shyly, embarrassed by her admission.

Personally, I don't see what the big deal is. We both have the same parts, and let's face it—naked women are pretty to look at. It's been scientifically proven that women can be easily turned on by another woman, no matter their sexual preference. The timid ones tend to get hung up over what they *think* they should be thinking or feeling based on societal standards.

"What's your name, sweetheart?"

"Gabby. And that handsome man over there is Rick."

"Gabby, would you like me to dance for Rick? Would you like to watch that?"

"Um…" She lifts her chin after a moment and nods confidently. "Yes. Yes, I think I would like that."

I grin knowing that Gabby and Rick are going to have a great time when they get home tonight.

I'm exhausted by the time I pull into my parking spot but I have to drop next month's rent check in the slot before heading to Gavin's. He's been in Sausalito all week so I've been staying at his place with Frodo. Despite my fatigue, my body's humming in excitement from all the money I made tonight. It's definitely a great way to end the week when you have enough to pay for two months' rent. I open the door to my apartment and find Cybil passed out on the couch.

"Oh, geez," I mutter as I kick the back of the couch. "Cybil, get up. What are you doing here? You don't live here anymore in case you forgot."

She mumbles incoherently.

I round the couch and shake her foot. "Cybil, seriously. You can't just come back here whenever you need a place to pass out drunk. *You left me*, remember?"

She rolls over and falls on the floor. That's when I notice that her eyes are closed and there's a tourniquet tied around her arm.

"Oh, fuck!" I cry as I run over to her side. I shake her gently. "Cybil, wake up."

She still doesn't respond so I lightly tap her cheek. "C'mon, Cybil. Don't do this." I move closer to her ear. "WAKE UP! MOM! *MOM!* Damn it, *WAKE UP!*"

I start shaking her shoulders violently when she does not react to my screaming in her face. Her lips have a bluish tint to them and she has vomit down the front of her shirt. *Oh, God.* I dig through my purse for my cell and dial 911.

"Hello 911 Emergency. Do you need police, ambulance, or fire?"

"Hello," I respond frantically. "I need help. My mom...my mom overdosed, I think. Heroin. She does heroin." My eyes dart around the room and sure enough, I spot the needle on the floor.

"Ma'am, what is your address?"

"211 Collins Street. Apartment 3."

"Help is on the way, ma'am," the operator says calmly. *How can she be calm right now?* "Is your mother breathing?"

"Um…" I look at Cybil and see her chest rising and falling. Barely. "Yes, I think so. But she doesn't look good."

"I'm going to stay on the phone until the ambulance gets there. While we're waiting for them, we're going to try to help her together. Okay?"

"Okay," I sob.

"Is your mother conscious?"

"Mom, wake up. Can you hear me?" The tears fall freely down my face when she doesn't respond. "No, she's not. She mumbled a few minutes ago but now she's not saying anything."

"Okay, ma'am. We're going to try to stimulate her with mild pain. All I need you to do is rub your knuckles into her sternum. That's the spot in the middle of her chest where her ribs meet. You need to use enough pressure to cause mild discomfort. Do you think you can do that?"

I clench my hand into a fist and rub the spot she's indicated. When Cybil doesn't flinch, I do it a little harder.

"Nothing's happening," I cry. "*Why is nothing happening?*"

"Is she still breathing?"

I place my head on her chest. It scarcely rises every ten seconds or so. "Not much. Her breaths are really slow."

"Do you know how to perform CPR?"

I nod, thinking back to freshman year health class.

"Ma'am? Are you still there?"

"Yes, I'm here. I think I know how. I've never done it before."

"I'll walk you through it step-by-step. Can you put your phone on speaker?"

I do as she says and place my phone on the dingy carpet. "Okay, you're on speaker. What do I do?"

"She needs to be on her back," she says. "Is she on her back?"

"Yes."

"Okay, tilt her chin up and check inside her mouth to see if there's anything blocking her airway. If you find anything, remove it if you can."

I tilt my mom's chin up and pry her lips open to sweep my finger inside. I go from cheek to cheek and feel nothing so I look down the back of her mouth as far as I can.

"There's nothing. Nothing's in her mouth."

"Okay, we're going to start mouth-to-mouth but no chest compressions. You'll need to plug her nose with one hand, and give two even, regular-sized breaths. Blow enough air into her lungs to make her chest rise. If you don't see her chest rise out of the corner of your eye, tilt the head back more and make sure you're plugging her nose sufficiently. Tell me when you've done that."

I press my lips to Cybil's and gag as I taste the remnants of her vomit. I follow the operator's instructions and watch as her chest inflates and subsequently falls. I hear sirens roaring in the distance but I feel no relief as you might expect. All I can think about is the fact that my mom is lying here unconscious while I'm literally trying to breathe life into her.

"I've done it twice," I shout. "But she's still the same."

"Okay, ma'am. Paramedics will be there to assist at any moment. I want you to continue giving your mom one breath every five seconds until they arrive."

I count to five four more times before there's a knock on my door. I run to open it and step aside as a man and woman dressed in paramedic uniforms cross the threshold. Since my living room is right inside the door, they easily locate my mom and get to work. Everything is a blur as they assess her condition and do what they can to treat her. They do some more breathing and inject something into her thigh but they're moving so fast I can't decipher much else. I step over to the small table and take a seat as they raise their gurney and strap her in. The woman looks back at me while she takes up the rear and starts pushing my mom through the door.

"The town clinic isn't set up for this type of emergency. We're taking her to Lincoln City Memorial. Do you know where that is?"

I nod. Lincoln City is only a ten-minute drive north. Like any small coastal town, nothing is really hard to find.

She gives me a sympathetic look. "Would you like to ride with us?"

I wipe the tears out of my eyes to clear my vision. "No, I'll follow you."

The paramedic nods. "Okay, check in with the front desk at Emergency and they'll direct you to the right place."

I numbly grab my purse and watch as they load my mom into the back of their rig. I'm not even sure if I remember to lock the door as I climb in my car and turn the ignition. The ambulance lights flash as it pulls onto the road while I go into autopilot and shift my car into gear to follow.

thirty-nine

"Hi, I'm here for Cybil Kennedy. The paramedics said she'd be here."

The hospital receptionist clicks her fingers on the keyboard, searching for Cybil's room number, I'm guessing. She purses her lips. "Are you a family member?"

I nod. "I'm her daughter."

The woman looks down for a moment before coming from behind her desk. She places her hand on my elbow with compassion in her eyes.

"It looks like they're blocking all visitors at the moment but her doctor should be able to speak with you soon. Let's go into the private waiting room. It's right down the hall."

I look around at the main room filled with at least a dozen people who seem to be waiting as well.

"Um, I can just wait right here."

She gently nudges me forward. "It's best if we go to a private location, dear."

She leads me down a narrow hallway and places her employee badge against a sensor. The door clicks open and she steps aside to let me in. The room is small, maybe four feet by ten feet. Six chairs are lined up against the wall with a small television hanging in the corner. "It shouldn't be too long," she says.

I nod as I sink into a chair. "Thank you."

She closes the door softly, leaving me to myself. I tap my leg and pick at my nail polish while I wait. It feels like at least thirty minutes have passed and I'm starting to think they forgot about me. Right before I get up to go check, I hear the lock engaging. I frown when I see Marcus coming through the door instead of a doctor.

"What are you doing here?" I ask him.

"The hospital called me," he says. "Your mom listed me as her emergency contact when we got married."

There's no way I heard him correctly. "I'm sorry; when you *what*?"

His brows knit together. "She didn't tell you?"

"That you got *married*?" I shriek.

"Yes," he nods. "Two weeks ago. We flew to Vegas for the weekend. I thought you knew."

"Unbelievable," I say as I slouch into the chair.

He takes a seat two chairs over. "Have you heard anything yet? The lady on the phone wouldn't give me any details. She only said it was urgent."

"Not yet." The tears start falling again as flashes of her lying unconscious run through my head.

Marcus slowly rises from his seat and takes the spot right next to me. I'm too numb to question him as he puts his arm around my shoulders. "What happened?"

I grab a tissue from the side table and blow my nose. "Maybe I should ask you that. Why was she at my apartment?"

He releases a deep sigh. "We had an argument. She said she was staying the night with you."

I tense. "When did she start using again? She told me she's been clean for months."

Marcus looks confused. "What do you mean? She hasn't touched anything besides pot since we met. She knows illegal drugs are a hard limit for me. I'm not going to spend my time with a junkie."

"But marrying a cheap hooker is okay?" I scoff.

"Don't talk about her that way. There is nothing *cheap* about Cybil." He adjusts in the chair to face me better. "Look, Katherine. Regardless of what you think, I love your mom. She has this spunk that's hard to find. Our relationship might not be...traditional in your eyes, but it's a relationship nonetheless. It works for us. I would've never married her if it didn't."

"I can't believe she got married and didn't tell me."

He winces. "I'm sorry; I really thought you knew."

"That doesn't matter right now. I just want her to wake up."

Marcus tilts his head to the side. "She's asleep? What exactly happened, Katherine? Tell me what you know."

I start crying harder. "She was...she was unconscious when I found her. So pale and clammy. And she had...a rubber strap around her arm. She was shooting up and I think she took too much, Marcus. She was hardly breathing."

He rockets out of his chair. "You're wrong. I need to see the doctor. Why the fuck is the doctor not here right now?"

"I don't know," I reply as I blow my nose again.

"Well, I'm going to find out." Marcus spins on his heels and opens the door. Inside the threshold is a fifty-something man with salt and pepper hair and a white coat.

"Cybil Kennedy's family?" the man asks.

"I'm her husband," Marcus says as he thumps his chest. "And she's her daughter. Are you her doctor? When can I see my wife?"

"Mr. Kennedy—" the doctor begins.

"Moore," Marcus corrects. "We just got married; she hasn't changed her name yet."

The doctor gulps. "*Mr. Moore*, please have a seat so we can talk about your wife."

"I don't want to have a fucking seat!" he shouts. "I want to see my damn wife!"

I'm frozen watching Marcus in such a state of panic. If I had any doubts about his feelings before, I don't now. This is clearly a man worried about the woman he loves.

The doctor adjusts his round-rimmed glasses. "Mr. Moore. I will explain everything. Please, take a seat."

Marcus sits with a huff. "Well, go ahead, Doc."

The doctor closes the door and pulls up a chair in front of us. "My name is Ben Miller. I was the attending physician when your wife arrived by ambulance." He looks at me. "I understand you're the one who found her?"

I nod. "How is she? Is she awake now?"

"When the paramedics arrived on-site, your mother was in severe respiratory depression."

"Speak English, Doc," Marcus barks.

Dr. Miller straightens his spine. "Heroin affects the Central Nervous System. That's the part of your brain that controls the ability to breathe and keeps the heart beating. She wasn't getting enough oxygen. That's why she passed out."

"But you fixed her, right?" I ask. "That's what you do; fix people." When the doctor remains silent I add, "*Right?*"

Dr. Miller lowers his voice a notch. "I'm sorry, but your mother passed away en route to the hospital. There was nothing we could do. She had the hallmark signs of an acute heroin overdose. We'll know for certain when the results of the toxicity workup come in."

My chest seizes. I'm in such a state of shock that I

can't make out what Marcus is saying to Dr. Miller. I can hear my heart beating in my ears. It feels like I'm underwater, fighting against a strong current. I don't realize that I'm holding my breath until I start feeling faint. I take a giant gulp of air and clutch my chest as a sharp pain jolts me out of my daze.

"Can I see her?" My voice is so quiet I'm not sure if anyone heard me. I take a fortifying breath and try again. "I'd like to see her. Can I see her?"

Dr. Miller and Marcus exchange glances. Marcus looks as incredulous as I feel. I don't think either of us will believe she's gone until we see it for ourselves.

"Of course," Dr. Miller replies. "You can go in together if you'd like. We have her in a private room."

I glance at Marcus and he seems to read my mind. "It's okay, Katherine. Go in by yourself. I'll wait."

"Thank you," I whisper.

Dr. Miller stands and opens the door. "Mr. Moore, I'll send a nurse over to bring you back when she's done." His eyes meet mine. "Miss Kennedy, I'll take you there now."

I stare at the back of his white coat as we wander down one long hall, then another. Each room we pass is closed off by glass doors with curtains added to give their patients privacy. There seems to be a never-ending stretch of linoleum as we round another corner. Dr. Miller stops at the first door and slides it open.

"Take as much time as you need," he says as he opens the curtain and steps aside so I can enter.

The room is sparse—a small sink on one side and a few machines on the other. I can't take my eyes off the gurney sitting in the middle. A tall, svelte body is clearly outlined under the white sheet that covers it.

"Would you like the lights on?" Dr. Miller asks.

I hadn't realized they were off until that moment. "Um...no, that's okay. There's enough light from the hall." I timidly step further into the room.

He nods. "Very well. Let us know if you need anything."

Dr. Miller closes the curtain and steps out. I can't seem to look away from her body lying in front of me. Her face is covered so I can't see anything besides her shape. The logical part of my brain tells me that my mom is under there. The illogical part tells me that she's not. If I don't see her face or feel her chilled skin, then she'd still be alive. Once I pull down those covers, there's no going back; I'm sealing my fate of being without her forever. I'm not sure if I'm ready to face that.

I take another two steps and carefully pinch the top of the sheet with my fingers. I squeeze my eyes shut as I lower it just enough to uncover her face. I take several deep breaths before opening them and seeing her pale features.

"Mom," I croak.

God, she's so beautiful, even in death. It almost

seems like she's sleeping…like she's going to wake up at any moment and tell me this was all a horrible joke. I know that's not going to happen though because I can sense that something's not right. Never mind the fact that her body remains completely still; it's more that I can no longer feel her *presence*. Marcus was right when he said she had a spunk like no other. She knew how to command attention when she walked into a room. I know we've had our problems but I relied on that dysfunction. It was the one constant in my life. And as ridiculous as it may be, a small part of me had always hoped that she would clean up one day and actually want to be my *mom*. Not just Cybil—the woman who gave birth to me. One day, we would actually have a normal mother-daughter bond.

As I press my hand to the top of her head and smooth out her bleached hair, that hope dies. The heat has already left her body. The spark that was always inside of her is no longer there. My fingertips press against her scalp, feeling her solid form, but at the same time, it's hollow. Her body may be here physically, but this is no longer Cybil Kennedy. *Cybil Kennedy has moved on to another place.* I'm not a religious person, but I hope that wherever she is, she's finally at peace. She hid it well, but I always knew she was slowly dying on the inside. Her addiction constantly ate away at her. She fought her demons daily. I try finding solace in the fact that she no longer has to suffer.

"I'm so sorry," I sob. "I'm so sorry you couldn't fight hard enough. That you no longer have a chance. I didn't mean it when I said I wanted you gone. I *never* wanted you gone; I just wanted you to be *better*. I wanted you to be my mom. *Why couldn't you just be my mom?*"

I fall to my knees and cry as I clutch her arm over the sheet. I'm not sure how long I'm there before a nurse walks in.

"Is there anything I can get you, hon?"

I wipe my face on my sleeve. "Um...no, thank you. I think I'm done." I stand up and look at the bed one more time. "I love you, Mom." I bend over to kiss her forehead before pulling the sheet up again.

The nurse gives me a sad nod and steps aside so I can exit. Marcus is waiting outside the door.

"Katherine, are you okay?" he asks.

"I will be. You can go in now; I'm done."

He quickly glances into the room then back to me. "The hospital needs to know what to do with her... remains. Do you have a preference?"

I shake my head. "I don't know. I don't think she'd want a burial."

"Neither do I," he says. "Okay...I'll tell them we'd like cremation. We can decide what to do after that. Do you need a ride home? I should only be a few minutes."

"I'm not going back there," I sniff. "*I can't*...not right now. I'll be okay; I can stay with a friend."

He takes a deep breath and exhales. "I'll be in touch soon."

"Okay."

"Katherine, this probably goes without saying, but I'm taking some time off from the club. I suggest you do the same. Just let me know when you're ready to come back."

I nod silently before turning around and walking away. Numbly, I make my way through the corridors to the parking lot. I don't even remember the drive to Gavin's as I put my key in the lock and open the front door. Frodo is waiting for me in the foyer. He rubs himself against my legs, trying to get my attention.

I bend down to pick him up. "Hi, buddy."

He mews in response. I cradle him to my chest and carry him to bed. I'm exhausted but every time I close my eyes, I see my mom's face. Instead, I focus on Frodo's rhythmic purrs as I stroke his soft fur. It's well after sunrise before I'm able to sleep.

forty

"Happy New Year," Gavin whispers as he softly kisses the back of my neck. "Did you miss me?"

"What time is it?" I mumble.

"Just after three. Are you feeling okay? It's not like you to sleep in so late."

My eyes are so swollen from crying that I have trouble prying my lids open. I stretch as I roll over to face him and squint at the brightness assaulting my eyeballs. I must look as bad as I feel because Gavin's eyes widen when he gets a good look at me.

"Kat, what's wrong? Why do you look like you've been crying?"

I sit up and scrub a shaky hand over my face. I'm surprised I have any tears left as my eyes begin to fill. "Because I have."

He gently places his palm on my cheek. "What happened?"

"My mom died last night," I explain with an exhale. "Technically, early this morning, I guess."

Gavin's mouth falls open in shock. "What? How?" He pulls me into his chest and wraps his arms around me as my tears break loose. "Shh, baby," he says. "We don't have to talk about it until you're ready."

I pull away from him and wipe my eyes. "No, that's okay. I have to get it out eventually." I take a deep breath. "I went to drop off my rent check after work this morning. My checkbook was inside the apartment so I went in to grab it. That's where I found her."

He raises his eyebrows. "She was at your apartment?"

I nod and try to swallow but my mouth feels too dry. My throat too tight. "She and Marcus had a fight. I thought...I just thought she was drunk. I thought she was passed out. But she looked..." I choke back my sob. "There was nothing they could do. It was too late. *I was too late*. She...she was so bl-blue."

"Oh, Kat," Gavin breathes as he pulls me into him again. "I'm so, so sorry."

I sob as he runs his fingers through my hair and over my back. I sniffle. "I can't get the image of her lying there out of my head, Gavin. Every time I close my eyes, I see it. How am I supposed to go back to my apartment without seeing her dying on my living room floor? How do I make that go away?"

"I don't know how to make the images go away." He squeezes me tighter. "You don't have to go back there if you don't want to, though. I can get anything you need from the house and you can stay here as long as you need to."

"That's fine for now, but what about later? There's a reason why we've lived there so long. It's the cheapest place in town. I just can't imagine going back."

"Shh," he coos. "You don't have to worry about that now. We'll figure it out later."

"I can't figure it out later!" I argue. "Don't you get it? I have to figure out a plan *now*. If I don't have a plan, if I don't have something to focus on…I don't know how I'm going to make it through this! I *need* something to focus on, Gavin."

He pulls me down with him until we're both lying on the bed. "Kat, I'm right here with you. I will help you in whatever way you need me to. You're not alone, baby. You don't have to go through anything alone anymore."

I clutch his shirt in my fist and take a few moments to breathe.

"She's being cremated," I mumble into his chest. "I have to figure out what I'm going to do with her ashes."

"We'll figure it out *together*, Kat." He continues rubbing my back. "Can I ask you something?"

"Of course," I sniff.

"Why didn't you call me? I could've taken an earlier flight. I could've been here with you."

"I didn't think about it," I answer honestly.

He tries masking the pain I've inflicted but I see it. He braces his hands on my face and says, "Kat, we're a *team*. I know you're not used to leaning on someone, but you can count on me. I promise I will do everything in my power to take care of you. To be someone that you can depend on. You need to let me in. Okay?"

"Okay," I whisper.

I have a sickening sense of déjà vu as I make my way into the frigid waters. There are a few differences this time though. For one, the box clutched tightly to my chest is a little heavier. And the ocean is colder—so cold that my legs are already numb after being submerged for only a few seconds. I'm older now too. Only by a few years, but I've gained significantly more wisdom since the last time I did this. Since the last time I poured someone's ashes into the sea. *How many times can one person do this and survive?* I ask myself. I certainly wouldn't wish this dread on anyone. There's so much finality in this one act. Turning over the box is the hardest part, you know. Lifting the lid, rotating your wrists, and emptying the contents of the urn into the water. I had trouble doing it the first time, and this time is no different.

The waves are crashing against my thighs, trying desperately to kick me out or pull me in further. The wind whips my hair as saltwater splashes onto my face, mixing with my tears. I begin to sway so I plant my feet deeper in the sand to stabilize myself. If only physically withstanding the elements could calm the inner turmoil raging inside of me. With each wave that comes, I experience a moment of panic. I know that I *should* get this over with; that I can only stay in the water for so long before hypothermia threatens, but I *can't*. In this cardboard box lies the remains of the only family I have left. I truly am alone after this. Just me, myself, and I. As another wave ebbs, I contemplate leaving. Going back home with the box intact. Pretend this isn't happening. That this isn't my reality. Until I feel large hands encompassing my own.

I blink rapidly to clear my blurry vision. I look into Gavin's eyes and I'm reminded that I'm not alone after all. I know from the depths of my soul that this man would never abandon me. I'm instantly granted the strength I need to do this. The courage I need to face the truth.

He nods toward the box. "We'll do it together on the next wave. Okay?"

I nod in agreement, unable to form words through the thickness in my throat.

Gavin looks out toward the sea, and back to me as the next one rolls in. "Are you ready, Kat?"

I nod once again.

He lifts the lid and tightens his fingers around mine. The wave pounds against us, knocking us back a couple of feet before it begins to pull away. I know this is it; that I need to release the ashes as it's going out. My hands falter as I begin to tip the box but Gavin lends me the force I need to complete the motion. Together, we invert the container and release my mother's ashes into the Pacific. I breathe a sigh of relief that it's over, and in the next moment, my knees buckle and I'm being swept away.

"I've got you," Gavin promises as he wraps his arms around my torso, pulling me back. "You're safe with me, Kat." His hold doesn't waver as he pulls me into shore. "You'll always be safe with me."

The conviction in his voice leaves no room for doubt. We towel off and change into the dry clothes we brought. Gavin grabs a blanket and wraps it tightly around our bodies as he pulls me into him. I curl into him as we sit on the rocky beach watching the sea. His warm breath fans across my face as he clutches me to his chest. I'm not sure how much time passes as we sit there in silence, but it's enough to watch the sun descend across the sky. As the final rays of light dance across the water, I finally speak.

"This is where I released my daughter's ashes. This is where I go when I need to think. I've never brought anyone here before."

He squeezes me tighter. "I'm honored that you trusted me. That you let me see this part of you."

"Sometimes I feel like you see *every* part of me." I shiver from the dropping temperature.

He rubs his hands over my arms to create warmth. "Is that a bad thing?"

I turn my face toward him. "No...I don't know. It's just...different. I try really hard not to be so transparent."

He places his palm on my cheek. "You don't have to do that. I understand wanting to guard your secrets, but you never have to be someone you're not. Not when you're with me."

I sigh. "I worry that we've grown so close because of our circumstances. What happens when things calm down? When we no longer have to hide?"

"I don't know," he replies earnestly. "What I *do* know, is that no one has ever made me feel the way you do. No one has ever compelled me to be a better man like you do. Hailey and I were together for almost five years and I never felt this strongly about her. I can't imagine my world without you in it, Kat. That's how I know you're different. I *hate* that we can't be together publicly. I can't wait for the day when that's no longer true. I want to show you off to the world; scream from the rooftops that you're mine. Until that day comes, I just ask that you give me the chance to prove myself."

I turn into him fully and wrap my arms around his neck. "You've *already* proven yourself, Gavin. It's crazy how fast everything has been, but I can't imagine my life without you either. I've been burned so many damn times that I need you to be patient with me, though. I can't magically make the doubt go away when it's been instilled in me for so long. I *do* trust you. And I believe in *us*. It's life in general that I worry about. Circumstances beyond our control. Fate has really fucked with me in the past and I just need time to get over that."

He presses his forehead against mine. "I'm not going anywhere, Kat. You can have all the time you need."

forty-one

Today is the first day back from winter break. Gavin thinks I should take some time considering I just laid my mom to rest two days ago but I disagree. I need some semblance of normalcy right now. Focusing on schoolwork and the everyday minutia within these walls will help keep me distracted. I'm still not ready to go back to the club but it's only a matter of time before that needs to happen as well. For now, I can't bear the thought of running into Marcus. He would, undoubtedly, remind me of my mom which is something I don't need. By no means am I in denial that she's gone, but I can't afford to allow that fact to control my emotions. I lost it when I met him at the funeral home to pick up her ashes. Seeing the grief so openly reflected on his face ripped me apart. When I invited him along to the beach, he refused. He said that his wife was not in that box. Her spirit and effervescence were not contained within a bunch of ashes. He wanted to remember her as she was and he couldn't do that if he watched her remains being washed away by the ocean. Quite frankly, I don't blame him. It's certainly not an event that I'll *ever* forget.

"Oh, honey, there you are!" Bree pulls me into a hug. "Kat, I'm so sorry."

I pull back and take a deep breath to collect myself. "Thanks, Bree. What are you doing here?"

She's standing right outside my second period class. *Gavin's* class. "I was waiting for you. I got in right before the bell rang for first, so I had to wait until second period to find you. I stopped by your apartment several times but you weren't there. Where've you been?"

I shrug. "I've been staying with a friend."

Bree looks confused. "*What* friend? As far as I know, Dylan and I are it. And I know you weren't with him because he's been worried too."

"I've been...seeing someone," I say quietly. "I'm crashing at his place for a while."

Now she looks shocked. "What? Who? And since when?"

"A little while," I say and shrug, trying to make my relationship with Gavin seem much more casual than it is. "You don't know him. He's...older."

"Why am I just finding out about this now?" She looks hurt and I can't really blame her. "Kat, I'm sorry; I don't mean to question you like this after what just happened, but I've been worried about you. *Really* worried about you. When can I meet this guy? It's my job as your bestie to make sure he's good enough for you." She adds a smile at the end, obviously trying to inject some levity into the situation.

Shit, how am I going to say this without making her feel even worse?

"Um...you can't meet him. Not right now, but I promise you will soon. Things are...*complicated* right now. We're not ready to go public."

She scowls. "What the hell, Kat? Is he *married*?"

"No," I say vehemently. "Bree, please just trust me on this. He's wonderful. Probably the best thing that's ever happened to me. But I can't tell you any more than that right now. When the time is right, you'll understand. I just can't say more *now*."

The warning bell rings, indicating that we only have a minute before the next class begins.

"Shit, I need to haul ass to math." She pulls me into another hug. "We'll talk more about this later. I'll see you at lunch. Okay?"

"'Kay," I nod.

"Kitty!" I stop right before walking into class when I hear Dylan's voice. I turn around and see him jogging down the hall.

"Hey, Dyl."

"Come here."

He braces his hand on the back of my head and pulls

me into him. He's almost a foot taller than me so my face is smashed into his chest. I choke back the sob that's threatening to break loose as I fall into the comfort he's offering. This is one of the things that I love most about Dylan. We don't need to fill the silence with words. We can just *be*. Despite all of the tension between us since Gavin and I got together, he's still one of my best friends. I really don't know what I'd do without him. He pulls back when someone clears their throat behind me.

"Miss Kennedy," Gavin says. "Mr. Taylor. Please take your seats so we can begin class."

Dylan frowns at him but wisely doesn't say anything to draw attention to us. As I'm walking through the door, I feel Gavin's little finger hooking onto mine.

"You okay?" he whispers.

Serenity washes over me from the innocent gesture but that disappears the second our fingers disengage. I nod discreetly and walk past him to the back of the classroom and take my seat.

Gavin shuts the door behind him and walks to the podium to address the class. "Welcome back everyone. Did you enjoy your break?"

A chorus of mumbled responses scatters throughout the room. Gavin briefly makes eye contact and gives me a sad smile before averting his gaze.

"I hope you're all feeling refreshed because we have a lot to do. This week we're focusing on college admission and scholarship essays. Since this is the time of year when most applications are sent in, it's important that we dive right into it. The essay is one of the most important components of your application. It's a chance to add depth to something that's important to you. Ultimately, it should convey to the committee why that particular university or scholarship would be a good fit for you. It also gives you a chance to showcase your personality and how you might contribute to the campus community."

Gavin walks over to the projector and flips the switch. "Essays should use this formatting unless specified otherwise."

I read through the bullet points listed on the white board as he continues.

He presses a button on his computer. "These are two common writing prompts that you'll see out there: *'Who has been the most influential person in your life?'* and *'Describe a major hurdle or obstacle you've had to overcome.'* I want you to choose one of these prompts and write your own essay. I'm passing out a packet with six examples of what worked. They are distinct and unique to the individual writer; however, each of them assisted the reader in learning more about the student beyond the transcripts and lists of activities provided in their applications. The purpose of these examples is to inspire you as you prepare to compose your own personal statements. The most important thing to remember is to be original and creative as you share your own story, thoughts, and ideas. Any questions?"

I tune them out as Gavin distributes handouts and fields several questions from other students. I ponder my topic choices for what seems like hours. I cringe as I stare at the whiteboard, thinking about how loaded each question is, with both carrying the potential to expose something supremely raw. Something I definitely don't want to share with anyone, especially a group of strangers deciding whether or not I'm fit to attend their university. I guess I'm going to have to bite the bullet, though, if I have any chance of getting out of Coastal Oregon. I read through the examples and see that two of them talk about their moms. Both women suffered from cancer. One made it; one did not. The words begin to blur as tears roll down my cheeks and drip onto the paper. I don't even realize that I'm crying until I see the first drop hit the page.

I look up when I hear my name being whispered and see several of my classmates staring at me with equal parts pity and discomfort. That's the funny thing about death, or any horrible event really. Your pain makes other people uncomfortable. They tend to think they should follow some unspoken protocol when bad things happen yet they have no idea what that may be. So instead, they avoid you, try pretending like nothing happened, or offer useless words. I look away from them and wipe my eyes just as the bell rings. I see Dylan approaching me but I shake my head causing him to change course. I leap out of my chair and into Gavin's arms the second I hear him close the door.

"I feel like such an idiot," I mumble into his chest.

He wraps his arms around me and kisses the top of my head. "Shh, Kat. You're allowed to be sad."

"Was I making a big scene?" I ask. "Honestly, Gavin... how bad was it?"

He strokes my hair. "It wasn't that bad, I swear. It was only the last minute or so of class. I was about to pull you into the hall but then the bell rang."

I pull away slightly so I can look him in the eyes. "God, I feel so stupid."

Gavin braces his hands around my face. "Don't, Kat. You have nothing to be ashamed of. Why don't you take the rest of the day off? Go crawl in my bed with Frodo and get some rest. You shouldn't be here. It's too soon. It's okay to take time to heal."

"I can't," I sniff. "I have to—"

"Gavin, do you have a moment—" We break apart the second we hear the woman's voice.

Gavin clears his throat. "Sure, Tara. What can I do for you?"

Tara, AKA Ms. Roberts, looks at us suspiciously. "I'm sorry; I didn't realize you had a student in here. I can come back."

I do everything in my power to avoid eye contact as I walk to my desk to gather my things.

"No need," Gavin assures her. "Miss Kennedy was just leaving."

I throw my bag over my shoulder and make my way toward the door. "I'll see you tomorrow, Mr. Cooper. Thanks for answering my questions."

"Of course," Gavin replies.

I leave the room with as much urgency as possible, hoping I'm not being suspicious. I don't risk looking back because I'm sure Ms. Roberts is watching me carefully. I know Gavin will find a way to explain what she saw, but I feel shitty for putting him in that position. I need to get my act together and I need to do it pronto.

I take Gavin's advice and head back to the house. Frodo is sleeping on the couch when I walk through the front door. He stretches languidly as I sit next to him and bumps his head into my arm, begging for attention.

"Hi, buddy," I say as I run my fingers through his soft fur from head to tail. This spurs him on even more—he moves to my lap and starts rubbing his body against my chest. I smile softly at what I assume is his attempt to comfort me. I once read that animals can sense when you're in distress and they instinctively offer their support. I know he's doing his best, but it's not enough to lift the crushing weight in my chest.

As tenuous as our relationship was, Cybil's death has left a gaping hole inside of me. I've never felt so *alone*. I realize how stupid that is—the people that I have left are closer to me than she ever was. But they can't identify with loss like I can. They don't know what it's like to have your entire family ripped away in an instant. I hope they *never* know such devastation which is why I refuse to burden them with my problems. I just need to find a way to hold myself together on the surface until this feeling fades. It has to go away sometime, right?

forty-two

The sun has barely risen as we make our way north on Highway 101. Gavin woke me up ridiculously early telling me I had twenty minutes to shower and dress before he was throwing me in the car. We've been on the road for almost an hour and he still hasn't told me where we're going.

"C'mon, Gavin. At least give me a hint."

He gives me a boyish smile. "Like I told you the first three times, no."

I huff. "Can you at least tell me how much longer we'll have to drive?"

"Thirty minutes or so. That's all you're getting."

It's been six weeks since my mom passed. I think I'm doing a pretty good job pretending I have this coping thing down. At school I've managed to avoid any additional outbursts. And while my return to the club was difficult, that too, was uneventful since Marcus has yet to show up. To be honest, most days are a blur and those days bleed into weeks. The only moments I can clearly recall are when something reminds me of my mom and I cry in the shower until the water runs cold. And when I come out, Gavin is always right there, taking me into his arms. He's the one person I can't fool. No matter what, he knows when I'm having a bad day, and he's determined to make it better. Sometimes we make love, other times we simply hold each other. The one constant is how therapeutic those moments are. How I always feel a little less fragmented when I wake up the next morning.

I start contemplating our possible destinations when Gavin veers off the main highway and heads east. *Where in the hell is he taking me?* The only clue I have is the big pile of stuff hiding under a tarp in the back of his SUV. I anxiously tap my fingers as we travel down the two-lane road. I'm trying really hard not to be a bad sport but I *hate* surprises. In my experience, they're rarely a good thing. I have to keep reminding myself that Gavin is one of the few trustworthy people in my life.

As promised, approximately a half hour later, he's turning down a dirt road. I read the sign as we approach the gates to the Siuslaw National Forest campground. Gavin rolls down his window as we pull up to a small ranger's station.

"Good morning," the woman in green says. "Will you be needing a day pass?"

"We have reservations under Cooper," he replies.

She punches a few keys on her computer and stares at the screen for a moment. Then she grabs a small envelope and rectangular piece of paper that she passes through the window. "Make sure you leave this card on your dash. Right around the corner, you'll find the visitor's station with a map of the grounds. We're open from seven to seven each day. It's not much but you can get bundles of wood, water, and a few other necessities. You're in yurt A-12; the door key is in the envelope. There's supposed to be a storm tonight so make sure anything left outside is anchored down really well."

"Will do," Gavin nods.

I wait until he rolls the window up before speaking. "We're going *camping*? Seriously?"

"Yep. What's wrong with camping?"

"Besides the fact that it's the middle of February? You heard the lady—a storm is coming."

"Relax, Kat," he chuckles. "The yurt has electricity and heat. We'll be fine."

"What if the storm knocks the power out?" Not uncommon in these parts when it gets really windy.

He smiles. "I'm sure we can think of some way to generate body heat if we need to."

I roll my eyes. "What about Frodo? We can't just leave him alone."

"Frodo's fine," he assures me. "I put out extra food and water. He'll be okay for one night."

"But...why?"

Gavin parks the car in front of the visitor's center and grabs my hand. "Because I want to spend time with you outside of the house. I want to stop hiding our relationship from the world, even if it's only for the weekend. Let's be honest, Kat; you've just been going through the motions day in and day out. It kills me seeing you like this. I thought it might help to get away...to regroup. If you really don't want to stay, we can leave." He tightens his grip around my fingers. "I'd really like you to say you'll stay, though."

Tears fill my eyes from his thoughtfulness. "I'll stay."

He grabs my face and pulls me in for a quick kiss. "You won't regret it; I promise." He opens the car door. "Stay here. I'm just going to run inside to grab some firewood then we'll find our campsite."

"Okay."

A few minutes later, we're driving around a narrow loop looking for our space. I have to admit the park grounds are beautiful. The area is backed against a large creek and dominated by giant Sitka spruces and Doug firs. I love the smell of the forest, especially when a storm is brewing. There's this static charge in the air that electrifies your senses. It seems as if it crawls under your skin and breathes life into your blood.

"Here we are; number twelve," Gavin says and points as he pulls the Tahoe onto the small parking slab.

Yurts are a big thing in the Pacific Northwest.

Although our winters are fairly mild temperature-wise, the winds can be pretty fierce, especially this close to the coast. Yurts allow for year-round camping while being protected from the elements. You still get to experience the great outdoors with hiking and campfire cookouts but when it's time to go to sleep or if the weather gets really nasty, you have a roof over your head that won't get pounded by the storm. The canvas shell is secured around a wooden frame with wooden floors. I've only stayed in one once but it was certainly the most comfortable camping trip I've ever had.

Gavin places the key in my hand. "Why don't you check out the inside while I grab our stuff?"

"I'll help you."

He hops out of the car. "Okay, Stubborn One. You can put the bedding on while I get a fire started."

I join him at the back of the car and start grabbing bags. "What if *I* want to get the fire started?"

"Do you?"

I smirk. "No. I said what *if*."

Gavin swats me on the ass. "Go put the sheets on, woman, so we have a spot to have all the sex."

I laugh. "Awfully confident that you'll get lucky, aren't you?"

"Nah, just hopeful."

"Well, keep being cute like this and I'd say your odds are pretty good."

He smiles. "Good to know."

Gavin really has thought of everything. We're roasting marshmallows over the campfire to make S'mores. Well, I should say *Gavin* is roasting the marshmallows since I can't seem to keep mine on the stick. After the fifth one fell, he decided to take over. You'd think I would've learned considering there are three charred hotdogs sitting at the bottom of the fire pit. That's what I get for being so determined to prove my wilderness expertise, I suppose. Or *pretend* I have any expertise, rather.

"Coming in hot," Gavin warns as he pulls the marshmallow out of the fire.

I hold out my cracker and allow him to set it down before I mush the two parts together. Chocolatey marshmallow graham cracker goodness explodes in my mouth as I take the first bite.

"Mmm, soooo good."

Gavin swoops in for a quick kiss. "Mmm, I agree."

"It's even better when it hasn't been bathed in my saliva."

He smirks. "I happen to like your saliva."

I roll my eyes but inwardly smile at his sweet, yet somewhat pervy comment. We sit by the fire eating an obscene amount of S'mores. Every once in a while a strong gust of wind blows but the flames are keeping us warm for the most part. After the last S'more has been demolished, Gavin stands up and reaches out his hand.

"Dance with me."

I laugh. "There's no music."

"Does it matter?" He raises his eyebrows.

I take his hand and raise up. "I guess not."

He pulls me into him and cradles my head to his chest as we lightly sway to the rhythm of our heartbeats. The breeze is picking up but I'm barely affected being in his arms, soaking in his warmth.

Gavin stops moving and lifts my chin so we're face to face. "Kat, I need to say something. And I want to preface it by saying that I don't expect you to respond. In fact, I'd probably prefer that you don't. It's something I've wanted to tell you for a while now but I don't want to scare you. So promise me you won't be scared. Okay?"

What on earth is he talking about? "What..."

He presses his index finger to my lips. "Kat, please don't overthink it. Just promise me you won't freak out."

"Okay..." I say hesitantly. I don't like making promises unless I'm sure I can keep them but this seems important to him. "What is it, Gavin?"

He palms my cheeks with both hands and blows out a breath. "Okay, here goes. Kat, I love you. I mean, I'm *in love* with you."

I gasp. "Gavin, I"

He holds his hand up. "Please just let me get this out. I know this is still new but I also know this is real. I feel like I've known you my entire life. I can't tell you why, but when I'm with you, I feel whole. When you're not around, your absence is tangible. The best part of my day is when we're together. I don't want you to say it back right now, but I know you feel this way too. I have faith that you'll tell me when you're ready—I don't care how long it takes. I just couldn't go another day without telling you."

"Gavin…"

"Wait…one more thing," he interrupts. "I'm going home for Spring Break next month. I want you to come with me, Kat. I want you to meet my family. What do you say?"

I take a deep breath as he watches me expectantly. "Am I allowed to talk now?"

He laughs. "Yes, of course."

"I'd be honored to meet your family."

"You would?"

I smile. "I would."

He pulls me into a bear hug. "They're going to love you as much as I do."

"I hope so."

He crouches down to my level. "Hey, none of that. They'll adore you; I'm sure of it. Have you ever been to San Francisco?"

"No. I've never been outside of Oregon or Washington. Will we be flying? I've never been on a plane before."

"Never?"

"Never," I confirm.

He grins. "Well, hot damn! I get to pop your plane cherry."

"You're an idiot," I tease.

He grabs my face. "And you're beautiful." His eyes dance across my face. "I love you, Kat."

"I—"

My reply is silenced by a kiss so scorching that my toes curl inside my boots. I'm not sure how long we stand there making out but at some point, the storm rolls in, drenching us with rain. I shiver involuntarily but I'm not sure if it's from the cold or the intensity of the moment. Gavin was right to be concerned. I can't say I'm not scared, but he makes me want to stick around and see what happens anyway. I couldn't have put my feelings into words any better than he did. He's right; I do feel the same. My love for him is soul deep. But I'm not ready to say those three little words and I'm thankful he understands that about me. I've only uttered them to one other person I was dating and look how that turned out. I know Gavin would never do anything to harm me, but I promised myself I would be careful saying the L word going forward. I think people throw the phrase around too casually and I'm not going to be one of them. When I'm ready to reciprocate, he'll know that I mean it. He'll know without a doubt that I no longer feel fractured, afraid of love's consequences. He'll know that I'm ready to put my demons in the past and love with my whole heart. I'm not there yet but with Gavin, I have hope that it will happen soon.

We walk backwards into the yurt and Gavin shuts the door behind us. Needing to feel his skin against mine, I pull the zipper down on his hoodie and push it off his shoulders. His shirt comes next while I'm kicking off my boots. He catches on quickly and removes my top and his shoes. Each article of clothing hits the floor with a wet plop as we undress each other. When we're finally skin to skin, we tumble toward the full-sized bed against the wall. His lips move down my throat, over my collarbone, to the swell of my breasts. He smells like marshmallows and chocolate and the tiniest hint of wood smoke. We scoot up the mattress together until my head is resting on a fluffy pillow. My thighs part as he settles between them. I nearly lose all cognitive abilities when he starts grinding against me, lightly tracing his finger over my flesh. His feather-soft touch sets all of my nerve endings ablaze. My heart gallops each time he tells me how much he loves me...how beautiful I am...how much he needs me.

When he enters my body, I wonder how I could ever be whole again without him.

Without this.

Everything is right in the world when our bodies become one. I have no past. No pain. No grief. All I have is this moment.

This man.

Our love.

We lay in bed afterwards, the howling wind the only sound in the room. We've burrowed under the covers, our limbs intertwined as much as they can be. I'm drowsy and content. *Happy.* More at peace with the world than I've ever been and I owe it all to him.

"Kat?"

"Hmm?" I mumble.

He strokes my hair. "Thank you for saying you'd stay."

I smile. "Thank you for bringing me here. Today's been perfect, Gavin. It's exactly what I needed."

"Good night, Kat. I love you."

I love you too, I think as I drift off to sleep.

forty-three

Spring is rolling in. So are the college acceptance letters. So far I have five, all offering really great financial assistance. I still haven't heard back from my top choice—U.C. Berkeley. Gavin doesn't even know I applied yet. I didn't want to get his hopes up in case I don't get in. But *if* I make the cut, Gavin and I wouldn't have to be apart. He could move back home and we could be together every day. I never thought I'd be that girl who'd let a guy influence her school of choice, but here I am all the same. It's not like it'd be a compromise, though; it's a great school that offers many different programs. It's a win-win in my opinion.

We've just boarded the plane to San Francisco and I am nervous for my first flight. It's a short one—under two hours—but Gavin's had to assure me many, many times it will be uneventful. I'm not so afraid of the flying *per se*; it's more the crashing and burning part that I'd like to avoid.

"Flight attendants, please prepare for departure."

I white-knuckle the armrest as the captain's voice comes through the intercom. We've taxied to the runway and our speed is picking up quickly.

Gavin grabs my hand and laces his fingers through mine. "Relax, Kat. This part's fun."

We're going faster and faster as we bump down the airstrip. I'm pushed back into my chair as the nose of the plane tips up and we lift off the ground. We're swaying recklessly from side to side as we climb into the sky.

"Is this supposed to happen? Why is it so choppy?"

Gavin chuckles. "Kat, *relax*. It's totally normal. The ride will smooth out as soon as we get to our cruising altitude."

I squeeze my eyes shut. "And when's that going to happen?"

I feel his hand on my cheek. "Hey, open your eyes."

I find Gavin's face inches away from mine. "Do you think I'd let anything bad happen to you?"

"You can't control the pilot," I argue. "And what if something malfunctions? It happens all the time."

He smirks. "First of all, it doesn't happen *all the time*. They check everything before takeoff. And two, statistically, flying is safer than driving. You're not afraid to drive, are you?"

"No, of course not."

"Well, then trust me. We'll be fine." He pushes the armrest back and pulls me into his side. "Listen to your music if you need to. We'll be there before you know it."

"Promise?"

He kisses the top of my head. "Promise."

It turns out I was being a drama queen for nothing. We landed safe and sound at SFO and now we're walking around Fisherman's Wharf hand-in-hand.

Gavin inhales deeply. "God, I love the smell of this place."

I wrinkle my nose. "It smells fishy."

"Well, yeah, but it's more than that. The salty breeze coming into the pier...fresh clam chowder in sourdough bowls...hell, even the sea lions add to the appeal."

"So you like stinky things?" I joke.

He shrugs. "It's nostalgic, I guess. I've had a lot of good memories here."

"With Hailey?" I ask hesitantly.

"No, strangely, Hails and I never spent any time down here. She thought it was too touristy but I've always loved the vibe."

I look around, taking in the eclectic group of people mixed with the charming architecture and breathtaking landscape. "It does have a good vibe."

"Right?" he smiles. He tugs on my hand and points

to the large Ghirardelli sign in the distance. "C'mon, let's get you some real hot chocolate and the perfection that is an Earthquake Sundae."

"You had me at hot chocolate."

After spending an incredible afternoon in the city, we're now pulling up to Gavin's family home. Nestled in the heart of Sausalito's Historic District, the house is a stately affair; a tri-level with dark shaker siding and sweeping views of the bay and city lights. He parks our rental car on a sunken parking slab beneath the house and turns off the ignition.

"Are you ready to do this?"

I take a deep breath. "I think so."

Gavin pops the trunk and exits the vehicle to grab our luggage. I step out with my carry-on bag over my shoulder and look around.

"So...electronic gates and underground parking, huh? Pretty fancy."

He shrugs like it's no big deal. "It's pretty common for the neighborhood."

"A swanky neighborhood."

My nerves ratchet up quite a few notches when I realize how outclassed I am. Gavin clearly comes from wealth. He grew up in this posh neighborhood filled with multi-million dollar homes. I would've never guessed; he's such a simple, laid-back guy. What if his family isn't the same? What if they take one look at me and decide I'm not good enough for them? I'm suddenly feeling very out of place. Gavin senses my hesitation when he grabs my hand and I dig in my heels.

"What's wrong, Kat?"

"I don't know about this...how do you feel about staying in a hotel?"

He laughs. "Yeah, right. My mom would kill me." His expression sobers when he takes a good look at me. I'm sure my face is broadcasting how uncomfortable I am right now. "Kat, seriously; it will be fine. They're going to love you."

I fling my arms out, gesturing to our surroundings. "Gavin, look at this place!" I spot something to the left of the parking area and gasp. "Oh my God, is that an elevator? *Your house has a freaking elevator?*"

He obviously senses my impending meltdown because he drops the bags and grabs both of my hands.

"Kat, look at me. Breathe."

I take some much needed air into my lungs and look into his eyes pleadingly. "Gavin, this house is so...*extravagant.* I couldn't be more out of place if I tried. Your parents are going to take one look at me and want to throw me out with the trash. Can we *please* stay somewhere else?"

His jaw hardens as he grabs my face with both hands. "Kat, please don't do this. Don't lessen your worth just because they have money. My parents couldn't care less if you were homeless or deep-ass in debt as long as you make me happy. *And you do*. I'm happier than I've ever been and they know that. They can't wait to meet you."

"But…"

"But, *what*?" he challenges.

"But…I can't possibly live up to their expectations."

He sighs. "Kat, think about what you're saying for a minute. You're telling me that you think my parents are going to judge you based on your bank account?"

"No, that's not what I'm saying." I shake my head furiously.

"That's *exactly* what you're saying," he argues. "Do you honestly think I was raised by people who are that shallow?"

"No, of course not."

"Kat, they're good people. Some of the best people I know. They adopted me for Christ's sake—they took me into their home when they had no need to other than the fact that *I had a need* and they wanted to help." He pulls on the ends of his hair. "Look, my dad is a software developer…he got into the business at the right time and did very well financially. But there's much more to them than their money. Quite frankly, Kat, it's judgmental of *you* to assume the worst of them."

His words shock me. Mostly because they're true.

I hang my head in shame. "I'm sorry, Gavin. I don't know why I'm being so anxious."

He pulls me into him. "There's nothing to be sorry about. I get that you're out of your element but you need to trust me. I would've never brought you here if you had any reason to worry. Okay?"

I nod and force a smile. "Okay." Gavin lightly pokes my ribs where I'm ticklish, making me laugh. "Hey!"

"*There's a real smile!*" He taps the end of my nose. "You ready to go up?"

I smirk. "Yeah, let's do this."

He picks up our bags and leads me to the gate, punching in a code to unlock it. He gestures for me to go through first.

"After you, milady."

"Always such a gentleman."

He swings me around and places his hands on my ass. "Not *always.*"

He punctuates his statement by pulling me into his growing erection. My bag falls to the ground as I wrap my arms around his neck and get lost in a deep kiss. As I'm trying to climb him like a tree trunk, a deep voice crackles through the air.

"Dude...I can't say I blame you, but you'd better tone it down before Mom walks in here and sees you trying to hump your girlfriend in the garage."

I pull away, breathless. "What the hell was that?"

Gavin groans and reaches behind me. Pressing a

button on an intercom that I'm just now noticing, he says, "If you don't want to see it, don't look at the monitor, you perv."

"Hey, buddy, I'm enjoying the show. I'm just saying *Mom* wouldn't. I'm sure she'd still like to think her precious Gavie's virtue is intact."

"What is going on?" I whisper. "Who is that?"

Gavin jerks his head to the video camera perched above the elevator and presses the talk button again. "Kiss my ass, Jack."

A smooching sound comes through the speakers. "Bend over, baby."

Gavin throws his hands in the air and laughs. "And that, ladies and gentlemen, is my brother, Jack. Ignore him; he's an idiot."

I wiggle my fingers at the camera and smile. "Hi, Jack." I didn't press the intercom button but I'm hoping it was simple enough for him to read my lips.

"Get up here and say that in person, Gorgeous," he says through the speaker. "And bring the dumbass standing next to you up too."

I laugh and give him a thumbs up in reply. Gavin pushes the call button and the elevator doors slide open a moment later. He takes my hand as we ride up to the level marked, S.

"Street level," Gavin explains.

I hold my breath as the doors open to a covered walkway. We only take two steps onto the brick pavers when the door in front of us opens and a beautiful, petite blonde runs out with her arms open.

"Oh, my baby's finally here," she shrieks as she pulls him into a hug.

Gavin blushes, which is quite possibly the cutest thing ever. "Mom, it hasn't been that long since I've been home. You're acting like it's been years."

She pulls back a little and smooths out the imaginary wrinkles on his shirt. "Oh, hush," she admonishes. "*Any* amount of time is too long. I don't like you being so far away. We miss you."

"I miss you too, Mom."

I'm smiling like a fool as I watch them interact. Every bit of anxiety I had about meeting Gavin's family has been erased within seconds. These people clearly love each other and don't have a pretentious bone in their bodies. His mom steps out of their embrace and turns her twinkling eyes in my direction.

"You must be Kat," she says while covering my hands with her own. "It's so nice to finally meet you, dear."

I smile shyly. "It's nice to meet you too, Mrs. Cooper. Gavin says such wonderful things about all of you."

"Oh, I don't believe that," she says and rolls her eyes in Jack's direction. "But I'm sure he says nice things about *most* of us. And please, call me Carolyn."

I didn't even notice he had joined us. *Wow.* Jack definitely isn't lacking in the looks department. His build is slightly bigger than Gavin's and, like their sister, he has dark hair and smoldering brown eyes. They must take after their dad.

I laugh as Jack whines, "*Mom!* Quit playing favorites!"

She chuckles as she takes both Gavin and me by the elbow and walks us toward the house. She stops when we reach Jack and pats him gently on the cheek. "Oh, Jackie. You know you're my favorite."

Jack beams until she leans over and whispers into my ear, "He's so sensitive. Sometimes I have to stroke the poor boy's ego." Considering Jack is standing right next to us, she obviously intended to be heard.

Gavin claps his brother on the back. "Tough break, dude. Time to play second fiddle for a couple days."

"Asshat," Jack grumbles.

"Dickhead," Gavin retorts.

"Boys!" his mom scolds. "Language!"

I laugh. "Oh, this is going to be *fun*."

Gavin winks at me in response.

Jack glares at him and throws his arm around my shoulder. "Welcome to California, Kat. It's going to be *so nice* getting to know you."

"Uh..." I stammer.

Gavin picks his brother's heavy arm off my shoulders and pulls me into him. "Keep your hands to yourself, Jack Off."

Jack punches Gavin playfully on the arm. "Just giving her options, Bro."

Gavin punches him back. "She doesn't *want* options."

Carolyn takes my arm and pulls me through the door. "Ignore them, Kat. They always act like children when a pretty lady is around." She looks over her shoulder. "Gavin, why don't you show Kat to your room so she can get settled? I have you two in the guest suite."

"Kat, my apartment is only a few minutes away if you want to shack up with a real man," Jack offers. "Just go down the Excelsior, take a right, and I'm one block away."

"What's the Excelsior?" I ask out of curiosity.

Gavin rolls his eyes. "Kat, don't encourage him. It's the large staircase to the left of the house. It leads into the downtown area. We can head down there in the morning and walk around the shops."

Jack smirks. "Bro, it looks like Gorgeous here *does* want options."

Gavin shoves him to the side and catches up with me. "C'mon, Kat, let's go get settled in our room."

Now that I'm no longer distracted by their sibling rivalry, I actually take a look at the inside of the house. "Wow," I say. "This is incredible."

I'm guessing this is the main level because it's an open floorplan showcasing a gourmet eat-in kitchen, a dining room, and a large living area with double doors framing the San Francisco skyline off in the distance. The entire space is decorated in shades of white, gray, and beige with red and dark blue accent pieces. The ceilings have to be at least twenty feet high.

"Is that a library?" I point to the sunken room off to the side that features a large stone fireplace and floor-to-ceiling bookcases.

"It is," Carolyn confirms. "It was always Gavin's favorite room in the house."

"I can see why." I've never seen anything this nice in my entire life. I honestly only thought it existed on those home improvement shows. I can't fathom actually spending your childhood here.

Gavin saves me from embarrassing myself with excessive gawking when he tugs on my hand. "C'mon Kat, the guest suite is downstairs."

I clear my throat. "Okay."

"Gavin," his mother calls. "Your sister and father should be here shortly. Don't take too long; dinner will be ready by seven."

"Okay, Mom," he replies and then he ushers me down a staircase until we reach another living area filled with several puffy recliners. "This is the theater room," he says. "The bedroom is toward the back."

"You have a *theater room*? Holy shit, Gavin! You realize how amazing this house is, right? I can't believe you grew up here."

"Yeah, I was definitely a lucky kid. They always made

sure we knew the meaning of hard work, though. Nothing was ever handed to us."

"They sound amazing."

"They are," he agrees. He leads me toward the back through a double doorway. I step into a large bedroom complete with a sitting area, a king-sized bed, a fireplace, and a private balcony. I'm pretty sure this room is bigger than my entire apartment.

I set my bag by the doorway and sit on the edge of the bed. "I can't get over this place."

He walks toward the bed and leans over me until I'm forced to lie back on the mattress. "I can't get over *you*."

I lift my head up to nip his bottom lip. "You're such a big softy."

"If you want hard, I can give you hard."

I laugh. "Oh, wow. That was cheesy. Soooo cheesy."

"You know you love it."

"I do," I chuckle.

He runs his hands through my hair. "I love *you*, Kat. I'm so happy you're here with me."

I almost return the sentiment but bite my tongue at the last second. I think Gavin can see my internal struggle because he gets a sad look on his face before he masks it. "It's okay. You know you don't have to say it back."

My eyes get watery. "But I should be able to. *I feel it*, Gavin; you know I do. I'm so fucked up because I can't just *say it*."

"You will," he says with confidence. "Just give it time."

"How can you be so sure?"

"I just am." He shrugs.

"You're too good to me."

"Nah, it's the other way around." My body arches off the bed as he starts kissing my neck, making me forget all about my issues. Just as things are really starting to heat up, someone barges into the room.

"Knock knock, kids! I hope you're decent."

Gavin groans in frustration. "Goddammit, Jack! The door was shut for a reason."

I laugh as Gavin rolls over and flops onto the mattress. "Hi, Jack."

He winks. "Hi, Gorgeous. Sorry to interrupt play time, but Mom wanted me to tell you to get your asses upstairs. Dad and Elle are back from the store and dinner's ready."

Gavin and I stand up and straighten our clothing. "We'll be right up."

Jack gives me a good once over. "Let me know if you change your mind, Gorgeous. I'll show you what a real man is like."

"Jack, go!" Gavin shouts.

Jack laughs. "Okay, Bro, I'm going. See you two upstairs."

"So...your brother is...*interesting*." I smirk.

Gavin rolls his eyes. "He's harmless. He's just flirting with you to drive me crazy. It's this thing we do."

"Oh, really? I'd love to hear more about that."

"Maybe later. Right now, we have some home cookin' calling our names. If we don't hurry up, the food will be gone with my dad and Jack in the house."

We all convene in the dining room around a fully set table, covered in delicious smelling dishes. I recognize Gavin's sister from when we met before but I haven't met the man who looks exactly like a silver fox version of Jack. This must be their dad.

"There you are!" the man's husky voice booms across the room. "Son, welcome home."

"Hi, Dad," Gavin replies. "Kat, this is my dad, Neil. Dad, this is my girlfriend, Kat."

It's so strange hearing him to refer to me as his girlfriend in front of other people. I could definitely get used to this.

Neil pulls out a chair and gestures for me to sit. "Welcome to our home, Kat. Please have a seat."

"Thank you."

"Kat, it's nice to see you again," Elle smiles from across the table. "Didn't I tell you I'd see you around?"

"Hi," I reply, slightly embarrassed about the first impression I must have made with her back home. "You certainly did."

"I'm glad to see my little brother didn't screw up and scare you off."

"Oh, Elle, leave your brother alone," Carolyn says. She's making her way around the table with wine. "Kat, would you like red or white?"

"Oh…um…" Shit, how do I answer this? Do they know how old I am? I wouldn't think so if she's offering me alcohol. "Neither, thanks. I'll stick to water."

Gavin must sense my discomfort because he squeezes my thigh under the table.

"Okay, dear. The bottles will be on the table if you change your mind."

"Thanks."

We all pass the dishes around and fill our plates while making conversation. Gavin and his brother obviously like to rib each other, and their sister seems to get in on the action too, although I can't tell which side she's on. Their parents just laugh at their behavior as if it's something they've seen a million times, which they probably have, now that I think about it. The food is wonderful. Gavin's mom certainly puts that beautiful kitchen to good use. Neil has just opened another bottle of wine as the conversation comes to a screeching halt.

"So, Gav, how did you two meet?" This is from Jack who's smirking like he already knows the answer. *Does he?* Fuck, why didn't I think to ask Gavin how much they know about us? Why didn't he think about it?

Gavin glares at his brother, confirming my suspicion that he does know exactly how we met. "We met in a bar, actually. Kat was celebrating her birthday and I offered to buy her a drink. But I've already told you that."

"Oh, that's right," Jack taps his chin thoughtfully. "Kat, which birthday was it again?"

"Uh…"

"Jack, it's rude to ask a lady her age!" Carolyn scolds.

Jack rolls his eyes. "Oh, please, Mom. That only applies to women over forty. And we all know Kat is nowhere near that benchmark. So, Kat, which birthday were you celebrating?"

"Jack, drop it," Gavin growls.

Their dad sets down his fork and, frowning, turns his attention to his sons. "What am I missing?"

"Nothing, Dad," Gavin lies.

Elle swats Jack on the arm. "Quit being an ass, Jack."

"Ow!" Jack whines. "That hurt."

Elle rolls her eyes and glances my way. "Kat, ignore these two. They've always been competitive about everything and they love to rile each other up. I think it's some sort of twin, not really a twin thing."

"A what?" I laugh, thankful to Elle for breaking up the stiffness in the room.

"The whole same age thing," she gestures between her brothers with a fork. "They have this freaky twin-like bond because they grew up in the same grade, with the same friends, but as you know, they're not actually blood-related. Hence the twin, but not really a twin."

Jack tears off a piece of his dinner roll and throws it

at Gavin's head. "Yeah, this guy wanted to be me so badly that he actually wormed his way into our family."

"What?" I feel like there should be tension in the air after that comment but everyone at the table chuckles, confusing the hell out of me.

"Gavin and Jack were friends before we adopted him," Carolyn explains. "They were in the same class since first grade. They were best friends, actually, along with Joey. We called them the Three Amigos. Gavin was always at our house anyway so we decided to keep him when we were blessed with the chance to do so." Carolyn smiles at Gavin lovingly, making me a little misty-eyed.

"Oh, that's really great." My voice catches a little on the last word.

"So, Kat, what do your parents do?" Neil asks.

"Um..." A sob gets stuck in my throat.

Gavin grabs my hand under the table, giving me strength to reign in my emotions. "Kat's mom passed away a few months ago," he answers on my behalf. "She never had a chance to know her father."

Carolyn places a hand over her heart. "Oh, honey, I'm so sorry about your loss."

Neil clears his throat. "I'm sorry, Kat. I wouldn't have brought it up if I knew."

"It's okay," I wave him off. "Really."

The room is completely silent until it's interrupted

by a loud thump. I look up, startled, and find Jack standing on his chair.

"Who's up for a game of strip poker?" Jack's chest is puffed out and he raises his eyebrows comically.

"Jack Anthony Cooper, you get down from that chair right now!" Carolyn rushes to his side and tugs on his arm. "You'd think you were raised in a barn!"

Jack gets down and holds his hands up. "Sorry, Ma."

She rolls her eyes. "You boys! I swear you're responsible for every one of my gray hairs."

"Mom, you don't have any gray hair," Gavin says.

She tucks a blonde strand behind her ear. "Only because I visit Ricardo every six weeks on the dot."

Neil wraps his arms around his wife and pulls her into his chest. "You'd still be the sexiest MILF I know; gray hair or no gray hair."

Carolyn's face turns beet red while her kids all groan in unison.

"And on that disturbing note," Gavin announces, "we're turning in early. Goodnight everyone!"

He grabs a bottle of wine and tugs me behind him.

forty-four

We've spent the morning walking around the downtown waterfront visiting quaint little shops along the way. Gavin suggested we stop for lunch so that's where we're at now—a locally-owned café with the best sandwiches in town according to him. The weather is abnormally warm so we've selected an outdoor table, giving us the opportunity to enjoy the sunshine while we wait for our food.

"So...exactly how much does Jack know about us?"

I meant to ask him this last night but when we got to our room, Gavin pulled me in for a kiss and I was rather *distracted* for a while. Not that I'm complaining.

He takes a sip of his coffee. "I still can't believe that asshole tried calling me out at the dinner table."

"That doesn't exactly answer my question," I say with a grin.

"He knows everything."

I raise my eyebrows. "Everything? As in?"

"Well, not *everything*, everything," he says. "It's not like I call him every night to gossip about what happened that day."

I playfully kick him under the table. "So what exactly *did* you tell him?"

Gavin rubs the back of his neck and his cheeks flush. "He knows how we met, how old you are, and that we're together, despite the fact that you're in one of my classes. He also knows we're keeping things quiet until after your graduation."

"Wow." I take a moment to think before asking my next question. "What happened to not telling anybody?"

He gives me a sheepish look. "I may or may not have been heavily intoxicated when I spilled my guts. It was when I came home for Thanksgiving. I wasn't exactly thinking at the time."

I laugh as I picture Gavin as a blabbering drunk. "You're different here. It's...cute."

"What do you mean?"

"You're so serious back home," I explain. "Here, you're more carefree—you smile and laugh a lot more. You seem...less stressed."

He grabs my hand over the table. "I think you being here with me—out in the open—has a lot to do with it. I feel like myself for the first time in a long time."

"Well, whatever it is, I like it."

"I like it too." He brings my hand to his lips and places a soft kiss on my palm.

"So, your parents don't know any of the sordid details?"

"No, they don't know *all* the details. Notice how I left sordid out of the sentence?"

I roll my eyes. "Yes, *Mr. Cooper*."

"Is it totally wrong that I get turned on whenever you say that?"

I get up and walk to the other side of table and take a seat on his lap. I loop my arms around his neck and lean in to nip his earlobe. "As long as it's okay that I get uncomfortably wet every time I'm sitting in your class watching you command the room. You know all those bathroom passes I've asked for over the months? I was really sitting in a stall, touching myself, wishing it were you."

I feel his growing erection beneath me. He groans as I wiggle against it. "Kat, I think you need to get back to your side of the table before we get arrested for public indecency."

I laugh. "You're such a—"

"Gavin?" a female voice calls behind me.

Gavin's posture instantly goes rigid so I know he recognizes this woman and isn't happy to see her. He lifts me off his lap and I quietly take my seat, looking up at the beautiful blonde standing next to our table.

"What are you doing here?" he asks.

"I could ask you the same thing," she replies indignantly. "I didn't know you were back in town."

"You lost the right to that knowledge a while ago." His tone is angry. *What is going on right now?*

The blonde eyes me curiously as I sit there silently doing the same. I'd place her around Gavin's age, maybe a few years older. She's wearing a navy shift dress with pearls around her neck and red-soled stilettos on her feet.

"Aren't you going to introduce me to your friend, Gavin?" she asks.

Gavin sighs. "This is my *girlfriend*, Kat. Kat, this is my ex-wife, Hailey."

Oh, shit. What is one supposed to do in this situation? Her arm is outstretched so I awkwardly shake her hand. "Nice to meet you," I murmur.

Her eyes shift back to Gavin. "So...how long have you two been seeing each other?"

"Since last fall," he answers. "Why does it matter?"

Hailey looks surprised. "Really? That long, huh?"

She places her French-manicured hand on her stomach which pulls her dress against her body. My eyes widen at the same time Gavin's do when we notice her small, yet obvious baby bump.

"*You're pregnant?*" Gavin says, staring at the spot where her hand is resting.

Hailey rubs a little circle over her bump before dropping her hand to the side. "Yes, I am. In a few more weeks, I'll know the sex of the baby."

"Congratulations," I offer lamely.

Hailey turns her attention back to me and smiles. "Why, thank you, Kat. That's very kind of you to say."

"How far along are you?" I ask.

Jesus Christ, could this situation be any more awkward? The only reason I'm even talking right now is because Gavin has turned into some kind of mute.

"A little over four months," she says. "I can't believe I'm showing so quickly. My OB says everything is perfectly normal, though."

"Well, you look great." I clear my throat. "Gavin, don't you think she looks great?"

He's staring into space. "Huh?"

I kick his shin under the table. "Earth to Gavin!"

He winces and rubs the spot where I may have hit a little too hard. "Sorry, I was lost in thought. What did you say?"

Before I get the chance to repeat my question, Hailey speaks. "Gavin, I didn't mean to interrupt your lunch. I was just walking back to my office anyway. We'll catch up another time. Okay?"

He finally lifts his gaze and makes eye contact with her. "Yeah...*we will.*"

I wait until Hailey is out of earshot. "What the fuck was that, Gavin?"

Instead of answering me, he stands up, pulls money out of his wallet and throws it on the table. "Let's go."

"What?" I ask. "Our food hasn't even arrived yet."

"I lost my appetite. I can get you something back at the house if you'd like."

"What is going on with you? Why are you in such a shitty mood all of a sudden?"

He gives me a look that seems to say, *do you really have to ask?*

"Okay, I understand how seeing your ex-wife could do that, but why should we let it ruin our lunch? We were having a perfectly nice time before she showed up."

He rakes his hand through his hair. "Kat, please. I'd just really like to go back to the house right now. I'm... tired. I think I'll take a nap. *Please* don't fight me on this."

"Fine," I huff as I grab my purse. "Let's go."

So much for carefree, stress-free Gavin.

"Gavin, please tell me what's going through your head," I beg.

"For the millionth time, there's nothing to tell. When I have something to tell you, I'll tell you."

"What do you mean, *when* you have something?"

He shakes his head. "I meant *if* I had something."

I groan in frustration. Gavin's been acting strangely since we ran into his ex-wife almost a month ago. I keep trying to talk to him and he keeps brushing me off with the same pithy response. I know something's wrong; he's pretending everything's fine but my gut says otherwise. Things between us have been strained. *Why won't he talk to me?* Is he upset because Hailey's starting a family with someone else? Does he wish it were with him? Honestly, the only way we've really connected since we've returned from Sausalito is sexually. It's the one thing we seem capable of doing right. As irritated as I am with him, my body still craves his without fail. I know he loves me; I can feel it in his touch. But I can't help but wonder if he has regrets about leaving Hailey. I can't think of any other explanation for this distance between us.

"I'm going back to my apartment after school," I announce. "I can't keep having this conversation with you. You let me know when you're ready to talk about it."

"What? Kat, no. Don't leave."

I start pulling my clothes out of the drawers and shoving them in my bag. At some point over the past few months, I seemed to have inadvertently moved in with Gavin. Maybe some space will be good for us.

I put my hand on my hip. "Are you going to tell me what's going on with you?"

He looks torn. "There's nothing—"

I hold my hand up. "Please don't."

He bites his lip. "Kat, please stay."

My eyes fill with tears. "I'm not breaking up with you, Gavin. I just need space. I never intended to stay as long as I have anyway."

He looks at his watch. "Damn it! I have to get to work. Please just hold off until we can talk about this later tonight."

I move to the closet and remove my dresses from their hangers. "I work for the next three nights but you know where I'll be afterwards if you want to talk."

"Kat…"

"*Go to work, Gavin.* I'll see you in second period."

A tear rolls down my cheek as he closes the front door.

"Miss Kennedy, I need to see you for a moment."

Goddamn him. The bell just rang indicating the end of second period. Gavin's been trying to make eye contact with me throughout the entire class but I've managed to avoid him. I'm trying not to have an emotional breakdown at school again. If I look at him, I'll think about him. And if I think about *him*, I'll think about *us*. I was planning to run out of the room as fast as possible but now I can't pull that off without looking insubordinate.

I clench my jaw and stare at my desk as the other students filter out. Gavin moves toward the door, I'm guessing to close it, but he pauses mid-stride and gets a strange look on his face.

"Hi, Gav," the familiar voice begins. "Do you have time to talk?"

Gavin walks backwards and looks at me nervously out of the corner of his eye. I sink a little lower into my chair and release my ponytail to hide my face with my hair.

"Hailey," he clears his throat. "What are you doing here?"

She shuts the door behind her and steps further into the room. "I'm sorry I haven't returned any of your calls. I've needed some time to think."

Wait...what? He's been calling her? Why? I hold my breath, pleading with God that she doesn't notice me.

"Um...Hails, now's not the best time to talk. Maybe we can meet after my last class? How long are you in town?"

"That depends on you, Gavin." She rubs her notice-ably larger belly. "We have some things to discuss."

Oh my God, does she want to get back together? Would he even consider that if she's pregnant with another man's child? I gasp as a sharp pain moves through my chest.

Her eyes immediately hone in on the sound. "Oh, I'm sorry. I didn't realize any students stayed behind."

At least something's going right; my hair is appar-ently hiding my face well enough.

"Um, that's okay. She was just leaving."

I take my cue from Gavin and grab my stuff, trying to weave my way to the other side of the room before making my exit. Clearly escaping notice was too much to ask because I drop my book less than five feet away from our surprise visitor.

"Shit!" I mutter under my breath. I bend down to pick it up and start walking briskly toward the door.

"*Kat?*" Hailey says. "Oh my God, *it is you!*"

I freeze. I should just walk right out the door and act like I didn't hear her but something inside of me won't let me leave. I straighten my spine and turn around to face her. "Hello, Hailey."

She looks between me and Gavin and gasps as she connects the dots. "Oh, Gavin, she's your *student*? What were you thinking?"

"*Hailey, not now,*" Gavin growls. His eyes meet mine and he adds, "Kat, I'll find you later, okay?"

I'm pissed about his dismissal but at the same time, I'm thankful for an excuse to get out of here. There is no way in hell I'm prepared to have a rational conversation right now. I narrow my eyes at him. "Yep, I'll talk to you later." I spin on my heels and rip open the door. It takes every ounce of willpower I possess to avoid looking back as I walk away.

I barely make it to the nearest restroom before I fall to my knees and cry.

forty-five

It's been three days since Hailey's arrival and I still haven't seen Gavin outside of class. We've been texting but whenever I press for information, he tells me he's still *gathering information*—whatever that means—and he'll fill me in as soon as he knows more. He apologizes for being so vague but he swears it's only because he doesn't want to bring me into it until he knows the whole story. The one thing I do know is that whatever he has to say, it has something to do with his ex-wife and the possibilities terrify me.

I look down as the text alert chimes on my phone.

Gavin: Can you come over tonight after work? We need to talk.

I take a deep breath before typing my reply.

Me: TALK talk? About what's going on?

Gavin: Yes.

I just walked into the dressing room of the club to start my shift. How in the hell am I going to get through the next four hours worrying about what he has to say?

Me: It will be late. I don't get off until 2 in the morning.

Gavin: I'll wait up. I need to see you.

Me: Okay.

Gavin: I love you. No matter what, just remember that. Okay?

Well, that was cryptic. Nausea bubbles in my stomach as I try reading between the lines.

"Lass, you're not even dressed yet?" Shawn shrieks as she walks into the room. "You're on stage in five. Hurry!"

Shit!

Me: Work is calling. I'll see you a little after 2.

I shove my phone in my locker before I can see another text come through. It's better to push all thoughts of Gavin aside right now. I grab my stage costume and quickly change my clothes. *Okay, Kat, you can do this*, I tell myself. I take one last deep breath to gather my bearings, finding that special place inside of me that allows me to anesthetize all of my thoughts and feelings. I'm thankful for that place; it's helped me get through some really bad days.

"Red, you're up," Shawn announces.

I square my shoulders and strut out of the room ready to perform.

I let myself into Gavin's house a little after three in the morning. I really needed a shower after work so I made a pit stop at my apartment. Yes, I could've showered here, but if I'm being honest with myself, I'm stalling. I can't shake the feeling that whatever's about to happen is going to really fuck with me. I should be excited right now; my acceptance letter from Berkeley came in this morning. I'd been waiting for the moment where I can surprise him with it—been daydreaming about all the creative ways I could break the news to him. Instead, I find myself not wanting to tell him at all. Not until I hear what he has to say first.

"Gavin?" I hang my purse and coat on the hook in the foyer and make my way into the great room.

"In the bedroom," he calls.

I walk down the darkened hallway, only slightly lit by the blue lights coming from the TV in the bedroom, and pause in the doorway. My heart wallops at the sight of Gavin sitting up in bed, shirtless, with the covers pooled around his waist. You'd think I'd be immune to seeing his bare skin by now, but I'm just as affected as I was the first day we met.

I gulp. "Hey."

He gives me a sad smile. "Hey."

"So...you wanna go out in the living room to talk?"

I think he's agreeing as he steps out of bed wearing a

pair of low-hanging basketball shorts. Jesus, I want to run my tongue over the V on his lower abdomen. *I love that V.* He joins me by the door and tugs on both hands, pulling me further into the room.

"No."

"No?" I repeat. "Why not?"

His hands move to each side of my face as he crouches down. "God, I've missed you so much."

"Gavin," I chide. "You said you wanted to talk. That you have something to tell me."

"I know." He lightly presses his lips to mine before pulling back. "And *I do*. But first, I need you. We can talk in the morning."

Oh, God, I'm tempted. *So tempted.* "I really don't think that's a good idea."

He smirks before tugging on my bottom lip. "Yes, you do."

Damn it, I do. *I really do.* I hate that he can reduce me to nothing but a pile of hormones with that sexy smirk of his.

"Gavin, we can't keep using sex to communicate with each other," I argue. "We need to start using some actual words."

He pulls me toward the bed and I'm not doing much to protest. "I know. And we will; I promise. *In the morning.*"

"Gavin, I don't think—"

"Kat, do you want me?" he interrupts.

"That's not a fair question," I whine.

"It's a yes or no question. Do. You. Want. Me."

"You know I do," I whimper.

"Then let me have this moment," he begs. "Let *us* have this moment. All your questions will be answered in the morning."

I know I'm being weak but I can't deny him. *I don't want to* deny him. "Okay."

He flashes a blinding smile before branding me with his lips and tongue. I give into the kiss without the slightest bit of resistance as my entire body comes alive with desire. He rips his mouth from mine and gazes at me breathlessly. Neither one of us says a word as he undresses me, peeling away each layer of clothing with this crazy mixture of gentleness and impatience. There's something so tender about the way he looks at me while he's kneeling on the floor, removing my panties.

He lowers me to the bed, fully naked, while he's still wearing his shorts. He spreads my thighs and trails one finger down the center of my body before lowering his head. I practically jump out of my skin the moment his mouth touches my heated flesh. I squirm and moan as his tongue swirls around and around. A shudder runs throughout my entire body so fast it surprises both of us as I'm crying out in ecstasy.

I'm still trembling when he crawls up my body for a kiss. I can taste myself on his lips which drives me into this wild frenzy of lust. I pull on his hair and hook my toes into the elastic band around his waist, pushing the shorts down. I reach down to take his length into my hand and guide him into my body. As he settles in as deep as he can be, he grabs my hand and flattens my palm over his left pec.

"Do you feel how fast my heart is beating?" he asks. "*Only you* do this to me, Kat. You own my heart and every piece of my soul. *Nothing and no one* will ever change that."

His words are everything that a woman wants to hear from the man she loves. From the man she can't imagine living her life without. Yet as I feel the steady thumping of his heart, my world feels like it's shifted on its axis. There's a crushing weight on my chest because I can't shake this horrible sense of foreboding. Gavin must see the anguish in my eyes because his fingers curl around mine and he kisses me like I've never been kissed before. He steals my breath, my thoughts, *my entire being* with this kiss.

Our lips never part as he moves in and out of my body, burying himself deeper and harder with each thrust. He plays my body like a maestro, bringing me to new heights that I couldn't have ever dreamed possible. With one final grunt, he stills inside of me and remains that way for several long moments while we catch our breath.

"I love you, Kat," he whispers against my lips. "I love you so fucking much it hurts."

He kisses me softly one last time before pulling out and collapsing to the side, cradling my head against his chest. I'm not sure which is more overwhelming: the emotion from everything that just happened, or the complete sense of dread for what's to come.

"Gavin—"

"Shh, Kat. Just sleep for now. We'll figure everything out after we've had some rest."

I want to argue but my body and my brain are so exhausted I can't summon the strength. So instead, I snuggle into him and allow his heartbeat to lull me to sleep for what I fear may be the last time.

I hear Gavin moving around in the kitchen when I wake and inhale the aroma of freshly brewed coffee. I crack my lids open and take a good look around the room. Physically, everything looks the same but I don't feel at ease like I normally do. Everything from last night comes back to me at once. I roll out of bed and run to the bathroom, locking the door behind me.

I stare at myself in the mirror and see sheer panic reflected back at me. My eyes are wild and unfocused, my fists are clenched, and my shoulders are tight. I sit on the floor with my head between my knees and focus on breathing. In and out. In...and out. Right when I feel I've calmed my frayed nerves to a manageable level, there's a knock on the door.

"You okay in there?"

I rush to the counter and run the sink. "Yep, I'm just freshening up. I'll be right out."

There's deafening silence on the other end. I imagine Gavin resting his head against the door, maybe with his hand on the doorknob, waiting for permission to turn the handle.

I hear him clear his throat. "When you're done, I have breakfast waiting in the kitchen."

"Okay, I'll be there in a minute."

I smooth out my hair and gargle some mouthwash before stepping back into the bedroom so I can dress before heading down the hall. Gavin is standing behind the counter setting a plate of eggs and bacon on the breakfast bar when I get to the kitchen.

"Have a seat," he offers.

I pull out a stool and begin moving the eggs around my plate. I can feel his eyes on me but I can't seem to lift my head up to know for sure.

"Kat, please look at me."

Well, so much for that idea. Hesitantly, I raise my eyes and freeze when I see the misery he is wearing, clear as day.

"So..." he begins.

"So..."

He sighs. "As you know, Hailey's pregnant...just over five months now. She's having a boy."

"How nice for her," I deadpan.

"Kat, the baby...the baby's mine."

I drop my fork. "*What?*"

His eyes fill with tears. "I'm the father of Hailey's child."

"But...how? When? How is this possible?"

He grips the edge of the counter and hangs his head. "The day after Thanksgiving, I went to a bar by my parents' house. I was miserable after seeing you at the club. I knew we couldn't be together because it goes against every moral code in the teaching handbook, but I couldn't get you out of my head. *I was trying to get you out of my head.*"

"*So you slept with your ex-wife?*"

"I didn't plan to," he insists. "She was at the bar drowning her sorrows when I walked in. Apparently she and Joe broke up—she caught him cheating. Ironic, huh?"

"Get to the part where you impregnated her, Gavin!"

He winces. "We both had a lot to drink. I don't remember much, but there's bits and pieces. Kissing in a cab...going back to her place. After that, it's pretty much a blank until I woke up in her bed the next day. Kat, you have to remember we weren't technically together back then. I would never betray you like that."

He's right. Logically, I know he's right but the confession is still ripping me apart.

"How do you know the baby's really yours?"

"The timing is perfect, Kat. Hailey is a lot of things, but she would never lie about something like this."

"Oh, so she can lie about having an affair but not about this?" I mutter.

He pulls on his hair. "I really don't think she would do that. Not when a child is involved."

"But how can you—"

He holds his hand up. "I'm not that naïve; I've asked for a paternity test. She's agreed to it as soon as the baby is born."

"She can't take one before?"

"She's too far along," he replies. "Even if she wasn't, there'd be a risk for miscarriage so I would never ask her to do that. But again, I don't think she would lie about this. I know her; she wouldn't have agreed to the paternity test so readily if she had any doubt."

"Couldn't a judge force her to take one if you pursued it?"

"They could," he answered. "And being an attorney she knows that, Kat. She's been trying to make partner in her firm for the past two years. She wouldn't risk a scandal like this. Yet another reason why I think she's telling the truth."

"What are you trying to say, Gavin? What does this mean for us?"

He sighs. "Hailey wants me to move in with her. For the baby."

I clench my jaw. "And what did you tell her?"

"I told her I'd think about it."

"So she wants to get back together?"

"I don't know," he says and shrugs. "I know she doesn't want to do this alone and she knows how I feel about fatherhood. How I swore I would always be there for my kid after my birth father gave up his rights to me. I can't have a child and not be actively involved in their life, Kat."

"You don't have to live with his mother to be a part of his life, Gavin."

He grabs my hand. "Kat, can you really see me being a part-time dad? I can't imagine raising my kid without both parents under the same roof."

"So you're getting back together with her?"

"I didn't say that," he says quickly. "That's not what I want. *I want you. I love you.* I don't know what to do. This is all so fucked up."

I move my plate to the side and rest my head on the counter. "Wow...just wow."

"Tell me about it," he mumbles.

We sit there in silence, neither one of us knowing what to say. After who knows how long, I decide that I have to get out of here. I can't just sit here while he decides so I jump down from the stool.

"What are you doing?" he asks.

I join him on the other side of the counter. Despite my best efforts, my tears break loose and I can't seem to stop them.

"I'm leaving, Gavin."

"What do you mean, you're *leaving*?"

I stand on my toes to kiss him on the cheek. "I mean, that you have a big decision to make and I can't just sit here while you're considering moving in with your ex-wife."

"Kat—"

"Don't, Gavin. You need to do what you feel is right; I get that. But I can't be here while you decide. I just *can't*." I begin backing away. "You let me know when you figure it out."

"But—"

"You know where to find me when you're ready. Until then, please respect the fact that I need some space."

forty-six

It's been a week since Gavin told me about the baby. A week that I've been hanging in limbo trying desperately to have some semblance of normalcy but failing miserably. I can't eat. I can't sleep. I've called in sick to work because I can't stop crying. I can't even force myself to show up for second period. The Monday after he told me, I walked through the door of his classroom, took one look at him, and ran out. I can see this is killing him as much as it's killing me. He looked *awful*, something I would've never thought possible before now. His hair was disheveled, he hadn't shaved in days, and he had dark circles under his eyes. Ever since then, I've spent my time in the library putting the finishing touches on my senior project.

Should I tell him about my acceptance to Berkeley? Should I give him another option to consider? I think about what he said to me the last night we spent together. How I own his heart...how nothing will ever change that. Then I think about the very real possibility that he could grow to resent me if *I'm* the reason he's not with his son every day. The reason why he misses his son's first words, first steps, and all those amazing little milestones. I know from my own experience that having a baby completely alters your perspective on life. He says that he wants me now, but will he still feel that way when he realizes how much he's missing?

I had to get out of my apartment so I'm spending the afternoon window shopping downtown. I wander into of one of my favorite boutiques to look through their selection of locally made lotions and soaps. As I'm sampling a vanilla lavender cream, something catches my attention out of the corner of my eye. I walk over to the display without thinking and pick up the tiny blue knit booties and hold them in my hand. I blink wetness away from my eyes as it really hits me that *Gavin's having a baby with another woman.* He's going to have a son in a matter of months. He should be excited about that, not completely unhappy like he is now.

I think about the last time we made love. How it felt so different from any of the other times we've been together. *Why is that,* I wonder. And then it hits me. That was Gavin's way of saying goodbye. Even if he hasn't consciously made a decision yet, he's already made one in his heart. He knows he can't live without his son. And he knows that he'd never forgive himself if he didn't at least give this thing with Hailey a shot. That's when I know what I have to do. *I have to be the one to walk away.* Because I know deep down he would never leave me willingly, but I can't bear the thought of him resenting me because of it.

I walk up to the cashier and place the booties on the counter. "I'll take these, please."

"Oh, what a lovely selection, dear," the gray-haired woman remarks. "One of the ladies from my crochet club made these. Are they a gift?"

"Yes," I nod, choking back a sob. "A *friend* of mine is having a baby in a few months."

"How nice." She punches some keys on her register. "Would you like these gift wrapped?"

"Um, sure."

She smiles. "Great, that will be $17.50 total, please."

I pull some cash out of my wallet and hand it over. She wraps the booties in white tissue paper and places them in a small box. I watch as she ties an intricate gold ribbon into the shape of a bow on top.

She offers the package to me. "Here you go, dear. Have a lovely day."

"Thank you."

I dart to my car and take several fortifying breaths. I glance at the box on the passenger seat before putting my car in gear and reversing out of the parking spot. I fight back tears the entire drive, knowing what I'm about to do is going to cause so much pain. As much as it hurts right now, though, I truly feel it's the right thing to do. I pull into Gavin's driveway and exit the car with the gift in hand before I talk myself out of it. I knock on the door, bracing myself.

"Kat, wh-what are you doing here? I thought you said you needed space."

God, he looks even worse than the last time I saw him. "Can I come in?"

He steps aside and allows me to pass through the doorway. "Of course. Here, let me hang up your coat."

"No, I'm not staying." I thrust the box forward. "Here, this is for you."

He shuts the door behind him and gives me a questioning look. "What is it?"

"Open it and find out."

He releases the bow and breaks the seal. I hold my breath as he lifts the lid and moves the tissue paper to uncover the contents. I know the second he figures out what they are because he gets a pained look on his face and closes the box.

"Kat...what is this? Why did you get this for me?"

"*Because you're going to be a dad, Gavin,*" I sniff. "And you should be happy about that. You should be excited about buying things like clothes, and cribs, and all the things that a baby needs."

"I don't understand where this is coming from."

"This is a big deal. *You're having a baby*. And I'm glad that you're going to have this opportunity."

"I sense a 'but' coming."

"But..." I wipe the moisture away from my cheeks. "But I'm not going to be there to see it."

He drops the box and grabs my shoulders. "Kat, no. You can't do this."

"I've accepted a full scholarship from Florida State."

"You w-what?" he stutters.

"I was going to tell you last week."

"God, that's really far away. I thought you only applied to schools on the West Coast?"

"I applied on a whim," I lie. "I wanted to keep my options open."

He narrows his eyes at me. "What does that mean?"

"Well, I thought it would be a good opportunity for me to get the full-blown college experience. You know, being so far away from home."

"The full-blown college experience," he repeats. "And where do I fit into this equation?"

"I thought you could find a teaching job in Florida," I shrug. "Or we could do the long-distance thing and visit each other on breaks and stuff. We would've figured out a way to make it work."

"We *would have* figured out a way? As in, we *can't* figure out a way now?"

I choke back the sob that's dying to be set free. "Gavin,

I don't see how that's possible now. You have a baby on the way. You have to focus on being a father. I would *never* take that away from you. You're going to be busy with your son. Besides, when I really think about it, there's no way I could keep up with all the demands of my school-work while flying back and forth to see you. I'm going to be busy in my own way. I've worked so hard to get out of this town and I can't turn down an opportunity like this."

"So what are you saying?"

I place my hands on his cheeks. "I'm saying that I'm making the decision for you. You're going to move in with Hailey and I'm going to school in Florida."

"There are two people in this relationship, Kat. You can't just make a decision like that on your own!"

I place my palm over his heart. "You see, that's where you're wrong, Gavin. The old me would have never had the strength to do this. But you changed that. You showed me what loving another person really means. Because of you, I know that I'm worthy of love and respect. Because of you, I know what it's like to love someone so much that you'd sacrifice your own happiness for theirs. Because of you, I am strong enough to survive the...*heartbreak of losing you.*" I choke on the last few words when I see tears rolling down his face. I place a soft kiss on his lips before saying the words that I couldn't speak until now. "I'm so in love with you, Gavin. Thank you for loving me...for *fixing me.* I truly wish you nothing but the best in your future. I'm sorry I won't be a part of it."

"Kat," he croaks. "Don't do this. This isn't what I want."

I give him a sad smile. "You know it's the right thing to do, Gavin. Deep down, you know it. Please don't make this any harder than it already is." I place my cheek against his and whisper, "I love you. *I think I was born to love you.* Goodbye, Gavin."

I spin around and run out of the house without looking back. My fingers are on the door handle to my car when he calls my name. I stop moving but make no effort to turn toward the house.

"I think I was born to love you too," he confesses.

I shove my fist against my mouth to stifle my cries as I get into my car and drive out of his life.

Well, the day is finally here. I'm officially a high school graduate. As Principal Edwards utters his final words, we graduates remove the caps from our heads and throw them up in the air to resounding cheers and applause.

"Kitty, get over here," Dylan shouts as he makes his way through the crowd.

I smile as I fall into his embrace. "We did it, Dyl."

He picks me up and twirls in a circle. "Of course we did! Have you met us?"

"What am I going to do without your cocky ass every day?" I laugh. "I can't believe you're going to school in Georgia. It's so far. Are you sure you can't come to Cali with me and Bree?"

He brushes the back of his knuckles against my cheek in a surprisingly intimate gesture. "You know I can't do that, Kat. I need some space to get my shit together. You're a tough act to follow, babe."

I gasp. "Dylan—"

He places his index finger over my lips. "It's okay, Kitty. I know you don't feel the same way and you shouldn't feel guilty about that. We can't control who we love. If we could, I don't think either one of us would feel so shitty right now."

I wrap my arms around his waist and squeeze. "I'm going to miss you so much."

"I'm going to miss you too." He pets my head while we hold each other, occasionally jostled by the crowd.

A man clears his throat. "Kat, do you have a minute?"

Dylan and I both stiffen at the sound of Gavin's voice. It's been just over a month since we broke up and Dylan has seen firsthand what a mess I've become. Gavin was never his favorite person but he holds even more resentment toward him now.

"I don't think that's such a good idea, *Mr. Cooper*," Dylan snaps.

I pull out of Dylan's arms and look at Gavin. "It's okay, Dyl. Can you give us some privacy?"

"Oh, hell no!" Dylan growls. "Not after what he did to you."

The crowd is disbursing so Dylan's words garner the attention of a few onlookers.

"Dylan, it's fine. Give me a minute."

"What the fuck ever," Dylan grumbles as he takes a few steps to the side. "I'm giving you five feet of space and no more."

I roll my eyes at Dylan but appreciate his protectiveness all the same.

"How are you?" Gavin asks in a hushed tone.

"I'm good," I lie. "Busy packing and stuff. I'm heading to Florida in a few weeks so I can get settled before school starts."

"Oh...that will be nice, I guess. I hear the summers are pretty hot there."

"Yeah...I guess," I hedge. "How's Frodo?"

"He's having a blast with all the moving boxes."

"Oh...so you're leaving soon then?"

He nods. "Next week."

"I'm going to miss the little guy."

"He's going to miss you too. We both will."

I stare at my shoes. "Gavin, please don't do this. It's too hard."

"Kat—"

"All right, that's enough time," Dylan announces as he rejoins us.

Gavin ignores him. "Kat, please just talk to me. It doesn't have to be like this."

My throat thickens. "I don't think—"

"Kat!" Bree shouts. "There you are!" She runs up to me and pulls me into a hug. "We did it!"

Dylan tugs on her elbow. "Bree, come to the vending machine with me to get a drink. I'm thirsty."

Bree is undeterred. "Oh, keep your pants on, Dylan. There will be plenty of tequila to wet your whistle at the bonfire."

Gavin clears his throat again, getting Bree's attention.

"Oh, shit!" she shouts. "I mean...uh, hi, Mr. Cooper. I didn't see you there."

Gavin smirks. "I picked up on that, Miss Hanson. Congratulations."

"Thank you," she beams. "Oh my God! You have to get a picture with Kat while you're here!"

"What?" Gavin and I shout in unison.

She gives us a strange look. "Well, Kat's been going on all year about how you're her favorite teacher. I think she should at least have a picture to remember you. Don't you?"

Gavin gives me a sad smile.

"Bree, don't be dumb," Dylan says. "I'm sure Mr. Cooper has better things to do."

"Aw, c'mon," Bree whines. "I'll be quick; I promise."

"Kat, are you okay with that?" Gavin asks.

"Uh...sure." What the hell am I supposed to say? There's still enough people standing around us that I don't want to cause a scene.

"Great! Mr. Cooper, just stand next to Kat and I'll take a picture with my phone."

Gavin sidles up to me leaving a respectable distance between us.

Bree's holding her phone camera toward us. "I need you guys to move in just a little bit."

Gavin awkwardly puts his arm around my back and pulls me into his side.

"That's perfect!" Bree squeals. "Now *smile!*"

We paste on fake smiles as she takes several pictures, insisting that she needs a variety of angles. Dylan stands next to her, glaring at Gavin the entire time. When Bree is finally satisfied she has *the* shot, she tucks her phone away.

"Thanks for being such a good sport, Mr. Cooper."

Gavin says nothing as I pull away and look up at him. We're facing each other now, having some sort of sad, silent exchange.

He tugs on his hair. "Well, I guess I should get going."

"Yeah...I guess so."

He starts to turn away but then comes charging toward me at the last second and pulls me into his chest.

I'm so stunned that I just stand there with my face nestled against his hard body, my hands hanging limply at my sides.

"I'm so sorry," he whispers. "I'm so damn sorry, Kat."

I pull away from him and turn my face away to wipe my tears. "Please go," I say meekly.

Gavin clears his throat and briskly walks away without another word. I'm left there with a very pissed off Dylan and a confused Bree staring back at me.

"Um, Kitty. What the hell was that?" Bree asks.

"Uh…he, um…do you remember that guy I told you about? The one I had been dating?"

"Yes," she answers. "What about him? I thought you guys broke up."

"Well…" I fling my arm toward Gavin's direction. "That was him."

"What?" she shrieks.

"Quiet the fuck down, Bree," Dylan admonishes.

Bree looks around the crowd wildly; I'm guessing in search of Gavin. "Mr. Cooper was *the* guy? The older one? Are you fucking with me right now?"

"I wish I was."

She gasps. "Holy fuck! Oh my God, I can't believe this!" She looks at Dylan and narrows her eyes at him. "Holy shit! *You knew!* You're such an asshole! Why did you know when I didn't?"

"I didn't tell him," I insist. "He caught us and I swore him to secrecy."

"How long?" Bree presses. "How long has this been going on?"

"Since last August." I hang my head. "We met before school began."

"Oh, Kitty, you've been with him for *almost a year* and you didn't tell me? Don't you trust me?"

"I do, Bree. I swear it had nothing to do with you. There was just too much at stake for both of us. Please understand."

She gives me a sympathetic look. "Oh honey, you're in love with him, aren't you? It's written all over your face."

"Yeah," I sniff.

She pulls me into a hug. "What happened? Why did you guys break up?"

"I really don't want to talk about it right now. I swear I'll give you all the details soon, just not now. Okay?"

Dylan surrounds us with his arms and nuzzles into my head. "Why don't we blow off the bonfire and have a mini graduation party just between the three of us?"

I put my arm around his waist. "That sounds perfect."

forty-seven

"That's the last one."

I've just finished loading the final moving box into my car. I'm not taking much; mainly clothes and stuff. I bought an older, yet reliable, 4Runner with my savings so, thankfully, I have room for cargo. Plus, I won't have to worry about my vehicle breaking down on the way. That's always a plus.

"I can't believe you're leaving me," Bree whines.

"It's only a month," I say. "I want to get into town before everyone else so I have a better chance of finding a job. I've been looking online; several coffee shops around campus are hiring right now."

"Why do you need a job right now? They gave you a full ride." Bree is perched on the hood of my car so I jump up to join her.

"Not completely," I correct her. "My scholarship only

covers tuition, the room, and books. Well, once classes start anyway. I'm paying out of pocket for early admission to the dorms. Then I'll need to cover my own personal expenses on top of that."

"But didn't you save a bunch of money from the club? Can't you use that to pay for your car insurance and stuff?"

"I could...for a while at least, but I need to stay busy, Bree. Being idle isn't a good thing for me right now."

"But SFS is right across the bridge! You'll have *me* to keep you occupied!"

I laugh at the pouty look on her face. "Honey, we're not going to be able to see each other every day with our class schedules, especially when traffic's bad. Plus, I'm sure you'll meet new people you'll want to hang out with."

She frowns. "None that will be as good as you."

"Ditto. You'll always be my favorite." I pull her into a side hug.

Our heads are pressed together while we watch the sun setting. The elevation is a little higher the further you go back, so my complex has a distant peekaboo view of the ocean. Orange rays peek through a break in the clouds and warm my face. I'd like to think it's some sort of sign that I won't always be so sad.

"Pretty sunset tonight," I remark. "I'm gonna miss seeing it disappear into the sea."

"The sun sets over the bay too, Kitty," Bree reminds

me. "You're the one who told me how pretty it was when you went down there with...uh, never mind."

I give her a sad smile. "It's okay, Bree. You can say his name. It's not like I'm going to forget about him any time soon." *I don't think I'll ever forget about him.* "It's different though when you don't have a city surrounding you. It seems so much bigger here."

"Yeah, I can see that," she agrees. "Are you having regrets about leaving?"

I shake my head. "God, no. I *need* to get out of here. I've lived in the same town my whole life, Breanna. It's time to start the next chapter. *Especially* after recent events. I'm the new and improved Kat Kennedy now. I should have a new city to go along with that."

She bumps her shoulder into mine. "I liked the old Kat too, just for the record."

"I know you did, babe. But I can't be her anymore. Not after everything Gavin showed me was possible." My eyes blur as I stare off into the distance. "*There's no going back after that.*"

"Kitty, are you sure about this?"

I furrow my brows. "About going to school?"

She chews on her lip. "No...about not telling Mr. Cooper, er, Gavin about *where* you're going to school. Do you really want him to think you're three thousand miles away when you're really living on the same bay? What are you going to do if you run into him?"

I'll admit; it's not the first time I've considered the possibility.

"The odds of that happening are highly unlikely, Bree. There are too many people in and around the city. *If* it does happen, I'll deal with it then."

She sighs. "I don't know, Kat. I'm worried you're going to regret this."

"It's the *right* decision, Bree." It's my turn to sigh. "As much as it hurts now, I'm not going to regret making it."

"I just hate seeing you like this," she says sadly.

I shrug. "It won't always be this way."

"Soooo....whatcha' doing with your furniture?"

I'm thankful for her not-so-subtle change in subject. "I'm donating it. Someone from the thrift store is coming to pick it up in the morning."

"So you're all ready to go then?"

"Yep," I confirm. "I'm heading out first thing in the morning. The landlord will let the Salvation Army guys in."

She throws her arms around me. "You're such a good person, Kat. Not many people would be so noble in this situation."

I squeeze her tighter. "Wow, I don't know if anyone's ever described me using that word."

She pulls back and gives me a wry look. "Well, that's because most people are judgmental assholes. But the people who know you, know better."

"It's going to be a long month without you." I blink

back tears. "Hurry up and get your sweet ass down there."

She laughs. "We're going to have the best college experience ever, Kat. I promise."

I sure hope so.

forty-eight

FOUR YEARS LATER

I can't believe the wedding is in a few days!" Bree exclaims. "It's crazy how fast time flies."

It sure is. In some ways, it seems like these past four years have passed at the speed of light. But in others, mostly when I have time to myself to think, the day seems to drag on and on. Thankfully, I never have too much down time. My classes keep me insanely busy, especially since I chose to major in education. It still boggles my mind that I'm going to be a teacher. After two more years in grad school, I'll officially be certified for secondary ed. I chose an English/Lit specialty because my love for the written word is stronger than ever. I hope I can inspire others to appreciate the value of getting lost in a story—just like the man who inspired me to teach.

I file the catering contract in the wedding organizer.

"Are you still riding with me to pick up the dresses on Friday?"

"Of course. Am I still the DD for your big birthday blowout tonight?"

I groan. "Bree, please tell me you're not making a big deal of this. I told you I just wanted a quiet dinner with my bestie."

"Ha! Like that's going to happen!" she laughs. "Dylan and Rae flew in early so we could celebrate your birthday before the wedding. We *have to* go somewhere fun."

Dammit! I thought I actually had a shot at bypassing a party with all of the last minute things that needed to be done for the wedding. My partying days are long over—the desire to numb myself with boys and booze disappeared at the ripe old age of eighteen. I can't say I haven't had drinks during my college years, or men in my life for that matter, but it's not the same as it used to be. I don't drink to forget and I haven't slept with anyone I wasn't seriously dating. All two of them.

I flop my head onto the table dramatically. "What are my chances of getting out of this?"

"Zero to none," she replies. "C'mon, Kat. It won't be that bad. Evan reserved a VIP room at *Obsidian*. It's just a small group of friends and their lov-ahs—nothing more."

I lift my head up. "Promise?"

She grins. "Promise."

"Fine," I grumble.

"Oh, cheer up, Buttercup!" she shucks me on the chin, making me laugh.

"You're lucky I love you, weirdo. I wouldn't put up with this crap from anyone else."

"You wouldn't know wh—*holy shit!*" Her eyes are practically popping out of their sockets looking at something over my shoulder.

I try turning around. "What are you—"

She digs her fingernails into my arm. "No, don't turn around!"

I pull my arm away from her and rub the sore spot. "What the hell is wrong with you, Breanna? Are you becoming a Bridezilla all of a sudden?"

"*This has nothing to do with my wedding!*" she whisper shouts. "Kat, you have to promise not to freak out."

"Well, when you put it that way...of course I won't," I mock.

She squeezes my fingers. "No, Kitty; I'm dead serious. You have to be strong."

I cross my arms over my chest. "Will you please tell me what the hell you're talking about?"

She continues staring behind me. "What if I told you that someone from the past is about to invade your present?"

I roll my eyes. "Will you please stop being so cryptic? Just spit it out already!"

"*It's Gavin,*" she sighs, "he's standing in line for coffee right now."

I freeze. "*What?!*"

"*Gavin Cooper* just walked in the door and he's the third person in line at the register!" she repeats. "What are you going to do? What if he sees us? Are you going to talk to him?"

This is the moment that I've feared since moving to the bay. I haven't heard from him once since graduation day. I'm not going to lie; a small part of me had wished he would reach out, despite the fact that I knew it'd be wrong. When a year had passed without contact, and then another, I pushed that hope aside, knowing it was pointless. Gavin has a family to take care of. Hell, he probably already has another kid by now. There's no room in his life for me.

"Is he looking over here?" I ask.

Bree shakes her head. "No, he's staring at the menu on the wall."

I discreetly turn my body so I can follow her gaze. A loud gasp escapes my mouth the second I see him. Fuck, he still has the power to take my breath away. He's dressed casually in a dark t-shirt and jeans, very similar to what he wore on the day we met. His sandy blonde hair is slightly longer than it used to be and there's a healthy amount of scruff on his jaw. He looks older—the little crinkles by his eyes are deeper—but that only makes him more handsome. He's slightly more built too;

not by much, but enough to see that his clothes are a bit more fitted. I can't force myself to look away as he waits for his turn at the counter. I think about Bree's question. What am I going to do if he sees me? How am I going to act unaffected when I'm so obviously the exact opposite of that?

"Shit," I mutter. "What do I do, Bree?"

"What do you *want to do*?"

"I should go up and talk to him, don't ya think? I mean, it'd be rude to not at least say hi after all these years, right?"

"Are you sure?"

I gulp. "Yeah, I think I have to."

"Do you want me to stay?"

I turn back toward her. "No, honey, you can't be late for your meeting with the minister. I'll be fine; I swear."

"Kat, I can call Evan and explain. It's okay if I'm late."

"No," I shake my head. "I'm twenty-three-years old; I can put my big girl panties on and do this by myself. I'm just going to go up there, be cordial, and be on my merry way. Simple."

She looks skeptical. "Kitty—"

"Bree, really; I'm fine. Call me after you're done with your appointment and I'll tell you everything that happened."

"Are you sure?"

I nod my head resolutely. "Positive."

"Okay..." Bree rises from her chair and pats me on the shoulder before walking away. Gavin is now off to the side waiting for his drink. He does a double-take when she passes right by him and walks out the door. He takes his coffee cup from the barista and turns in my direction. I hold my breath as his long strides bring him closer and closer to my table. I realize he must be heading to the little stand off to my right that holds creamers and sweeteners. He's only about three feet away when recognition washes over his face.

His step falters and his jaw drops. "*Kat?*"

I smile as I stand up. I don't miss the quick scan he gives my body when I do. I give myself a mental high-five for wearing cut offs with a fitted tee today.

"Hi, Gavin. How've you been?"

He gulps. "Wow, you look...uh...you look *incredible*. What are you doing in San Francisco?"

"Do you remember my friend, Breanna?"

"I do. She was just here, wasn't she? I thought she looked familiar."

I nod. "Yeah, she's getting married this weekend at Golden Gate Park. She and her fiancé live here in the city." I don't think right now is the best time to tell him where *I* live.

"That's nice for her. Tell her I said congratulations. Are you flying out after the wedding?"

"Um..."

He gestures to the table. "Do you have a few minutes to talk?"

"Uh, sure." I sink back into my chair as he takes his place across the table.

"I'd offer to buy you a drink, but it looks like you're all set."

I grab my latte and take a sip. "I am, but thank you anyway."

A myriad of emotions runs over his face as the shock of seeing me begins to wear off. "Happy Birthday," he says softly and smiles.

I raise my eyebrows. "I can't believe you remembered."

"How could I forget the day we met? It changed my life."

I turn my face to hide my blush. Damn this man and the effect he has on me.

"The Sunshine State really agrees with you, Kat. You've always been beautiful but...wow. You're *stunning*. Your hair is shorter. I like it."

"Thanks. You look great too."

He smiles. "So, how's school? Wait...you just graduated, didn't you?"

"Yeah, but I'm going back for my master's so I still have another two years."

"That's great." I notice that he's not wearing a wedding band when he takes a drink. "What are you majoring in?"

"Education."

He gulps audibly. "*Really?* You're going to teach?"

"I am," I smile. "Middle School English/Lit hopefully."

His gorgeous green eyes twinkle. "You're going to be a fantastic teacher."

"You think so?"

"I do," he nods. "Although, you might want to consider an all-girls school. If you were my teacher at that age, I would've never had a chance of concentrating in your class. Probably would've failed."

I laugh. "I think I'll manage. I can relate to being distracted by your teacher."

He gives me a thoughtful look. "What are we doing, Kat? This is bullshit, right?"

"*What's* bullshit?"

He gestures to the space between us. "This entire conversation. We're acting like we hardly know each other."

"I *don't* know you anymore, Gavin," I argue. "And you don't know me. A lot's changed."

"Like what?"

I narrow my eyes at him. All right, if he's going to force the subject...here I go. "How's fatherhood? And Hailey?"

He bites his lower lip and leans back in the chair. "I wouldn't know."

Wait...what? "What does that mean?"

"It means that I haven't heard from Hailey in years." He clenches his jaw. "The baby wasn't mine."

I stare at him open-mouthed. "She lied? How did you find out? Did you have a paternity test?"

He pulls on the ends of his hair. "I didn't have to. When Christian was born—that's what she named him —it was obvious. He has his dad's skin and hair."

"I'm sorry, but I feel like I'm missing the point here."

"Kat, I didn't need a paternity test. Joe is African-American. And so is Christian...at least half anyway. I'm guessing she was hoping his skin would be much lighter and it wouldn't be so obvious. Hailey and I were never together—that night or any time after. She broke down and admitted everything after Christian was born. She was mad at Joe...hurt, I guess, so she wanted to get back at him. She says things...*happened* between us but she put a stop to it when I called out another woman's name. *Your name*, actually. Anyway...when Joe found out she was pregnant, he assumed the baby was his. Until she told him it was mine. Things were really tense for a while."

I don't know how to respond. How could Hailey do that to him? To Joe even? *To me*? My God, the entire reason I left him was based on a lie! I'm shocked. Angry. Incredulous. *Disgusted*. How different would my life be right now if we hadn't broken up? I want to cry when I think about all of the wasted possibilities.

"Kat, please say something."

"Why…why didn't you call me as soon as you found out? It couldn't have been more than a few months at that point."

He releases a sigh. "I wanted to. God, I wanted to more than anything. But I kept thinking about what you said to me one time. That you needed to experience life… to know that you could make it on your own before you'd be ready to settle down. I knew how important that was to you and I didn't want to rob you of the opportunity. Things were already so fucked up; I didn't want to make them worse. I didn't want to cause you any more pain."

I feel like there's a ton of bricks in my stomach. I left him because I thought I was doing the right thing. He never contacted me because he thought *he* was doing the right thing. How can two selfless acts cause so much hurt?

"I don't know what to say, Gavin."

"Can I ask you something?"

I brace myself for his question. "What would you like to know?"

"Are you seeing anyone?"

I meet his eyes and see so much loneliness reflected back at me. It's the same look I see in the mirror every day. "No, I'm not."

"Can I take you out for a drink tonight? I have this work thing later but it shouldn't take too long."

Is he actually asking me on a date? After everything

that's happened? I can't help it; I shake my head and laugh.

He grins. "What's so funny?"

I give him an astonished look. "Sparkles, are you seriously asking me out on a *date*? Don't you think we're a little past that point?"

"God, I never realized how much I missed that stupid name."

It takes me a moment to catch on. I replay my statement in my head and realize that I called him Sparkles. It was my favorite term of endearment for him; mostly because it drove him nuts, but it really is a perfect name for someone with his eyes.

"It just slipped out," I blush.

"I wasn't complaining, Kat. So...drinks?"

"I can't...I have this thing. A birthday thing."

"Oh," he breathes. "Okay, sure. Of course you already have plans. Maybe next time you're in town then."

I lightly tap his shin under the table. "Hey, Gavin?"

He looks up in surprise when my foot touches his leg. "Yeah?"

"Would you like to come to my party? It's at 9:00 at a club called *Obsidian*. Do you know where that's at?"

"I do," he nods. "I'd love to come...as long as you're not inviting me simply to be polite."

"I certainly wouldn't kick you out if you decided to show," I say with a smirk.

He grins. "That's good enough for me."

"Okay. I'll leave your name at the door. We have a VIP room."

I try acting cool but I feel like I'm about to explode. I haven't felt this kind of attraction to another man since...well, *since him*. Christ, I have to get out of here before I do something stupid like mount him in public.

I stand up. "Well, I should get going. I have a few things to do before tonight."

He stands as well. "So, I'll see you later?"

"Right," I say, nodding nervously.

"I'm *really* looking forward to it, Kat."

I do my best to leave the coffee house on steady legs but I miss a step when I look back and see him watching me like he wants to eat me alive. All the way to my car, I have to remind myself to put one foot in front of the other and breathe.

What did I just get myself into?

forty-nine

I answer my phone the second it rings. "Hey, how'd the meeting with the minister go?"

"Who gives a fuck?" Bree shrieks. "Bitch, I want details and I want them *now*!"

"Calm down, Bridezilla."

"Kat," she growls. "Tell me what happened with Gavin! I've been dying over here! I'm pretty sure I didn't hear a single word the preacher had to say. For all I know, he plans on performing our ceremony in Swahili."

I chuckle because I'm fairly certain that wasn't an exaggeration. "I don't even know where to start, Bree. I wasn't with him for very long, but so much happened."

"Try beginning with the part where you said hello."

I proceed to tell her about my conversation with Gavin. How I'm freaking out because every feeling I've ever had for him came rushing back to the surface. How the sparks flying between us could've burned the coffee house to the ground. How I realize that I never really got over him, which in retrospect, explains why my other attempts at a relationship never took.

"So what happens now?" she asks.

"I don't know," I sigh. "I know I need to be cautious–I can't just jump back into a relationship with him. Too much has happened, ya know? I keep telling myself that now is not the time to be impulsive–I need to go really slow and make sure I'm not making a mistake. Besides, I don't even know if he wants to try again."

"Well, that's stupid," she scoffs. "Of course he does. He asked you out, didn't he?"

"For all I know, he just wants to catch up," I argue. "Maybe he wants to be friends."

"Oh, Kitty, I think you're both smart enough to know that you could never be just friends. You're each other's lobsters."

I smile at her *Friends* reference. She used to program old episodes on her DVR and we'd binge watch them together on rainy days.

"I don't think I'd survive another fallout with him, Bree. I barely made it through the first time."

She sighs. "I get it, Kat; I really do. But you'll never know if you're too afraid to try."

"I know," I grumble. "So what would you do in my situation?"

"You can start by asking him to be your date for the wedding," she suggests.

"I can't do that!"

"Why not?" she challenges. "It's a perfect opportunity. Your maid-of-honor duties won't take up too much time. You'll have almost the entire reception to talk to him. Dance with him. Get freaky in the coat closet...you know, whatevs."

"I am *not* getting freaky with him in the coat closet!" I shriek.

"You never know," she chuckles. "Just ask him, Kat. What's the worst that can happen?"

"He could say no."

"He *won't* say no. Trust me."

"I don't know Bree..."

She sighs. "Okay, look. How about this? You said he's coming to the party tonight, right?"

"Yeah. And?"

"So, why don't you just play it by ear? Talk to him and catch up...whatever. You can decide if you want to ask him to the wedding then."

"I guess that sounds okay..."

"Great!" she exclaims. "It's decided then. If by chance, Gavin decides to be a dick, I'm sure Evan and Dylan won't mind kicking his ass."

"Har, har," I say.

"All right, it's settled. Go pick out a sexy dress and I'll be there to pick you up at 8:30."

"Okay, I'll see you then."

"Kitty, it will be okay; I promise."

"I hope you're right."

"Here you go," Dylan says as he slides the shot in front of me. "Drink up, Princess."

I tilt the glass and pour the whiskey down my throat. "Damn it! That burns! What the hell did you give me, Dylan?"

Evan, Bree's fiancé, pats me on the back. "That's how you know it's good shit."

I glare at him. "No, *good alcohol* is smooth. That crap was rocket fuel."

Dylan throws his heavy arm around my shoulder. "Oh, Kitty. I couldn't resist. It was for old time's sake."

"Baby, that was plain ol' mean," Rae chides with her sugary drawl.

Breanna isn't the only one that found love. Dylan and Raelynn met at the University of Georgia and have been together for over two years now. He really thinks she's *the one*. He plans to propose on her birthday in a few months. I'll admit, when he first told me he met someone special, I was skeptical. I thought there was a possibility he was using her to get over his feelings for me. Until I met her and discovered that she's a fiery redhead with no qualms about putting Dylan in his place. That poor boy never saw what hit him when he fell for her. I really like her though—we've seen each other on several visits now. She's your quintessential Southern Belle—a perfect blend of beauty, impeccable manners, and sass.

I gulp some ice water. I rarely drink anymore so I make a point to down two waters for every glass of liquor I have. We've been here for almost an hour now and there's been no sign of Gavin. I'm trying not to get worked up about it, but it's a lost cause. Breanna gives me a sympathetic smile every time she sees me checking the time on my phone.

"Hey, Kat, do you want to dance?"

This comes from Alex, a guy that I met in my Educational Psychology class. He's made his interest in me clear but he usually maintains a respectable distance. He knows that I'm not big on the whole dating thing so we usually hang out as a group. He's really cute and sweet so Bree invited him before my run-in with Gavin. I think she's trying to push me back on the horse, so to speak. When Alex showed up, I was concerned about him having an awkward encounter with Gavin. I guess I don't need to worry about that now since Gavin's a no-show.

"Um…" I chew on my lip debating my answer. Alex has had several drinks at this point and he's getting pretty handsy. Exhibit A: said hand is on my thigh right now. I'm not sure if I want to put myself in a position where that could get any worse.

"Hi, Kat."

I shiver when I hear his deep voice. I look up to find Gavin leaning against the railing, assessing the situation in front of him. I immediately stand up, leaving Alex and his wandering hands on the couch with Evan.

"Gavin...I didn't think you were coming."

"I'm sorry I'm late—I had a dinner meeting that ran over. I got here as soon as I could."

"A meeting for what?"

He smiles. "I just accepted a position at the University of San Francisco. I was having dinner with the dean of the English department."

"*You're a professor?*"

"I am now...completed my PhD last spring." He nods toward the group of people currently staring at us with curiosity. "Are you going to introduce me to your friends?"

I loop my arm through his as if it's the most natural thing in the world. "You already know Bree and Dylan. And that's Breanna's fiancé, Evan, Dylan's girlfriend, Rae, and Alex. Alex and I know each other from school." I point to each one as I make introductions. "Guys, this is, Gavin. An old...*friend* of mine."

"Nice to meet you," Gavin offers the group.

Dylan is glaring daggers at Gavin right now. He may have muttered something to the effect of *what the fuck.*

Bree senses the tension and jumps up from her position on Evan's lap. "Gavin! I'm so happy you could make it. Would you like a drink? We just need to order on this tablet and they'll bring it up." She hands the device over to him.

"Sure...thanks." Gavin moves his finger over the screen for a few moments and places it on the pub table closest to us before turning toward me. "Would you like to dance, Birthday Girl?"

I don't even need to think about it. "I'd love to."

He leads me to the metal staircase that connects the main floor of the club with the upper VIP areas. I look over my shoulder as we're walking down and see Bree giving me a big smile with a thumbs-up.

We make our way to the dance floor right as the song switches to a slow, sensual beat. *Obsidian* lives up to its name with black walls, black furniture, and glossy black flooring. The only break in the theme is the brushed silver tabletops and a wall of blue lights behind the bar.

Gavin gives me a sexy grin as he pulls me into his arms. One hand spans almost the entire width of my bare back and the other rests on my hip. I knew it was going to test my resolve, but I wore this dress specifically with the hope that I would feel his fingertips on my skin. It's pretty conservative from the front with its high neckline but the back dips down to my waist, barely covering the top of my ass. I wrap my arms around his neck and begin swaying with him to the beat.

"I love this dress." His mouth is right against my ear so I can hear him over the music. "You look fucking edible."

I suppress another shiver and lift my chin so he can read my lips. "Thank you."

I'm not sure how long we stand there, completely motionless amongst a sea of writhing bodies. Gavin's grip becomes tighter as his eyes flash with awareness. I'm blown away that he can still read my body like no other. I'm absolutely certain that my features do not betray my thoughts to the average onlooker—it's a skill that I've honed to perfection over the years. But *this man* knows that I'm fighting a whirlwind of emotions from being in his arms again. He studies me carefully as an inner battle wages inside of me, waiting to see which one will become the victor.

He pulls me forward until my chest is flush against his. We simultaneously suck in air, proving that it's futile to deny this crazy connection we have. I don't know if it's his heartbeat or mine, but there's an erratic thumping between us, more powerful than the bass being emitted from the large speakers. Gavin's pupils dilate as he lowers his head toward mine. I'm mindlessly pulled into his orbit until our lips are practically touching. We're breathing the same air but neither one of us attempts to close the gap. My eyes glaze over as I picture us in a tangle of lips and limbs. It may be my imagination, but I think I moan.

I feel Gavin's finger under my chin. "Kat."

Isn't it remarkable how one word can speak volumes? My name—that single syllable, is filled with so much want, and regret, and hope. I know this because it's what I feel whenever I speak his name. If I'm being honest, I only need to *think* about him and everything I've been repressing for years threatens to drown me with emotion.

"*Hey, Teach*, mind if I cut in?" I'm jolted out of my trance as Dylan speaks.

Gavin stiffens but then steps back and composes himself. "Of course not." Before releasing me entirely, he leans into my ear and adds, "I'm not going anywhere. Come find me upstairs when you're done."

I nod in reply.

Dylan waits for Gavin to leave before he pulls me into him and snarls, "What the hell are you doing, Kitty? Why is he here?"

I clench my jaw. "I'm not discussing this with you, Dylan. He's here because I invited him. That's all you need to know."

He grabs my arm and leads me down the hallway to the restrooms. "Don't bullshit me, Kat. Why is he here after everything he did to you? Why in the hell would you want him back in your life?"

I cross my arms over my chest. "Dylan, don't be so quick to pass judgment. There's a lot you don't know."

"Well, enlighten me then."

"Don't you need to get back to your girlfriend? Where does she think you're at right now?"

"*She knows where I am*! She knows that you're acting like an idiot and I'm trying to prevent you from getting hurt!"

My expression softens but I keep my mouth shut. Mostly because I'm pissed that he called me an idiot.

He sighs. "Kat, this is not me being a jealous dick. I'm in love with Rae; you know that. She's the best thing that ever happened to me. But you're my closest friend so *I hurt, when you hurt*. I saw how you were after he left. I can't watch you go through that again."

I thread his fingers with mine. "Dylan, I know what I'm doing. I'm not jumping into anything with blinders on. The Gavin situation isn't what we thought. He never got back together with his ex and he doesn't have a kid." I hold my hand up when he tries to interject. "I'll explain the rest later but just give me some credit. Okay? Do you think you can do that?"

"Hey, guys, everything okay here?" I didn't even see Breanna until she spoke.

I give Dylan a pointed look. "Well?"

"Fine," he grumbles. "I'll give you the benefit of the doubt. But I swear to God, if he hurts you, I will be on the first plane from Atlanta to beat his ass into a bloody pulp.”

I smile. Dylan may be an overprotective ass sometimes, but his intentions are good. Besides, his threats are pretty empty. I don't think it went unnoticed that Gavin is even bigger now.

“We're good, Bree.” I step between the two of them and loop my arms into the crook of their elbows. “Shall we go back upstairs?”

“That's probably a good idea,” Bree says with a guilty look on her face. “Before things get any worse.”

I scowl. “Breanna, what did you do?”

She waves her hand. “Oh, *I didn't do anything*. But Gavin *may* have chatted Alex up and Alex *may* have mentioned where you two go to school.”

“Fuck,” I mutter.

“Aw, this is gonna be good!” Dylan smiles.

I glare at him. “Bite me.”

He leans down to peck me on the cheek. “Nah, Kitty. Been there, done that. You're old news.”

My mouth gapes. “I can't believe you just said that!”

He and Bree share a laugh. “Oh, c'mon, Kat. I'm just playin' and you know it.”

“Asshole.”

He pulls me into a side hug. “I love you too, babe.”

I cringe when I see Gavin waiting at the top of the stairs as we make our way to the VIP lounge.

He circles my wrist. “Can we go somewhere to talk?”

I give Bree an apologetic look. "Do you mind? I know it's my party, but I really think we should go somewhere a little quieter."

Bree makes a shooing gesture. "Honey, you're the guest of honor. You can do whatever you want. Just text me if you need anything, okay? We'll probably hang here for a while since we have the room."

I grab Gavin by the hand. "There's a diner a few doors down."

He nods and follows me down the stairs and through the club. When we step outside he says, "My place isn't far from here if you'd rather go somewhere more private."

I laugh. "Gavin, no offense, but I am *not* going to your place right now. Being alone with you is the last thing I should be doing."

He looks confused. "Why not? Do you not trust me?"

"I don't trust myself," I answer honestly.

That earns a smile. "Okay...the diner it is then. Lead the way."

We head down to the corner and walk into an all-night retro diner. The sign up front says to seat yourself so we grab a booth over by the window.

Gavin begins flipping through the dessert menu. "Shall we see if they have any birthday cake?"

"And we've officially come full circle," I say with a laugh.

He grins. "So we have. Why don't we put in our orders and then we can talk?"

The waitress arrives and takes our order for two pieces of pumpkin pie, extra whip, and two hot chocolates.

I stir the whipped cream before taking a sip of my cocoa. "Wow, talk about dejá vù."

"Speaking of talking," he says, "do you want to start? Or should I?"

"What would you like to know, Gavin?"

"How long have you been at U.C. Berkeley?"

Of course he'd go straight for the hard question. "A little over four years."

"Four *years*?!" he repeats. "What happened to Florida State?"

I begin fidgeting with my silverware. "I never exactly...applied to Florida State. And since I never applied, it kind of would've been hard to go to school there."

"Jesus, Kat." He looks pained. "*Why?* Why did you tell me you were going to school so far away? Did you even know you were going to Berkeley at that point?"

I stare at the Formica tabletop. "Yeah, I knew."

"Why didn't you just tell me the truth?"

"Because I thought it would make it easier to walk away," I say and shrug.

"I can't believe this," he sighs. "Kat, if I knew...if I knew you'd be so close, I would've—"

"You would've *what*, Gavin?"

He rubs his hand over his face and groans. "I don't know. My God, I can't believe you've been right here this whole time!"

"Gavin, would it have really mattered? Or would you have been walking around looking for ghosts the entire time, like I have? You already admitted that you weren't going to call me after you discovered the truth. Because you thought you were doing what was best for me. Well, *I was doing the same for you* when I made that decision! Do you know what it feels like to wonder if today was going to be the day that I ran into you? To feel hope every time I saw someone that resembled you, only to be crushed when it turned out it wasn't? I knew what I was signing up for, but it wouldn't have been fair to put you through that too with a baby on the way."

"There was no baby!" he whisper shouts.

I throw my hands up. "I didn't know that, Gavin! If I did, I wouldn't have been terrified these past few years that we'd cross paths and I'd have to see you with someone else. I wanted you to be happy—I swear. I just couldn't bear the thought of seeing it firsthand if it wasn't with me." I hang my head in my hands.

"There hasn't been anyone else."

My head snaps up. "*What?*"

"There hasn't been anyone else," he repeats. "Since we...since you left. I haven't *been* with anyone else."

"Are you trying to tell me that you haven't dated anyone since me?"

"I've gone out on a few dates here and there," he replies. "But no one interested me enough to take it any further."

"Are you really saying you haven't had sex since we were last together?"

He shrugs. "I didn't really see the point. I knew those women couldn't hold a candle to you."

I slam my hand over my mouth as my eyes fill with tears. "Oh. My. God. You've been *celibate* for four years? Because of me?"

"I suppose it's too much to hope that you have been too," he says with a sad smile.

"Gavin—"

He holds his hand up. "No, it's okay; I don't want you to answer that."

"I was trying to move on," I explain anyway. "I thought you had a family. You could've been married again. I was in two short-term relationships but that's it. They were the only ones."

He winces. "Kat, please don't say any more. I really don't want to picture you with anyone else either."

"I'm sorry," I sniff. "I was just trying to move forward with my life. I thought about you every day— you were the only one in my life that made everything better."

"Even when I broke your heart?"

"Even then," I wipe the corner of my eye. "Being with you made me a stronger person, Gavin. I would've never made it through the past few years if I wasn't. God, I'm so sorry for this entire shitty situation."

He grabs my hand over the table. "Please don't apologize; you have nothing to be sorry for. There wasn't a day that went by when I didn't think about you too, you know."

"Yeah?"

"Yeah," he nods. "So...where do we go from here?"

I decide to take Bree's advice and spin the wheel of chance. "Do you have any plans on Saturday night? I need a date for a wedding."

He grins from ear-to-ear. "I can't think of anything I'd rather do."

epilogue

GAVIN

I'm the luckiest bastard alive.

I glance to my left and see Jack smiling at the flower girl, little two-year-old Emma, as she's walking down the aisle. About halfway into her march, she dumps the entire basket of red rose petals over and begins twirling in circles, bringing soft chuckles from the crowd. Breanna steps away from her maid-of-honor post to collect her daughter and deposits her into a chair with her daddy. She gives me a small smile as she takes her place again, knowing how eager I am for what's about to happen.

I stand up a little bit straighter, craning my neck toward the house when the music changes to Canon in D Major. My parents have transformed their backyard into the perfect intimate wedding venue. Three rows of white guest chairs line both sides of the garden with meticulously manicured lawn in between. I'm standing up front under the pergola, along with our minister, my brother, and Kat's best friend. Our ceremony is small—only family and close friends. I tried encouraging her to go big—something so grand that she will remember it for the rest of her life—but she declined, saying that no matter what the day holds, she'll remember it forever because of the man waiting for her at the end of the aisle. As I said before: Luckiest. Bastard. Alive.

Our guests shift in their seats as the French doors open, signaling the bride's arrival. Dylan steps out first, reaching his hand over the threshold to help Kat down the steps. My dad offered to walk her down the aisle, but she insisted that Dylan should be the one to give her away. It may seem odd given our history, but I couldn't think of anyone better to fill the role. It's no secret that Dylan and I had...*issues* when we first met. That's what happens when you're both in love with the same person. But when all is said and done, he's been by her side no matter what. He was there for her when I wasn't and I'll always be thankful that she had someone watching out for her. Besides, when he met the *true* love of his life, he realized that his affection for Kat was misplaced, and that they were always better as friends. He and I finally cleared the air last year when we had a long overdue man-to-man discussion.

I'm staring through the doorway, anxiously awaiting the first look at my bride-to-be. When she finally makes an appearance, an audible gasp washes through the audience. Their murmurs fade into the background as she steps onto the porch and searches me out. *My God, she looks like an angel.* Her strapless gown is understated —a layered flowy material falls to her feet, barely hugging the curves beneath. Dark curls tumble over her shoulders with small white orchids strategically pinning the sides of her hair back. I laugh when I see that she's barefoot; clearly her anxiety about getting her heels stuck in the grass won. When our eyes meet, I have to blink back tears from the overwhelming happiness I'm feeling right now. In a matter of minutes, the woman of my dreams will become my wife.

She loops her arm through Dylan's and they begin walking toward the altar. It takes every bit of willpower I possess to avoid running down the aisle to meet her. When they finally make their way to the front, she flashes me a blinding smile, silently telling me that she's just as excited as I am.

"Who gives this woman to be wedded to this man?" the minister asks.

Dylan takes her hand and places it in mine as we rehearsed. "I do."

I squeeze her fingers as we take our places to recite our vows. "You're breathtaking," I whisper.

She winks. "You're not so bad yourself, Sparkles."

I smile. She once confessed she only called me that to drive me crazy, but what she doesn't know is that I secretly love it. I haven't bothered to correct her because I don't want to risk never hearing it again.

As the reverend speaks, I think about how much we've overcome to make this day possible. The beginning of our story was less than ideal but I wouldn't change it for the world because it brought us to where we are now. It's been three years since she walked back into my life and I've never taken for granted that we were given another chance. This woman breathes life into me—she gives me a reason for being. And just last week, she gave me another reason to look forward to each new day. I glance at her toned stomach and imagine what it will look like swollen with our child. She's almost three months along now so I know it will only be a matter of time before I find out. Kat squeezes my hand, clearly knowing what I am thinking, and smiles.

I love you, I mouth.

"I love you," she whispers.

As the ceremony continues, vows are recited, rings are exchanged, and pronouncements are made. When the minister finally begins the part I've been waiting for, I cradle her face in my palms, anxiously waiting for his final instructions.

"You may now kiss your bride."

"It's about damn time," I mutter. Our kiss is less than chaste, because...well, have you seen my wife? We finally break apart when the wolf whistles drown out the applause.

Kat bites her lower lip. "Wow, that was some kiss, Dr. Cooper."

"You seem to have that effect on me, Mrs. Cooper," I say with a wink.

also available by laura lee

Dealing With Love Series (Interconnected standalones)

♥ Deal Breakers (Devyn & Riley's story)

♥ Deal Takers (Rainey & Brody's story)

♥ Deal Makers (Charlotte and Drew's story)

Bedding the Billionaire Series (Interconnected standalones)

♥ Billionaire Bosshole

♥ Billionaire Bossman (Formerly Public Relations)

♥ Billionaire Bad Boy (Formerly Sweet Temptations)

Windsor Academy Series (Books 1-3 <u>must</u> be read in order)

♥ Wicked Liars

♥ Ruthless Kings

♥ Fallen Heirs

♥ Broken Playboy (Bentley's story-can be read as a standalone)

Standalone Novels

♥ Beautifully Broken

♥ Happy New You

♥ Redemption

GO TO: https://www.subscribepage.com/LauraLeeBooks to sign up for Laura's newsletter and you'll be the first to know when she has a sale or new release!

Laura Lee is the *USA Today* bestselling author of steamy and sometimes ridiculously funny romance. She won her first writing contest at the ripe old age of nine, earning a trip to the state capital to showcase her manuscript. Thankfully for her, those early works will never see the light of day again!

Laura lives in the Pacific Northwest with her wonderful husband, two beautiful children, and three of the most poorly behaved cats in existence. She likes her fruit smoothies filled with rum, her cupboards stocked with Cadbury's chocolate, and her music turned up loud. When she's not chasing the kids around, writing, or watching HGTV, she's reading anything she can get her hands on. She's a sucker for spicy romances, especially those that can make her laugh!

For more information about the author, check out her website at: www.LauraLeeBooks.com

You can also find her "working" on social media quite frequently.

Facebook: @LauraLeeBooks1
Instagram: @LauraLeeBooks
Twitter: @LauraLeeBooks
Verve Romance: @LauraLeeBooks
FB Reader's Group: @Laura Lee's Lounge
TikTok: @AuthorLauraLee

acknowledgments

To my husband, Tad: We've been married for ten years and I can honestly say I love you more now than I did on our wedding day. This past year has been one of the saddest and most challenging we've ever faced. You were my rock during the darkest days and I'm honored to have been yours. Your unwavering love and support is what gets me through life. I couldn't ask for a better partner-in-crime.

To my children: Being your mom is the greatest gift. It never ceases to amaze me how your smile can melt my heart or how your hugs can brighten my day. I am so proud of you and I love you to the moon and back.

To my critique partner, fellow author, and most importantly, my friend, Jen (J.L.) Durfey: Thank you for helping me see Kat and Gavin's story come to life. (And for letting me use your son's awesome name!) Your feedback throughout the entire process was more helpful than I could've ever imagined. You are the best and quite possibly, the most psychic brainstorming partner a gal could ask for. It's seriously freaky how well you can read my mind when I can't figure out what I'm trying to say.

To my lovely betas Jamie and Michaela: Thank you for reading through yet another book and giving me your invaluable feedback throughout the early stages.

April Wells: Thank you for never failing to entertain me. Justin and I will always BELIEBE in you!

To all the seriously awesome bloggers in the book world: Thank you for everything you do to help spread the love of reading! You make it possible for people like me to do this for a living and I could never thank you enough.

To my editor, Erin Potter: Thank you once again for squeezing me into your schedule despite all of my crazy delays. I will always recommend your services at Shamrock Editing!

Last but never least, to my readers: Thank you for sticking with me through this crazy thing we call life. I know I drive you crazy when one book gets delayed because another story won't stop speaking to me. Your patience does not go unnoticed nor unappreciated. Each and every one of you are so special to me. I could never do this without you.

Beautifully Broken, while fictional, represents real problems within our world.

If you have been a victim of sexual assault, please seek help. IT'S NOT YOUR FAULT!

RAINN (Rape, Abuse & Incest National Network) is the nation's largest anti-sexual violence organization and was named one of "America's 100 Best Charities" by Worth magazine. RAINN created and operates the National Sexual Assault Hotline (800.656.HOPE and online.rainn.org) in partnership with more than 1,100 local sexual assault service providers across the country and operates the DoD Safe Helpline for the Department of Defense. In 2015, the Online Hotline expanded to offer services in Spanish at rainn.org/es. RAINN also carries out programs to prevent sexual violence, help victims and ensure that rapists are brought to justice.

If you or someone you love suffers from an addiction, you're not alone.

Nar-Anon (Family & Friends of Addicts)

http://www.nar-anon.org

Al-Anon (Family & Friends of Alcoholics)

http://www.al-anon.alateen.org

Narcotics Anonymous (Self-help for drug abuse & addiction)

http://www.na.org

Alcoholics Anonymous (Self-help for drinking problems)

http://www.aa.org

www.ingramcontent.com/pod-product-compliance
Lightning Source LLC
Chambersburg PA
CBHW070811190726
48292CB00006B/1969